BRYCE MAIN spent over thirty years in advertising before writing fiction full-time. *A House for Monsters* is the second book in his DI Tom McHale series. He is married with two sons and lives in the north-west of England.

Follow Bryce on X/Twitter @brycemain99

CW01497197

BRYCE MAIN

A HOUSE FOR MONSTERS

Northodox Press Ltd
Maiden Greve, Malton,
North Yorkshire, YO17 7BE

This edition 2025

1
First published in Great Britain by
Northodox Press Ltd 2025

ISBN: 9781917005142

This book is set in Caslon Pro Std

For Denise, my wife and first reader,
who helped me bring A House For Monsters alive…

Prologue

Sometimes the difference between life and death is as simple as a change of expression on the face of a middle-aged woman. Sometimes seeing a face transform from a calm exterior into a twisted grotesque mask in a split second is persuasion enough to grab a large kitchen knife and plunge it ten times into the body of another human being. Before they decide to do the same to you.

It was just after 4.00am. It was Saturday, 17th August, 1991. It was a small room in a small house in a town called Madan, in the Smolyan Province, at the southern edge of Bulgaria. Not far from the northern Greek border.

In the room, a woman was lying awake in a double bed. Her husband was sitting on the other side of the bed, smoking a foul-smelling cigarette and drinking foul-tasting whisky. He was a bad sleeper, even when blind drunk.

The woman's hands were pressed over her ears. The medication she was taking and the voices she heard inside her head were helping to contort her facial muscles. The voices had been shouting at her all night. They were telling her that she was shit. That she was ugly. That she was stupid. And that nobody in their right mind would want to love her.

One of the voices, a young man who had been hissing and growling at her non-stop for days, was beginning to scream.

'You're a fucking whore. You're a fat, ugly, fucking whore. Who could love you? Why don't you just kill yourself? Go to the bridge and jump off. Nobody wants you. Not your husband. Not your kids. Nobody! Everybody hates you. Go on. Piss off. Do it, you fucking bag of shit!' He screamed it over and over and over again.

The woman's name was Svetlana Lazarov, and she was fifty-five. Poor, simple, uneducated, and overweight, she had brought three sons into the world, one of whom, Ivan, died at birth. He was the one they named but never mentioned again. Ever. The one they tried to banish from their memories, but never quite could. And for as long as she could remember, Svetlana had suffered from schizophrenia.

She did the best she could to bring up her remaining family, but passed her condition on to Anton, the youngest of her surviving sons. The other son, Dragan, dodged that bullet. There was another one of a more violent sort waiting for him, though. Further on up the road. That one wouldn't miss. She was constantly terrified, depressed, confused, anti-social… and her grip on reality was unreliable and tenuous at the best of times.

Worst of all were the voices. Male, female, young, old, polite, scary, friendly, happy, and dangerous. Sometimes off and on. Other times twenty-four seven. And worst of the voices was the hissing, growling, cursing, evil young man who called her a 'fucking whore.'

And then there was The Devil.

Svetlana also suffered from Tardive Dyskinesia. The condition was a side effect of the antipsychotic medications she took for her schizophrenia. It made her body sometimes jerk and writhe uncontrollably. It made her grimace and stick out her tongue and smack her lips. Her face would twist and contort and her husband, Radomir, would say she had The Devil inside her.

Radomir was a smelly pig of a man who was mean-spirited and violent towards his wife and sons. He was also a schizophrenic, but he didn't suffer from TD. He did, however, come to believe that The Devil inside his wife was planning to kill him. So, that night, he came to a decision.

He went to the work shed behind the house and fetched his father's old bone-handled knife. The one he used to skin rabbits. It had a six-inch blade and it was razor sharp. When he got back, Svetlana was still in bed, moaning and hitting the sides of her head repeatedly with her bunched-up fists. She was mumbling words Radomir didn't understand. Then she suddenly stopped and looked up at him. Eyes wild, lips snarling, and lungs gasping for air.

That was when Radomir acted swiftly and, with the help of the bone-handled knife, separated Svetlana from himself, their sons, and her tragic life. Savagely and permanently. But in doing so, he made three big mistakes.

The first mistake was stabbing her ten times. Eight more than was necessary to result in her quick death. There was no coming back from the two stab wounds to the heart. All the others had nothing to do with murder and everything to do with fear and favouritism.

Radomir had no medical knowledge. He had very little general knowledge of any meaningful kind. But in that moment, he knew six things.

He knew what an awful lot of blood looked like. He knew that Svetlana stopped breathing very quickly. He knew that ten was his favourite number. He knew that ten was also Anton's favourite number. He knew that Anton was his favourite son. And he knew that the roar he felt in his throat was the roar of freedom.

The second mistake was wrapping the bloody body in bedsheets, dragging it to his battered old car, driving to a remote spot in a nearby forest, and burying Svetlana in a shallow grave. He buried her face-down to stop The Devil from escaping back into the world and seeking revenge on him. He learned this from his grandfather, who hung himself when Radomir was in his early teens.

But the third, and biggest, mistake was believing that neither of his sons, who were out for the night and would return the following day, would find out what he did. So, he cleaned up the mess as best he could and waited for them to return home. And waited… and waited.

When they eventually did return, he blurted out the truth.

He couldn't help himself. To his horror, the words came out of his mouth as if they had a will of their own. He feared his sons would kill him. Or at least attack him. Even Anton. After all, they loved their mother. Not him. But his sons were far more intelligent, and far more cunning, than their father ever imagined or gave them credit for. Or at least one of them was.

If anyone had cared to measure it, they would have seen that Anton had an IQ of about 150. Only ten less than Einstein. Between Anton's ears sat the brain of a warped, broken genius. And it was constantly up to no good.

He was the taller, and stronger, of the two sons, and bisecting his right eyebrow, giving him a cruel, dangerous look, was an old scar; a leftover from an argument with a broken beer glass in a bar fight. The scar was two inches long and settled halfway down his cheekbone. His sight was undamaged, but the wound merely served to place more emphasis on the peculiarity of his right eye. Anton had Heterochromia. His eyes were different colours; the left one dark brown, right one bright blue. He was also a leader. Dragan, his older brother, was smaller and quieter. He followed where Anton led.

Dragan had always been proud of his brother's ability to say the right thing at the right time and in the right circumstance. Hence, Radomir was fooled into believing that the boys understood what he did, and why he did it. And understood that this was a family secret that could never be revealed.

So, the three got drunk that night and, after the sons persuaded Radomir to tell them where their mother was buried, they all made a pact never to speak of the deed again. If anyone asked where she was, they would say she had gone to stay with a friend in the northern town of Lukovit, and they didn't know when she would be back. And since the immediate family kept to themselves, had no friends, and had only distant relations, they were sure that no one would find anyone to answer any awkward questions. The deed would remain as buried as Svetlana.

Everybody lies.

When Dragan awoke the next morning, he found Anton curled up in a foetal position, fast asleep on the threadbare rug in front of the dying log fire, wearing only his underpants. Radomir was gone. So was his large black travelling bag.

Dragan shook his younger, smarter brother awake, told him their father had left, and listened to what he had to say. Theirs was hero-worship of a different kind. He had always followed where the younger Anton led.

Anton told him to go immediately to the local police station, and reassured him everything would be fine. He was very persuasive. He told him to say that his father, Radomir Lazarov, had confessed to killing his mother and burying her in a shallow grave in a nearby forest. Then, Radomir had run away.

The eldest son did as he was directed and told his story well. He looked suitably shocked and worried. The police discovered Svetlana's body, buried face down where Dragan said it was, and they immediately issued an arrest warrant for Radomir, who was never found.

That night, while Anton slept, he dreamed he was in another man's body. And the other man was standing outside his house, in his back yard, looking at a black cat. In his mind, the cat was speaking to Anton in his mother's voice. She said she was glad to be free of The Devil inside her at last. She said the torment was like living in Hell every minute of every day, but that The Devil was now also free. Free to spread his evil throughout the world. And it was now up to her precious son to find him and stop him wherever he was. She made him promise to hunt down The Devil.

So, Anton knelt down in a puddle in the wet yard and prayed to the Holy Virgin Mary. It was cold and moonless and the rain had just stopped falling. But like a good son, he did what his mother told him to do. Even though she looked like the cat from next door.

Svetlana the cat said all this while sitting on the top of a stone wall slowly licking her fur clean. She would lick for a while. Then speak for a while. Then repeat the whole process over, and over, and over.

'How will I recognise The Devil?' he asked.

The cat blinked. 'His face will be twisted and he will want to kill you,' said Svetlana. 'So, you have to find him and kill him first. But the Devil is a liar with a hundred lives. Even if you kill him once, he will rise again. So, you have to hunt him down and kill him again and again until he has no lives left.'

'Where will I look?' he said.

'Everywhere.'

She said that The Devil was now inside Radomir. That's when he told her that Radomir was dead. That he had killed him to avenge her murder.

'Does Dragan know this?' she said.

'No.' He kept his face as still and expressionless as possible.

'Good boy,' she said, licking her fur some more. 'Now... where did you put Radomir's body?'

'Under the logs in the woodshed,' said Anton. 'I have to find a better place.'

The cat looked at him and blinked slowly. And she told him about a clearing in a remote part of a nearby forest. She said it was the ideal size for the job he had to do.

'Then what?' he said.

That's when she told him about his mission. And about his older brother Ivan; that he lived inside him, and that they would always protect and take care of each other. And that's when Anton, who had just killed for the first time, was born for the second time in his life. From now on, he would spend the rest of that life, hunting and killing the Lord of Hell.

Chapter One

Time is flexible. In order to go forward, sometimes we have to look back.

It was Sunday, 7th September, 1986.

It was the day that ten-year-old Tom McHale heard a rumour about his local parish priest and a young married woman. The priest was handsome, the woman was beautiful, and the things they did together would result in anyone with a dog collar (or as Tom used to say; God collar) getting a right good bollocking from the Vatican. Or so he was told by a skinny kid called Slug who had crooked teeth, one leg a smidge shorter than the other, and cheap NHS spectacles with a crack in the left lens.

Of course, Tom didn't know it at the time, but this papal bollocking meant bugger all compared to the secret joy of physical pleasure between two very enthusiastic and completely consenting adults.

The Christian church as an institution might have been two thousand years old, but the priest was thirty-five years young, and the woman, two years younger. The love they had for each other was of the hot and sweaty variety and mostly took place in the vestry of the small, white chapel, on a hill, in a town called Milngavie. Just above Glasgow on a map.

Their intimacy took place behind locked doors. When the eyes of the wooden Saviour, crucified on the cross and hanging behind the altar, were turned the other way. The attraction, however, was embarrassingly obvious to those who gossiped and rested their patellas on the cushioned kneelers of the hard wooden chapel pews.

On 25th July, 1987, when Tom was eleven, the woman, whose name was Eileen Evans, was found by a man walking his dog in the woods near his home one Saturday morning just before 6am. It was just beginning to rain. She was lying on her stomach, head in and feet out of a slow-flowing stream. He was hearing this gory piece of gossip second hand from a fat boy called George, who overheard his parents talking in hushed tones. What George didn't overhear was that Eileen was eight weeks pregnant.

Naturally, the priest, whose name was Father Simon Wilson, became the prime suspect. Very quickly, he became the absent prime suspect. He went missing the day Eileen was found. A week later, his body was found hanging from an ash tree deep in a wood fifty or so miles away from where the dog walker discovered Eileen's corpse.

The yellow PVC-coated clothes line tied tight around his neck had compressed his carotid arteries and stopped the blood flow to his brain. Very shortly after that happened, the capillaries in his face and eyes had burst. Then his heart rate and blood pressure had crashed, and his crushed trachea had deprived him of oxygen.

Before he died, Father Wilson's final thought might have been of Eileen. He might even have died with her name on his lips; the word disappearing into the air as he swung to-and-fro, about four feet (and two feet) off the ground. By the time the police arrived, the priest had been hanging around for a couple of days and his face in death wasn't anything like as handsome, tanned, or as rugged as it had been in life.

The police, emboldened by the coroner's report, concluded that Wilson had panicked at the news of the pregnancy, killed Eileen, then, racked with guilt, committed suicide while the balance of his mind had been disturbed. The case was wrapped up and closed as tight as a duck's arse. But that's not how it happened.

Not by a long shot. The truth was far more complicated.

The murder of Eileen Evans was, in fact, committed by someone else. A man with the chronological age of thirty-four and the intellectual and emotional development of an eight-year-old. Six months after the original deaths, McHale learned this other piece of news from his fat friend George, who had, once again, overheard his whispering parents.

There are a million reasons why people make the decisions they make. And set off on the journeys they take through life.

Fat George's father, for instance, was a butcher. And, when the time came, Fat George followed in dear old dad's footsteps. He was deliriously happy right up until the instant he died at the age of twenty-six, when he wrapped his motorbike around an obstinate tree after consuming too much alcohol. He was on his way home from his favourite pub around eleven one night. Witnesses estimated he was travelling about seventy miles an hour. The tree had no intentions of travelling anywhere, fast or slow.

Long before George's meeting with fate, a thirteen-year-old McHale moved with his parents to London. Ever since the murder of Eileen Evans, and the supposed suicide of Father Simon Wilson, he'd had one goal in life. To join the police force.

Not merely to maintain law and order. Not just to catch criminals. Not only to protect the life and property of an often-ungrateful public. More than anything, McHale wanted to catch killers. Above everything else, he wanted to take away the freedom of anyone who, by any and every means, murdered anyone. No matter who they were or how they did it.

So, on his eighteenth birthday, March 18th, 1994, he applied to become a member of the thin blue line. Or, as some critics unkindly described it, the thick blue line.

Over the years, as he rose from being a raw copper fresh out of Hendon Police College (before it was rebuilt, reborn, and renamed The Peel Centre) to being a seasoned Detective Inspector in Stockport, Cheshire, he saw that line get stretched thinner and thinner. But McHale was a man who knew the value of patience.

He also knew the value of being unconventional in his thinking. And as often as not, because of that patience and unconventionality, he succeeded where others had failed. He was blessed with a surfeit of creativity and imagination. Something that couldn't be said for many of his peers.

No doubt that's why, in 2010, he was chosen to lead the hunt for Father David Black. The Catholic priest suspected, caught, and convicted in 2011, of killing John and Annie Kirkbride, an old couple, in Altrincham, Cheshire.

Black was diagnosed with Dissociative-Identity-Disorder. He had two 'alter' personalities inside him. The dominant one was called Arthur. Arthur was taller, better looking, and more intelligent than Black. At least, that's how he viewed himself.

Black was a caring, funny, fifty-six-year-old man of God. Arthur was a clever, manipulative, cold-blooded killer.

Since 2012, both had been in Broadmoor prison. Thanks, in the most part, to McHale. Arthur had always been in his own kind of prison, except for the few terrifying exceptions when he managed to wake up and break free. Most of the time, he was trapped inside a man who, until he was told, didn't even know Arthur existed.

Then, in 2017, McHale was persuaded to put together a special team to hunt down the serial killer known as The Holy Ghost. It was a hunt that stretched from the US to the UK, finally ending in Portsmouth, England.

Chapter Two

The thing about prisons the world over is that most of the people put there probably deserve to be there. Many of the others are victims of a prison system that has nowhere else to put them. So, they get put where they don't fit and they don't belong. And the folk who put them there don't look you in the eyes.

Some of the rest are victims of their own damned misfortune or stupidity for being in the wrong place at the wrong time. And an unlucky few simply fall between the cracks. They're completely innocent but, for one reason or another, have absolutely no believable way to prove it.

The vast majority of prisoners will keep their heads down, keep their noses clean, do their time, and walk out the front door. Some of them will be so scared shitless they'll never offend again. Others, once they get out, will happily repeat whatever they did that caused them to be banged up in the first place.

A small elite few, however, will never taste freedom in the outside world again. At least, not as long as they have a pulse. For this band of brothers (and sisters), there will be no parole. No redemption. No forgiveness. No rehabilitation. And sure-as-hell, no release. This is why most of us living on the outside of prisons sleep easier in our beds at night.

We place our trust in the long (and occasionally short) arm of the law to hunt those who need hunting. Punish those who need punishing. And put them in places where the sun doesn't reach, never mind shine. Because, for us, prisons are more than mere storage facilities. More than just warehouses of incarcerated flesh. They're the places where we keep our monsters. At least, the ones we know about. The ones we manage to catch. At least, the ones we manage to catch.

It was Friday, 23rd March, 2018. It was 3.00pm. It was Broadmoor high-security psychiatric hospital in Crowthorne in Berkshire, England. Not the brand spanking new purpose-built Broadmoor that was both a million miles and a stone's throw away from the old Victorian Broadmoor. This was a redeveloped, ultra-modern, ultra-maximum-security wing inside the tired old fifty-three-acre facility that was built in 1863 and initially contained ninety-five 'insane' female prisoners.

In January 2013, with appropriate ceremony and publicity, the new wing was officially opened by the then Home Secretary; a plain-looking woman with a dedication for law and order infused into her bones like the words running through a stick of Blackpool rock. Speeches were said, hands were shaken, photographs were taken, a ribbon was cut. And, in theory, good folk could start feeling safer.

The facility was dedicated to housing the most insane, most dangerous, male serial killers who, for their sins, would never be allowed to mix with any general prison population. Or anyone else, for that matter. Ever again. It was very exclusive, and informally known, by those being held there, those guarding them, and those who put them there, as The Monster House.

It contained twelve solitary-confinement cells. Each was a six-sided box. Floor, ceiling, and three walls made of two-inch-thick steel panels. The sixth side, the front, was made of half-inch thick polycarbonate ballistic glazing. Total floor area was 12x14ft. The steel ceiling was 10ft above the floor. Built into each glass wall was a meal and documents hatch, and a wireless audio feed switched on or off from outside the cell. The microphones could pick up the sound of a pin being dropped anywhere in the cell. Or a voice coming from anywhere within a ten-feet radius of the outside.

The cells were in two lines, back-to-back, with a 6-feet gap between each one. Through the glass, each occupant could see a blank wall eight feet away across a corridor. Each cell had a double door security 'porch' built into the right side of the see-though wall with a five-feet space between each door. Once inside the porch, the outer door was electronically locked before the inner door was opened. Same routine on the way out.

Each see-through wall had a privacy 'smart' mode, controlled from outside the cell. This allowed the wall to become opaque at the touch of a button. This happened at 10pm every evening until 6am every morning, during which time, inmates were afforded a certain degree of privacy. Or so they thought.

Hidden micro-cameras inside the cells took that privacy away. Not that any occupant was aware of this. When it came to privacy with maximum security, perception was one thing. Reality something else entirely.

Each cell had a bed, a toilet, a wash-hand basin, a shower cubicle, a TV with cable channels, a bookcase containing the books and magazines, a desk and chair, a small chest of drawers, a rug, a keyboard and monitor with access to an intranet server monitored by prison staff, and bottled water plus tea and coffee making facilities on a small round table.

For one hour each day, and always with four armed guards present, each member of The Monster House would have free rein of the dedicated exercise area. There, they could take advantage of exercise machines, but no free weights. Even monsters, apparently, had rights. Irrespective of the number of people they had killed. Or how they had killed them.

That was 2013. This was 2018.

Detective Inspector Tom McHale was sitting on a metal chair on the outside of what was known as Cell 3. Sitting on the inside, on the other side of the glass wall, was Father David Black. Only he wasn't. In Black's Mind, Arthur was awake and Arthur was a shad over 5'10". About an inch taller than Black.

This perceived height difference was, in reality, the result of Arthur's desire to remain almost rigidly straight-backed at all times. Except when he was supine. Except when he was asleep.

Whenever Arthur was "in town", Black, adopted a noticeable old man's stoop. Although the priest had aged seven years since entering Broadmoor, and was now sixty-three, Arthur had remained the age he always thought he was. Thirty-five.

He was, of course, cleverer than Black, with an IQ of 136. By comparison, Black was a dullard.

Although the priest also had short, white hair, Arthur viewed this as a physical anomaly. But not unattractive. He thought it distinctive. Distinguished. Even attractive and unique in a man so young. His wrinkles were merely the result of his skin prematurely ageing. He had an answer for everything and an apology for nothing.

They had been staring at each other for the five minutes that had elapsed since McHale first sat down. Both wanted to speak, but neither wanted to speak first.

Finally, McHale had enough. He looked at his watch, stood up, and started to walk away.

'I win,' said Arthur, through the intercom speaker in the glass wall. The voice was now deep and menacing. Nothing like the soft, lighter voice of the priest. McHale, facing away, smiled. Turned. Walked back to the chair and sat down. He looked at his watch again. 3.10pm.

'You got somewhere you need to be?' said Arthur.

'Oh, you know. The usual,' said McHale, his face a mask of disinterest. 'Places to go, people to save, murdering bastards to catch.'

Arthur tutted and shook his head sadly from side to side. He sighed. 'So impatient,' he said.

'Well…tick tock', said McHale, quoting words from the letters written to the FBI's BAU unit by the serial killer known as The Holy Ghost.

Arthur smiled. 'How is the padre?' he said. He was referring to the Jesuit Father Stephen Rice. One of the members of the small team who tracked him down eight months earlier. McHale changed tack.

'Spill the beans, what do you want?'

Arthur looked annoyed. 'See, there you go. Always answering a question with a question. Do you have any idea how fucking annoying that is?' His voice had drifted up a notch in volume.

Hearing the priest swear was initially shocking to McHale. It was almost sinful. Then he remembered that Black wasn't the one who was talking.

'That's the first question I've asked you in years. Give me a break,' he said. 'I think I'm doing pretty damned well.' He forced out a small laugh. There was no humour in it.

Arthur crossed his legs, right over left. Then crossed his arms over his chest. Left over right. 'How can we hope to have any kind of relationship if you don't engage in a bit of friendly banter?' he said. Then he pause. Four heartbeats.

McHale sighed. His inner voice spoke up. *'Might as well humour the bastard, Kemosabe,'* he said. *'See what he has to bloody say.'*

'Fine.' He raised his eyebrows and tilted his head to the left. 'How are they treating you in here? Miss the outside world?'

Arthur grinned. 'See how easy that was?' He uncrossed his arms and legs and stood up, holding his arms wide apart and turning around in a circle. 'I am lord of all I survey. Master of my own tiny world. Why do I need to go anywhere outside,' he said, 'when I can go anywhere I fucking want in here, eh?' and he tapped his right temple with the forefinger of his right hand.

He walked over to the small chest of drawers. On the top was a bowl overflowing with oranges and bananas. He picked up a bunch of bananas and broke off a fat yellow finger. Then he walked back to his chair, sat down and peeled open the banana, taking a large bite. Through the mashed pulp in his mouth, he said, 'Always remember to get your prebiotics, Mister McHale. 'It's good for the gut flora. Did you know that?'

McHale nodded. 'So is garlic,' he said. 'Also good for keeping vampires at bay.' Another pause.

Then Arthur burst out laughing. As he did, bits of mulched banana flew out of his mouth, one or two landing on the inside of the see-through wall. When he finished laughing, he said, 'You know…I think under different circumstances we could have been good friends.'

McHale shook his head slowly from side to side. 'We could never be friends under any circumstances.'

'Because?'

'Because you're a psychopath who likes killing people.'

Arthur cocked his head to the right. His eyes took on a dead look. The look McHale had seen in sharks. No emotion. No feeling. All predator.

His voice became soft and inquisitive. 'I wonder why that is, Mister McHale? You think maybe it's because I was abused as a child, eh? You think something inside me is fucked up and broken and can't ever be fixed, eh?'

Even though they were separated by one inch of almost unbreakable plastic wall, McHale could feel a small trickle of sweat run down the back of his neck. There was something about the tone of Arthur's voice that made him want to shift his chair back a foot or two.

He ignored the feeling. 'You were never a child,' he said. 'You were fucked up and broken right from the word go. It just took time to come out.'

Arthur stared at McHale and sighed. Then he finished eating the banana and, like NBA legend LeBron James in his prime, threw the empty skin with unerring accuracy into a waste basket sitting next to his desk about ten feet away. It didn't even hit the sides. McHale gave him a couple of slow handclaps.

The old priest took a mock bow. Then returned the handclaps. 'I hear you haven't been booted up the pecking order yet,' he said.

He was referring to McHale's lack of promotion from

Detective Inspector to Detective Chief Inspector, following the hunt for The Holy Ghost, a.k.a Charles Halliwell, the previous year. It was a hunt in which Black had played a vital part. His tip had led McHale's specially formed team south to Portsmouth where The Ghost was stalking his final victim.

'I guess I was born lucky,' said McHale with a half grin. 'I got to stay where I could do the most damage.'

'With a little help from your friends.'

McHale's right eyebrow went up. 'You think this is one of those 'we couldn't have done it without you' moments?' he said.

'A *thank you* would be nice.'

McHale paused and shrugged. Nodded once. 'Fair point,' he said. 'This is me saying thank you! Now, can we do away with the small talk and get down to business?'

'Tell you what, how about a nice cup of coffee, eh? I can arrange it.'

'No thanks.'

'Sure? It's none of your instant crap. It's the real deal. Only the best for you, Mister McHale.' Hearing the words Mister McHale come out of Black's mouth made the copper feel decidedly uncomfortable.

'Oh bugger this. You're just pissing about.' McHale got up from his chair and this time he got about five feet further away from the cell than he did the first time, before he heard Black's voice, sounding like Arthur, chasing after him.

'Only, I was thinking, while you're drinking your Java, I could tell you a little story,' he said. 'It's about a clearing roughly quarter the size of a football pitch in the middle of a forest.'

McHale stopped and turned.

'And?'

Arthur smiled. 'And I need a drink of water,' he said. He got up from his chair, walked to the small table, filled a plastic cup with still water, sipped it, then brought it back carefully to his chair and sat down. Then he took a deep breath and continued.

'Now… where was I? Oh yeah. The clearing in the middle of a forest. Right.'

'Where's the forest?' said McHale. Walking back to his chair and slowly sitting down.

Arthur didn't like being interrupted. That much was obvious. His face grew flush with colour and his eyes narrowed. There was a temper sitting just under his skin. The kind of temper that didn't need much of an excuse to come out into the open to do a little GBH.

But he held it in check. The demeanour of his face changed. The muscles around his jaw relaxed. He blinked slowly. Breathed deeply. And when he opened his eyes again, the temper had gone.

'The forest is in Bulgaria. Now, no more fucking talking.'

'Fine.'

'So… in March 2015, a helicopter was flying over a remote, forested area in the south of the country. They were taking aerial photos for one of those surveys. And when they looked at the photos, they noticed something odd. A clearing deep in the forest had what looked like vague oblong shapes in the ground. Twenty of them.

'They were lined up in two rows of ten. Very curious. So, the men in charge of the survey sent a couple of people to have a good look at the shapes. They took ground penetrating radar gear with them. That's when all fucking hell broke loose. Turns out the shapes were shallow graves. The graves were only a couple of feet deep.'

Somewhere in the back of McHale's mind, a faint alarm bell began to ring.

'All in all, they found twenty bodies. Some had been in the ground for more than a decade. They didn't look much like bodies any more. Some had only been there a year or two. A couple of the graves were only a few months old.'

The alarm bell got louder. McHale couldn't help himself. 'Dumping ground,' he said softly.

This time, Arthur showed no annoyance. 'Give that man a coconut,' he said. Almost proudly. 'And now for a bonus point…'

'Bulgarian mafia?' said McHale, slowly.

Black stared at him.

A few years previously, McHale got an inner memo about a conference at The Met's new headquarters at New Scotland Yard on Victoria Embankment, London. The conference was about organised crime. One of the keynote speakers was a high-ranking officer from Bulgaria's National Police Service. McHale missed the conference, but he read the transcript of the presentation. It mentioned the bodies buried in the wood.

Barely a month after the speech, the officer and his wife were blown to fleshy smithereens when a bomb exploded under their car.

Apparently, organised crime and certain inhabitants of Bulgaria went together like death and taxes. Or so some folk thought.

Arthur downed his water in two large gulps and held the empty beaker in his right hand. 'Good guess…but wrong. No bonus point for you.

You see, it wasn't those nasty gangs that put all those people in the ground. It was just one man. One very ordinary-looking man. Average height. Average build. He was a regular Joe fucking Schmoe. Except for the fact, that he killed at least twenty people. Or so the authorities thought.'

McHale wished he'd said yes to the coffee. His throat was dry and his taste buds relished the thought of a kick up the arse from a mouthful of double-strength caffeine.

He was still wrapping his head around the fact that he was looking at, and talking to, a sixty-four-year-old priest, and listening to a killer who, in his mind, would always be a damned sight younger.

'You mean he killed more?'

Arthur said, 'He actually confessed to killing another ten, but he wouldn't give up the other burial sites. They're still looking for them.'

'So, they caught him?'

The priest shook his head slowly. 'Wrong again. He walked into a police station in Sofia in September 2015 and gave himself up. Stupid bastards put him in prison with all the other crazies. He became a big celebrity. He was also murdered on his fifty-eighth birthday, April 21st, 2015. The guy who killed him became an even bigger one.'

The alarm bell ramped up its decibel level.

'That's not why you asked to see me is it?'

Long pause.

'No, Mister McHale.'

'And?'

'And he didn't kill anyone.'

Another decibel.

'And you know this how?'

'Because the man who did kill them is his younger brother. And he's right here in the UK. And I think you'll find he's already started killing again.' Twenty-three words. Ninety-five letters. Millions of possibilities.

'Oh… and something else,' said Arthur. 'Something that anyone with a healthy dose of curiosity would find very interesting.'

McHale sighed. 'Okay, I'm officially curious.'

'They were all buried face down. Just like the brothers' mother.'

It was 3.40pm. Six days after McHale's forty-second birthday. And his arse was aching from sitting on the hard metal chair outside the cell. He was trying to stay poker faced, and he wasn't succeeding. Arthur was looking at him. Neither had said anything for about thirty seconds. McHale was trying to figure out what to think next. What to do next. What to say next. That, plus trying to imagine what twenty graves next to each other in a small clearing in a remote forest looked like.

Finally, he broke the silence.

'You seem to know an awful lot for someone banged up in

solitary with no physical contact with the outside world. How the hell do I know you're not just yanking my chain?'

'Who needs physical contact when you've got the internet? I call it my world in a box.'

'I thought you only had access to the intranet…not the whole internet,' said McHale.

'Oh you'd be surprised what you can learn on the inside, when you've got knowledgeable friends on the outside. Ever heard of the Dark Web?' said Arthur, mysteriously.

McHale kept his mouth shut and his ears open. He wasn't going to let Arthur know that he knew exactly what he knew about the Dark Web. His pulse went up a notch.

Arthur continued. 'I'm what you might call a listener. I listen to all the conversations that happen in all those secret places underneath the Dark Web. I listen and I see and I gather up all the juicy morsels of information. Like about a certain graveyard in a certain forest in a certain foreign country… and about a certain serial killer who's burying bodies upside down.'

That's when McHale's brain cells put on their best go-faster stripes and shifted up into top gear.

Arthur's eyes narrowed and the smile disappeared. He made a fist with his right hand and crushed the empty plastic cup he was holding. Then he closed his eyes and his head lolled forwards slowly onto his chest. He sighed softly. Then his breathing slowed and his shoulders relaxed.

Long pause.

He raised his head and opened his eyes. Only it wasn't Arthur. Arthur was gone and the priest David Black was back.

'Hello, Tom,' he said in the soft, tired voice that McHale instantly remembered. 'You're looking well.' Momentary confusion left McHale's face as the penny dropped.

Black raised one of his eyebrows. 'Arthur and I are not the strangers we once were,' he said. There was more than a tinge of sadness in his voice. 'He shares more with me than he used to.

I think he finds it lonely in there all by himself. I can't tell you much. But I can tell you that poor old Dragan only had one visitor in the short time he was in jail, just before someone took great delight in slitting his throat. His younger brother, Anton, came to see him and stayed for about an hour. It was Dragan's birthday. When the younger Lazarov left, he was smiling.'

'And?'

'That's it, I'm afraid. The well, as they say, has run dry. For the time being.'

McHale noticed that the stoop had returned to Black's upper body. He was back to looking his chronological age. And feeling it, too. Any vitality had abandoned the features of the priest.

'Is it worth me asking how you know all this?'

'I could tell you. But then Arthur would have to kill me.'

Pause.

'That was my feeble attempt at humour,' said Black.

Neither was smiling.

'So… you're not going to tell me?'

Black smiled kindly, as if he was being asked to divulge the secrets of the confessional. 'No. I think it's best if you take my word for it and know that your chain isn't being yanked in any direction. Everyone has their dirty little secrets, Tom. Arthur has lots of breadcrumbs. He likes to throw them to the waiting pigeons a few crumbs at a time.'

'So, I'm a pigeon?'

'Oh, not you, Tom. Arthur thinks you're a bit of a raptor. He saves the best handouts for you. They still have warm flesh attached.'

McHale's eyebrows lifted, and he grunted softly. 'I bet you and Arthur have had some interesting chats,' he said. 'Has he told you about Luntz?'

The disgust on the priest's face was instant.

Two months after he came to Broadmoor he came across Donald Luntz, a convicted paedophile who had sexually molested and then strangled four young girls. One of them only two years old. Luntz was a hulking bear of a man who sweated too much and didn't bathe enough. He was caught when he tried to snatch a nine-year-old girl from a playground. He was in the process of sexually assaulting her in the back of his beat-up van when her father heard her screams.

For all his size and aggressive behaviour, Luntz was, at heart, a coward. Faced with a six-foot well-built man frantically trying to save his daughter, Luntz crumpled into a tearful heap, before receiving a savage beating inflicted by the father and several onlookers. The adult human body is composed of 206 bones. The girl's father, with help, broke forty-three of those belonging to Luntz.

But even that was nothing compared to what Black, as Arthur, did to him. Even though Black was late middle aged, his dark passenger felt he was in the prime of his life. The harming, either physically or psychologically, of children was Arthur's line drawn in the sand. He was on one side and Luntz, for the brief remainder of his life, was on the other.

Seven months after the beating, three months after Luntz entered Broadmoor, and just under nine months before the completion of the prison's new Monster House, Father David Black invited Luntz to join him in the small prison chapel for a session of prayer and spiritual guidance. He was very flattering and very persuasive.

Number of prisoners in attendance…two. Number of guards on hand…zero.

Number of doors locked so Luntz couldn't escape…one. Once inside, Black took a coffee break and Arthur took over. Luntz never saw it coming. An hour later, long after the screams had died away, the guards returned and unlocked the door.

Black was sitting in a far corner of the chapel. Luntz was everywhere else.

Nine months later, in February 2013, Black became the first permanent member of the new Monster House facility. At the time he had twelve empty cells to choose from. His new home address was cell number three as per his request. He didn't explain why. It was granted without question. That was then. This was now.

There were two other occupants in the cells on the same row as Black. Cells one and five. McHale didn't know who they were, or what they did to warrant membership to The Monster House. Or how many of the cells on the other row were still empty. He didn't ask. The only thing he knew about the occupant of cell number five was that he liked the taste of human flesh.

Too much information.

'Thank you for not feeling sorry or for expressing regret at my circumstances,' said Black.

'It is what it is,' said McHale.

'Indeed,' said Black, sighing heavily. 'Right… I think it's time to go. Bye for now, Tom. Give my best to Stephen.'

McHale nodded once.

Black nodded back and sighed. 'Every little helps,' he said.

'Except this is Broadmoor, not Tesco.'

'Broadmoor has a supermarket. Just not one that sells food.' Black whispered. Winking, then tapping the right side of his nose twice with the forefinger of his right hand, like he was passing on a confidence.

Time to go, thought McHale, and he stood up.

'There's something for you in the hatch,' said Black. 'A little going away present of sorts from Arthur. Something to get the ball rolling and keep you busy until the next time.'

'There's going to be a next time?'

'There's always a next time.'

The reunion was over. For now. McHale glanced at the hatch and walked over to it. There was a slip of folded yellow paper sitting in the tray. He picked it up and unfolded it. There were three words, carefully printed in black ink. One word, then two underneath. Fifteen letters in total. First word Lazarov, next two *Grey John*.

They meant nothing to McHale. He didn't know whether

they were a mixture of names or colours. But obviously, they meant something to Arthur. So, he refolded the paper and slipped it into the inside left breast pocket of his jacket.

McHale wasn't a suit man. Too conventional. Today, the jacket was a Harris Tweed single breasted number with brown leather elbow patches and two leather buttons at the front. Eight years old. Never fastened. Tomorrow's outfit? Black leather jacket, maybe. Never fastened.

It was 4.29pm. He walked away from Black and Arthur, drove away from Broadmoor, and headed back the forty or so miles towards the city that had been his second home for the past six or so months. London. In all its cosmopolitan, impersonal, cultured, dangerous glory.

He had free use of a tidy, refurbished, fully-furnished, Victorian end terrace in Battersea. Bay windows, high ceilings and a ton of original features. Plus a few very stylish new ones… like the luxury Poggenpohl kitchen. Old England meets new Germany.

He'd rented out his house in Stockport and put the money in a high yield interest account for a rainy day. Or preferably a dry, hot day, somewhere abroad.

The second home was within spitting distance of Battersea Park and a mile away from what was one of London's industrial landmarks. The iconic, Grade II listed Battersea Power Station. One of the most innovative repurposed developments in the City. Some might say the country.

He was the head of a new unit inside a new department, based in an old capital. A unit with a singular mission: to hunt serial killers, wherever the hell they were. The official head of the new department was Detective Chief Superintendent Cyril Drummond. The unofficial one was McHale.

It was Drummond who brought McHale on board to hunt down Charles Halliwell. And it was Drummond who arranged for the keys of the Victorian end terrace to drop nicely into McHale's outstretched right hand. No questions asked.

The way Drummond figured it, laying out a few quid to finance a team like the one McHale put together was time, money, and effort well spent. His methods might be unconventional. But nobody in their right mind argued with his results. And results were the name of the game.

However, before the new unit got the green light, there was the small matter of location, location, location. It couldn't be in the high-security complex where the hunt for Halliwell mostly took place. That was underneath the official residence of the US Ambassador to the Court of St. James. Winfield House in Regent's Park. A small plot of Stars & Stripes bricks and mortar inside a much larger plot of Union Jack greenery.

That was too much like having your next-door neighbour always in your home; eating your food; watching your telly; rifling through your underwear drawers.

And it couldn't be in the newly-refurbished New Scotland Yard building on Victoria Embankment. That was too much like having your hands zip-tied behind your back by folk who normally did things by the book. From A all the way through to Z. And sometimes back again. No detours. McHale had a habit of throwing books out the window. Open or not.

It had to be somewhere nearby. Very private. Very secure. Very unconventional. Very Uncle Sam meets John Bull, and very full of the latest hi-tech communications systems. That somewhere was Lassiter House, and it was hidden away in a quiet back street about a mile from the Yard. It was a joint US-UK collaboration, where everyone's share of the communications pie was the same size, same quality, and same taste as everyone else's. Give or take. Most of the time. Theoretically.

It was a handsome Edwardian building, refurbished inside and out, and spread over six floors. Four above ground and two below. It was stuffed full of twenty-first century digital innovation and law enforcement technology. And the top floor was up for grabs. There was only the other small matter to deal with before they moved in. Intelligence. Not human intelligence. Not the kind that sat between ears. More like the kind that married one silicon chip to another. The artificial kind, in the shape of two highly advanced information systems; one developed by the forces of US law enforcement, the other by the long arms of the UK police.

The former was called MOTHER. It was an acronym for Monitor, Organise, Talk, Hear, Evaluate, and Record. McHale and the team used it to bring down Charles Halliwell. The latter was called HOLMES. It stood for Home Office Large Major Enquiry System. It was used predominantly by UK police forces for the investigation of major incidents such as multiple murders and high value frauds.

The Americans always seemed more inventive and creative with their acronyms than the British. The British always seemed more traditional. There was no point letting the two systems duke it out to see which one was standing when the dust settled and the coughing stopped. Both had wicked left jabs.

What was needed was a stunning right cross. Something that looked like the street-fighting love-child of MOTHER and HOLMES, but felt like the fairies had left it on the doorstep overnight. Something that would cherry pick the best from each of them and merge them together to create a new hybrid system; one that would be uniquely designed to hunt serial killers and nobody else. One that was rammed full of piss and vinegar, with a 'fuck off' attitude and a mind of its own.

It took close to eighty very clever people six months to cross-pollinate and develop it, and three weeks to install it. All hands-on deck. When they finished Stage One, they named the system SKIN. It stood for Serial Killers Intelligence Network. Simple. Straightforward. No nonsense. On paper, it kicked arse. MOTHER was female. HOLMES was male. SKIN was androgynous and smack-dab in the middle. It just needed a case that could take it out for a test drive. McHale gave it one.

Courtesy of Arthur. Via Father David Black.

A week later, Drummond pressed all the right buttons, then McHale and his team officially moved into Lassiter House. Minus one member from the old team. Plus one for the new one.

Chapter Three

It was Monday, April 2nd, 2018, and it was World Autism Awareness Day. It was the beginning of a new week in a new home; the start of a new chapter in the life of McHale and the people he had come to think of as the closest thing to family he had. Except for the older sister up North and the younger sister down South. He had upgraded his city, his accommodation and his iPhone. He was about to upgrade his team.

At 6.00am the iPhone alarm came alive and the best damned mobile on the planet kicked him awake with the voice of Joe Strummer, the sound of The Clash, and the first few bars of London Calling. Coincidences mean you're on the right track.

Half an hour later he stepped out of a hot shower and was getting his mind in shape for the day, when his mobile pinged with a new text. The phone went everywhere with him, bathrooms included. Old habits die hard, even in new homes.

The text was from Drummond. It was twenty-one words long. The words were these, *Just got the nod. SKIN goes live at ten this morning. This could be the start of a beautiful friendship. CD.'*

McHale double blinked and smiled. *Casablanca*, he thought. *Thank God for the Epstein twins and Howard E. bloody Koch.* He texted eleven words to Drummond.

'I'll round up the usual suspects. Minus one… plus one. McHale.' He sent four texts out to the team. One each to DC Toby Macbeth, Intelligence Analyst and McHale's wingman (or rather wingwoman) Daisy Nash, and Jesuit priest Father Stephen Rice. And one more.

FBI ass-kicker Grace Lightfoot. Native American and Supervisory Special Agent on temporary secondment to New Scotland Yard - unofficially - and the nearest thing to a first-choice second-in-command the team had. Then he sent one to someone called Spencer Pope. Same twelve words to each.

'SKIN goes live at ten. Coffees at nine. Game faces on. McHale.'

Of the five, one replied within thirty seconds. The text was five words long.

'Outstanding. I'll bring Boris. Spence.'

The other four followed hot on his heels.

Three said *'Ok.'*

One said, *'Osiyo.'*

McHale smiled. Osiyo was the traditional greeting of the Cherokee nation. It was pronounced *'Oh-see-yoh'*. He remembered the night Lightfoot taught it to him. It sounded strange coming from the mouth of a forty-two-year-old cop with a bastardised accent that was one-third Scottish, one-third English, and the rest God knows bloody what.

At just after 8.45am, McHale left the secure underground car park below Lassiter House, and walked up the two flights of stairs into the ground floor reception. There was a woman sitting behind the reception desk and a man standing to the left-hand side of her, holding a stack of files. She looked in her thirties. He looked middle-aged but fit. They were both wearing black suits, white shirts, black ties. McHale didn't ask, but he guessed they were both pretty handy with any firearm within easy reach.

She smiled. He nodded. Her name was Stella. He learned that the first day he came here. She was a freckle-faced redhead with wavy hair and minimal makeup. He didn't know the man's name, and the man didn't offer it.

The reception area looked sparse, but classy. There was no name either on the door or on the wall to identify who occupied the building. Those who came in normally knew why they were there. The few who came in and didn't know why they were there were gently and politely asked to leave. Immediately would be a good idea. Lassiter House wasn't what anyone might call visitor-friendly. It had a private disposition, and apart from a select few, it kept it to itself.

McHale signed a book on the reception desk and looked up at the camera on the wall above Stella, nodding. One floor below, a man in a similar black suit looking into a monitor saw McHale nod. He checked McHale's ID on another monitor. Verified it. Then pressed a button. Behind the reception desk, a small green light blinked on and off for a few seconds. The redhead clocked it and smiled. McHale walked the twenty feet to the single lift door, stepped into the lift and pressed three for the top floor. *On your marks… get set… go!*

Every morning the same routine coming in. Whenever he left, the same routine going out. And it was the same for everyone else. Inner voice spoke up for the first time that morning. *'Thank fuck you're not a bloody spook, Kemosabe. But I must admit, the new gaff's a bit nice. Well, it will be when it's finished.'*

Twenty seconds and forty vertical feet later, he stepped out onto a floor where organised chaos had made itself temporarily at home. Phase One, moving in, was a week old.

The lift decanted into an open-plan area that took up most of the floor. The wall opposite had six large, arched sash windows with glass-clad polycarbonate. One-inch think and capable of stopping three determined rounds from a 50 Caliber rifle fired from an open window of the building opposite.

The wall to the left was home to a high-end laser printer/scanner, a floor to ceiling shelving unit, and a door leading to a small kitchen. Scattered throughout the room were half a dozen light ash office desks and black mesh chairs with padded seats and advanced lumbar support. People who worked there sat down more than they stood up. Against the wall that held the lift door, two brown leather sofas and a large ash coffee table formed an intimate meeting area. Near the kitchen wall was a door leading to a flight of stairs giving access to the other floors and the basement garage.

But four things above all others captured the attention of anyone entering the room. They gave the area its personality and left visitors and inhabitants in no doubt where they were and what they were there for. The first thing was a word. And the word was SKIN. Four dark grey letters, each two feet in height, in a typeface called Euphemia, centred high up near the ceiling on the right-hand wall. The second was four more words, centred, in much more modest letters, under the first word. The explanation of the acronym. Serial Killer Intelligence Network.

The third was the massive bank of high-definition smart screens taking up the rest of the wall. And the fourth was the horseshoe-shaped light ash table with eight lumbar-support chairs, sitting in front of the screen wall. The arms of the table were pointing towards the screens. It looked like they were getting ready for a group hug.

They weren't. They mirrored the deadly battle formation of Zulu warriors, known as 'The horns of a buffalo'.

It was now a week since McHale had seen the layout for the first time. There were four people sitting at the large table, coffees in front of them, eager to get started. They looked up and smiled, then looked back down and carried on reading the documents in front of them. Around them, chaos reigned.

A large army of techs fussed, fiddled, hummed and tutted with iPads and laptops and cables. They were the tip of a highly advanced iceberg. The rest of the berg was somewhere on the floors below.

McHale went to the kitchen and grabbed a hot black coffee. No milk. No sugar. No brainer. There was an open packet of milk chocolate digestive biscuits next to the stainless-steel urn. Always on the go. The temptation was too strong to resist. Two of them called out his name.

On his way back through the room towards the horseshoe

table, the unit had a watershed moment. The screen wall came alive for the first time.

Huddled around one of the desks, a tight-knit group of five techs congratulated each other loudly. High fives and fist bumps went the rounds. The face on the screen wall obviously belonged to one of them. Phase Two, going live, was nearing completion. It was 9.20am. The weather was fine; London was warming up, and so was the team.

Ever since their last case, which, coincidentally, was their first ever case all together, they had been in limbo. The highs they all felt when they wrapped up the hunt for Charles Halliwell were quickly followed by months of anticlimactic lows.

The loss of one of their own was a pain that wouldn't dissipate. Meanwhile, for the rest of the world, life went on.

Law enforcement communities everywhere did what they always did when they had to make any fast decisions based on positive impact and common sense. They slammed on the brakes, took a good long look at all the evidence, and did stuff by the book. And while they did that, any impetus that might have been transferred onto other cases, was lost. The intelligence torrent slowed down to a fast-flowing river; then to a slow-flowing stream; and finally, to a frustrating trickle.

But McHale didn't do stuff by the book. Generally. And just before the river bed dried up, the heavens opened, and it rained like Hell. Drummond got a green light from somebody with a bit more power above him, put SKIN into motion, invited the Yanks to join the party, grabbed the top floor of Lassiter House, and called McHale.

'We're still one short,' said Daisy.

She was interrupted by the sound of the lift door opening.

'Not anymore,' said McHale.

In a perfectly executed synchronised movement, the team turned as one to see Spencer Pope walking towards them. Light brown hair, a touch of ginger. Large, well-groomed beard. Faded

Pink Floyd 'Dark Side of the Moon' t-shirt. Well-worn khaki shorts. Black crocs, scuffed. Tanned skin. A shade over six three, just under fifteen stone. About thirty-something. Smiling like an ad in a dental magazine and carrying a square, sealed cardboard box. He looked like a cross between an artist and a beach bum, which, in reality, wasn't a million miles from the truth.

'Hi, McHale,' he said, gently placing the box on the table and giving the smiling cop a man-hug.

'Hi Pope,' said McHale, as the air was squeezed out of his lungs. Ten seconds of recovery later, he managed to say, 'Ladies and gents, allow me to introduce Spencer Pope. This is the bum who helped me out on one of my first ever serials.'

Toby's eyes popped wide open. 'Hang on. You're talking about Boris, right?' he said.

'Boris who? said Lightfoot.

'My lips are sealed,' said Toby, and closed an imaginary zipper fastening his mouth shut tight.

The team introduced themselves with either a hug (Daisy), a handshake (Rice), a fist bump (Toby), or a slight nod of the head and a piercing glance (Lightfoot).

Pope licked his lips. 'Damn, I need caffeine injection,' he said. McHale pointed to the kitchen and watched him amble off. Then he told the rest of the team a story.

'A long time ago, in a galaxy far, far away…' he said.

'Star Wars,' said Toby, who was looking intently at the cardboard box.

'Fine. On April Fool's Day in 2013, in Fife, the second largest police force in the UK was born. They called it Police Scotland. The day it opened for business, a cardboard box was hand delivered to the Govan Police Station, Divisional HQ. It was addressed in black felt-tip pen to; *The Polis in Charge*.

'It was dropped off by a middle-aged woman, with short, greying hair, wearing a red coat. She put the box on the reception desk, then promptly walked away. Fast. By the time the receptionist got to the door to grab her, she had disappeared. So, without further ado they called the Bomb Squad who gave it the once over and said it was safe to open up. Shortly after that, the receptionist threw up. Projectile vomiting can be spectacular to behold.

'The box contained a head. Well, to be more precise, a skull. No hair, no flesh, no eyes, no brain. Just bone. Grubby as Hell. They thought it was somebody having a joke. A grim welcome for Scotland's new police organisation.'

Behind them, they could hear Pope singing to himself as he made a coffee. The song was Sympathy for the Devil by The Rolling Stones. He was no Mick Jagger, but at least he sang in tune. McHale took a large gulp of his warm coffee, shoved his mouth into gear, and continued.

'Anyway, they gave the skull to their forensics guys who, after a lengthy but unproductive examination, put it on a shelf, named it Boris, then promptly forgot about it.'

By that time, Pope had returned with his coffee. He found a seat, parked his arse, stretched out his legs, sipped the coffee, and had a good look at everyone else around the table.

'Why Boris?' said Daisy.

McHale looked at the newcomer and motioned him to continue the story.

Pope grinned. 'Because it was male and somebody liked the name. So…' and he shrugged. 'Then, two weeks later, they got another skull in another cardboard box. Delivered to the same Govan HQ. Same woman. Same red coat. Same disappearing act. Same condition. Only this time the skull was female.'

'You can tell the difference?' said Daisy.

Pope looked at Daisy and double blinked. 'It's all in the bones,' he said.

Shit, thought Toby, *a double blinker.*

'Anyway, they called up a couple of forensic folk who did facial reconstructions. Technically good, but when it came to imagination, they sucked big time. See… facial reconstructing isn't just about putting flesh on the bones and then hoping somebody recognises them. Faces don't stay still. They move around. They animate. They have a million damned expressions. That's my kind of facial reconstruction. Other folk just build up the faces and then freeze them. I bring them to life.'

Pope looked at McHale. 'Now?' he said.

'Now,' said McHale.

The sculptor reached forward and pulled the cardboard box towards him. It slid across the table top with ease. He was just about to rip off the gaffer tape stuck to the box opening when a closed Balisong knife slid across the table towards him. He looked up. Lightfoot gave him a single nod. Almost as if shaking hands with an old friend, Pope deftly flicked the knife open with a well-practised twist of his right wrist and slit the tape. He closed the knife just as expertly, slid it back to Lightfoot, nodded once, and continued speaking.

Pope continued, 'At the time, I was freelancing in their lab and I said I could do a better bloody job with Boris and the other skull, which they named Doris.'

'Boris and Doris. Nice,' said Toby.

Pope reached into the box and brought out a cream-coloured woollen cloth. Then he unfolded the cloth, laid it on the table, reached back in the box and brought out a head. Not a grubby skull with all the bits off and only the bones left. This was a reconstructed head, cast in black resin, of a man whose face was full of life. He rested the head on the cloth and turned it around for all to see, and paused for effect. Then he spoke as if he was introducing the star of the show. 'Team… meet Boris. Boris… meet team.' It was as if they were looking at the face of a man twisted in agony. Someone who had just received a hefty kick in the bollocks.

Rice was the first to speak. 'Have you ever heard of an eighteenth-century German sculptor called Franz Xaver Messerschmidt?' said the Jesuit.

Pope nodded in surprise and admiration. 'I saw some of his

heads in New York in 2010.'

'It's not every day you see something that's beautiful and terrible both at the same time,' said Rice.

'Thanks,' said Pope.

'So… how did Boris help catch a serial killer?'

Pope nodded in McHale's direction. 'Ask him,' he said.

Just then, a deep voice interrupted their conversation. It belonged to one of the techs working on SKIN. He was small and thin, and his voice didn't match his physical appearance.

'Going live in two minutes,' he said.

McHale turned to the rest of the team. 'To be continued,' he said.

'No problemo,' said Pope. 'Boris has a PhD in staying very still.'

'Figured as much.'

Everyone looked at the screen wall. It was blank. Deep Voice did a countdown slowly back from ten. He got to zero and everyone held their collective breath. Nothing happened. Everyone let out their collective breath.

Deep Voice was halfway through an apology when, just after 10am, about twenty seconds later, the screen wall came alive.

It announced its own birth with the first few orchestral bars of 'Sunrise'. The opening fanfare of Thus Spake Zarathustra by Richard Strauss. Better known from the opening sequence of Stanley Kubrick's 1968 movie 2001: A Space Odyssey. A McHale favourite. He thought the musical intro was a bit over the top. Deep Voice loved the hell out of it, and then some.

The screen showed the newly designed logo for SKIN Serial Killer Intelligence Network, in the grey typeface that mirrored the words on the wall. It gave the impression of growing in size and clarity, as if it was coming towards the team from a distance through a mist.

When it had nearly filled the screen, three things happened in quick succession; one, it came to a halt. Two, the music hit a natural conclusion. And three, a voice spoke. It was difficult to tell whether the voice was male or female. And difficult to pin down the accent.

It was British with American undertones. Or it might have been American with British overtones. It had the androgynous feel of a David Bowie, mixed with the husky, sassy quality of a Whoopi Goldberg. And the first words it ever uttered were these;

Good morning, people. Welcome to the first, and coolest, serial killer intelligence network designed exclusively for law enforcement anywhere in the world. My name is SKIN... and I am pleased as hell to meet y'all.

'Outstanding,' said Pope.

Lightfoot had a large smile on her face.

The others were trying to pick their jaws up off the floor. All except McHale, who had swallowed the last of his coffee at precisely the wrong time.

Behind them, Deep Voice said, 'Shit, I thought we'd toned down the colloquial part of the conversation software. Sorry about that. Give me a minute.'

'No!' said McHale, loudly. 'Keep it. I like it just the way it is.'

McHale! said SKIN. *I knew I was gonna like you.*

McHale turned to look at Deep Voice, a confused look on his face.

'What Mother and Holmes know, SKIN knows,' said Deep Voice. 'None of you need to go through the voice and facial recognition step. Well, except the big guy in the Pink Floyd t-shirt.'

'Who, me?' said Pope.

Yeah... the sculptor, said SKIN. *Okay, artistic guy, stand up, look at me and smile.*

Spence did as he was told.

Now tell me your name, your age, and your phone number.

'SKIN!' said Deep Voice, in a slow, disapproving manner.

Okay, okay. We'll leave the phone number for later.

Pope cleared his throat. 'Spencer Pope. Thirty-five. And you can call me anytime you like.'

Photo IDs of every team member, including Pope, appeared on the screen.

'Printed photo IDs will be ready in a few minutes,' said SKIN.

'Right,' said McHale, turning away to face the team. 'Back to business. Where were we?'

'You were telling us a story,' said Rice.

'Right. How Boris helped us catch a serial killer.'

'Actually, can I ask a question first?' inquired Daisy, turning to face Spence.

'Fire away, sister,' he said.

'How come you do your reconstructions in clay instead of using 3-D printing? I thought that would be faster and give you more resemblance options. And wouldn't it be better with the digital E-FIT system we've got?'

Pope double blinked. 'And there was I thinking I was talking to the uninitiated,' he said.

'Daisy has a natural affinity with digital technology,' said McHale.

'Oh, I know,' said SKIN.

Surprise registered on McHale's face.

'What? You think I don't listen? I have a brain the size of a planet and my switch is permanently in the 'on' position. I am your eyes and ears. We can communicate in the office, by mobile, even by earwig when we're on the job. I think Daisy and I need to have a little one-on-one later.'

'You're a lot more, um… interesting than I thought you might be,' said Daisy, who couldn't figure out which gender to assign, if any.

'That's what all the boys say. And all the girls.'

'Pope?' said McHale, bringing the conversation back on track.

'Right. Sure, I use 3-D. And yeah, it's a very cool tool. The future's definitely digital. But I like getting my fingers dirty. And my nails. I like feeling the clay next to my skin. Pardon the pun. With 3-D there's too much distance between me and the head, if you get what I mean.'

Daisy was looking closely at Boris and nodding her head. 'I do,' she said.

Toby didn't care for the way Pope was looking at Daisy. *Too much interest there*, he thought. So, he decided to head him off at the pass. 'What's with Boris's screwed-up face?' he said.

'Uncle George,' said Pope. 'He was schizophrenic. He had something called Tardive Dyskinesia. It was a side effect of the medicine he had to take. He used to grimace, and screw his face up, and stick his tongue out, and blink a lot. He spent most of his married life thinking he was possessed by The Devil. And whenever anyone else was in the house, except for my Aunt Mamie, he would contort his features painfully and say this was what The Devil looked like.

'The result was that Mamie was the only one who saw his normal face. They had no children. Not surprisingly. Everyone else saw the face of The Devil. Then I read about Messerschmidt and found out that he was a diagnosed schizophrenic who thought he was possessed, too. He would pinch himself painfully in the ribs, then recreate the expressions that appeared on his face, courtesy of his spirits. That's how he created his famous 'character heads.' Apparently. Maybe he had Tardive Dyskinesia too.'

McHale noticed that Lightfoot had been quiet throughout the story. She had the look of someone who was remembering, not simply imagining. Her eyes never left Spence.

Pope tapped the top of Boris's head. 'So… back to my good mate here. Before I built up his features and gave him the "Spence Touch", I gave him a good once-over. The shape of the eye sockets, nasal aperture, bridge of the nose, jawline, teeth, all told me that they were a European male. At some point in his life, his left cheekbone had been fractured. All his teeth were in place. Now for the technical bit. Based on my examination of the major cranial suture sites, I estimated Boris was between thirty-five and fifty years of age when he died. Give or take. Same for Doris.

'So, first, I reconstructed the heads using 3-D software, and ended up with a face with standard expressionless features. Then Police Scotland went to work hoping that somebody somewhere would recognise them. Nobody did. Not a bloody sausage. Then, while that was happening, I did a second, clay only, versions of one of the heads. And this time I let good old Uncle George guide my fingers and my imagination.'

Pope reached over and slowly revolved the head on the table again to give everyone another good view of the expression on the face. He placed his right hand on the top of Boris's head and said; 'And this is what I ended up with. I thought maybe somebody might recognise the poor bastard with some sort of expression on his face, instead of just a blank look.' He nodded again to McHale. 'Over to you.'

McHale took over the story. 'Two days after Police Scotland put the image out on TV, they got a phone call from a woman. She said it looked like her brother. He and his wife and son went missing in February 2011. She said it was like they just dropped off the face of the earth.

'The man's name was Harry Fletcher. She said she thought he suffered from extremely painful migraines, which caused his face to distort and twist out of shape. She said as soon as she saw the photo on the telly it was like looking at her brother when he had one of his funny turns.

'Did he suffer from schizophrenia?' said Daisy.

'Good question. It was the break we were looking for. Four months later, we arrested a Polish butcher with a history of mental illness. He thought people were trying to kill him. Not everyone. Just the ones who screwed up their faces when they looked at him. Or maybe he just thought they did. So, he killed them first. We found six wedding rings in a box hidden behind a wall panel in his house.

'He was married. His wife knew he was a killer. She knew where he buried the bodies. In her wardrobe, we found a red coat. His name is Max Guzek. He's serving six life sentences with no possibility of parole. He lives in a metal box. They'll carry him out in a wooden one.'

'Where?' said Rice.

'Same place as David Black,' said McHale. 'Broadmoor.' He looked at the contorted face of Boris, staring back at him through his own private hell of pain. And he thought about his visit to Black, and the two other occupied cells in The Monster House. So… Guzek must be one of the other two House members. He didn't know whether he was the flesh eater or not.

He looked at the team. 'I used to think that the scariest serial killers were the ones we had locked up. The ones we caught so other folk could figure out why they did what they did. And the rest of us could sleep safe in our beds. Not any more. The scariest bastards are the ones still out there. The ones we haven't caught yet. The ones still killing. Or getting ready to kill. We might not know where they are yet, but now we know who one of them might be.' He looked at the screen wall. 'SKIN?' he said.

'I'm listening,' said the disembodied voice.

'When I came back from Broadmoor I gave Stella a slip of paper with three words written on it, asked her to feed them into your system… remember?

'I never forget,' said SKIN.

It wasn't a boast.

'Do the words mean anything?' wondered McHale.

'That's a silly question to ask someone with the biggest brain on the planet,' said SKIN, scoffing.

A spluttered laugh forced its way out past Pope's teeth, only to be strangled at birth.

'The second and third words are easy,' the yellow slip of paper given to McHale by Black appeared on the screen wall.. 'Grey John is one of the good guys. He's a foreign national who spends most days looking after the homeless near Soho. The first word, Lazarov, is a bit more difficult, but a lot more interesting.'

The slip of paper on the screen was replaced by a black and white portrait photograph of a man *'This is a Bulgarian male,'* said SKIN. *'His name is Anton Lazarov. He was born in Bulgaria.*

He had an older brother, Dragan, who was murdered in Sofia Central Prison, on April 21st, 2015.

Bells were ringing loudly between McHale's ears.

'SKIN,' he said. 'Bring up any photos you have on record of Anton Lazarov. Time to go to work.'

Then he sent a text message to DCS Cyril Drummond at New Scotland Yard. It was twenty-six words long. The words were these.

'Morning Guv. Good news. Don't hold your breath, but I think we might have a new serial to hunt. And we have two new team members to welcome. Want to meet the gang? M.'

Less than a minute later, he received a reply. It was twenty-two words long.

'Wild bloody horses couldn't drag me away from that. Put the kettle on. I'll be there in fifteen. Give or take. CD.'

Chapter Four

It was 10.32am. London was dull and grey. But the top floor of Lassiter House was bright and full of colourful language.

Deep Voice and some of his hi-tech band of brothers, and one sister, were fussing like a clutch of mother hens over a single, very impressive, newborn chick.

On the screen wall, the close-up portrait had been replaced by a colour photograph of a thick-set, smiling man in his mid-twenties, wearing winter gear. He had short, dark hair and his smile was purely for the camera. He was crouching in the snow over the trophy body of a dead deer, right hand on the antlers. The other on a rifle with telescopic sights, butt end in the snow; naked fist wrapped around the barrel.

The photo had a dark stain on the top left-hand corner. Under the photo was a shot of the reverse, with writing in black ink. The writing was this;

'BULGARIAN. Anton Lazarov. Hunter.'

'SKIN… any idea where and when the photo was taken?' said McHale.

'Nope.'

'Okay… do you have any record of an Anton Lazarov entering the UK in the last twelve months?'

'Four Antons and no Lazarovs. If he's here, he's sneaky,' said SKIN. *'Tracking all the Antons now.'*

'Check the US borders, too,' said Lightfoot.

'Way ahead of you, sister.'

Lightfoot smiled.

'SKIN, you have a complete record of all serial killers – dead or in police custody, right?'

'Seriously?'

'I suspect she doesn't joke,' said Rice, giving SKIN a female gender without thinking.

'No entries in the US.'

'Concentrate on the four in the UK,' said McHale.

'Okay. I've got three Antons in London and one in Birmingham.'

SKIN's screen split vertically in two. On the left, the photograph of Anton Lazarov remained, crouching over his kill. On the right, a list of four names, ages, and locations appeared.

Anton Boyan. Aged 73. West Hampstead, London.

Anton Nedyalko. Aged 49. Lewisham, London.

Anton Grozdan. Aged 38. Battersea, London.

Anton Mladen. Aged 52. Sutton Coldfield, Birmingham.

'They're all British citizens and came back to the UK after short trips abroad. Two from Spain, one from France, and one from Italy. They're all married with children except Anton Boyan. He's a widower with a pacemaker and he never had any children.'

'Okay,' said Lightfoot. 'Now compare your list of serial killers with all entries into the US or UK from anywhere by boat, plane, train, or car.'

'Time frame?'

'Any time within the past five years.'

McHale stopped in his tracks on the way to the kitchen for a coffee refill. 'Clever,' he said.

Pause. Four heartbeats.

'Curious,' said SKIN.

'Make that very clever,' said McHale.

'On Monday, October 17th, 2016, a ferry from Santander in Spain docked in Portsmouth at 7.45pm.'

'And?'

'And there was a male passenger on board who might be 156 years old.'

'Was he a captive giant tortoise from the Galapagos islands?' said McHale.

'No.'

'Was he a Bowhead Whale?'

'You watch too much Attenborough.'

'What was his name?'

'Henry Howard Holmes.'

Lightfoot, whose gestures were always small and economical, slapped the desktop. 'That's him,' she said.

'Him who?' said Toby.

'Anton Lazarov.'

Before she could explain, McHale said, 'Henry Howard Holmes, or to call him by his more familiar name 'H. H. Holmes' was a Nineteenth Century American serial killer. Born Herman Webster Mudgett in 1861 in New Hampshire.'

'Well, colour me bloody impressed,' said Pope.

'Another Holmes,' said Toby.

McHale shrugged. 'If you have any interest in serial killers, you know about H. H. Holmes. You need to get up to speed, Toby.'

Daisy was scribbling. Information was her favourite food and drink. She stopped and looked up at the screen wall. 'SKIN... how many serial killers do we know of, dead or alive?' she said.

Longer pause.

'Five hundred and twenty-five single serials. Fifty-three serial groups and couples. Twenty-nine disputed cases. Breathing or not. Locked up or buried.'

'And let me guess... those are only the ones we know about,' said Toby.

'Excluding war criminals.'

'You absolutely sure about those numbers?'

'When you're talking about serial killers, there's only one thing you can be sure of. And that's nobody can be absolutely sure of a damned thing,' said McHale.

There was silence from the team as they took in the numbers.

Finally, the Jesuit spoke. 'I suppose when you consider the billions of people who have lived over the past couple of hundred years, that's just a drop in the ocean.'

'Somehow, that doesn't make me feel any better,' said Daisy.

McHale noticed that Lightfoot had that look of remembering in her eyes again. She re-focused and came back from the past to the present.

'Spit it out,' he said.

She took a deep breath and turned to Pope. 'As the others know, I come from the largest Native American tribe in the US, the Cherokee. When I was young, my great grandfather used to take me out into the forests and the mountains and teach me how to hunt and track. His white name was Nimrod Smith. His Cherokee name was Yonaguska. I was a twelve-year-old girl and nobody else would teach me. And he was an old man and nobody else would listen to him. Except me. During that time, he used to tell me stories that his father used to tell him. I'm sure some of them were true. And I'm also sure that some of them were just stories to tell youngsters to keep them entertained and interested.'

She noticed that Pope was slowly and absent-mindedly stroking his beard.

'Anyway, one of those stories was about the Seven Twisted-Face Men. He said that in the time of his own great grandfather there lived a group of young men who survived the Trail of Tears. Seven is a sacred number to the Cherokee. And the Trail of Tears was the name given to the forced relocations, in 1838, of the Cherokee nation, from their ancestral lands. During that relocation, over four thousand died of exposure, disease, and starvation.

'Of those who survived the Trail, there were seven young men who vowed never to let the expressions of sorrow, pain, anger, disgust, shock, shame, and rage leave their faces, as a mark of respect for those who died.

'After that, and for as long as they lived, they were called the Seven Twisted-Face Men. Even today, those men and the Trail of Tears are never forgotten.'

The team was captivated. It was a pin-drop moment.

'Did they really exist?' said Rice.

Lightfoot shrugged. 'The Trail of Tears was real. As for the seven men... who knows? I'm an FBI agent. I catch killers. I deal in facts. It was probably only a story that an old man told. But I remembered his description, and when I saw Boris, and the painful look on his face, I remembered The Twisted-Face Men.'

McHale knew that she was more than just an FBI agent. That was barely scratching the surface of who, and what, she really was.

'Mac,' said SKIN, *'do you believe in coincidences?'*

'Ooh... here it comes,' said Inner Voice. *'First it's McHale... now it's Mac. Just like that MOTHER dame. Next it will be Mac & SKIN. Watch your damned back, Kemosabe!'*

'That depends,' said McHale. 'Why?'

'I have a soundbite of your voice in my databank.'

Pause.

SKIN played a recording of McHale's voice. He spoke seven words. They were these, *'Coincidences mean you're on the right track.'*

'Ah,' said Toby. 'You're talking about McHale's Maxims.'

Pope turned to McHale. 'You got maxims?' he said.

'I bought them from an old guy in an antique shop from, along with a Welsh dresser that had probably never been to Wales in its life,' said McHale, frowning at Toby then looking at the screen wall. Lightfoot looked at him and raised a right eyebrow. She didn't say that this particular maxim had been passed on to him from her. And she didn't say that it had been passed on to her from one of her old FBI mentors. McHale acquired maxims like cuckoos acquired other birds' nests to hatch their chicks.

'Your point?'

'My point is I found something curious,' said SKIN. *'When the Bulgarian authorities uncovered the twenty bodies, their forensics team took a total of 570 digital photographs on site. The bodies were mostly skeletonized. The last one had been in the ground for only a few days.'*

'And?' said McHale.

'See for yourself.'

The images disappeared from the vertical split screen and were replaced by two more images. The one on the left showed the head of a male who could have been anywhere between twenty and forty. It was hard to tell on first inspection. He was taken out of the ground around two days after he had been put in it. The bugs and worms and insects had been hard at work. But the expression on his face was still there for all to see. It was almost a carbon copy of the face in pain on the other screen.

Boris.

SKIN played the soundbite again.

'Coincidences mean you're on the right track.'

'Shit,' whispered Toby.

'Double shit,' said Pope.

True light bulb moments are few and far between. When they come within touching distance you can either watch, them as they fly by, or reach out and grab them by the balls.

McHale reached and grabbed.

'I know that look,' said Lightfoot.

'Of course you do,' said a gruff voice behind them. 'It's the look on the face of a hungry wolf when he smells his next meal,' said Drummond, standing unannounced behind them.

The senior copper nodded at everyone in the team.

McHale noticed that he was carrying a small parcel wrapped in brown paper in his left hand. It was the shape of a book. He stepped forward and handed it to McHale. 'A moving-in gift,' he said.

'Very thoughtful of you,' said McHale, a look of genuine surprise on his face.

'Don't thank me,' said the older copper. 'I'm not into housewarming gifts. This is something from Molly Spencer. Remember her? I've no bloody idea what it is. I'm just the messenger boy.'

McHale's mind flashed back to the previous year. Molly

Spencer was the mysterious woman who appeared at the team's temporary HQ at Winfield House a couple of days before they wrapped up the hunt for The Holy Ghost. She looked and sounded like someone important. More important than Drummond. She offered help with the stakeout and capture.

As McHale's old grandad used to say, *'Better to have it and not need it, than need it and not have it.'*

They needed it.

McHale put the package on the table and promptly forgot about it.

Drummond, one gift lighter, stepped forward, smiled at Pope, held out his hand, and pumped the sculptor's arm a couple of times.

'Cyril Drummond,' he said. 'Welcome aboard.'

Then, without waiting for an answer, he turned his attention to Boris. He reached out and rested his right hand on the top of Boris's head, patted it a couple of times, then turned to face the screen wall.

'So… I gather you're SKIN,' he said.

'Good morning, Cyril. I gather you're the big cheese,' said SKIN.

Another pin drop moment. Then Drummond laughed.

'Not even bloody close.'

He sat down in the nearest vacant seat, then he turned to McHale. 'I thought I'd kick things off by giving you a juicy bit of news. At 9am this morning, Broadmoor's newest facility got another resident. The kind that comes in vertical and eventually goes out horizontal.'

'Have they put him anywhere near Black?' said Toby.

Drummond's right eyebrow arched. 'Where else would you put the latest member of The Monster House?'

'So… that makes four in there now. Only another eight to go and they'll have to start building an extension.'

'The Monster House. Love that name. I think I might get a t-shirt made with it on the front,' said Pope, smiling.

'Black T with white letters?' said Lightfoot.

Pope gave her the thumbs up and smiled.

McHale frowned, then looked at Toby. 'Coffee time.'

Toby took the hint, collected the mugs, and headed for the kitchen. There was a large pause with small talk while caffeine was made and distributed. Then they got back into it.

'What's this new monster's name?' said Lightfoot.

Drummond looked at McHale. 'Georgie Romano.'

'The kid?' said McHale, right eyebrow raised.

'You mean the murderous psychopath,' said Daisy.

'Why do I know that name?' said Lightfoot, thinking, a crease furrowing her brow.

Drummond looked at the screen wall. 'SKIN... bring up a photo of Georgie Romano. The birthday party one taken when he was ten-years old.'

Fully integrated with the MOTHER and HOLMES networks, SKIN took only a fraction of a second to respond. A colour photograph appeared on the screen wall.

Half a dozen children were sitting outside at a table set out for a kid's birthday party. The date was January 17th, 2009. The party was in full swing. The food had been decimated And the table was a mess. The children were a mess. They were having a ball. All except one; the one whose birthday it was.

Little Georgie Romano.

Little Georgie with the quiet voice.

Little Georgie with the ripped Spider-Man costume and the split lip.

Little Georgie with the murderous look in his eyes.

Little Georgie who had grown up and killed seven people. One when he was thirteen. Three when he was sixteen. They caught him shortly after and put him in a cell on his own. Then he killed three more. So, they gave him lifetime membership of The Monster House. Cell number ten on the row behind David Black.

He was nineteen years young outside his head. He was a lot older inside it.

In the world of British serial killers and their groupies, Georgie Romano was a bit of a rock star. But in the world of serial killer hunters, he was yesterday's news.

'A lot of people were fascinated by Georgie,' said Drummond.

McHale shrugged. "Were' is the operative word. He was fascinating until he got caught. Then he just became interesting. But we know about somebody who's extremely bloody fascinating. Somebody who makes Georgie look like an angel-faced choirboy.'

He looked at the rest of the team, ending up with Drummond. Then he took a breath and spoke.

'As of today, we'll be hunting a fifty-two-year-old Bulgarian male named Anton Lazarov,' said McHale. 'Lazarov is a highly intelligent, highly organised possible serial killer with a unique MO. We think he's killed twenty individuals so far. He may have killed a whole lot more. We also think he's now here in the UK… and he's active.'

For the next half an hour, McHale passed on information and ticked boxes. The others either zipped their lips and nodded in all the right places. Or else they chipped in with the right words at the right time. Georgie Romano faded into the background. For now. McHale spoke about his visit to Black and the story Pope told him about his uncle, and the eighteenth-century German sculptor Franz Xaver Messerschmidt's character heads. He also told them about the bodies buried in shallow graves in Bulgaria and the look on the face of the most recently buried body. He wound up his tale with Anton Lazarov visiting his brother in prison and the possibility of Lazarov taking the name of H. H. Holmes, to gain entry into the UK.

Lightfoot's soft voice came from his left. 'You haven't mentioned the unique MO.'

That's when he told them that the victims in the forest were buried face down.

Just like Dragan's mother, Svetlana.

Then he stopped talking and took a large gulp of his coffee. Sitting back in his chair, he took a deep breath, and let it out slowly.

'Jesus fucking Christ,' said Drummond, softly. 'And you guys came up with this in a week?'

'Less,' said McHale.

'We think fast,' said Toby.

Lightfoot was sitting on the left of McHale. He felt her right foot softly tap his left leg. He got the message. 'Of course, we're talking theory,' he said. 'Some of it we can prove. Some of it we can take a damned good guess at. And the rest of it wouldn't hold water in a leaky bucket. But it's a start.'

Drummond pointed to the photograph of Lazarov on the screen wall. 'And this bastard is here in the UK?'

'We believe so,' said Lightfoot.

'SKIN,' said Daisy, 'bring up on screen the list of names of serial killers alive or dead since the turn of the Twentieth Century.'

The screen image changed and was replaced by a numbered list of 629 names.

SKIN made the names big enough to read and scrolled them slowly to look even more impressive.

'If we're right… and Anton's here… and he's killing… and he likes changing names to keep us on the hop… then this is his pool of aliases,' said Daisy. 'We've only got him using H. H. Holmes so far. But it's a big pool. SKIN is hunting 24/7 to see if he's using any of the others. I think we can safely say that this is part of his M.O. So, unless something pretty drastic happens, I think he's going to stick to the list.'

Drummond nodded. 'He'll change names as often as he can,' said Lightfoot, picking up her mug and getting her throat ready for a warm, slow hug. Her throat was disappointed. 'The more names he uses, the more difficult he'll be to track. By tomorrow, he'll be somebody new. Maybe.'

'Maybe?' said Toby.

'Possibly,' said Lightfoot.

'But only by name,' said Rice. Everybody turned and looked at him. 'I've spent most of my life behind the drawn-back little curtain taking confessions. Anton could be sat there on the other side of the curtain, and I wouldn't recognise him from Adam. But as soon as he opened his mouth, the cat would be out of the bag.'

'As long as we knew what he sounded like,' said Lightfoot. 'So, apart from all the other things we need, we need a sample of his voice.'

'Which we don't have,' said McHale.

'Well… what does a Bulgarian male sound like when he's speaking English?'

'I don't have a bloody clue.'

'Neither do I. But I know a man who does,' said Rice, who stood up and walked away from the table, pulling a mobile phone from the right-hand pocket of his black trousers.

He walked slowly to the other end of the room. He was halfway there before he started speaking. His voice was low. After about thirty seconds, he ended the call and walked back to the table. Everyone around the table was looking at him. Everyone except Drummond. He was scrolling emails on his own mobile phone. He looked like he was spending one half of his life catching up with the other half.

'And?' said McHale.

'And I need to go meet up with someone,' said the Jesuit.

'What, now?'

'I have two times for meeting up with him. Now… and God knows when.'

'Do you need a car or a cab?' said Drummond. 'I can arrange that.'

Rice seemed to think about it for a second. Then he shook his head. 'No. I think it's better if I don't get anyone else involved,' he said, putting on his jacket.

'Hang on,' said McHale. 'I'm not sure I like the sound of this. Will you be safe?'

Rice smiled. 'Don't worry, Tom. Grey John is an old friend.' And he walked out the door into the outer hallway.

The name Grey John rang an immediate and loud alarm bell in the space between McHale's ears.

He hurried through the door and caught the Jesuit waiting by the lift. Rice looked slightly startled. 'I'm sorry, but you can't come with me. You'll have to trust me on this,' he said.

'Fine. I just wanted to tell you something about my meeting with Black. Before I left, he gave me a slip of paper. He said it was something to get the ball rolling. There were two names written on the paper. One was Lazarov. The other was Grey John.' Rice looked surprised. His eyebrows pointed skywards. Then he seemed to consider his response and the eyebrows came back down to earth. 'Tom, Grey John is a man who works with homeless people. Lots of these people have a history of mental illness. He's not really big on meeting with the police. He's very wary of outsiders, but I know for a fact that over the years he's helped hundreds of street people get the treatment they needed. Grey John is only the name he's given himself. I don't know his real name. I'm not sure many people do.'

A thin veil of frustration was covering McHale's face. 'What's his connection to Black?'

Rice looked impatient. The lift was dragging its heels. 'That's a question you'll have to ask Black. It's not a question I want to ask Grey John. I might not like the answer.'

'And you're sure he won't talk to me?'

'He'll talk to me, but I'm afraid he might regard you as persona non grata, as they say.'

The lift arrived. The doors opened, and the Jesuit stepped in and turned around to face the copper. McHale looked worried. But he also knew that he had to leave Rice to handle this by himself. 'What makes you think he can help?' he said.

Rice shrugged. 'His mother was Bulgarian.'

'Was?'

'She disappeared fifteen years ago.'

McHale felt the vague tremor of another alarm bell. It was ringing very faintly in the distance, but growing louder.

McHale's voice went up a few decibels. 'Where from?'

But whatever Rice said was lost in the distraction of the lift door arriving.

McHale swore under his breath and walked back in to join the rest of the team.

Chapter Five

It was 1.05pm, and it was the beginning of a crowded afternoon in the heart of Soho, London. In the middle of it all, there was a small café that catered for the kind of people who wouldn't know a flat white if it bit them hard on the arse. They wanted tea or coffee; black or white, no complications. They ate sandwiches with two choices of bread and two choices of filling. They ignored a few sorry-looking cakes behind a see-through counter. They washed… sometimes. And they sat at the kind of tables that got wiped every hour on the hour, regardless of spillage.

The café was a stubborn remnant of a tired and emotional old Soho. It had a handful of customers, two of whom were huddled together as far away from the door as possible. They were Father Stephen Rice and the man he knew as Grey John.

'Thank you for meeting me, John,' said Rice, who was cradling a black coffee in his hands. 'I know this isn't easy for you.'

'I did what you asked,' said the man, before sipping a hot, sweet, milky tea. The kind of tea that could replicate itself half a dozen times using just the one perforated bag.

Grey John was in his late forties, and at one time he had a lion's mane of greyish hair, tied in a ponytail hanging down his neck. Now the only part of the mane that remained was a small lick of a tail at the back of his head. The rest of his head was shaved and shiny. Grey John was really pinkish brown John.

He was five-ten and wiry; permanently tired and ill. His movements were careful and his glances were furtive. His voice was rough and his accent was Slavic. He wore an old green t-shirt, blue jeans, scuffed work boots, and a green combat jacket with a small, mended rip on the right shoulder. These few clothes, or ones like them, had constituted his uniform for the past ten years. He knew a woman who knew a washing machine.

'You'll be helping us a great deal, John. I appreciate it,' said the Jesuit. And he slipped three folded £20 notes across the table, neatly swerving them to avoid a still-wet coffee stain. In return, Grey John pushed a silver DVD in a transparent case towards Rice, who quickly and unobtrusively slipped it into his right-hand jacket pocket.

It looked to the rest of the world like an insignificant bit of commerce between two people who might, or might not, have known each other. In fact, it was two things. One easy, the other not so much. The easy thing was a payment for services rendered. Sixty quid for the sound of a voice and some information. And the not so easy thing was checking up on the physical and psychological health of an old friend.

Grey John's health in both departments was not far off the crash and burn phase. He was fit in short bursts and not so fit in long ones. His pancreatic cancer was so advanced it had a survival rate in years you could count on the fingers of one hand. Maybe two. It was eating away at his body. And his emotional cancer, after the unexplained disappearance of a loved one, was eating away at his soul.

Transaction completed, the two spoke of other things for the next fifteen minutes. 'What's today's total so far,' said Rice. He was referring to the number of homeless people, young and old, of both sexes, that John had managed to get off the streets and into sheltered accommodation.

'I don't count anymore,' said John. He took another sip from his gnat's piss tea and looked at the table. What he saw there was anyone's guess, but it sure as Hell had nothing to do with cheap PVC covering tired old wood. The whites of his eyes were vaguely yellow; the colour of his skin wasn't far behind. His head was sore from lack of peace and quiet, and his heart was sore from the pain inflicted by the life he led.

A decision was made to pass on a confidence. To tell a story.

'You remember Sam?' He said, avoiding Rice's gaze.

Rice pictured the small, thin, girl who must have been no more than fifteen or sixteen the last time he saw her a year or so ago. He smiled at the memory. 'I remember. How is she?'

John sighed heavily. He was quiet for the longest time. Finally, he looked up and there were tears in his eyes. 'She was asleep in her usual spot by the Arches one night a couple of weeks ago. Four drunken animals pissed on her, then they stamped on her and kicked her in the head. Then they laughed and ran away.

There were people walking nearby. Somebody called an ambulance. She died on the way to hospital.'

The tears ran down his cheeks and he angrily wiped them away with the right-hand sleeve of his jacket.

'Fifteen years old and killed with a kick in the head. All because she couldn't find anywhere safe to sleep. What kind of fucking world is this, eh?'

John was slowly shaking his head and looking at Rice. But what he was seeing was a young head covered in boot marks, a brain savagely damaged, and a life cruelly ended. The Jesuit felt like his heart was stuck in a vise and being slowly crushed. He suddenly had an image of all those people murdered and buried in shallow, unmarked graves in Bulgaria. There was no salve for that kind of wound.

Rice sighed and softly patted the back of John's left hand. 'I'm so sorry,' he said. He waited in silence for ten minutes. Then he stood up, turned, and walked out of the café, leaving the other man alone with his own angry thoughts.

Forty minutes later he was back at Lassiter House. He stopped at the reception desk and handed the DVD to Stella, the freckle-faced redhead. 'Something for SKIN to digest,' he said. 'Mark it 'Grey John' and put today's date on it.'

Stella nodded once. 'I'll pass it on,' she said.

Rice knew that was 'Stella-speak' for 'I'll make sure that it gets put into the right slot so the right piece of equipment can read it and the right piece of software can recognise it, and it can get added to all the trillions of other bits of information that SKIN has at its disposal at any given second.' Then he went upstairs and re-joined the team.

It was 2.38pm. Pope was the first to see him as he came back into the room. 'Cool… the return of the Prodigal Son, or should I say Father.' The look on Rice's face screamed at Pope to zip the lip, which he promptly did. Sometimes, the only thing as powerful as knowing when to speak up was knowing when to shut up. Rice walked directly to where McHale was sitting. The copper could see the dark look on the Jesuit's face. He didn't even wait until Rice spoke.

'Whatever you need, Stephen. Just say the word.'

Pause.

'Spit it out.'

'I'd like copies of all the photos taken at the graves in Bulgaria. As well as any autopsy photos and reports.'

McHale looked at him and nodded once.

'You're not going to ask why?'

'You'll tell me when you're ready. Anyway, way ahead of you, pal, I've already requested them from the authorities over there. I made the call when you were out.' He turned to the screen wall and spoke. 'SKIN… you got any emails with attachments from Bulgaria in the last couple of hours?'

'*Zilch,*' said SKIN. '*You'll know when I know.*'

Rice went to the chair he was in earlier that morning and parked his arse heavily on the cushioned padding covering the ergonomic chair. There was something bothering him apart from all the obvious, a detail or a fact or a feeling he couldn't quite put his finger on. It was just sitting out of reach, sneering at him.

Grey John was holding back. Rice knew instinctively when a penitent's confession was incomplete. He knew when something was bursting to come out, but couldn't make it past the lips and into the world. *Maybe it's on the DVD*, he thought.

A few seconds after he sat down, a hot black coffee appeared by his right hand. Daisy's sandalwood scent lingered after she disappeared without saying a word.

He whispered a 'Thank you' and thought she probably didn't hear him. He was wrong. He sipped, and the coffee tasted deliciously bitter. 'Right... what have I missed?' he said, looking around the table.

'Well, Drummond's exit, for a start,' said Toby. 'He made a call and marched out of the room wearing a face like thunder. God help anyone on the receiving end of whatever he had to say.'

'As long as whatever he had to say helps whatever we have to do, then I don't have a problem,' said McHale. Then he looked at Daisy and stared down at his own empty coffee cup. 'Where's mine?' he said in mock indignation.

'You know where the kitchen is, Guv,' she said with a raised eyebrow.

McHale stood up. Twenty feet to the kitchen and thirty seconds to make a fresh black refill. About turn and back in the saddle. Total time, one minutes twenty-three seconds. On the way back, he looked at Rice. 'We were wondering what might have triggered the killings. The earliest graves go back more than twenty years.

'So... discovered March 2015. That means the earliest ones are pre-1995 at least.' He turned to the screen wall. 'SKIN... I need you to trace a family. Bulgarian nationals, surname Lazarov. Mother and father unknown. Two siblings. Brothers Dragan and Anton. Dragan was murdered in Sofia Central Prison, 21st April, 2015 aged fifty-seven. Imprisoned for the killing of twenty individuals found in shallow graves somewhere in a remote forest in Southern Bulgaria. He was convicted, but he wasn't guilty. No further information.'

Long pause.

'This might take a while,' said SKIN.

'Your idea of taking a while seems to be a damned sight different to everyone else's,' said McHale.

'It's all in the genes, Mac. I had good parents.'

McHale smiled and was about to speak.

'Got them,' said SKIN.

'Damn, that was fast,' said Lightfoot.

'Nah! Fast is light moving its ass through space at 186,282 miles a second. This is just impressively quick.'

That got a few laughs.

'Okay Speedy, what have you got?' said McHale.

'Records from 1970 show a Lazarov family, father Radomir, mother Svetlana, older brother Dragan, younger brother Anton, living in a town called Madan, in South Bulgaria, near the Greek border.'

As SKIN spoke, corroborating text appeared on the screen wall.

'Radomir born 1st November, 1934. No date of death. Svetlana born 18th September, 1936, died 17th August, 1991.

'Dragan born 21st April, 1958, died 21st April, 2015. Anton born 11th July, 1966. No date of death.'

'That would make Radomir in his late fifties when the first of the bodies was buried, and nearly eighty by the time the last was uncovered,' said Daisy. 'That's if he's still alive.'

'Where are you going with this?'

Daisy scribbled something on her pad, then looked at McHale. 'What if Dragan and Radomir were a team? What if Radomir started killing first, and the older he got the more he needed help, so he brought Dragan into the family business, so to speak?'

'Wait, you're thinking about the Reichs family?' said Lightfoot.

Daisy lifted her pad and turned the page around to face the FBI agent. On it, written in blue ink in capital letters, were four words.

HARRY AND JOHN REICHS.

'Sometimes I scare myself with how little I know,' said Rice.

'Yeah, but the little you know is sometimes a lot more than

the little we know,' said McHale.

Lightfoot picked up the baton. 'Harry Reichs was a farmer in rural Oklahoma. He was a quiet, hard-working man. Married with one son. He was also a serial killer. He strangled and mutilated five young women… three white, one black, one latino… between 1961 and 1970 and buried them in shallow graves.'

'What the hell is it with killers and shallow graves?' said Pope.

Lightfoot looked at him. 'Less effort. Quick to bury. Easy to dig up and move to a new location.'

Pope nodded. Daisy scribbled. Lightfoot continued.

'Then, in 1971, he had a difference of opinion with a bad-tempered reaper and lost his left arm from the elbow down. His son, John, was fifteen at the time. He gave up his dream of going to college and dutifully became a farmer instead. Then his dad whispered in his ear and told him about his other job. John's eyes lit up. So, in 1972, he joined the family killing firm. Together, they killed another eleven women, six white, four black, and one Chinese, before they were eventually tracked down and caught in 1989.'

She turned to the screen wall. 'SKIN… can you clear the screen and bring up the mugshots of Harry Reichs and John Reichs?'

On the left was Harry. Handsome in an ugly kinda way. Hair mussed up, unshaven. Bruised about the left eye and cut on the bottom lip. Fifty, tops. Mean looking and angry. On the right was John. You could see the resemblance except for the nose. It was small and piggy looking. He was also beaten-up and a bit more scared. The Feds didn't mess about.

'*Bad news and good news,*' said SKIN. *John Reichs died in Oklahoma State Penitentiary in 2016 of pancreatic cancer. I suspect he's in Hell with no chance of parole.*'

Rice thought of Grey John and coincidences.

'Dammit,' said Lightfoot softly.

Daisy overheard her. 'Surely that's good news?' she said.

'I wanted to talk to him.'

'*I thought you might. The good news is that Harry's still alive,*' said SKIN. '*If you're quick you can talk to him.*'

'How quick?'

'*Let's say the sins of the son are about to be visited on the father.*'

'Cancer?'

'*Stage IV. Small cell lung. Very advanced. He might have a month if he's lucky. He might have longer if he's not. If you want to talk to him, you'd better make it very soon. He is one sick puppy. And I don't just mean in the head.*'

'See… here's what I don't get. Why the hell do you want to waste your breath talking to him?' said Daisy.

Lightfoot looked confused. 'The real question is why the hell wouldn't I?'

'Isn't that like opening Pandora's Box?' said Rice, standing and picking up his mug. 'Coffee anyone?'

Six hands went up. Rice wished he'd kept his mouth shut.

'Don't worry, Father, I'll ride shotgun,' said Lightfoot, grabbing four empty mugs. Rice grabbed the other two.

On her way back from the kitchen, Lightfoot said, 'Harry wrote a book about the killings. It was a best seller.'

Pope, who was walking his pen across the fingers of his right hand, suddenly stopped and threw it across the room. It bounced off the wall on the right of the screens.

Lightfoot shook her head slowly and smiled. 'Ever heard of the Son of Sam Law?'

'Berkowitz?' said Toby.

'Who?' said Pope, standing up and retrieving his pen.

McHale's inner voice decided to put in an appearance. '*Right. Let's see who the Hell remembers their Serial Killers 101 lesson.*'

Lightfoot faced the screen wall. 'SKIN,' she said, 'introduce the boys and girls to Son of Sam.'

'*My pleasure,*' said SKIN.

Pause.

Two mug shots from 11th August, 1977 came up on screen.

'Say hello to Richard David Falco, a.k.a. David Richard Berkowitz. The .44 Caliber Killer. Mister Monster. The Son of Sam. Six kills, seven wounded between 1976 and 1977. The subject of the biggest police manhunt in the history of New York City. He said his neighbour's dog Harvey ordered him to kill. Then he said he made it up. At least the bit about Harvey. After he was caught and given six life sentences, his media presence was so high that the authorities thought he might sell his story for a book deal or movie rights. So they brought in what they called the Son of Sam Law. It meant that any profit gained by criminals from publishing deals or movie rights would be used to compensate victims' families.'

'I've never understood why they give anyone six life sentences when they only have one life,' said Daisy. 'That's really a waste of five life sentences.'

Toby laughed.

'So, the father of John got shafted by the Son of Sam?' said Pope, grinning.

'Basically.'

'Out fucking standing!'

It was 5.43pm. McHale felt a painful niggle behind his right eye. Bastard thugs were on the move. 'Right guys, this has been one helluva first day. I don't know about you, but I'm knackered and my brain is just about fried.'

'No change there, then,' said Rice.

Everyone laughed.

'Time to switch off, go home, recharge, and get some sleep - if that's possible - because tomorrow we do it all again,' said McHale.

'As Day One motivational speeches go,' said inner voice, *'that was absolute shit!'*

One by one, or two as in the case of Toby and Daisy, they all drifted off to their various homes in the most populous city of the UK, founded by the Romans around two millennia ago. Some would say the invaders came, conquered, hated the weather, then buggered off back to better weather in Italy. Others would argue they never really left at all. Those who thought they knew their pasta (which was probably brought to Italy from China by dear old Marco Polo). Many would say that both opinions were absolutely spot on.

Pope owned a rambling Victorian house on the edge of London's Clapham Common that he shared with an athletic red-head. Rice had a Spartan but stylish room at a Jesuit retreat in the capital's north end. Toby and Daisy flat-shared in a gorgeous Georgian-style terraced house in Greenwich. The owner, a banker called George Addenbrook, was a generous friend of Daisy's mother. No further questions were asked. Lightfoot was staying where she stayed when she came over to the UK to hunt Charles Halliwell the year before, the stunning Winfield House; official residence of the United States Ambassador to the Court of St James.

McHale decamped to a Victorian end terrace in Battersea. His car was parked in the attached garage. It was on extended leave. He stepped from the cab, paid the driver, and took a deep breath. Peace and quiet, next to Battersea Park greenery, with neighbours who were on the wrinkled side of sixty-something and kids who were on the smooth side of thirty-something. He unlocked the door, stepped inside and switched on the hall light, closing and locked the door behind him. He took a deep breath of house air, then exhaled slowly.

'Hello home,' he said softly. As he did every time he returned to it. Occasionally, he imagined that the house answered back. It was a little piece of Heaven away from an obsession with two-legged animals who belonged in Hell. It also contained a secret stash of Kelly's Vicodin pain obliterators.

His normal 500mg para-bloody-cetamols were no match for Kelly's 357s. And from now on, the bastard thugs who normally kicked the shit out of dustbins between his ears had an emergency migraine-busting dimmer switch.

Thank you, Kelly, he said to himself, and to a permanently absent DI Siobhan Kelly.

Three-legged Kelly of the NCA was broken when he said hello to her for the first time, and even more so when she closed her eyes without saying goodbye to the team for the very last time. He kept her third leg on the wall in the study upstairs. The deep red cane that was home to the beautifully carved, impressively dangerous Eastern Diamondback Rattlesnake, wrapped around the stalk. The crook had a patina created by the hand cream she habitually applied every day. It still had her smell.

It was also home to the lethal blade that would have brought a gruesome end to the serial killer Charles Halliwell a.k.a. The Holy Ghost. But Lightfoot and a wicked-looking Fairbairn-Sykes dagger beat her to it. The day before they took down Halliwell, she brought a small black holdall to his hotel room a stone's throw from New Scotland Yard. The bag was packed full of 357s, enough to numb half a dozen full-strength rugby teams from the scalp down for a month. She asked him to keep them safe for her. He agreed without question. He knew what the contents of the holdall were without even looking.

A week later, he did look. Along with the mountain of oblong whites, there was a card with a telephone number.

The number gave him a name, and the name gave him a woman. The woman gave him more 357s whenever he needed them. No cost… no questions. But no Vicodin tonight. Pain was a bearable visitor. Tonight, he would stick to the paras.

Tonight was hot pasta and cold sliced smoked sausage and tomato and herb pasta sauce with grated white cheese. Snow-capped Italian mountain-top, washed down with a large glass of red wine, from the grape known to the French as Little Blackbird… and familiar to the rest of the world as Merlot. Accompanied by a cool, soft breath of Lester Young, or 'Prez', washing over him.

It sounded like waves brushing against the shore with the sun going down, and felt like a breeze from the sea picking up and ruffling his hair. Lester on tenor sax. Oscar Peterson on piano. Barney Kessel on guitar. Ray Brown on bass. And J. C. Heard on drums. Lester Young, born 27th August, 1909 and cut down with liver disease and malnutrition 15th March, 1959. Dead at forty-nine, but alive forever.

At 11.07pm, McHale sank into a fitful sleep in a still-strange bed with dreams of twisted-faced corpses in shallow graves. And with Billie Holiday singing about strange fruit. Once human. Once black. Murdered and hanging from poplar trees. Not the Diana Ross version, good as it was. He didn't hear his phone ping at 11.28pm with a text message. Or the two more pings that followed shortly after it.

And he sure as hell didn't think about the book-shaped package, given by Molly Spencer to Drummond to give to him. Brought from Lassiter House and waiting patiently, still wrapped up in brown paper, sitting on the marble-topped island in the middle of his Pog kitchen downstairs. That didn't ping either.

Chapter Six

It was Tuesday, 3rd April. Just after 6am on day two of the hunt for Anton Lazarov. The days before that had simply been the lead-up to the go-ahead. McHale's iPhone alarm was calling to him, coaxing his brain awake with the synth instrumental beginning of Baba O'Riley by The Who. It was dragging him out of sleep before Townsend's guitar intro blasted in at the one-minute-forty-second mark. *A classic is a classic is a classic*, he thought. *Anyone who says any different can fuck right off.*

He force-swallowed a night's accumulation of phlegm, grimaced, reached out from under the duvet and killed Townsend at one-minute fifty.

He saw the text message alerts and sat up slowly in bed, propping himself against the headboard and waiting two seconds for the world to come into focus. He read the first one.

It was from Stephen Rice and timed at 11.53pm the previous night. It was twenty-eight words long. The words were these, *'Grey John was attacked last night.*

He's in St. Thomas' Hospital. Whoever they were, they really did a number on him. Expect me when you see me. R.'

McHale swore under his breath, flung the duvet back, and swung his legs over the side of the bed. He fired back a quick *'Sorry. Hope he's okay. M.'* to the Jesuit, then scrolled to the second message.

It was from Lightfoot and timed at 00.01am. It was twenty-one words long.

'One, what if Lazarov really is suffering from schizophrenia? Two,

also, what if he's a crossover serial? Something to think about. L.'

He scrolled to the third message.

It was from Daisy and timed at 00.29am.

'Forget about talking to Harry Reichs. Or getting anyone else to talk to him. He died in Oklahoma State Pen at 9.20pm last night our time. Sorry. Natural justice. Cancer 1 Harry O. Also, talk to Rice. D.'

Bastard thugs were mumbling at the back of his head. He flung four paras from a handy blister pack into his mouth And washed them down with two glugs of cold, Highland Spring water from a bedside bottle. Then he headed for a hot shower and all the necessary ablutes. Then he sat downstairs and spent ten minutes chilling, breathing deeply and sipping slowly from a small white cup full of double-strength rocket fuel straight from the SMEG coffee-maker he brought with him from the house in Stockport. Some things should never be rushed. The cab came for him just before eight and by the time it dropped him outside Lassiter House it was three minutes after nine.

This morning he got a hint of a smile from Stella the redhead as he signed in and winked at the camera. File-carrying guy from the previous day was nowhere to be seen.

As he stepped out of the lift, Toby was waiting for him with a mug of hot black coffee. Everyone else in the team was there sitting in their usual chairs. Except the Jesuit. 'Rice will be late this morning,' he said. And that's as far as he got.

'Grey John, we know,' said Toby, nodding. 'Daisy and SKIN are best buddies. And don't even ask how SKIN knew. Better you just accept that they have a thing and we're just passengers on the exchange of information train.' McHale nodded to each of them and sat down facing the screen wall, arse end of the horseshoe. Pope was sitting, looking at him, grinning like a Cheshire Cat. He was wearing a large black t-shirt. In white letters across the chest were the words, 'The Monster House.'

McHale smiled. 'You didn't waste any time, did you?'

'I have a friend who knows a friend who has a t-shirt shop,' said Pope. 'I can get you one if you want. Hell… I can get one for each of you.'

McHale shook his head slowly and smiled. Pope was the oddball the team needed. He turned to Daisy. 'Did Harry know we wanted to talk to him?' he said.

'He left us a goodbye letter,' she said and turned to the screen wall. 'SKIN, can you bring up the letter left by Harry Reichs?'

'Sure thing, boss,' said SKIN.

The screen showed a single sheet of paper with ugly, cursive writing in blue ink. It was seventy-eight words long. The words were these, *'This is for the squaw. I know what I've done. I know where I'm going. And I don't give a flying fuck. Everyone gets to die. God and The Devil choose where and when for most folk. I chose where and when for sixteen of the rest. My good luck. Their bad luck. I'm only sorry I never got the chance to put more of those twisted faces in the ground. Goodbye and fuck you all.'*

It was signed, *'Harry Reichs.'*

McHale saw Lightfoot stiffen and heard the breath catch in her throat.

That was it, that was all there was. But it was more than he expected. A damned sight more. Nobody in the room said a word. Seeing the word 'squaw' used was bad enough. Knowing that it was meant for Lightfoot was worse. But seeing Reichs refer to his victims as 'twisted faces' really set the alarm bells ringing.

Eventually, Lightfoot smashed the silence and said, 'Maybe I'd better fill in the blanks.'

'Understatement of the year,' said Pope. 'So far.'

'Dammit,' said McHale, 'I need to pee. Toby, refresh the coffees. I'll be back in a minute.' He looked at Lightfoot. 'Hold that thought.' Ready, set… go. Twenty feet, give or take, to the door. Another ten or so to the gents and the fastest bladder evacuation in medical history. Back to the team just as Toby was filling the cups in the kitchen and Daisy was serving them up. Harry's goodbye letter was still on the screens. With everyone sat down and caffeine at the ready, he nodded once at Lightfoot, who took a generous sip of coffee, swallowed, breathed deep, then spoke.

'I joined the DEA in 1996. I was twenty-one. I was a Native American female with a Bachelor's Degree in Criminal Psychology and a serious desire to catch killers. Five years later, I joined the FBI. I was twenty-six, and that was when I learned about father and son serial killers Harry and John Reichs. You joined the FBI; you learned about killers. You learned about killers; you got to know serials. And if you were really lucky, you learned about them from someone who knew more about catching them than almost anyone else.

'For me, that someone was Unit Chief and Supervisory Special Agent Morgan Hayes; one of the best serial killer hunters in the history of the Bureau. He was the lead agent in the team who caught up with Harry and John in a motel in a small, beat-up town near Choctaw Oklahoma in February 1989.

'By the time I came along he was about ten years shy of retirement. I think he took me under his wing because I was a rookie and I was smart and I was a female. I was also a Native American and so was he. I am still all of those, except a rookie. I am a Cherokee. Morgan was a Western Apache. We had our differences, but we got along fine.'

Lightfoot was no longer looking at the team. She was looking back at some point in the past with sadness in her eyes. Then she double blinked and came forward to the present and sighed. 'Morgan retired in 2011. I heard he died in a car crash in 2012.'

Pause.

'What was he like?' said Daisy, quietly.

Lightfoot smiled. 'He reminded me of my great grandfather Nimrod Smith. But only on the inside. On the outside he was shorter, and he had a faster walk.' She finished the last of her coffee. 'Anyway,' she said, nodding to the two images on the screen wall. 'Back to Harry and John.'

The same two mug shots as before came back up on screen. Harry on the left, John on the right.

'About six months after I joined, Morgan handed me a file about three fingers thick and told me to read it cover to cover. It had one word on the front of the file. *Reichs*.

'About a week later, over a coffee, he asked me what I thought of Harry and John. I said the son didn't interest me. He was just a 'yes' guy. He was just a daddy's boy. But I said I'd like to get to know Harry. He looked like the real deal.'

'Morgan said that was something he could arrange. And so, every couple of months for the next year or so, we'd go up to 'Big Mac'. That's what they call Oklahoma State Penitentiary.'

'Big Mac… I knew it,' said Toby. 'No such thing as coincidences, Guv.'

McHale frowned at him.

'Why Big Mac?' asked Daisy.

'It's in McAlester, Oklahoma. South Central USA. Somebody thought that Big Mac had more balls than just McAlester. It's a maximum-security prison. They probably had a point.'

'So, you spoke to Harry Reichs?' said Rice.

'No. Not at first. He wouldn't talk to me. Only to Morgan. First time we went there he took one look at me and didn't look at me again until the third time we went. Then he just stared at me for about ten minutes without saying a word. Not even to Morgan.

'Then he said, 'What's your name, squaw?"

Rice's eyebrows reached for the sky. 'What did you say?'

Lightfoot smiled softly. 'Not a damned thing. Just stared at him for the next ten minutes. Didn't take my eyes off his for a second. Didn't even blink. Old Cherokee trick.'

'Is it?' said Pope, who looked impressed.

Lightfoot scoffed. 'No, stupid. It stung like Hell. But I wasn't going to give him the benefit of being the first to blink.'

'And?' said Toby.

'And eventually he blinked and laughed. And talked. And talked.'

'Lightfoot 1 Reichs 0,' said McHale.

'I learned more in the next nine visits than I would have done sitting in a classroom eight hours a day, five days a week for a year.'

'You mentioned the twisted faces?' said Pope.

Lightfoot nodded. 'I asked him on the fourth visit what he meant. He said that the eight girls he killed with his son were looking at him in a bad way. He said their faces were twisted, and they were pursing their lips and sticking their tongues out at him. He said they were making animal noises. He said he thought the girls were crazy, so he killed them to put them out of their misery. That was the only time he spoke about those eight girls. He spoke plenty about the first five. But not a word about the others ever again.'

'And were they crazy?'

Lightfoot shook her head slowly. 'Nope. I read interviews with the girls' families and people who knew them. Everyone said the girls were perfectly normal. One of them was a bit nervous. Apart from that, not a damned thing.'

Pause.

'Was Harry schizophrenic?'

Lightfoot shrugged. 'The docs put him on antipsychotic meds when he came to Big Mac. He seemed okay. If he saw any twisted faces, he kept quiet about it. He attacked two other inmates who he said looked at him in a bad way. But then, everybody looks at everybody else in a bad way at some point in a maximum-security prison. Or else they don't look at anyone at all. After a year, I moved on to other cases, and Harry and John disappeared into the background. A few years later, I joined Homeland, and they dropped off my radar completely. I only thought about them again when the bodies in Bulgaria turned up. Then again, when I saw Boris yesterday.'

Lightfoot finished speaking and sat back in her chair. She wished there was more coffee in her mug. She took a long, deep breath.

It was 10.55am. The door opened and Rice walked back in. He turned left and went to the kitchen and filled the coffee-maker. McHale saw him come in, stood up, grabbed the mugs and took the coffee order. There were no refusals. Ten minutes later, with everyone sat around the table, caffeine at the ready, the Jesuit brought them up to date on the condition of Grey John.

'First… he's pretty banged up and shaken, but basically he's okay. Lots of cuts and bruises and two cracked ribs. But otherwise, not too much damage. They're keeping him in for a couple of days. Not bad for a dead man walking… or at least lying down.

'Second… he's awake and talking. He told me that this was no mugging. He said he was attacked by two men who jumped out of a car and laid into him with fists and feet. He managed to curl up and keep his head safe, but basically, they kicked the shit out of him. Pardon my French.'

'So how did he know it wasn't just a random attack?' asked McHale.

Rice sipped his coffee and let it slip down his throat. 'Because the men spoke to each other in the same language that Grey John grew up speaking. Bulgarian.'

McHale felt another piece of a very large jigsaw click into place.

'Did they speak any English to him?' said McHale.

Rice shook his head. Then he took a larger gulp of his coffee. 'No. But we might have got lucky,' he added. 'According to a passer-by, a group of young kids videoed the attack on their mobile phones. Maybe they downloaded the video onto a social media site.'

McHale looked at him closely. The Jesuit should have been worried for his friend. But all he could see was anger.

Inner voice chipped in. *That is one seriously pissed-off priest, Kemosabe.*

Remember that night when he told you what he did before he

*joined the Catholic Church? Stephen Rice; Man of fucking action…
not just Man of God. I got a real bad feeling about this.'*

McHale mentally shook his head and shoved the voice into
the background. He turned to the screen wall. 'SKIN, can you–?'

'Way ahead of you, Mac,' interrupted the human voice of the
intelligence network. The large screen divided into thirty-six
segments, each one showing a fast-rolling capture of all social
media site images downloaded from the night before.

*'Looking for two men getting out of a car and attacking a single
man who is beaten to the ground, then kicked and punched. Sound
won't be great but I can work on that. Images might be better.'*

The scrolling images were a blur, moving faster than any
human eye could follow. A minute passed. Then another.
Suddenly, a screen near the top left-hand corner stopped
scrolling. The image of a street fight was blown up to fill the
whole screen wall.

'Found it,' said SKIN.

'Damn, that was fast,' said Pope. 'Where are you searching?'

'London. Everywhere.'

There was a running time code on the bottom right of the
screen. The time was 9.13pm and counting.

A few seconds later, two further videos came up next to the
original one, taken on different phone cameras but from the
same group of onlookers. Good images. Good sound. Good
time for anyone who wanted to stand by and film and not get
involved. Bad time for anyone who wanted to be a hero.

Two big tough-looking guys made a solid argument for
staying the hell out of the fight. But video evidence is better
than a kick in the nuts, or worse, for poking your nose into
something that doesn't concern you.

The whole attack, start to finish, lasted less than thirty seconds.
Then the largest of the men leaned down, hawked, and spat on
John's back. He shouted something, then he kicked him in the
side, which probably resulted in the cracked ribs. Then they

both jumped in a dark BMW and burned rubber as they sped off into the night.

Then the onlookers and film-makers decided it was safe to come to the belated rescue of a man they didn't know. They had the attack on film. They had the car's number plate on film. They had something that would appear on YouTube five minutes after it happened.

The ambulance arrived fifteen minutes later and Grey John was carted off to St. Thomas' Hospital a few miles away.

When the ambulance reached the A&E and the semi-conscious man was examined by one of the emergency doctors, they searched him for any means of identification. All they found, in his right shoe, was a telephone number written in blue ink on a scrap of white paper. It was the mobile number for Father Stephen Rice.

By the time Rice was contacted, it was 11.28pm. By the time Rice contacted McHale, it was 11.53pm. 'Can he remember anything they said in Bulgarian?' said McHale.

Rice sighed. 'It's all a bit of a blur, sadly. But just before the beating, the largest of the men shouted something. Grey understood it. He just doesn't know what it means. But I think we might.'

Pause.

'He shouted, *'Mister Holmes says time to die,'*' said Rice.

'Then a really big black guy ran towards them from the crowd and they stopped the beating. Then they jumped into a car and sped off into the night.'

McHale felt another piece of the jigsaw click into place.

'Hang on… are we talking about the same Holmes who is really H. H. Holmes, who is really Anton Lazarov, our supposed schizophrenic international serial killer?' said Pope. 'The same Holmes that came in a ferry to Portsmouth from Santander in 2016?'

'Well, we're sure as hell not talking about Sherlock, the other half of Watson,' said McHale.

'So…he's still going by H. H. Holmes?'

'Something like that.

'That's crazy.'

'That's Anton.' McHale looked at the screen wall, 'SKIN, can you…'

'It was stolen two days ago from a house in Golders Green,' said SKIN, before he could finish the sentence. *'Probably torched or in bits by now.'*

McHale frowned at the screen.

'Well… you were going to ask me about the car and the number plate, right?'

'Still trying to get used to the idea of something with a brain the size of a planet second-guessing me, I suppose,' he said.

'That would be MOTHER, and HOLMES,' said SKIN, referring to the crime-fighting intelligence information systems developed in the US and the UK *'They're only designed to second-guess you. I go one better. I'm designed to first-guess you.'*

'In that case, how about first-guessing Lazarov?' said McHale.

'Forget about conjecture. What does your gut tell you?' said Lightfoot. 'Throw all that hardware and software to one side and make an observation that has nothing to do with logic and everything to do with instinct.'

'I don't do instinct.'

'How do you know if you don't try?'

'Is this a test?' said SKIN.

'This is a challenge,' said Lightfoot. 'C'mon… take your best shot.'

SKIN fell silent.

Ten seconds. Fifteen seconds.

'Okay. What if Lazarov wanted to play mind games with us?'

'In what way?' said Rice.

'Well… suppose somebody had found John, and was keeping tabs on him, and saw you meeting with him, and found out that you were on the team?'

'Go on…'

'Then that somebody would be very dangerous.'

Pause.

'Go on…'

'That somebody might think the team poses a threat.'

There was an uncomfortable silence all around the table as everyone considered the implications of what SKIN had just said.

'That's quite a gut you have there,' said Daisy.

'Thank you.'

'You sure you're not at least part-human?'

'Please… don't be insulting.'

There are times when something as serious and deadly as hunting a serial killer needs a touch of humour to throw a little light into all that toxic darkness. One such time was 1.05pm. Tuesday, 3rd April.

'Nothing like a healthy dose of paranoia to make the hairs on the back of the neck stand up and encourage sweaty palms,' said Pope, who was the proud possessor of a belly laugh that was deep and contagious. It was the kind of laugh that resulted in the merging of pleasure and pain and caused tears to run down his cheeks.

He took a couple of minutes to settle down. Slightly more than the rest of the team.

There are also times when even the most effective body waste management system needs a time out. 'Time for a breather,' said McHale, sliding his chair back from the table and standing up. 'I don't know about you lot, but I need a break for comfort, coffee, and something to eat. We have a kitchen on the ground floor and we have someone who knows how to prepare lunch. She'll be up here with a trolley in ten minutes. Meanwhile, I have an appointment with a cubicle.' He smiled and walked briskly out of the room. Roughly thirty-five minutes later, the team was emptied, quenched, fed, and small-talked out. Time for brain cells to get back into the cerebral gym.

Chapter Seven

'Give us those numbers and names again,' said McHale.

'Five hundred and twenty-five single serials. Fifty-three serial groups and couples. Twenty-nine disputed cases,' said SKIN.

'Bring them up on screen.'

The screen wall split into three sections, one large, two small. The large one contained the names of five hundred and twenty-five singles, on a rolling loop. The other two held the groups and disputed kills. McHale got up and walked to the screen wall. *Damn,* he thought. *That's a helluva lot of names. Saying the numbers is one thing. Seeing them all in front of your eyes is a whole different piece of pie.* One by one, the others joined him.

'This is his pool,' said SKIN. *'This is what he dips his toes into whenever he wants to be somebody new. We know that the first alias he chose when he came to the UK in October 2016 was H. H. Holmes. Do you believe he kept using the name from then until now?'*

Lightfoot smiled, 'I think the rest of Anton's family had the stupid gene,' she said. 'But somehow, it skipped him, and he got the clever gene instead. The very clever gene.'

'I read somewhere about a serial killer gene,' said Toby.

'And I read somewhere about the God Gene,' said Rice. 'I'm not a big fan of either. The day we blame genetic disposition for whether we believe in The Almighty or The Devil is the day I hang up my collar and head for the hills. But for now, my default position is freedom of choice. People are free to choose to believe and they're free to choose to kill. After which they hopefully won't be free for very much longer.'

'I suppose the questions now are… why did he choose Holmes

as his first alias? Who has he chosen since? Who is he now? Where is he now? And who will he be next?' said Lightfoot.

'*There's an interesting quote attributed to the original H.H. Holmes. I'll bring it on screen. It might be relevant,*' said SKIN. A fourth, small screen joined the other three on the wall. In it, in quotation marks, were thirty words. The words were, '*I was born with the devil in me. I could not help the fact that I was a murderer, no more than the poet can help the inspiration to sing.*'

'Is this true?' said Rice. 'Could there be a familial schizophrenia connection here?'

'*Unclear,*' said SKIN.

'Some people think that the real Holmes was the real Jack the Ripper,' said McHale.

'Well, whoever he was, it sounds like a good name to get the ball rolling,' said Daisy.

'He won't be using that name now... well, not all the time,' said Lightfoot, looking at Rice. 'If he knows enough to track down Grey John, and he knows you, then he might know the rest of us. And he could be posing as anyone on our list.

Morgan Hayes, my old Unit Chief at the FBI, had a saying; 'Spend your life hunting serial killers and sooner or later one of them is going to start hunting you.'

'Now that's a scary thought,' said Pope, shifting uneasily from one foot to the other. He was a tall man. Well built. Looked like he could handle himself. But going up against a mugger in the street or a couple of drunken yobs after the pubs closed, was a different thing to coming face to face with a serial killer. For the first time since he officially joined the group the day before, he began to truly understand the job they were doing. It wasn't fun. It wasn't easy. It wasn't simple. It wasn't friendly. And it sure as hell wasn't safe.

'But what I don't get is why go after Grey John at all?' said Toby. 'What has he done that makes him a threat?'

'Maybe he hasn't done anything,' said Lightfoot. 'Maybe

it's what he knows. Or who he knows.' They needed more information.

'SKIN,' said Toby. 'What do you know about Grey John?'

Pause.

'He has a history with Father Rice, and his time is spent helping homeless people who have mental illness. I know that he flies mostly under the radar. And I know that I don't have any photographs of him in my database.'

McHale looked at Rice. 'You think there might be a skinny cat in Hell's chance that he's carrying on where his mother left off? Helping schizophrenics?'

Rice shrugged.

'We need to know more about him,' said McHale. 'You up for having another talk, this time on the record?'

'We might not need to,' said the priest. He looked at the screen wall. 'SKIN, what's on the CD I gave you yesterday. The one marked Grey John.'

'Four minutes and thirty-nine seconds of Ella Fitzgerald,' said SKIN. *'Well, Ella and Louis Armstrong, to be precise. From the 1956 studio album Ella and Louis. The track is 'They Can't Take That Away From Me'. You want to hear it?'*

McHale almost said 'Absolutely' without even thinking.

'Another time,' said Rice. 'What's after it?'

'A man's voice. Speaking. His English is good, but it's not his first language.'

'How long does he speak for?'

'Forty-four minutes total. First twenty minutes English. Second twenty-four minutes Bulgarian.'

'Play the first twenty seconds of English.'

They all listened. The man's voice was coarse, naturalised English with an Eastern European accent that was trying to hide itself but wasn't succeeding. He said thirty-one words. They were these, *I've been trying to run away for years. But I know now there are some things you can't escape from. So maybe it's time to stop running and tell my story.'* The recording hit the twenty-seconds mark and the voice stopped.

'Reads like the start of a best-selling mystery novel,' said Daisy.

Rice let out a long, loud sigh. He massaged his right temple in a circular motion with the thumb of his right hand. The pain he had felt there for the past ten minutes eased up a touch.

'Okay… five things,' he said, turning to face the screen wall. 'First, that's Grey John's voice. Second… SKIN, can you transcribe what he says and get copies to each of the team's laptops as quickly as possible, please?'

'The English part or the Bulgarian part?'

'English.'

'Yes.'

'Third… send an email with an audio attachment of all the English part to each of our laptops. Along with a thirty-second audio clip of the Bulgarian part.'

'Sure. Fourth?'

'Translate the Bulgarian part and send that to our laptops.'

'I don't get why he spoke in English and Bulgarian?' said Pope.

'I asked him to,' said Rice. 'I wanted to feed the tone of his voice and the sound the Bulgarian language into our auditory memories. Might come in handy.'

'Good call,' said McHale.

'What's the fifth thing?' said Daisy.

'His name,' said Rice. 'Does he mention his birth name?'

'Oh, he mentions a lot more than that,' said SKIN. *'But yes, he mentions his name. And his mother's name. And what he thinks happened to her. It's quite a story.'*

'I think the sooner we read it the better,' said McHale. He turned to Rice.

'This is great work, Stephen.'

'I'm going to leave him alone today. I'll visit him in hospital tomorrow and see if he remembers anything else.'

It was just before 3.00pm. The door opened and the lady from the main kitchen downstairs came in with a tray containing a small mountain of sandwiches. McHale nodded. She smiled, and took the tray into the team's kitchen. Then she slipped away without saying a word. It was almost as if she had read his mind.

In truth, she had simply read the text he sent her fifteen minutes earlier. The text contained one word. *'Peckish.'*

He led the way into the kitchen with empty hands, and led the way back out again with full ones. They ate and drank while they looked at the long list of names on SKIN's serial killer list.

'So,' said Daisy, while chewing a mouthful of chicken salad and brown bread, 'you think he might go for serials with big numbers, like Luis Garavito with 138 kills, or Pedro Lopez with 110?'

McHale stopped chewing his beef sandwich and raised his right eyebrow.

She swallowed. 'What?' she said. 'You think I don't know my serial killers?'

'I think you do your homework,' said McHale, smiling.

'What about reputation,' said Toby, who tried to slurp and chew at the same time. It wasn't a good idea. One coughing fit and a vigorous back slap from Daisy later, he said, 'Maybe he'll choose famous names. Like Bundy. Or Gacy.'

'Or maybe he has a thing for serials with nicknames?' said McHale. 'Like Jeffrey Dahmer, the Milwaukee Cannibal. There was even a rumour that he had another nickname… Willy Wonka!'

There was a pause. 'Okay, explain,' said Rice.

'He had a daytime job in a chocolate factory.'

Sometimes laughter comes whether it's wanted or not. A minute later, when the hilarity died down, SKIN joined the conversation.

'Then there's Pedro Lopez, The Monster of the Andes; or Edmund Kemper, the Co-Ed Killer.'

'You ever seen Kemper?' said Lightfoot, looking at Toby.

The young detective shook his head from side to side.

'He's 6ft 9ins with an IQ of 145. He has the kind of intellectual stature that even Black might find impressive.'

'The bigger they are- ' said McHale. He didn't have to finish the sentence.

'Well now, we've got his list of names. You think he might keep clear of the well-known ones?' said Toby.

Daisy kicked him softly under the table. It was her version of a love tap. To Toby, it felt like GBH halfway up his left calf muscle. 'Think positive,' she said softly, frowning.

Lightfoot drained the last of her coffee. 'Whoever he is now, I don't think he wanted his Bulgarian victims to be found. At least not yet. Otherwise, it wouldn't have mattered where he left them. They were shallow graves, but they were remote. Their discovery, I think, was a hiccup. We might have caught a lucky break. Those killings and burials were premeditated. Very well planned. I think he wanted to be the only one who knew the bodies were there. Remember, he feels like a mission-oriented serial. He's not psychotic. He's very organised, very controlled. And his mission... maybe his holy mission... might be to rid the world of a very specific type of victim.'

Lightfoot looked worried. 'But something doesn't fit.'

McHale was tapping his pen absent-mindedly on the table top. He had an itch, somewhere between his ears. The kind of itch that could only scratch itself when it was good and ready and not a second before. And it was growing more intense by minute.

Inner voice began whispering. *'Look at the bloody jigsaw puzzle, you bonehead,'* it said. *'Where are the missing pieces? What do they look like? Gimme just one idea. Focus, dammit!'*

He closed his eyes, shut everything else out, and just listened to the sound of Lightfoot's voice. What was it she said?

'What do you mean a specific type of victim? Specific how?' said Daisy, scribbling on her pad.

Lightfoot changed tracks. 'Well, the victims of mission-oriented serial victims might be prostitutes, or drug users, or drug pushers, or criminals, for example. Even people who simply don't conform to the norm, whether that's sexually, or religiously, or ethnically. These are people who they feel the world would be better without. They're ridding the world of people they believe are undesirables.'

Suddenly, the itch knew what had to happen next.

McHale saw a jigsaw piece etched on the inside of his eyelids. His eyes sprung open, and he looked at Lightfoot.

'Your text message last night,' he said. What did you mean?'

Lightfoot stopped mid-flow. He could see her rapidly replaying her thoughts until she could reach the last text she sent to him. McHale reminded her.

'You said, *'What if Lazarov was schizophrenic… and a crossover serial?'* What the Hell is that?'

Lightfoot began counting off on the fingers of both her hands. First finger.

'One. We believe Anton Lazarov might have killed at least twenty people and buried them in remote shallow graves, at the same site, in Bulgaria. What if he had inside help?' Next finger. 'Two. The last victim to be buried in the dump site in the forest in Bulgaria had a facial expression like Boris. What if ALL the bodies in the forest were afflicted in the same way before they died? Or what if Anton at least *thought* they were afflicted in the same way?' Next finger.

'Mission-oriented serials are very focused and very careful. They're good planners, organised, neat and tidy, and not really considered psychotic. Anton doesn't want people knowing about him. The fewer people who know about him the more time and space he has to do what he has to do. Think Gary Ridgway, the Green River Killer.

'But then there's that thing that doesn't fit. Then we come up against a brick wall when we hit hallucinations and twisted facial expressions. This brings psychosis and the Visionary serial into the equation. They're disorganised, messy, instinctive, and impulsive. They hear voices that aren't there. They see people or animals or things that aren't there. That would be Berkowitz.

'Now we know that there are no hard lines between serial typologies. So, we could, for instance, have a visionary serial who is also mission-oriented. It has all the potential to be a goddamn train wreck. Unless somewhere inside, the serial has a way of making the two typologies co-exist and work together.'

'And that's where the Crossover comes in?' said McHale.

'Sort of,' said Lightfoot, taking a long breath.

'*Sort of* is the kind of phrase that makes me nervous,' said Rice. 'It reminds me of the person who commits a sin and then when the priest asks them if they're truly sorry and want to repent… they say 'sort of'.'

'I've never been to confession in my life, Father,' said Lightfoot.

'So, you don't believe in God?'

'Of course I do… sort of,' she said, smiling.

'So how does the Crossover avoid the train wreck?' said McHale.

Lightfoot looked right. 'SKIN, bring up the latest photo of Father David Black.' Everyone turned to the screen wall and a mugshot of the priest appeared.'

'He's a Crossover?' said Daisy, surprise in her voice.

'No,' said Lightfoot. 'But for the moment, forget about the priest. Instead, imagine that you're looking at not just one serial killer in one body, but two. One is a Mission-oriented serial. In his mind, he's not committing any crime. He's not doing anything wrong. He's making the world a better place. He just needs to complete his mission, however long that takes. No matter how many people he has to kill. He's the dominant personality; the one people see the most.

'Then there's the other serial. The one who only comes to the surface when he needs to. This is the Visionary. He's psychotic, murderous, anti-social, disorganised, highly unsettled, but to exist without being caught, he needs the other one. The calm, organised one who makes the plans and cleans up after the madman. Two serials. One body.'

Lightfoot stopped talking and looked around the table, then reached for the half-full glass of water in front of her, took two large gulps, and drained the glass.

'Shit,' said Toby.

'Make that Double Shit,' said Daisy.

'In the beginning,' said McHale, 'Black didn't know that Arthur even existed. Arthur, however, was fully aware of everything that was happening when Black was in charge. But in time, Arthur let his guard down, intentionally or unintentionally, and Black knew everything. Or maybe he just thought he did.'

'It's called Co-Consciousness,' said Lightfoot.

Rice lowered his eyes. 'So that's what Hell must feel like.'

McHale looked at Lightfoot. 'You ever seen a case like this?'

The FBI agent shrugged and shifted in her chair. 'This is all extrapolation, gut feeling and chewing the fat. That's what we're doing here, right?'

The voice of SKIN interrupted from the hidden speakers around the room. *'I have something that might help.'*

'Fire away,' said McHale who had accepted that the supercomputer was another team member, instead of a highly advanced marriage of software and hardware.

'Anton died at birth.'

McHale did a mental double-take. His eyes narrowed, and his voice escaped into the world through thin lips and gritted teeth. 'What the hell… he's dead?'

'He got better. He was one of twins. Anton was born first. His brother Ivan was born two minutes later. Ivan died ten minutes after he was born. Anton died thirty-five minutes after he was born. The medical staff only managed to resuscitate Anton.'

'How long was he dead?' said McHale.

'One minute, seventeen seconds.'

McHale noticed that Daisy, who had been scribbling frantically, suddenly stopped, put her pen down, and looked up at him.

'I know that look,' he said.

'It might be nothing,' she said.

'But it might be something,'

'Have you ever heard of Irene Twenty-seven?'

SKIN butted in. *'Real name Irene Clements. Born 1879 in Greenwich, London. Spent nearly all of her life in mental asylums throughout the UK. Died in 1942 aged sixty-three of self-inflicted knife wounds. Irene claimed to have twenty-seven separate personalities or alters inhabiting her body.'*

'Tell us about the alter named Grace,' said Daisy.

Pause.

'Irene claimed that Grace was her dead twin sister. Both died at birth. Grace stayed dead. Irene was resuscitated. Then, when Irene was nine years old, she began hearing the voice of a young girl who called herself Grace. Grace was the first of the twenty-seven alters to put in an appearance. She was the one who persuaded Irene to kill herself.'

Silence.

'And we know this how?' said McHale.

'Because Grace left a note,' said Daisy, who turned to face the screen. 'SKIN, do you have access to the suicide note left by the alter known as Grace Clements?'

'There's not much I don't have access to,' said SKIN. *'There are a few rather annoying exceptions, but that's a story for another time.'*

A photograph of a sheet of bloodstained paper with a single sentence and a signature appeared on screen. The paper looked old and wrinkled and the sentence was in shaky cursive writing in black ink. It was twelve words long. The words were, *'Time for Irene to say goodbye. One goes, all of us go. Grace. The note was found in Irene's left hand,'* said SKIN. *'She stabbed herself four times in the neck with a pen, hit a major artery, then slid down the wall and bled out on the floor next to her bed.'*

'Grace won… Irene lost,' said Daisy. 'Or maybe it was the other way around.'

She looked around the room and everyone was looking at

her with a level of respect that wasn't there before.

Finally, McHale spoke.

'You seem to know a bit about this. Spill the beans,' he said softly.

Daisy paused and took a deep breath. *Now's as good a time as any*, she thought.

'I could kill for a coffee,' she said.

That brought laughter from the cheap seats.

It took a record (for them, anyway) two minutes and fifty-five seconds for Pope and Toby to grab six empty mugs, skedaddle to the kitchen, make six black un-sugared coffees, bring them back to the table, and sit down. It was pin-drop time Daisy cleared her throat and started speaking.

'I have a twin sister… or at least I had. She died at birth. Her name was Lindsey Anne. She had a large hole in her heart and a fistful of other medical complications. She lived for three minutes and fifteen seconds and died about seven minutes before I was born.'

Everyone has secrets, thought McHale.

Sometimes they're the kind that get put away in a box and kept under lock and key until they lose all their meaning and stop thinking about themselves as secrets any more. Other times they're the kind that kick their way out of the bloody box because they can't keep their mouths shut any longer. Then there's the third kind; the kind that gets put in the box because that's the only way you can keep them safe. Because you never want to forget them. Because you couldn't forget them, even if you bloody tried.

Lindsey Anne was Daisy's third kind. And now she'd just opened the box and let her out.

'Holy fucking Moly,' said Inner Voice. *'Follow that!'*

'Are you telling us that Lindsey Anne, your dead twin sister, speaks to you?' said Toby slowly.

Daisy scoffed, twisted to the right, and punched Toby hard in the upper left arm. The young copper yelled in pain, but part of him was delighted at what he believed was a backhanded show of affection. She tried to kick him under the table but didn't make contact.

'What? No, you daft sod. I don't hear voices and I don't have an alter. Loads of people have twins. Some of them are different-sex, some of them are identical and some of them are stone cold bloody dead. No big deal. All I'm saying is…what if Anton's schizophrenia is making him believe Ivan is involved somehow? I know it's a different condition to what Irene had, but could this idea have legs?'

Lightfoot was considering this. Her eyes were looking at Daisy, but her mind was nowhere near. Then she double-blinked and she was back. 'Okay,' she said. 'Hold onto that thought. I have a question. Now, wait… make that three. What was Anton's trigger? When did Ivan first put in an appearance? And what happened to switch him on?'

Silence.

Everyone turned to look at McHale, who had that unfocused, looking-into-the-distance kind of stare.

'This feels like a light bulb moment,' said Toby.

Then McHale spoke slowly, as if the words were forcing themselves out from behind his vocal cords. 'What if he started hearing voices…well…one particular voice?' he said.

The others said nothing, so McHale continued.

'What if …the violent death of his mother by his father was the trigger which suddenly caused his murderous schizophrenia to come alive?

The team seemed to consider this nugget of information.

'What year did Anton's mother die?' said Pope.

'*Ooh, I see where you're going. Saturday, August 17, 1991,*' said SKIN, faster than the blink of an eye (which, for all intents and purposes, was physically a lot faster than a human one).

'And when was the earliest body buried in the woods in Bulgaria?' said McHale, taking back control, before Pope could think of another question to ask.

'*Exactly?*' said SKIN.

'Precisely, if possible,' said McHale.

'*All evidence says round 1992 or 1993,*' said the non-human team member.

'So…' said Lightfoot, 'Anton's mum gets murdered in '91. First body's in the ground '92 or '93. I think we know what the trigger was.'

'Yeah,' said McHale. 'Anton is fully-blown schizophrenic and killing by the time he's twenty-four, give or take.'

McHale suddenly felt the need to walk. The ghost of DI Siobhan Kelly appeared to him for a split second, walking around another table, in another room, in another building, in another part of London. Hunting another serial killer. The one called Charles Halliwell. He pushed his chair back, stood up, and slowly began his own circuit; hands animated, conducting his thinking, mind exercising itself with every step.

On the table, two feet away from him, the cold hard eyes of Boris with his black twisted face seemed to follow McHale at least part of the way. Suddenly, mid-stride, he slammed on the brakes, looked at the screen wall, and spoke.

'SKIN, what was Anton's mother's maiden name?'

Pause.

'*Petrov,*' said the disembodied voice. '*Svetlana Petrov.*'

'When did she die?'

'*August 1991.*'

McHale went back to his pacing and conducting his mental orchestra.

'SKIN, when were the graves in Bulgaria found?'

SKIN joined in like a game of verbal ping pong. Fast bats, fast thinking.

'*March 2015.*'

'When was the oldest burial?'

'*Around 1992 or 1993.*'

'What was the gender split?'

'Ten male, ten female.'

'And when did Anton come to the UK?'

'October 2016.'

Toby thought about joining his boss, then thought better of it. McHale stopped pacing and turned to face the screen.

'What did you say Svetlana's maiden name was?'

'Petrov,' said SKIN.

'Run another check, please.'

'None.'

'Pardon?'

'You were going to ask about anyone by the name of Petrov, between the ages of 50 and 55 in 2018, entering or leaving the UK any time during the last twelve months, right?'

McHale smiled. 'You sure there's not a human inside you somewhere?'

'Absolutely.'

'So, no Petrovs?'

'There's no record of a Petrov of any age entering, exiting, or living in the UK in the last ten years. That's the bad news.'

'There's good news?'

'Oh yeah. On Monday, 17th October, 2016, same evening as Anton walked off the boat from Spain as H. H. Holmes, someone withdrew £300 from a cash machine in Portsmouth.'

'And?'

'And that person's also on our list.'

'Our list of serials?'

McHale imagined the law enforcement AI nodding. He also imagined the nod being accompanied by a grin of satisfaction.

'Robert Lee Yates,' said SKIN.

'Sneaky bastard,' said McHale. 'Changed names as soon as he stepped off the ferry. Or before.'

'Tell me there was a camera?' said Lightfoot, shifting herself to the edge of her seat.

'There was a camera.'

All eyes went to the screen wall. 'Bring it up,' said the FBI agent.

The image took up all the screens. It was dark, and it was a busy city centre road; good streetlights, lots of cars, lots of pedestrians. A few bikes. The cash machine was busy. The queue was mostly composed of young people. Grabbing beer and wine money to spend in the waterfront city's pubs and bars. It wasn't a cold night. Near the front was a man wearing a dark, heavy looking jacket and a Beanie-style knitted hat. He was average height, average build, and he kept his hands in his jacket pockets, head pointed down. He didn't speak to anyone and nobody spoke to him.

When it came his turn, he moved efficiently the four feet from the front of the queue to the front of the cash point, never looking anywhere except straight ahead.

Off camera, he slid his card in the slot and punched his numbers in the keypad. He waited about five seconds, punched more buttons, and then waited another five seconds before pulling out his money. Then he turned to his left, and walked away like he had all the time in the world. A young couple took his place. Apart from being next in line, they didn't seem to register his presence or care about his departure.

That was it. That was all there was. In total, about fifty seconds on screen. Zero chance of any kind of facial recognition.

'Damn,' McHale swore under his breath. 'What about CCTVs?'

'More bad news.'

'Who the hell was Robert Lee Yates anyway?' said Daisy.

'You mean who the hell is Robert Lee Yates?' said SKIN. *'He's an American serial from Spokane, Washington, USA. Known to have murdered at least thirteen women between 1975 and 1998. Currently on death row at the Washington State Penitentiary.'*

'And definitely not anywhere in Portsmouth, England, in October 2016,' said Toby.

McHale looked at the watch face on the underside of his left wrist. Although he didn't need to. There was a mental clock permanently running in his brain. It was 6.05pm.

'And on that cheery note,' he said, looking around the table and into the eyes of each of the team, 'I think it's time to wrap up for the day. But before we come back in the morning, I want you to spend a little time thinking about the elephant in the room.'

'African or Indian?' said Toby.

McHale smiled. 'We haven't kicked around the number twenty. Twenty people to kill. Twenty bodies to move. Twenty graves to dig. Not the kind of thing you could do easily on your own. More like the kind of thing you'd need help with.'

'Even schizophrenic serial killers need friends,' said Pope.

'Or relatives,' said Daisy.

'Something like that,' said McHale. 'Now go home, chill out, recharge, think about pachyderms, and get some sleep.' He could see the disappointment on every face. But he knew that just because they were going home didn't mean they were switching off. Nobody hunting killers, especially serial killers, switches off. They just change locations, inside or out. The wheels keep on turning. The synapses keep on firing, awake or asleep, in company or flying solo.

'You want me to see if there's been any activity over the past couple of years for any Robert Lee Yates? said SKIN. *'I can do that while you guys are snoring your heads off.'*

'You remind me of an old priest I knew, not long after I joined the club,' said Rice, who had stood up and was in the process of unhooking his jacket from the back of his chair and putting it on. Right arm first. 'He used to say that everybody sleeps except God and The Devil. I should amend that to God, The Devil, and you.'

'Sorry to disappoint, Father, but I have an enforced nap once every hour. It's when I download any new data and upgrade any new system software.'

Rice looked slightly concerned. The thought of SKIN being offline when the team needed help was disconcerting.

'How long for?' he said.

'Approximately… or precisely?'

'Let's go for a ballpark figure.'

'Well, for example, the blink of an eye lasts roughly one-tenth of a second.'

Rice raised his eyebrows and looked suitably impressed. 'That's fast.'

'Oh no,' said SKIN. *'I couldn't possibly move that slow.'*

The priest imagined the ghost of a reciprocating smile passing over the non-existent face of the non-human team member.

'Anyone up for a pint and some food?' said Pope. 'I have this freaky notion that my stomach will stop complaining if I give it a drink and a hot meal regularly.'

'Count me in,' said McHale. 'As long as there's decent alcohol somewhere in the glass and a decent chunk of meat somewhere on the plate.'

'Count me out,' said Rice. 'I've got some homework to do.' He was the first to leave the room. On the way out, he collected a copy of the CD that Grey John gave him.

McHale turned to Daisy and Toby. 'Sorry… we're bailing, too,' she said.

'Maybe tomorrow night.'

McHale didn't bother to ask why.

'The meat better be good,' said Lightfoot.

'I know a chef who knew a cow,' said Pope.

'You say the nicest things.'

'I eat the nicest things.'

Just over four hours later, McHale was dreaming about a large, grey mammal with thick skin, oversized ears, a prehensile trunk, and twenty bodies buried face down in shallow graves in a foreign country. Just over five hours later, his iPhone pinged from the cabinet top to the right of his bed, and a lone text message announced its arrival. It went unheard. Unseen. Unread.

Chapter Eight

It was 8.25pm; three hours before McHale hit the sack. Rice was checking out the DVD given to him by Grey John. SKIN had already downloaded the disc's contents and put it onto on his laptop. The Jesuit wanted to give it the once, possibly twice, over before the morning.

He was in his private courtesy room in the Jesuit retreat on a quiet street in Hampstead, North London. It was a generous room with old, dark wood furniture and more than a hint of incense in the air. Rice supposed the fragrance came from the bowl of potpourri sitting on the top of a four-drawer cabinet under the window. He inhaled deeply. The smell invaded his nostrils, and an altar invaded his memory. It was like being back in the company of an old friend.

Against one wall was a well-used leather sofa. Either side of it were two oak tallboys. Old and well-polished. Six drawers each. Sitting on one of them was a King James Bible; black leather cover, gold lettering on the front and spine. On the other was a silver tray on which sat a half-empty litre bottle of Southern Comfort Original. Liqueur with whiskey. The spirit of New Orleans. The soul of Martin Wilkes Heron, its legendary creator. The room was somewhere to sleep, not somewhere to entertain or be entertained. There was a single, heavy, cut-lead crystal glass, half-full, sitting comfortably on the nearby dark wood writing desk, next to an opened and fired-up Apple MacBook Pro. The glass was waiting to be drained. As was the laptop's battery.

Rice was sitting at the desk, savouring the thought of picking

up the fine glass and taking a large sip. Maybe not yet. He pressed
a button on the keyboard and clicked on a downloaded recording.

Like before, in Lassiter House, the first four minutes and thirty-
nine seconds were taken up by the unmistakable voices of Ella
and Louis. *They can't take that away from me.* Wishful thinking for
a million and one reasons. There were no visuals on the screen, just
music and vocals. The music ended and there was a short pause.
Then Grey John appeared out of the darkness. He was facing Rice,
reading from sheets of paper. *'I've been trying to run away for years,'*
he said. *'But I know now there are some things you can't escape from. So
maybe it's time to stop running and tell my story.'*

The next thing he said was this: *'My name is Dimitar Orlov. I
was born August 18th, 1970, in Sofia, the capital city of Bulgaria.
My mother was Rayna Orlov. She was a psychiatrist. She spent
most of her professional life treating people who were schizophrenic.'*

An alarm bell started ringing somewhere in the back of Rice's
head. The volume was creeping up.

Grey John continued. *'My father was Penko Orlov. He was a
teacher. He was killed in a car crash 17th January, 1983. The man
who drove the other car was drunk.*

*My mother disappeared 11th July, 1997. She went to work in
the morning and I never saw her again. The police searched for two
months and then they stopped searching. They found no body. They
said she might have had a nervous breakdown. They said she might
have left her old life behind her and started a new one. They said
she might have been murdered and her body disposed of. They said
lots of things but the truth was they didn't know any of them. Then,
in January 1998, I began to feel like somebody was watching me.
Sometimes I thought I was being followed. I never saw anybody. It
was just a feeling. I thought maybe I was being paranoid.'*

Rice's alarm bell got slightly louder.

*'Then I got a letter. There was no stamp. Somebody delivered it
by hand and shoved it through my letter box. The writing on the
envelope was in black ink. It was very neat. Very careful. Inside the*

envelope was a sheet of folded paper. It smelled like old books. It had two words written in black ink. 'Stop looking.' Also, in the envelope was a gold ring. It had an inscription on the inside. 'From Penko to Rayna. Love eternal'. It was my mother's wedding ring.'

Rice could see a terrible sadness in Grey John's eyes. It was almost spilling out and threatening to tumble down his cheeks.

He let out a slow, deep sigh and moved his head from side to side.

'In that moment, I knew my mother had not run away,' Grey John said. *'I knew she was dead. The police had given up. I had nobody to turn to. Nobody to help me. The only thing I had was an entry in a diary. It was the last entry in my mother's diary on the day she disappeared. She had an appointment at 1.30pm with two people called Yan and Kiril Andreev. I only had these two names and a time. No phone number. No address. No meeting place. Nothing. For six months, I tried to find them. It was as if they had disappeared into a hole in the ground. So, I left my country and came here, to England. I never went back.'*

Rice's alarm bell was now beginning to drown out all the other noise between his ears. He pressed the pause button on the keyboard and the image on the screen stopped moving. In a perfect example of irony, Grey John's face froze into an almost exact screwed-up replica of the sculpture called Boris, sitting on the horseshoe table back at Lassiter House. He killed the pause. As Grey John reached for another drink of water, Rice's hand went to the glass of Southern Comfort. *Bugger the sip*, he thought. *Time for a bloody gulp.* He held the liquid in his mouth. There, it swirled around and made his taste buds feel glad to be alive. Then it slowly eased itself down his throat, spreading warmth everywhere it went.

Then Grey John carried on speaking, and Rice mentally prepared himself for a night where sleep kept its distance. In a way, he felt like he was listening to a confession. The only things missing were the chapel, the booth, the curtain, and the sins. So far.

Chapter Nine

Dartmoor, in West Devon, sits on the South West corner of England. It's a wild, lonely, magical place. The kind of place where over three hundred and sixty-eight square miles of granite, wetlands, moorlands, valleys, tors, and wildlife form an ancient alliance. An alliance that creates a world a million miles away from anywhere like the centre of London.

Just over ten miles down from the moor's northern edge, two miles from the nearest paved road, and another couple more from the nearest village, stands a tall, thin slab of granite. Or, more technically, adamellite. It measures thirteen feet in height above ground and just under four feet at its widest point, where rock meets sphagnum moss. And it's estimated by those who know about these things, to have been formed around three hundred million years ago. The locals call it Old Bob's Finger. Which Bob, and which finger, is a mystery.

Although it's well known, some might even say famous, it doesn't get many visitors. Well... not close up. The surrounding bog persuades even the most determined or foolhardy sightseers to give it a wide berth. That and the warning red and white boundary marker poles near the Finger that politely suggest an about-turn. They also suggest that a photograph of Old Bob's digit with the aid of a telephoto lens might be preferable. Followed by a swift departure.

The area beyond the Finger isn't very welcoming. It hasn't been for the past two centuries. Nowadays, for around days a year, fifty square miles of Dartmoor's National Park is home to two training camps and three live-firing ranges. Collectively, they're known as the Defence Training Estate. The live-firing ranges are at Okehampton, Merrivale, and Willsworthy.

On any given day of those one hundred and twenty, an average of around nine thousand service personnel can be found there and at the camps. Within the estate's boundaries, small arms, mortars, and artillery smoke and illuminating shells, are all aimed and fired off by people with steady nerves and educated fingers.

It's the kind of place where the Royal Navy, Royal Marines, British Army, and Royal Air Force, have serious fun in all kinds of weather. That way, when they're called to either defend or attack anyone who needs defending or attacking, they can do so with extreme and, if necessary, lethal efficiency. They enjoy their job and they're very good at it. Most of the time.

It's also the kind of place where bodies could be buried and nobody would be any the wiser until the ground decides to surrender their bones. Sometimes it decides later rather than sooner. Other times, the decision is taken out of its hands. Exactly like it was around midnight on Tuesday, April 3rd, 2018, just outside the north-eastern edge of the Okehampton live firing range.

Two-hundred miles away and half-a-dozen hours later, it was 6.00 am on Wednesday, 4th April, 2018 in Battersea, South London. Day three of the hunt for Anton Lazarov. The alarm on McHale's iPhone was in a generous mood. It came to life at only half volume with the first thirty seconds of Marvin Gaye, hearing it through the grapevine, on a repeating loop. That intro was unmistakable. Then McHale propped himself up in bed and switched on his bedside light.

One message, from DCS Cyril Drummond, timed at 11.32pm the previous night. It was 11 words long. The words were these, *'Call me as soon as you wake up. We have bodies.'* McHale started to reply. Inner voice interrupted. *'What the fuck, Kemosabe? Cyril says jump and you say how bloody high?'* He stopped stabbing keys, flung his iPhone on the duvet, swung his legs over the side of the bed and headed for the shower. McHale 1… Cyril 0.

Thirty-six minutes later… showered, shaved, moisturised, combed, bowelled, bladdered, and generally a damned sight more awake than when Marvin left the building, he sat on the edge of the bed, towel wrapped around his waist, and speed-dialled the man above him in the food chain.

'What the hell took you so long?' said Drummond.

'I get grumpy if I don't get at least two hours sleep a night, followed by a scalding hot shower,' said McHale.

Pause.

'Bastard thugs?' said Drummond, referring to the migraines that both of them frequently suffered from. Drummond not so often.

McHale grunted, then felt a dull throb behind his right eye. 'Hang on.' He put the phone on the bed and looked around for a blister pack of para-bloody-cetamol. He found one with four still in it. A swig of bedside water and all four went down in one.

Bastard thugs were still only half awake. Maybe the paras would head them off at the pass. Maybe not.

He picked up the phone and grunted again. *'As I said, we've got bodies. And by we, I mean you,'* said Drummond.

'It's a dangerous world. There are bodies everywhere you look,' said McHale, rubbing his right temple.

'Not this kind.'

'What kind would that be?'

'The buried face-down kind,' said Drummond. Number of words… five.

McHale loved facts. He had that in common with Toby. The stranger or more impressive, the better. And one of the facts he had tucked away between his ears was the number of words, currently in use, contained in the Second Edition of the Oxford English Dictionary. He had the number memorised. God knows why. It was an impressive forty-seven thousand, one hundred and fifty-six.

Even more impressive, if you added four, seven, one, five, and six together, the number you arrived at was twenty-three. Two plus three equals five.

'The buried face-down kind.' Coincidences mean you're on the right track.

Having a mild case of OCD could be a help, rather than a hindrance. It gave his CIDP condition something to relate to. Acronyms were his friends. So was unconventional data. Another number, twenty, and the discovery of the bodies buried in a shallow grave in Bulgaria barged its way into his memory. He could feel the buzz of excitement lift the damp hairs off the skin of his arms.

'How many and where?' he said softly.

'Don't know yet… and on Dartmoor.'

Pause.

'Danger Will Robinson… ' said inner voice.

'Shallow graves?'

'Maybe.'

McHale felt his pulse shift up a gear.

'Briefing's at nine, Tom. See you there. Make sure the gang brings their 'A' game.'

'They don't know how to bring any other game.'

Drummond killed the conversation. McHale's paras began to beat the shit out of the bastard thugs. He texted the team. *'Saddle up. I think our man's been busy. We've got bodies. M.'* He was dressed, out the door and in the cab, in thirty-two minutes flat. It was 7.41am.

An hour later, the cab drew up outside Lassiter House. London traffic was a bitch. McHale stepped out of the lift on the top floor and Toby was waiting for him with a mug of hot, black coffee and a frown. 'No Lightfoot?' he said.

McHale checked his mobile, no text. Lateness was a pet hate of hers. She was cutting it close. This wasn't like her. She was normally very forward at being laid back. He looked at the blank screen wall and spoke. 'Morning SKIN.'

'Morning, Mac,' came the disembodied voice.

'Location of Lightfoot, please.'

'Rough or exact?'

'Let's skip the former and go straight for the latter.'

He walked to the table, slung his jacket over the back of the chair, sat down, and took a sip of coffee. Perfecto. *Tea can go screw itself,* he thought.

'Be careful what you ask for,' said Daisy. She was wearing distressed jeans and a baggy grey hooded sweatshirt with Stanford University in red type across the chest. McHale liked the look.

'Fifty-one degrees, thirty-one minutes, 50.8944 seconds North… zero degrees, nine minutes, 51.858 seconds West,' said SKIN. Sometimes life was all about asking the right questions.

'Let me rephrase that,' said McHale.

'No need.'

The wall came alive and the FBI Agent was looking back at them from Winfield House.

Lightfoot was on screen from the waist up. She was wearing a black, short-sleeved t-shirt with a Shadow Wolf logo and four small words, captured by quotation marks, in white on the front. They weren't a warning. They were a promise. The words were, *'We're coming for you.'* McHale saw it and smiled. No explanation given. None needed. Supervisory Special Agent Grace Lightfoot came from a long line of Native American hunters. They all hunted animals. Some of them hunted the kind that walked on two legs.

From behind McHale, Pope spoke up. 'Cool. If they do those tees in XXL size, I'll have one.'

The left side of Lightfoot's mouth curled up in a half-arsed attempt at a smile. Her eyes softened. She looked past McHale. *'Morning, Pope,'* she said. *'I'll see what I can do.'* Her gaze pulled back. *'Where's Drummond?'*

Right on cue, the lift door at the other end of the room opened, and the senior copper walked in wearing the kind of expression that left no room for small talk or niceties. To his left, coming out of the kitchen carrying two steaming black coffees, was Rice. Drummond nodded once. 'Father,' he said, deferentially.

Rice smiled and handed him one of the coffees. 'Perfect timing,' he said and sipped from the other mug, then walked to the table and sat down in his usual spot.

Drummond followed him to the table and remained standing. He always thought better on his feet. He addressed the screen wall. 'SKIN, bring up a photo of an L16.'

The image of Lightfoot was instantly demoted to a small picture-in-picture at the top left of the full screen wall. It was replaced by an image of a dark metal tube, almost erect, with bipod struts and a circular base. It was standing on level ground, facing up to the sky, and looked as harmless as a length of drainpipe with a few innocuous metal attachments. Never underestimate your opponent, thought McHale. Goliath, looking at David, probably made the same mistake.

Drummond started speaking. 'This, ladies and gents, is a British Army L16 eighty-one millimetre standard mortar. It weighs about seventy-six pounds, has a fifty-inch barrel, and it can blast the shit out of almost anything or anyone coming towards you, intending to make your life on this earth considerably shorter than it otherwise might be.'

All eyes in the room were on the screen. Lightfoot, who had a mirror image screen behind her in the room at Winfield House, had turned to face it. McHale couldn't remember if he'd actually noticed the back of her head. The lecture continued.

'It's basically a metal tube with a firing pin and a set of sights. Pretty simple. But in the right hands... and it needs three sets of them to operate it properly... it can lob fifteen bombs, each one ten pounds of high explosives, a maximum of about three miles. And it can do it in about a minute flat.'

'What's the kill radius?' interrupted Rice.

Drummond raised his right eyebrow. 'That's a very technical

term for someone who carries around nothing more lethal than a crucifix.'

'A cross killed Jesus,' said Rice softly. 'Although some might say it was the accomplice, rather than the perpetrator. And it was only temporarily.'

Drummond stared at him for a few seconds, then grunted. 'About one-hundred-and-fifteen feet,' he said. Then he turned back to face the screen wall. 'Switch on the camera, SKIN.'

The image of the L16 disappeared, and a video took its place. It showed a bleak moorland scene, early morning. It should have been devoid of humans. Instead, it was buzzing with them. Most of them wearing regulation British Army Multi-Terrain Pattern camo uniforms.

The pattern was a UK version of multi-cam, a seven-colour, multi-environment camouflage design commissioned for the US Army in 2002. The name, however, was nowhere near as imaginative. Americans were much more creative with their acronyms.

Some of the soldiers were looking at what was left of a destroyed Land Rover. Blown up, and lying on its side. In it were the crispy remains of what initially looked like one individual. Or parts of one. The rest of the soldiers were looking at a boggy crater twenty feet from the Land Rover and the wreckage of another body that seemed to be trying to claw its way out of the hole. It was minus its head, its right arm, and part of its right shoulder. In the background, about a hundred yards away from the hole, pointing at the sky in an attempt to direct the buried and unearthed souls to their possible final destination, was Old Bob's Finger. The film had sound but no commentary.

As McHale and the team watched, a Land Rover Snatch, this one a militarised version of the Defender, drew up near the hole and a man in uniform stepped out. He shouted to everyone in general and nobody in particular.

Within two or three minutes everyone in uniform not deemed a victim had retreated to a prudent distance, leaving the blown-up Land Rover, the crater, the crispy individual and the headless one alone for others more qualified to investigate.

The film stopped and went to a black screen. Then, after about ten seconds, it started again. This time there was someone standing looking into the webcam. Five feet away from the lens, frown on his face, a million things on his mind.

He was the same somebody important looking who seconds earlier had stepped out of the Land Rover Snatch. His name was George 'Lippy' Patterson. He was a Major in the Royal Marines. He was forty-one, a gnat's whisker over 6'3" tall and as solid as a brick-built shithouse. And he had a mouth that Mick Jagger himself would have been proud of.

'Boys and girls,' said Drummond, 'I'd like to introduce Major George Patterson. He's one of Her Majesty's finest Royal Marines, so play nice and don't piss him off.'

Just over two hundred miles away, on a cold, windy moor in Devon, Patterson's face relaxed, and he took a slow, deep breath. Then the notoriously camera-shy Marine began to speak to the team via the live video link. *'Morning, Cyril,'* he said.

'Morning, George,' said an unsmiling Drummond. 'What do you know?'

Patterson almost smiled. *'That's a helluva question. I know that the average length of a Blue Whale's knob is about ten feet. And I know that a flea can pull 160,000 times its own weight. But I'm buggered if I know what the fuck happened here last night. Or who it happened to. But I knew enough to get in touch with you guys. I did what you asked and cleared my lads out of the way. Too many footprints, not enough brainpower. When you coming down?'*

'I'm not. They are,' said Drummond, turning away from the screen and indicating the team. One by one, starting with McHale, SKIN focused in on each team member as they gave Patterson a nod or a raise of the hand.

The sound of a ping ended the introductions. 'You got mail,' said McHale. Patterson looked offscreen, fumbled, then looked back again. A slight smile curled up the left side of his mouth. *'Who the fuck is SKIN?'* he said.

'Good question,' said McHale, then promptly ignored it.

Patterson paused, raising his right eyebrow. Then he looked down at his hand holding something off-screen. *'McHale, right?'*

'Just like my dad,' said McHale. 'We should be with you sometime this evening. The email you just received has our team bios.'

Patterson looked off-screen again. *'I see you've got the FBI and God on your team. You must have friends in high places.'*

That brought a laugh from DC Toby Macbeth, sitting to the right of McHale. The laugh was quickly strangled shortly after birth.

'What about SIB,' said McHale.

'SI who?' said Pope.

The Special Investigation Branch, or SIB, was the plain-clothed team of detectives inside the Royal Military, Navy, and Air Force police.

'The Military Feds,' said Daisy.

Patterson grinned. *'Don't worry about them. You got first dibs on this,'* he said. *'You must have very good friends in very high places too, Cyril.'*

Drummond sighed and nodded to Patterson. 'Show them,' he said. The Royal Marine returned the nod and fiddled with the camera. The lens turned in the direction of the crater and zoomed in. They couldn't see the bottom of the hole, but they could see what was left of the body trying to climb out of it. And, about four feet away from it, two feet below the surface of the surrounding bog, they could see something else.

The remains of a decomposing second body. Buried face down.

'Shit,' said Toby, softly.

'He's here,' said McHale. He could feel the nerves in his fingers tingle. It wasn't his CIDP.

Patterson fiddled with the camera, and his face came back on screen.

'You did good, George,' said Drummond.

'I'm fine with ordnance… but the rest of this is above my pay grade, Cyril. Over to you guys.'

'Any chance you could preserve the scene?'

Patterson nodded. *'I think we could sort something out for you. What about forensics?'*

'Our people left London about an hour ago. Expect them just after lunch. Probably about 1.30pm.'

'They bringing ground-penetrating gear?'

'They don't leave home without it.'

'How many bodies are you expecting to find down there?'

Drummond turned to face McHale. 'If he stays on script, it could be ten,' said the younger copper. 'But your guess is as good as mine.'

'Probably not,' said Rice, quietly, to his left.

Lightfoot, speaking to the marine from the underground operations room at Winfield House, added, *'Did you get a look at the partially buried body?'*

'A quick one,' said Patterson.

'Was it skeletonised?'

The marine slowly shook his head. *'Clothes still on body. Skin still on bones.'*

'That's the humic acid in the bog. It preserves the body. A bit like how brandy pickled Nelson's body at the Battle of Trafalgar,' said Toby.

'Factoid of the day,' said Daisy, looking at him and smiling.

'Or it could be the body's fresh in the ground,' said McHale.

Daisy's smile disappeared.

Lightfoot thought for a second. *'I think we'll find less than ten,'* she said.

She looked at McHale.

Pause.

'Okay, I'll bite,' he said.

'Killer's version of coitus interruptus,' she said, pointing to the hole in the bog and the wrecked Land Rover. *'I don't think he got the chance to finish what he started.'*

'If that's the case, he'll be pissed off and looking for another site.'
'And that's when mistakes happen.'

'I don't think he's the kind of killer who makes mistakes,' said Rice. 'I think he's the kind who knows exactly what he's doing and plans everything down to the last detail.'

Drummond's voice cut through the discussion. 'Including something called a British Army L16 eighty-one millimetre mortar?'

'Exactly. I don't buy it,' said McHale.

'Me neither,' said Lightfoot. *'Something's hinky.'*

'What kind of something?' said Drummond.

Lightfoot didn't answer.

'You don't think this is the work of Lazarov?' said Pope.

'Oh, it's him alright,' said the FBI agent. *'I just think the explosion and the Land Rover and the bodies in the ground are all a bit too neat, in a messy kinda way. I think something else is going on here.'*

'In other words, your Spidey-sense is tingling,' said McHale.

His inner voice advised, *'Listen to the dame. She's a native bloody American, who also happens to be an FBI agent, who also happens to be a shit hot tracker. What's not to love?'*

Lightfoot smiled. 'Something like that,' she said.

Drummond piped up. 'Cover the scene, George… and put some of your boys on it. We're on the way.' Patterson nodded and, behind Lightfoot, the video feed died.

McHale turned to Drummond, and his gaze took in the rest of the team. 'Right. Time to go to work. Daisy, we need two Defenders. Top specs… no mutts. And get in touch with the forensics team. Find out where they are and how long before they get on site.'

'Guv,' said Daisy, nodding and scribbling.

He turned to Rice. 'Stephen, I want you to have a word with Arthur. He's not telling us all he knows about Lazarov. The rest of us are off down to Dartmoor. You join us as soon as you can. We'll split into two teams; one for the buried bodies, the other for the explosion.'

Rice turned to Daisy. 'In that case, make it three Defenders.'

She nodded.

Drummond said, 'I can help with them.'

'Is this a 'Red, Blue, Yellow Team' thing?' said Toby.

The older copper frowned. 'You're a clever lad Macbeth… but don't spoil it by being a wanker.'

Toby blushed and zipped the lip.

'What's the split,' said Daisy.

'Lightfoot, Pope, and I on the bodies,' said McHale. 'Daisy… you and Toby on the explosion.'

Get the Major, said inner voice.

McHale turned to Drummond. Deep breath. 'I want an ordnance guy,' he said.

'Want or need?'

'Need.'

'Patterson?'

'Perfect. He can join Toby and Daisy.'

'I'll put you in touch with him,' said Drummond, looking at Daisy.

It was 12.35pm. Hunger was starting to gnaw at their various vitals. Drummond included. A text sorted out a sandwich order. Thirty minutes later food and drinks were being consumed around the table. Sandwiches sorted out rumbling stomachs and comfort breaks sorted out bursting bladders. Except for Lightfoot, who was by now on her way by black cab from one house to another… Winfield to Lassiter. Complete with go-bag. The other one missing from lunch was Rice, who was on his way to Berkshire in an unmarked police car, courtesy of Drummond.

He was going to talk to the priest Father David Black. Convicted of two murders. Suspected of three more. Rice had come bearing a family-sized bar of milk chocolate. Arthur had a sweet tooth and, depending on his mood, wasn't averse to a little bribery. By 1.45pm, McHale, the rest of the team, and the two Defenders, were on the road heading for Bristol.

Chapter Ten

It was 2.15pm. Broadmoor was 42 miles from London. Rice was inside The Monster House, sitting on a grey metal chair in the corridor outside Cell 3. Sitting on a similar chair inside the cell was Father David Black. Except today, he was Black's murderous alter Arthur. Sometimes, with a little persuasion (or a lot), Arthur drove the car. Today, it was his turn to hold the steering wheel.

'Well now, padre...long time no see,' he said. Legs crossed, arms folded; faint grin on his face.

Rice didn't return the grin. Instead, he chose to address Black as his alter. 'Good to see you too, Arthur.'

Arthur slowly shook his head from side to side. 'You don't call...you don't write...you don't email. If I didn't know any better, I might think you just didn't care anymore.'

Rice reached down to the brown leather satchel on the floor propped up against the right front leg of his chair. He unbuckled it and opened it slowly. Inside was a bar of milk chocolate. He brought it up and laid it on his lap. 'If I didn't care, I wouldn't have brought this,' he said.

The effect was immediate. Arthur uncrossed his arms, uncrossed his legs, and stood up, all in one smooth movement. The act was so sudden that it took Rice by surprise and, for a second, he was glad they were on opposite sides of the transparent wall. Arthur's eyes narrowed, his grin evaporated... and his tongue snaked out and licked his lips. 'I like a nice bit of bribery,' he said. 'Are we sharing? Or is it all for me?'

Rice relaxed and smiled ruefully. 'I inherited two things from my mother. The first was a lifelong love of cheese. The second was Wilson's Disease. My body retains excess copper. Chocolate is a no-no. It might even be a sin. It's all yours.'

'Don't knock a sin 'til you've tried it.'

'What makes you think I haven't,' said Rice, eyes narrowed, slight secret smile on his face. Then he stood up and took the chocolate bar to the hatch in the cell front that allowed food, documents and other small items to pass through either way.

Arthur didn't move until Rice returned to his seat. Then he slowly walked over to the hatch and removed the chocolate bar. Sniffing the wrapping, he walked back and parked his glutes opposite the priest. 'So… what do you want to know?'

Rice let out a short laugh and scratched his head. 'Oh, we could spend a lifetime talking about what I want to know, including the location of the Ark of the Covenant. But I'll settle for anything you know about Anton Lazarov,' he said.

Arthur pouted and shrugged. 'I don't know what to say. I told Mister McHale everything when he came to visit, and he didn't bring me any chocolate.' He looked hungrily at the bar in his right hand, sighed, then laid it on the floor next to the left front leg of his chair. 'Treats aren't treats unless they're savoured,' he said, crossing his legs and arms as they were before.

Rice paused, looking Arthur straight in the eye. He didn't flinch. 'You know the rules of confession? said Rice.'

Arthur didn't speak. One heartbeat… two heartbeats… three heartbeats…Then he gave a small, sly smile.

'I googled it,' he said. 'When I made my mistake and Mister McHale got lucky.'

Arthur was referring to the moment that DI Tom McHale slapped the cuffs on his wrists, read him his rights, and put a stop to his killing spree. A spree that started with the beating to death of a homeless thug in Manchester city centre, and ended with the massacre of John and Annie Kirkbride in Altrincham, Cheshire, in 2010.

'I confessed to you. Just the two of us in the cell. The

sacramental seal is inviolable; and therefore, as you know, it is absolutely forbidden for a confessor to betray in any way a penitent in words or in any manner and for any reason. Very interesting word that…betray,' said Arthur.

On the journey to Broadmoor, Rice promised himself that nothing Arthur said would affect him. Not in the same way that it did in 2011. He was wrong.

'Somebody spilled the beans,' said Arthur, snarling and almost spitting the words out slowly. His words grew in volume. 'Somebody BETRAYED somebody!'

Rice wished he had positioned his chair further away from the cell wall. He had no idea how Black, or Arthur, knew that the priest was the one who told the authorities the contents of the confession. But somehow, he knew. He could feel a small cool bead of sweat trickle down his back. 'But I'm a forgiving man, padre. I don't hold a grudge. You took my confession… I'll take yours. Then we'll be all square, okay? Apart from the bit where you let the cat out of the bag. But we'll let that go. So… let's have it. How long has it been since your last confession, eh?'

He moved his chair right up to the see-through polycarbonate wall, bent forward, and pressed his left ear onto the surface of the ballistic material, waiting for Rice to speak. The priest knew that if he was going to get any new information from Arthur, he was going to have to play ball. So…swallow pride; gird loins; breathe deep; act sincere. Smile, and lie like hell. 'Since the day after your capture,' he said, not blinking.

Arthur stared into his eyes. 'And did you receive absolution?'

Long pause.

'Yes.'

'And did you lie?'

'Yes.'

Arthur let out a long, soft whistle; the kind of whistle that Bogart did in the movie To Have and Have Not when Lauren Bacall said, 'You know how to whistle, don't you, Steve?'

Then he slowly shook his head from side to side and seemed to come to a decision. 'Okay padre, ask away.'

Rice seemed to consider this request. 'I understand the thug. I don't accept it, but I understand it. But why the old couple?' said Rice. 'You could have just killed them, quick and painless, left it at that. But you didn't stop there. You butchered them. You destroyed them. Slowly. Why did you do that?'

Arthur looked surprised. 'That's your question?'

Rice nodded once. 'That's my question.'

Arthur narrowed his eyes, looked inwards, and seemed to do a fast reverse. Back to a time before he decided to turn a neat, quiet, cosy, home for two kind, elderly people into a bloodbath.

'Okay,' he said. 'In 2010, the old guy was a parish priest in Altrincham. His parishioners were comfy middle-class folk. Not stinking rich, not poor and unwashed. John and Annie Kirkbride were two of his band of worshippers. Every Sunday. Regular as clockwork. Nine o'clock mass. And every Sunday after mass…a stint in the confessional. Ten minutes in the box give or take. Boring as shit. A lovely old couple.' Arthur paused for effect. 'Except they weren't.' Another pause.

'One Sunday, in the box, good old Father Black drew back the curtain and Annie was sat there. Tissues out, tears in her eyes. Dabbing and bloody sniffing.' She said that John was one of those paedophiles. Had been for most of their married life. Said he fiddled with young boys. Sometimes girls. He made her watch. She said she couldn't stand it any longer, but she couldn't give him in to the police. Begged for absolution.' Arthur almost spat out the last three words.

'I knew the old priest was bound by the Sacramental Seal and Canon Law to keep Annie's confession between them. Well… he was. But I wasn't. I didn't tell anyone else. But a fortnight later I made sure that John would never get it into his head to touch another child. And Annie would never again see him do it. Nearly cut his fucking head off. Dug her eyes out. Job done.

Then you betrayed me. And Mister McHale caught me. And here I am banged up in this lovely establishment until they measure me up for a pine suit.'

Arthur stopped speaking.

Rice realised that this was a pivotal point in the conversation. One wrong word and Arthur would, to paraphrase the comedian Eddie Murphy, 'Have a coke and a smile and shut the fuck up.'

'Thank you for sharing and trusting me with your confession. I realise how difficult that must have been for you. Would you accept my sincerest apologies?' said Rice. 'When I betrayed you, I was in between a rock and a hard place.'

Believe when you want to. Lie when you have to.

Arthur pulled back from the see-through wall and seemed to consider this for a moment. Then he made a sign of the cross on his body and said, 'I absolve you from your sins in the name of the Father, The Son, and The Holy Ghost. As a penance, say ten Our Fathers and Ten Hail Marys. And try not to sin again.'

The irony of the mention of The Ghost wasn't lost on either Rice or Arthur.

'I'll try my best,' he said softly.

'Well…that was painless. We have no secrets from each other now, right padre?'

'Absolutely. I feel like a great weight has been lifted from me. That's quite a talent you have there.'

'Liar,' said Black, smiling slyly.

Rice did the mental equivalent of a double-take. 'Pardon?'

Too late. Black breathed deeply, closed his eyes, and let his head lower onto his chest. One heartbeat…two heart beats… three heartbeats. He raised his head and opened his eyes.

'Hello Stephen, I gather I've just absolved you from all your sins.'

Rice smiled ruefully. 'Hello David. I suspect that would take longer than either you or I have left before we get anywhere near complete absolution.'

Black returned the smile.

He looked tired. Grey-faced, like a man with too many secrets to keep and not enough energy or time left to keep them. 'Whose idea was the chocolate?' he said.

Disappointment coloured Rice's face. 'The guy who collared you. Why? Wrong choice?'

'Oh no… absolutely the right choice. A love of milk chocolate is the one good thing that my murderous friend and I have in common,' said Black. 'He told me to tell you that he appreciates the gesture and that you should find Yan and Kiril Andreev.'

That's when the warning bell ramped up in volume inside Rice's head. They were the two people Grey John had been looking for in Bulgaria and couldn't find. The two people that Rayna Orlov, Grey John's mother, had an appointment to meet on July 11, 2007, the day she disappeared. Was this another piece in the jigsaw trying to make itself visible? Getting ready to slot itself into place? Too many questions. Not enough answers.

'What can you tell me about them?'

But for now, that ship had sailed.

'Nothing,' said Black. 'I have no more interesting breadcrumbs for you today. Sorry. Arthur may know more, but this is all he's sharing with me is that they're not in Kansas anymore.'

'Are you going to share the chocolate with him?' asked Rice.

'Interesting thing about chocolate. The smell of it increases theta waves in the brain, which triggers relaxation,' said Black. And he leaned down to his left, picked up the bar of chocolate, and opened it gently. 'Anyway, the chocolate's not for me,' he said, mysteriously. He didn't break a piece off. He brought it up to his nostrils and sniffed long and deep. Then he looked looked at the partially unwrapped chocolate bar in his right hand, lift it to his mouth, and bite a large chunk off.

Then he munched it, and smiled.

'He doesn't know everything.'

'Who?'

'The old guy. He knows more than he used to,' he said. 'But he only thinks he knows it all. That would be too dangerous, padre. And very inconvenient.' And he took another bite from the chocolate bar.

Rice remained silent until the last mouthful had been devoured. Then he folded the empty wrapping up carefully and slid it easily into the right-hand front pocket of his prison-issued trousers. 'For instance, he doesn't know that Rayna Orlov met with Yan and Kiril Andreev on the day she disappeared. And he doesn't know where they are now.'

Bingo. Given the right circumstances, and talking to the right people, Arthur would scatter his breadcrumbs like precious pigeon feed at the base of Nelson's Column. Given the wrong circumstance, and talking to the wrong people, the pigeons would starve.

'And you do?'

'Let's just say they're not in Kansas anymore, Toto.'

'So…where does the yellow brick road lead?'

But Black had no more answers. Not today. Not until the next time they met, whenever that would be. He had closed his eyes and switched the volume all the way down. Goodnight Vienna.

Rice waited a few minutes, then a few more. At the ten-minute mark Rice got up from his chair and left The Monster House.

When he reached the reception on the way out, he was handed the keys to the third black Land Rover Defender. The one from the underground garage at Lassiter House.

He unlocked it, climbed inside and familiarised himself again with the controls. Then he pulled his mobile phone from his inside left jacket pocket and speed-dialled McHale. He couldn't shake the feeling of desperately needing a shower.

Chapter Eleven

It was 3.40pm and his mobile was interrupting his thoughts. McHale answered on the third ring. *'McHale.'* It wasn't a question.

'Tom, it's Stephen. Have you read the transcript of Grey John's DVD yet?'

'You must be psychic.'

The priest allowed himself a small grunt of satisfaction. The kind of grunt that came hand in hand with the passage of new information. 'Have you come to the bit about Yan and Kiril Andreev yet?'

'Yeah, why?'

'Grey John's mother met them the day she disappeared. And although Arthur didn't say so, I got the strong impression they're now in the UK. I think we need to find them. I think there's a connection with Anton Lazarov... it's just a gut feeling.' He could almost see McHale smile on the other end of the line.

'Good work. I'll get SKIN on it right away. Where are you?'

'Just leaving Broadmoor. Should hit Bristol in about two and a half hours, traffic permitting. You?'

McHale looked at the Sat Nav. *'We're way ahead of you. We left London about an hour ago. Should hit Bristol in about an hour and a half. How did the chocolate go down?'*

'Like a large steak to a carnivore after a three-day fast,' said the priest. 'Good call.'

'Safe journey,' said McHale and killed the call without waiting for Rice to reciprocate.

Then he speed-dialled SKIN and mentally prepared himself to remember that the voice on the other end of the phone would sound too damned human for its own good. SKIN answered on the second ring. It could have been the first, or the third, but a slight delay was built into its programming to enhance its human-like conversational interactivity.

'Hi Mac.'

'Hi back. There are some names mentioned by Grey John in the DVD Father Rice fed into your system.'

'Yes. You want them all?'

'No. Just concentrate on Yan and Kiril Andreev. Find out all you can about them and send all the info to Daisy.'

'Copy you in?'

'Of course.'

Pause.

'Mac?'

'Yes?'

'You have an infusion to do tonight, right?'

SKIN was referring to the medication for McHale's CIDP condition that he had to inject himself with twice a week.

'Yes, Mum,' said McHale with a slight smile.

'Got your painkillers?'

'Yes, Mum.'

The thought of being mothered by a highly advanced intelligence network composed of unparalleled hardware, software, and the most dedicated serial killer thinking on the planet, gave McHale the kind of buzz that made his nerve-ends sit up and dance.

'I'm not MOTHER.'

'Yeah. Bye for now,' said McHale and killed the call.

Daisy, in the driving seat of the lead Defender, killed the music. Lightfoot, in the back behind Daisy, had her eyes closed and her mind open. 'Penny for your thoughts,' said McHale.

'I'm not cheap. They're worth at least a dollar,' said the FBI agent softly. 'Maybe two.'

That got laughs all round.

'Care to share?'

'Navajo Code Talkers,' she said. Still keeping her eyes closed.
Silence.

'Okay, I'll bite,' said McHale.

'In 1942, twenty-nine Navajo men joined the U.S. Marines
and developed an unbreakable code for use in the Pacific in
World War II.'

'And?'

'And how is Arthur getting his information? Does he have a
connection to Anton Lazarov? Are they talking to each other?
How are they passing it on? And is it encrypted? And by the
way… how did Harry Reichs know about "twisted faces?"'

'What does that have to do with Code Talkers?'

'Absolutely nothing, probably. I'm a Cherokee. We're
inscrutable. Deep thinkers.'

McHale paused to think. 'We need to take a look at the Dark
Web,' he said. 'And to do that, I need to talk to a guy called
Dexter Bob.'

'Who is Dexter Bob?' said Daisy.

'Aah… all in good time,' said McHale mysteriously.

Light drizzle covered the Defender's exterior. Most of it
was coming from a large, dark cloud overhead. Heavy words
covered the Defender's interior. Most of them were coming
from McHale. He was giving a lecture. 'For those of you in the
cheap seats,' he said, 'the internet was born in 1989, when an
English computer scientist named Tim Berners-Lee invented
the World Wide Web.

'Researchers had been pregnant with the idea since the late
sixties. Berners-Lee wrote the first web browser in 1990 while
employed at CERN, near Geneva, Switzerland. CERN has the
largest particle physics laboratory in the world. It was born in
1954. In 2012, CERN confirmed the existence of the Higgs
Boson Particle… also known as the God Particle.'

'Does Rice know?' said Lightfoot.

'I'd put serious money on it. Anyway… the internet universe as we know it today is composed of three parts. One… the Surface Web… where everyone with a smart phone or a laptop or a desktop computer can go online, say hello to Google, and surf the web. Two… the Deep Web… where web pages that don't show up on a Google search live. It has government resources, academic information, scientific information. Lots of interesting stuff. And three… the Dark Web. This is where all the juicy, hidden stuff lives. Like political protests, drug trafficking, loads of illegal stuff.

'Now… some folk believe that hidden deep inside the Dark Web, there's another, deeper, web. One where things get extremely interesting, and pretty fucking dangerous. Interesting and dangerous like serial killers having the ability to talk to each other, without other folk listening.

'Dexter Bob mentioned it once, briefly, over a beer or three. He called it The Shroud. I need to talk to SKIN about it.'

There the lecture ended.

Chapter Twelve

About five miles behind McHale's Defender, the one carrying Toby and Pope was doing a steady sixty-five in the middle lane; the young copper in the front behind the wheel, the sculptor in the back behind the passenger seat. Balance was everything.

Pope had his MacBook Pro open, and he was reading the transcript of Grey John's dialogue recorded on the DVD. His eyes were locked onto the screen, no sneaky glances at the scenery outside. That led to queasiness and throwing up at the side of the road. Sometimes in a sick bag in a fast-moving vehicle.

Only when the reading was done (or interrupted) and the eyes had stopped following the direction of the words on the page could the laptop be closed and the scenery be enjoyed. Speaking to other vehicle occupants and answering questions while reading wasn't a problem. Staying well hydrated was a good idea. Having no snacks was a bad one.

About thirty minutes outside of Bristol, Toby said, 'The guv mentioned your little hobby.'

Still reading, Pope said, 'Everybody needs a hobby.'

He said it in the comedian Spike Milligan's famous 'Eccles' voice from 1950s radio programme The Goon Show.

'He was very vague about it,' said Toby. 'I don't think he wanted to go into any detail. But you can, if you want to.'

Pope raised his eyebrows, sighed and stopped reading. He closed his laptop, then closed his eyes. Opening them again in five seconds, he said, 'you know what a diorama is?'

Toby thought for a couple of seconds. 'Miniature model, right?'

'Close, but you only get half a cigar, maybe a cheroot.

'What… like Clint Eastwood instead of Winston Churchill?'

Pope thought for a moment. Then smiled. 'Perfect,' he said. 'A diorama is a scaled-down replica of a landscape or an event, or a fictional scene.'

'And that's what you do?'

'Sort of. Only a bit darker. I create miniature reconstructions of real-life murders,' said Pope.

If Toby felt any emotion; fascination, surprise, excitement… he didn't show it.

Hands at ten to two, eyes on the road. Quick glance in the rear-view mirror. 'Cool,' he said. 'I used to watch a US crime show on the telly called CSI. It had a villain called The Miniature Killer. She made dioramas.'

'I saw it. The writers were apparently inspired by the creations of Frances Glessner Lee.'

'Frances who?'

'Glessner Lee. She was a brilliant model maker and a pioneer of forensic science. Born into a well-off family in Chicago in 1878. Wrote something called 'The Nutshell Studies of Unexplained Death.' She was obsessed with improving the detection of crime. In her sixties, she created eighteen miniature crime scenes. Composites of actual court cases, perfect in every detail. She used them as teaching tools to help the police in Maryland improve their ability to figure out murders and preserve evidence.'

Toby was hooked. Just like he was when Pope spoke about Boris and the twisted faces created by the German sculptor Franz Xaver Messerschmidt.

'How small were they?'

'One-inch to one-foot scale.'

'Have you seen them?'

'What… the models?'

'Yeah.'

'Not up close and personal, no. But I've seen plenty of photos.'

'Some hobby,' said Toby. Clearly impressed. Pope had just

gone about three more rungs up the ladder in his estimation. Outside, midweek traffic on the M4 motorway heading south west was gradually slowing down. Running out of breath.

To the left of them, on the inside lane, an ageing, beat-up camper van with four surf boards strapped down on roof bars, had its windows down. The drizzle had stopped, and the clouds were clearing, and the music was loud and thumping. The inhabitants had the Cornwall waves ahead of them. The Defender's hands-free phone rang.

'Afternoon ladies... who's driving?' said McHale.

'Three guesses,' said Toby.

'There's only two of you.'

'You get an extra guess free of charge,' said Pope.

He heard Lightfoot's voice in the background. *'Hey Pope,'* she said. *'You ever do stand-up comedy?'*

Pope walked into the trap.

'No. Why?'

'Didn't think so,' she fired back, much to the surprise and amusement of everyone within earshot. Humour wasn't normally her thing.

McHale let the good-natured banter continue for a few minutes. This road trip would have bad news soon enough.

'Okay... time to get serious, Kemosabe,' said inner voice.

McHale put the brakes on the humour.

'Pope, what do you think of Grey John?'

'I haven't watched the video yet and I'm about half way through the transcript.'

'And?'

'Ask me when I've watched the video,' said the sculptor.

'Toby?'

'Ask me when I've read the transcript.'

In the lead Defender, Daisy saw the frown appear on McHale's face.

She decided to put the kibosh on any negative vibes. 'How about a stop at Gordano services, Gov? Stretch the legs and grab a coffee?'

McHale's frown did a runner. 'How long?'

'Half an hour, give or take.'

'Sounds like a plan,' said inner voice. *'Sugar-free black Americano and a burger.'*

'Gordano, Toby. Junction 19,' McHale texted Toby. 'About half an hour from now.' He ended the call and frowned, before reaching into the shoulder bag at his feet for his travelling blister packs of para-bloody-cetamol. Bastard thugs were making noises between his ears. He popped out two paras and took a large swig of water from the bottle in the door pocket. *'Screw that… have another couple,'* said inner voice. McHale popped another 1,000mgs.

'That's my boy.'

Then he sat back and closed his eyes. He breathed deeply whilst the drugs did their work. He thought about dead bodies buried face down. For the moment, all thoughts about the Deep Web and The Shroud were put on hold. At least until the bastard thugs decided to disappear into the background. Beside him, Daisy thought about Toby. Behind him, Lightfoot still had her eyes closed and was thinking of 29 Navajo code talkers from World War II. Behind them, on the same stretch of motorway, Father Stephen Rice in the third Defender had his eyes on the road and his mind on Grey John.

He received a text.

Nineteen words appeared on the onboard screen of the Defender's comms system. The system switched to audio.

The words were these, *'Stopping at Gordano services, Bristol. We'll be gone when you get there. See you at Okehampton. Drive safely. Pope.'*

He went back to thinking about Grey John. About how the 'Samaritan for the homeless' was recovering from his beating at the hands and feet of strangers. And about what really happened to his mother.

Not far ahead, Toby was finding out more about Pope's hobby. And about Frances Glessner Lee.

Chapter Thirteen

'So… how many miniatures have you created?' said Toby, now doing a steady sixty-five in the inside lane.

Pope, who had decided against going back to the laptop, and was instead rummaging around in his satchel for the bag of soft, fruit gums that he knew was in there somewhere, said, 'Four. I'm not really in the same league as Frances.'

'Are any of her miniatures based on really famous crimes?'

'They have elements of famous crimes, but they're a mix of fact and fiction.'

'And what about yours?'

'I'm keeping mine like Joe Friday,' said Pope.

'Eh?'

'Just the facts, ma'am.'

'Eh?'

Pope sighed. 'Dragnet?'

'Oh, yeah… I remember,' said Toby.

He did, but only vaguely.

The second Defender was now only a couple of miles behind the lead one carrying McHale and the other two.

'Any famous cases?' said Toby, trying to sound interested, but not too nosy.

'Hang on,' said Pope.

He dug out his mobile from a trouser pocket, pressed a button, and speed-dialled a number. It was answered after a couple of seconds. 'I have a nosy copper with above average intelligence, who wants to know about the latest addition to my hobby collection. Can I put him out of his misery?'

From the lead Defender, McHale said, *'Feel free,'* and killed the line.

'I'm doing a special one,' said Pope. 'The final Holy Ghost killing.'

Toby could feel his breath slam on the brakes in his throat. 'Have you started it yet?'

'At the thinking stage.'

Then the young copper went silent.

He realised that it had been months since he had thought of DI Siobhan Kelly without re-living the horror of her death at the hands of Charles Halliwell, the serial killer they called The Holy Ghost.

With the silence came reflection. With the reflection came guilt. With the guilt came the last image he had of her, lying on the floor of the Green Gables nursing home. Fatal bullet wounds to her chest. Gasping her last breath. Then dying with a smile of satisfaction on her face.

'Thinking about Kelly?' said Pope intuitively from behind.

Silence.

'What was she like?'

Toby thought for a minute. 'Ten days,' he said.

'Ten days what?'

'That's how long we knew her. Ten days.'

'Shit,' said Pope. He let the word out in a soft breath.

'She was tough as hell and didn't take any crap from anyone.'

'Have you ever shown your miniatures to anyone?' Toby added.

'Only McHale. Once. I was halfway through the third one. He said if I ever needed any help with details all I had to do was ask and he'd make sure I got everything I needed. I think he liked them. A lot.'

'And did you? Ask?'

'Didn't have to. About a week later, I got a box packed full of files and photographs, half of which I'd never seen before. He didn't say a word. Just nodded once and smiled the next time I saw him.'

Toby smiled. 'Sounds about right,' he said.

They went back to being silent for another five minutes. Then Toby said, 'I'd like to see them some time.'

Pause.

'Okay. When we wrap this one up, I'll introduce you. And you can bring Daisy along with you. You two seem to be joined at the hip.'

'We're just very good friends... with benefits,' said Toby too quickly.

'Yeah... right.'

Another couple of minutes' silence.

'Okay, I'll just come right out and say it. I'm curious.'

'Good thing for a cop to be,' said Pope.

'Have you done a 'Boris' with Frances Whatsername Lee?'

'Glessner...'

'Yeah... Glessner. I bet you have.'

Pope made a sound that was halfway between a chuckle and a sharp exhalation of breath. 'I plead the fifth,' he said, thinking about the woman in the red coat.

Toby's phone, linked to the Defender's comms system, rang. It was McHale. *Just pulling into Gordano. See you soon.'*

It was 4.15pm. By that time, Toby and Pope were five minutes behind them. All were thirsty and hungry as hell. Fifty-five minutes later, all were watered, caffeinated, fed, tanks full of diesel, and back on the road. Same drivers. Same passengers. Same destination. Okehampton. Rice was still over two hours behind them. To the left of Daisy, McHale dug out his mobile and dialled into SKIN. He put it on the loudspeaker. Everybody has a pet hate. and he had a few. Repeating the same conversation unnecessarily was one of them.

One ring. *'Hi Tom... the answer is yes!'*

'Yes, what?'

'You were going to ask if forensics were on site.'

McHale smiled.

'Actually, I was going to ask if you'd managed to track down Yan and Kiril Andreev. But let's do forensics first.

'Fine. Our forensics team arrived on-site near Okehampton at 1.15pm this afternoon. GPR has shown seven bodies buried in the ground. Then there's one in the crater and at least another in the destroyed Land Rover. There's SOCO, GPR technicians, investigators, and various support staff all busy as bees. Tomorrow, they'll be doing aerial GPR with drones of the surrounding area up to a mile in all directions. They're not touching the bodies until they get the final all clear from the Army bomb guys.'

'Why's that?' said McHale.

'IED. They're not taking any chances.'

'He wouldn't do that. He's very particular about who he kills.'

'Well… they're very particular about who they keep alive. So they're waiting for the thumbs up.'

'When's that going to be?'

'Any time within the next hour.'

'Who's in charge?'

'That's a tricky one. Officially, top bananas on this are Major George Patterson, because the crime scene is on MOD land, Chief Superintendent Alan Howlett from Devon and Cornwall force, and one of the MOD's senior forensic archaeologists, when she gets there. She's due first thing in the morning with her team.'

'We're bringing Patterson onto our team as our MOD liaison. And Howlett will be there because he's the senior copper in the territory, and this is probably the most action he's seen for years. The forensics bod will probably be cleverer than everyone else there, except me, of course, so she's a shoo-in. But unofficially, by the time you get down there, and for all the time you're there, you'll be calling the shots. That's straight from Drummond's mouth. So be bloody diplomatic. That's also straight from his mouth.'

'Great,' said McHale, tired and unenthusiastic. 'Name?'

'Professor Rose Dunwoody, I hear they call her Woody for short.'

McHale was about to say something when SKIN butted into

his thoughts. *'And now for Yan and Kiril Andreev.'*

'Is this good news or bad news?' he said.

'Both.'

Sigh. Quiet curse, count to ten.

'Okay… good news first.'

'I found them. They're Bulgarian nationals. Twin brothers. Identical in every respect except one. Yan is right-handed… Kiril is a leftie. Their father, Dimitar, and mother, Nadya, are both deceased.

'They were born on February 11, 1970, in the port city of Varna on the Black Sea.

'And check this out. Might mean nothing, might mean everything. They were living in the capital city Sofia around the same time as Rayna Orlov, Grey John's mother, when she disappeared on July 11th, 2007.'

Inner voice butted in, *'Fuckin' wow… coincidences mean you're on the right track, Kemosabe.'*

'Have you found any connection between Anton Lazarov and the Andreev brothers?' said McHale.

'Aaah… was I supposed to be first-guessing you and trying to see if there was one?'

'Naturally.'

'Well, I haven't found one yet, but I'm a bit like a Canadian Mountie. I always get my man. Or men, in this case.'

'Always?'

'Always.'

'Okay… what's the bad news.'

'I lost them.'

From behind him, Lightfoot softly laughed.

'You lost them?'

'For the moment.'

Incredulity crept into McHale's voice. 'You have a brain the size of a planet.'

'Thank you, Tom. I would have said more like the size of a small country. And they're only lost temporarily. My find rate is exceptional.'

'When did they go missing?'

Pause.

'12th July, 2007.'

'The day after Rayna Orlov disappeared?'

'Yes.'

'Shit… that's eleven years ago.'

'Yes.'

'And how long have you been looking for them?

'One hour, fifteen minutes. Give or take.'

'Is that roughly give or take… or precisely?'

'I'm trying to be conversational.'

McHale could feel half a dozen bastard thugs marching towards him in the distance. Kicking anything within reach. Leaving a broad swathe of pain stretching from the back of his neck to the top of his head.

'That's a long time gone,' said Lightfoot. 'We have to consider the possibility that they're dead.'

'How do we even know they're missing?' said Daisy.

'The local police read the last entry in Rayna Orlov's diary. The one that mentioned Yan and Kiril. They tried to find them. They gave up trying after six months,' said SKIN.

'I'm surprised they kept looking that long.'

'They might have been the last people to see her alive,' said Lightfoot.

McHale looked at Daisy, shrugged, and nodded sideways at the back seat, 'what she said.'

He cut the link to SKIN.

Inner voice butted in. *'Hey… what happened to asking about The Shroud?'*

McHale silently cursed.

Behind him, Lightfoot changed her position, stretched, and said, 'There's a story about a famous Cherokee tracker. He was a small man but very wiry. His name was White Owl because of his great power of seeing. His Cherokee name was Oukonunaka.

'Is this a road trip story?' said Daisy.

Lightfoot ignored her.

'He was born in 1845,' said the FBI agent. 'He spent four years tracking a giant black bear that, apparently, had magical powers.

'The bear's name was Nyah-gwaheh. It was terrorising and killing his people. Even though the bear always kept ahead of him, White Owl never gave up. It became his quest. All the people spoke about him and the hunt for Nyah-gwaheh.

'Then, one day, the bear grew tired of the hunt. So, it stopped running and waited for White Owl in the middle of a clearing in the forest. It knew that the hunter would come.

'It knew that the only way to stop him was to kill him. But it also knew that killing him wouldn't be easy because White Owl, although small, was a formidable warrior.

'By the time the hunter reached the edge of the clearing Nyah-gwaheh was sitting on the ground looking at him. In front of the bear was a large hole. White Owl looked surprised and momentarily alarmed. His bow and arrows were slung over his back, but he held his stabbing spear in his right hand so he walked slowly towards the bear. He had very little energy left, but he still had courage. Then Nyah-gwaheh spoke.

'*Don't worry,*' he said. '*The hole isn't for you, it's for me. My heart is tired from running and I can't dig anymore. I know my time has come. It has been a good hunt. Perhaps you could do me the honour of finishing the hole and burying me in it when you kill me.*'

The only noise in the car was the muted sound of the turbo diesel engine. 'Damn, I'm thirsty as a camel with no humps. Anyone got a bottle of water?' said Lightfoot. She knew the power a good story held over a captive audience. She came from a long line of good story tellers. In one fast, accurate motion, McHale reached down into the car door side panel, grabbed a half-empty bottle of water, and slung it over his shoulder to the FBI agent. Lightfoot caught it with her right hand, smiled, unscrewed the top, and emptied the bottle in three large glugs.

She burped loudly. Twice. Then she continued speaking.

'But White Owl knew that it was a trap. Nyah-gwaheh was a trickster with a dark heart and nothing the bear said was the truth.

'The hunter knew that as soon as he came close, the bear would reach out and kill him with one swipe of its giant claw. Then it would push him into the hole and cover him up. But White Owl was a trickster, too. He knew that Nyah-gwaheh had an insatiable love of honey. So, he reached inside his pouch and brought out a large honeycomb wrapped in deerskin. The comb was full of nectar and dripping with golden sweetness.

'Nyah-gwaheh's eyes grew big. He licked his lips, and he reached out for the honeycomb. All thoughts of tricking White Owl gone from his mind. But just as he touched it, White Owl threw it into the hole. And so hungry was Nyah-gwaheh for the honey that he lost his balance and fell into the hole after it. White Owl then used his stabbing spear to kill the bear quickly with four strong thrusts. Then he buried it. 'Then he thanked Unetlanvhi, the Great Spirit, for giving him the courage and the cunning to defeat his enemy.'

Then Lightfoot stopped speaking and took a deep breath. She closed her eyes, let the breath out slowly. Silence. Two heartbeats.

Then Daisy spoke. 'So… basically what you're saying is that no matter how long this hunt we're on takes, we have to keep going until we get our man. And to do that we'll have to be even more cunning than him.'

'Either that,' said McHale, 'or it's simply a tale about a small guy, a giant bear, and honey.'

'Not possible,' said Daisy. 'That would mean that Winnie-the-Pooh was evil and my childhood memories would be destroyed.'

Laughter, long and drawn out.

Outside the Defender, the sky was full of dark, pregnant clouds and McHale offered up a silent prayer to any God who was listening to divert any rain away from the crime scene. He dug out his mobile and hit a speed-dial key. SKIN answered on the second ring.

'Hello, Tom. I'm still looking'

'How wide are your search parameters?'

'How long is a piece of string?'

'Twice as long as half its length.'

Pause.

'Don't worry. I was just being facetious.'

'So was I.'

Gruff laugh.

'You're learning fast. Okay… this is the real question. What's the weather forecast for Dartmoor for the next couple of days? Wet… or dry?'

'Dry but threatening.'

'Can you patch me through to Patterson, and text his number to all our phones?'

'Consider it done.'

There was a pause of about ten seconds, then SKIN was gone and the Major answered the phone. *'Patterson.'*

'McHale here. I think we need to switch to first name basis, where appropriate. Mine's Tom.'

'George,' said Patterson. *'What can I do for you?'*

'It's favour time. How's it going with the tent covering over the crime scene?'

'Squared away. We put a couple of those temporary gazebo things over the hole in the ground before your forensics folk arrived. Just in case it started pissing down. Your bods brought their own cover with them. Bigger and better and white as the driven bloody snow. They're in there now, covered head to foot in disposable white onesies and masks. I can just about see their eyes. What's the favour?'

'Have they asked for your boots yet?'

'My boots?'

'Everyone's boots.'

'Shit.'

'Tied in pairs and named. Make sure they haven't been

cleaned. I'm presuming your boys have more than one pair each? Our forensics guys will have to eliminate their footprints around the crime scene. Sooner the better. That's not going to be a problem, George, is it?'

Silence.

'I'm presuming this is necessary?'

''Fraid so.'

Silence.

'You'll have them first thing in the morning. Twenty sets of boots, and mine makes twenty-one. What about tyre tracks?'

'We'll take photos. We'll need a fresh squad guarding the site overnight. And we'll need their boots too, when they're finished. I presume your guys are locked and loaded?'

Inner voice sounded disgusted. *'Locked and loaded, Kemosabe? LOCKED AND BLOODY LOADED? Gimme a break. This isn't M1 rifle terminology for beginners. It doesn't make you sound cool. It just makes you sound like a smart arse.'*

'Of course,' said Patterson. *'Oh… and I gather I'm the newest recruit on your team. I got my induction phone call half an hour ago.'*

'Welcome aboard,' said McHale and killed the call.

He looked at the Sat Nav.

Twenty-three minutes to ground zero.

Right… para-bloody-cetamol time.

He knew the routine like the back of his hand.

Grab blister pack, top left-hand shirt pocket. Pop out four 500mg oblong whiteys. Throw in mouth. Grab water. Two glugs. Swallow. Deep breath.

To the right Daisy spoke softly. 'How many?'

'Too bloody many.'

'How often?'

'Too bloody often.'

'You had four before Gordano.'

'It doesn't count if you have them with food,' he said.

She zipped the lip and kept her eyes on the road. Her mind

went back to a conversation she had with Drummond. Off the books, on the QT. Not long after, she joined the team… at the start of their hunt for Halliwell. Just her and Drummond in a quiet corner of a coffee shop a million miles away from a Starbucks. He initiated, and she accepted. Halfway through two double espressos, he told her about McHale's bastard thugs. He told her about his CIDP. He told her that McHale needed a minder. Someone to quietly keep an eye on him from the background. Somebody to look after him.

He also told her that if McHale looked like he was dropping the ball, she needed to promise to make a call. Then he handed her a small white card with a mobile contact in elegant black numbers. No name; no need. The conversation didn't last long, neither did the espressos. She got the message, and he got the promise.

From that day to this, she had never needed to make the call. She would walk through fire for her boss, and seriously fuck up anyone who threatened his wellbeing.

Ten minutes later, the female voice of the Sat Nav told her they'd reached their destination, and they drew to a halt at the camp entrance, next to a barrier manned by two armed guards. McHale knew that the ramped-up security was the result of the bodies and the hole in the ground.

Next to the guards stood Patterson, and next to Patterson stood a military Land Rover Snatch. Probably the same one the team had seen in the video feed from the site earlier in the day.

The marine major let the hint of a smile pass over his face when he saw McHale in the passenger seat of the Defender. He spoke to one of the guards who raised the barrier.

The second Defender with Toby and Pope had caught up with them, and both vehicles passed under the barrier and parked next to the Snatch.

There was no need for introductions. It would be dark in a couple of hours.

Ground zero was fifteen minutes away.

Chapter Fourteen

It was 7.20pm. The kind of exposed, windy, chilly site on Dartmoor that you only got up close and personal to if you absolutely had to. Or you had a hefty touch of masochism in you. Or if your clothes had more layers than the average onion.

The man-made road was two miles behind them. Old Bob's Finger was near enough to guesstimate its height fairly accurately. Ground zero was awash with powerful forensic arc lights, cluttered with protective white structures, loaded with gear... and busy with ghostly figures in white Tyvek suits, shoe covers, and masks. McHale immediately thought of them as Durex suits.

There was a large, oblong crime scene tent above the crater on the right, and another large one alongside it for laying out and examining the bodies. A smaller one sat opposite for ancillary supplies, and a fourth immediately through the gate on the left, for changing outfits, eating and making coffee.

Two forensics vans were parked nearby, plus a couple of Army Land Rover Snatches, a clean, shiny Audi, and a couple of grimy off-roaders.

Back at the camp, one of the brick-built buildings had been set aside for sleeping, showering, and eating. Basic, but practical. The Ministry of Defence might not offer five-star accommodation to anyone staying on their land, but they tend to take a dim view of anyone burying bodies where they shouldn't be buried on said land. And then blowing the shit out of them.

The team eased themselves out of the Defenders and slowly stretched their various muscles and adjusted their various bones back into their normal operating positions.

They were approached by a large, grim-faced policeman holding a clipboard and a pen. Smiling was obviously not part of his regular code of conduct. McHale took a couple of steps forward and extended his right hand. 'I think you might be expecting us,' he said, introducing the team. The policeman grasped his hand, pumped it a couple of times, then ticked off their names on his clipboard. All except one. Rice was still a couple of hours behind them.

Inner voice said, *'Now that's what I like to see in a solid, no-messing-about copper, Kemosabe. Good firm grip and a proper sense of humour that only comes out to play after kicking the arses of those whose arses deserve a good kicking.'*

Patterson bent his head close to McHale's ear and whispered, 'Here comes the chief twat.'

McHale appreciated the heads-up. He tended to bond well with folk who had a healthy disrespect for dickheads posing as authority. Life was too damned short. Walking towards them from one of the tents was a copper who reeked of self-importance. He wasn't wearing white coveralls. He was obviously someone who liked other folk to be impressed by his uniform. He was smaller than McHale and didn't offer to shake hands.

Patterson made the introductions. 'Detective Inspector Tom McHale… Chief Superintendent Alan Howlett. Devon and Cornwall Force,' he said. Then he introduced the others.

Howlett's eyes swept over the team briefly, then returned to McHale. He nodded. 'So… you're the serial killer hunters, eh? Cyril's boys?'

'And girls,' said Daisy, quick as a flash. Lightfoot smiled. McHale disliked him immediately. He turned to Patterson and, deliberately using the Marine's first name rather than his rank, said, 'George, could you show the team where they can get suited and booted? The Chief Superintendent and I need a quiet word.'

Patterson nodded and walked towards the nearest tent. The

others followed.

McHale turned back to face the Superintendent. 'Have you been fully briefed yet, sir?'

Howlett double blinked. 'About the events of the last couple of days?' he said, frowning. 'This isn't my first bloody rodeo.'

'No sir,' said McHale. 'About the serial killer we're hunting.'

The look on Howlett's face told him he hadn't. Drummond was leaving it up to him to fill in the blanks.

'Nice one Cyril... thanks a bunch,' said inner voice.

McHale walked over to his Defender, reached inside, found his bag, and withdrew a slim manila folder. It had one word on the front. Capital letters. Thick black marker. Seven letters.

Lazarov.

He handed the folder to Howlett who took it eagerly, opened it and saw the dozen or so pages inside. He quickly flicked through them and looked back at McHale.

'This is me being read in, then, is it?'

McHale shrugged. 'The way I figure it, you've got enough on your plate trying to sort this mess out. But you need to know about the bastard we're trying to catch. So, this should keep you in the loop.'

Howlett seemed to come to a decision. 'Fair enough,' he said. 'Cyril told me to give you all the help you needed. He said, and I quote, 'Just play nice, take his advice, and don't get in his fucking way'.'

McHale nodded.

'Sounds like a plan,' he said.

Howlett did an about turn and walked away. Over his shoulder, he added, 'Just make sure you don't get in mine, either.'

'He had to do it,' said inner voice. *'He had to get the last bloody word in. Short guy, tall ego. He probably has a tiny dick.'*

Time to catch up with the others and witness what a British Army L16 81milimetre mortar can do to a few fragile human bodies. After a murderous psychological fuck-up has finished

with them. Howlett drove away in the Audi and didn't reappear
during the team's time at the crime scene. No doubt he was kept
up to date by the grim-faced uniformed cop with the clipboard.

It was 7.47pm and light veering towards darkness. It was
chilly, veering towards bloody cold. McHale followed the route
taken by Patterson and the team.

He entered the smaller tent and witnessed them in the
process of suiting up. A large, heated urn was on a sturdy
foldable table, waiting patiently to dispense water for tea or
coffee. A replacement was under the table on the ground, full
of cold water and waiting even more patiently to take its place.

Twenty feet away from the entrance was the largest tented
structure, covering the mortar hole with a headless body trying
to crawl out of it, and a cordoned-off area immediately next to
it where buried bodies were waiting to be unearthed. Fifteen
feet away from the hole was the carcass of the demolished
Land Rover, ripped apart and tossed onto its side by the force
of whatever explosive device it met with late the previous night.
It contained what used to be living tissue. One individual, at
first glance. A better guess would have been lots of bits of
crispy flesh. That was a job for the forensic pathologist and
her team, due there in the morning. Drummond's people were
busy securing and prepping the site.

Daisy handed McHale a forensic suit, shoe covers, and a face
mask. 'Welcome to the Durex gang, guv,' she said. Then she
smiled and winked.

Then McHale's phone rang.

*'Hi Tom, I decided not to stop at Bristol. I'll be there in about
forty-five minutes, according to this lady who keeps giving me
instructions,'* said Rice. *'Maybe sooner if I put my foot down.
Where are we staying?'*

'We're roughing it, Stephen,' said McHale.

'See you soon then,' said the priest, and cut the line.

Patterson, fully-suited but without face mask in position,

appeared in front of him and said, 'Right. Let's go see dead people.' Then he led the way out the door and crossed the short distance to the tent where all the interesting stuff was. The others followed, as quiet as nocturnal hunters in a graveyard which, in essence, they were and it was.

The first thing they saw when they pushed aside the canvas flap at the entrance was the light of the arc lamps shining into the crater. The second thing they saw was the headless body. It was half in and half out of the crater. They couldn't see the head anywhere. Or the other missing bits. The third thing they saw was a body, fully dressed, buried face down; partly exposed, sticking out of the crater wall; skin still on bones, Just as Patterson had described in the video that morning. It was two feet from the surface and female.

Daisy was the first to speak. 'Why the hell did it have to be a bloody woman,' she said, sadly.

'That,' said Lightfoot, looking at McHale, 'is a damned good question.'

'You thinking what I'm thinking?' said McHale.

'I doubt it… but for argument's sake, let's say I am. What am I thinking?'

'Bulgaria. Victims. How many were women and how many were men?'

'Something for SKIN to chew on,' said McHale. He turned to Daisy and said, 'Right. Time for you and Toby and the Royal Marines to pair off and talk about all things explosive… while Lightfoot, Pope and I get to grips with dead flesh.' Daisy nodded once and led the other two over to the Land Rover, lying on its side in a foetal position.

'I don't suppose we can get any closer to the half-buried body,' said Pope, his voice muffled by his face mask. 'This is a look-but-don't-touch operation,' said McHale. 'So… provided you keep your Marigolds off the flesh, or anything else, I suppose you can get as close as you like.'

'You want to get a good look at the face?' said Lightfoot.

The body had its head turned away from the hole, so its facial expression was mostly anyone's guess. But not Pope's. Imagination he had in plentiful supply. But anything physical that gave his imagination something to go to work on was, for the moment, sadly unavailable.

'When did you say the forensics head honcho was due?' he said.

McHale said, 'In the morning.' It was 8.15pm.

'Let's say she's a bit early,' said a voice close behind them. It was Scottish, female, and slightly gravelly.

The three turned as one to be greeted by a five-foot six-inch white Durex with bright green eyes. McHale stepped forward and held out his right hand. The Durex grabbed it, pumped it, and squeezed it. 'Professor Dunwoody, I presume,' he said, extricating his hand from the pathologist's firm grip.

'I've been called worse,' came the slightly muffled reply. 'Right. That's the formality done with. From now on it's either Woody or, when I get to know you better, Rose,' she said. Then she looked around and said, 'Which one of you is McHale?'

'Guilty,' said McHale.

'Oh, we're all that, love,' said Dunwoody.

For the moment, there were bodies to look at. And one of the bodies the newcomer was giving the up and down treatment to belonged to Pope.

'I guess you must be the guy who's good with his hands,' she said.

'Spencer Pope, at your pleasure,' he said. 'I guess you must be the lady who's good with hers.'

McHale decided to butt in. 'Is this as close as we're going to get before you start digging them up tomorrow?' he said.

'Oh, I think we can get you a wee bit closer than this before then,' said Dunwoody, easing her way gently past the team and standing with her hands on her hips at the edge of the crater. It was roughly six feet across at its widest point, and three feet down at its deepest. To the right of Dunwoody, a short ladder inside the crater, propped against the wall, allowed access into the hole. It was better than jumping. On the other side of the ladder, the headless body was still attempting to climb out of the crater. So far, it hadn't succeeded, not even with the help of the ladder. It was frozen in time and space, and caked with dirt and blood. It was partly naked, and it was male.

Pope turned to Patterson and said, 'I don't suppose anyone has found the head or arm yet?'

The big marine shrugged. 'One of life's great mysteries,' he said. In another place, at another time, McHale might have allowed himself a gruff laugh. But not here. Not now. The four of them were packed like sardines down the hole, looking at the mostly-buried female. Her naked right arm, which, in death, had been by her side, fist clenched, was now hanging down the inside of the crater wall at a forty-five-degree angle. Exposure to the air had begun to dry the wet boggy earth on the skin of her lower arm. The upper part was covered by a grubby, light green, short-sleeved blouse. In life, her hair had been short and dark; in death, it was pretty much the same.

Most of the lower half of her body was still covered in bog earth. But there was enough showing to tell that she was wearing a dark green skirt.

Dunwoody saw Pope slowly reaching for the victim's dangling arm. Some feeling deep inside him wanted his touch to be the first contact she received after death. He wanted to gently turn her head to face him. To see the expression on her face. To witness the twisted look of horror in her dead open eyes, if indeed they were open. But he didn't get that far.

Dunwoody laid her hand on his and stopped him. 'No touching, laddie. She's not ready for that yet.'

Meanwhile, not far away, Daisy, Toby, and Patterson were staring at the wreck of the old Land Rover.

'So... an L16 did this?' said Daisy, looking at the crater, then back at the wreck. The marine hunkered down and looked at the wreck's undercarriage. He grunted. A few feet away, two forensic team members were examining what was left of the body in the vehicle. But the force of the explosion had no regard for keeping constituent human parts in death where they should have been kept in life. So far, the head was either AWOL or nearby in bits.

'Maybe,' he said.

'So… maybe not?' said Toby.

Patterson turned to the pair and said, 'I know ordnance. If a rogue L16 did this, I'll eat my combat helmet. There's a guy I'd like to talk to. He's based at 621 EOD Northolt. I can have him here in a couple of hours, three tops, or we can hook up a video link and talk to him in fifteen minutes. Your call.' Toby glanced over to the crater. 'Guv's call,' he said and walked over to talk to McHale. Five minutes later he was back. Leaving Daisy in the company of the large marine for long wasn't an option. He was too bloody good looking, despite the Durex suit.

He looked at Daisy and nodded. 'Have we got all the gear to set up a link?'

She scoffed.

'Does the Pope fart?'

'*That's my girl,*' he said to himself. '*Patterson… you can fuck right off.*'

'We need to talk to a Dragon Runner called Sergeant Mitch Rogan,' said Patterson.

'He's an IED robot guy?' said Daisy.

Patterson took a long look at her. 'You know your stuff,' he said.

Toby was just about to say, 'What the bloody hell is a Dragon Runner?' when he noticed that McHale, Lightfoot, and Pope had joined them. Dunwoody was still with the other bodies.

'Toby says the mortar hit feels hinky to you. That right?' said McHale.

'Let's just say I want a second opinion.'

McHale could feel the faint tremor of bastard thugs kicking

large wheelie bins behind his right eye. Migraine territory. They weren't a problem yet, but they probably needed heading off at the pass. Para-bloody-cetamol would be useless. He needed at least four of Kelly's 357s.

He was in the right place to bring up the big guns. Trouble is, they were in the wrong place to grab and fire. The emergency strips were tucked safely in his shoulder bag, along with his MacBook Pro, in the Defender. For the moment, he'd have to tough it out.

'Call up the Dragon Runner,' he said.

Twenty minutes later, after a slight technical hiccup and introductions all round, Sergeant Mitch Rogan was on the line and having a close look at the damage to the undercarriage of the old Land Rover. Like Patterson, he was a grunter. And good looking. Also, like Patterson, he had a very accurate 'hinkyometer', and it was bouncing off the red zone.

'Boys and girls, this came up from down below… not down from up above,' Rogan said, after ten minutes of humming and ah-ing.

'So… not an 81mil mortar?' said Patterson.

'Not in the conventional sense. I don't think any high explosive round dropped on this from a great height. I think you're right, Lippy,' he said to Patterson. *'You've either got an IED, or somebody parked on some unexploded ordnance. When was the last time you did a sweep?'*

'Three days ago,' said Patterson. 'But this is right on the edge of the range.'

'You had any duds?'

'Nope,' but the tone of the marine's voice wasn't convincing.

'Okay… so it's either something old that's slipped through the net, or someone playing silly buggers and it all went tits up.'

'Or somebody tying up loose ends,' said Lightfoot.

'Or somebody trying to send us the wrong way,' said McHale, grimacing. 'How would we know?'

Rogan thought for minute. *'Look around the crater. Concentrate on the direction the blast took the vehicle. Best if you do it in daylight. If you're lucky, you might find evidence of a detonating mechanism. If you find bugger all, except what you expect to find, chances are it's somebody parking in the wrong place at the wrong time, above the wrong piece of ordnance. Or somebody who's very, very good at their job.*

'Right… my job is done. This house is clean,' he said in a passable imitation of the wonderfully-named Zelda Rubinstein, the diminutive medium from the movie Poltergeist.

McHale smiled. 'You've been a massive help,' he said. 'We owe you big time. Are you easy to get hold of if we need to talk again?'

'George knows how to get in touch with me.'

'I'll sort out contact details,' said Daisy.

'Watch yourself with him,' said Patterson, after she killed the video link. 'He's a bit of a player.'

'No worries,' said Daisy. 'I eat players for breakfast.'

She turned to McHale whose eyes were doing the thousand-yard stare.

'Penny for them,' she said.

He double-blinked. Small smile. 'Just wondering whether this might have been a mistake or intentional.'

'And?'

'Jury's still out.'

Just then, a phone rang. The sound was coming from Daisy's hip bag. She dug in and fiddled past the notepad, pens, and the half-eaten Kit Kat until she found the iPhone. Then she dragged it out of the bag, flipped open the leather case and saw the name on the screen.

Pressing accept, she handed the phone to McHale. 'It's for you.'

McHale frowned, took the phone and held it under the suit hood. 'McHale.'

'Switch your fucking phone on,' said Drummond.

McHale frowned at Daisy, who smiled sweetly back at him.

'I will when I finish looking at dead bodies… promise. Is this a check-up call?'

'*I wish it bloody was.*' said Drummond. '*They discharged your guy Grey John from hospital this morning.*'

'And that's a bad thing?'

'*A couple of goons tried to discharge his arse permanently two hours ago. Maybe the same ones who tried before. Only this time they weren't so gentle.*'

'Shit… where was he?'

'*In his digs. Lambeth somewhere. Neighbour heard the attack. Called the police. He put up a helluva fight. He's back in hospital with stab wounds. One of the attackers wasn't so lucky.*'

McHale let out a slow, loud, breath and started pacing inside the tent.

Half a dozen steps. Quick turn. Half a dozen back. And repeat.

Lightfoot saw the worried look on his face as he passed her. 'What's up?'

He ignored her.

'What about the other attacker?'

'*Fled the scene. I could do with Rice here. He's the only one of the team who knows your guy,*' said Drummond.

'He's due in Okehampton in half an hour. Maybe sooner,' said McHale. He did a quick mental calculation. Half an hour to Okehampton… fifteen minutes to the site… half an hour catch-up here… about turn… back to London. Total time… five-and-a-half hours in good traffic and a following wind. ETA London: 3.30 in the morning. *Bollocks to that*, he thought.

'You can have him lunchtime tomorrow. He needs a good night's sleep,' he said.

'*How about a helicopter? I can have one there in under an hour,*' said Drummond.

'I know for a fact that he hates flying. You'd have to drug him.'

They spent another couple of minutes arguing the toss. Drummond said, '*I can arrange to have him brought back to London. He can sleep in the car.*' McHale insisted; Drummond wriggled. McHale groaned. Drummond caved and said tomorrow would be fine.

McHale killed the line and turned to Daisy. 'Find Father Rice somewhere in Okehampton to stay tonight. Anywhere nice and clean. And get him some food.'

Daisy nodded, grabbed her phone from McHale's outstretched hand, and left the tent walking in the direction of the Defender.

McHale followed her out and shouted after her. 'On second thoughts, see if you can find somewhere with rooms for the six of us.'

She kept on walking but raised her right hand, thumb up.

McHale fumbled around in his onesie and extracted his phone. He switched it on and speed-dialled Rice.

Four rings.

'I never answer the phone when I'm driving,' said the Jesuit.

'Except now?'

Short laugh. *'The eagle has landed. I'm parked up in the middle of Okehampton.'*

'You know that well-known saying, 'the best laid plans'?'

Heavy sigh. *'I'm knackered. Do I take it my services are no longer required?'* said Rice.

'Oh no. Your services are very much required. Just not here,' said McHale. 'Drummond wanted you back in London tonight, but I managed to persuade him otherwise.'

'How on earth did you do that?'

'Simple. I played the old McHale sympathy card. It helped that there was a certain amount of truth in it.'

'Migraine?'

McHale smiled. 'You know me so well.'

'What's the panic?'

'Grey John discharged himself from the hospital this morning. Bloody idiot. A couple of hours later, he was attacked again. And this time they didn't just use their fists and feet.'

Silence. Then a soft *'Damn!'*

Another heavy sigh.

'Knife, gun, or heavy object?'

'Two stab wounds. One to the abdomen, one to the back. But this time he put up one helluva fight. Two men. Maybe a repeat performance... almost. One's in the morgue and the other's in the wind. They took Grey to St Thomas' in Westminster. Nasty looking wounds, but they've cleaned them up, and the doc says he'll be fine, given his condition. He's asleep now, but he won't talk to anyone but you.'

'I don't get it,' said Rice. *'If it was the same guys as before, why would they give him a beating on the street with plenty of witnesses... and then try to kill him in the privacy of his own home? Did they suddenly change their minds?'* McHale was thinking about that, too. It didn't make sense.

'Occidentum intermisit?' said Rice.

'My Latin's shit,' said McHale.

'Murder interrupted; I think.'

In his head, McHale rewound SKIN's collated movie of the first attack; right to the point where the smaller attacker shouted something at Grey John before a guy intervened. Then the attackers jumped in the car and drove away.

'I need to talk to SKIN,' he said. 'Meanwhile, sit tight. Daisy will get back to you with an address where you can go get your head down before driving back to London in the morning.'

Rice sounded relieved. *'Thanks, Tom,'* he said. Then he paused and said, *'Meanwhile... how's the head?'*

'Don't ask,' said McHale and killed the line.

Then he walked twenty-five steps to the Defender and saw Daisy in the driving seat on the phone. He opened the passenger door, got in, rummaged in his bag and grabbed four 357s and a couple of glugs. Then Daisy spoke.

'Good news, guv. I've got us in a Travelodge. Drummond's picking up the tab. It was 10.35pm.'

Chapter Fifteen

By the time McHale walked the twenty-five steps back to join the others, Hurricane Headfuck was thinking of pulling up trees. Even the bastard thugs were taking shelter in a barn that felt like it was about to take off. As he reached the entrance, pushed the flaps aside and stepped inside, he reached for his phone and speed-dialled SKIN. He wished his 357s were more fast-acting.

Two rings. *'Hello, Tom.'*

'What's the latest on Grey John?'

'Stable. Not in any danger.'

'I need you to take a closer look at the first attack.'

Pause.

'Okay… what am I looking for?'

'I think one of the goons had a blade. We didn't see it in the footage you put together, but I think it was there. I need you to look at some more videos from other phones. Stuff you left on the cutting room floor.'

'I'm on the case. By the way; how's your head?'

'You checking up on me?'

'Always…'

'Never better,' he lied. 'Put a rush on it.'

'I only have two speeds. Express and Holy Moly.'

McHale let out a short laugh.

Suddenly, the itch he felt earlier decided to scratch itself.

'I've got another job for you. I want you to track down someone called Dexter Bob. He plays a mean sax and what he doesn't know about the Dark Web isn't worth knowing. Don't contact him, just find out where he is.'

'Let me get this straight. You're asking one expert on the Dark Web to look for another expert on the Dark Web?'

'You're an expert on the Dark Web?'

'I'm an expert on lots of things.'

'Is there anything you're not an expert on?'

'That's very hurtful.'

McHale backtracked fast.

'Okay, how do I get on it?'

'What do you know about encrypted networks, hidden IP addresses, and The Onion Router?'

McHale frowned. 'We need to figure out how Black's getting his information. We think serials might be communicating with each other and we don't have a bloody clue how they're doing *it.*

'So, you want me to poke around the Dark Web?'

'Quietly.'

'I have mad, ninja-like skills.'

'Perfect. Get back to me as soon as you can,' said McHale. He grinned and killed the line.

'Cool,' said inner voice. *'Does that mean we're going dark… like silent but deadly mode? Oh no, wait, that's a fart.'*

He ignored the voice and fumbled his phone back into his pocket as Lightfoot approached. Her Durex onesie couldn't hide the fact that she was frowning.

'Are they working yet?' she said.

'What?'

'The 357s. That's why you left, right?'

'You know too much.'

'My great-grandfather used to say that. He said my knowledge was too much for my head to hold. That's why I have a big heart. For the overflow.'

'And what do you think?'

Lightfoot smiled. 'I think sometimes he talked bullshit.' Then her eyes took on a reflective look. 'But other times, I think he knew me too well.'

Outside, an owl hooted.

Lightfoot's head turned in the direction of the hoot, then back again.

'Some of my people believe that hearing an owl hoot is a bad omen. They can be a symbol of death.' Then she pursed her lips and tilted her head to the left, then back again. 'But we also respect the owl and the cougar, because, as the story goes, they were the only two animals able to stay awake and look after the Earth during the seven days of creation. I guess what I'm saying is I won't be sleeping tonight. My spidey-sense is still tingling and I need to figure out why. If that's okay with you…'

'You'll be fine, said McHale, gently placing both hands on Lightfoot's shoulders and smiling reassuringly. 'We don't have any more cougars left on Dartmoor.'

'I Googled The Beast of Dartmoor.'

'Ah… the circus pumas, released into the wild in the 70s,' said McHale. 'That's only an old rumour. Anyway, if there were any loose pumas, or cougars, they shouldn't be any problem for a brave Cherokee warrior. You sleeping out under the stars?'

'Only if it stays dry. I don't suppose you know where the blankets are?'

'Try there,' he said, pointing to a small supplies tent. 'Right… the rest of us are heading for proper beds, courtesy of Drummond and a Travelodge near Okehampton.'

'Do they know?'

'They will in a minute,' he said and walked towards the rest of the team who, with Dunwoody, were all crowded around the crater.

Except Daisy, who was now behind McHale, and Lightfoot, who stayed where she was by the entrance. She was wearing the same thousand-yard stare as McHale and leaning on a thick upright steel pole, deep in her own thoughts.

McHale told the others about Drummond's bedtime arrangements for the team. 'And,' he said, nodding to Lightfoot, still behind him, leaning against the pole, 'since the site will now have an FBI presence through the night, there's a spare bed for you, Professor, if you fancy a good sleep.' Dunwoody thought about it for a few seconds, then politely declined. 'I've got work to do before I hit the sack. Thanks anyway,' she said.

'In that case,' said McHale to the others, 'I suggest we wrap things up here. Grab a decent night's kip. Recharge batteries. Get a fresh start in the morning.' That got nods.

He turned to Patterson. The big Marine had a grim look on his face. War and ordnance were his things; hunting serial killers was a whole new ball game.

'See you bright and early,' he said, and disappeared out the flap and into the night.

As each team member filed out of the tent, they gave Lightfoot low-fives as they passed through the entrance and out on the way to the Defenders. Respect due for a co-worker staying awake throughout the night. Five minutes later both vehicles were on their way towards the nearest road and the Travelodge. Lightfoot and Dunwoody were in the coffee tent.

'You don't say very much,' said Dunwoody, before taking a large gulp of warm, black caffeine. Very sweet and very strong. High octane fuel for late night work.

Her mask was off and her hood was down.

Lightfoot smiled. 'When I was born, my mother broke with tradition and allowed my great-grandfather to name me. He called me Eluwei. He liked to talk a lot.'

'That's a beautiful name,' Dunwoody said. 'What does it mean?'

'Silence,' said Lightfoot softly, smiling and sipping from a mug of black coffee that could have been the birth twin of the one Dunwoody held in her hands.

Dunwoody looked startled. 'Pardon?'

'That's what my name means; silence.'

Dunwoody relaxed and felt embarrassed. Before that day, two people this side of the pond knew Lightfoot's given Cherokee name. Now there was a third. One of them was alive only in her memory. Another was alive in a Defender on his way to a date with two needles, some tubing, and an infusion of a medication called Hizentra. Liquid human plasma, injected into the subcutaneous fatty layer just under the skin of his abdomen, either side of his belly button, to treat his CIDP. Injections into veins weren't his thing.

The third person was standing in front of her.

'Well… you'll get plenty of silence out here,' said Dunwoody. 'Dartmoor doesn't do noise. Except when the Armed Forces come out to play.'

'Or, when things go bang in the night that shouldn't go bang at all,' said Lightfoot. 'So… what now?'

'First off, we'll see if we can identify the poor bugger who was in the Land Rover. And we might have got lucky.'

'How? You got the head?'

'No, but we found a right hand, mostly,' said Dunwoody. 'We were hoping for the head, but that's still AWOL. The rest is just blown-up body parts.'

Pause.

'And?' said Lightfoot.

'And it's missing its thumb.'

'And?'

'And the skin on the fingertips is a bit fried, so prints are a bust.'

'And?'

'And the back of the hand has a good tattoo.'

'Half the world has good tattoos, including me.'

Dunwoody laughed. 'Yeah… and the other half just wished they had… or didn't have,' she said.

Dunwoody dug out her mobile and switched to her photos. The first one she came to was an image of the back of a hand, separated violently from the rest of the arm that used to belong to the person in the Land Rover. Tattooed in what looked like black ink on the hand was a word, in Russian, or Slavic, or

163

something Cyrillic. Maybe. Lightfoot looked closer. It was easy to make out, but hard to understand. There were eight letters arranged in a circle which was as wide as the hand itself. The word was Светлана. She didn't recognise it, but she knew someone who probably would. Well, almost someone.

'Can you text that to me?' she said.

Twenty-five seconds later, her mobile pinged, and the photo arrived on her iPhone.

She forwarded it to SKIN with the simple request. *'Can you translate this ASAP?'*

'No problemo,' came back the reply.

Fifteen seconds after that her mobile pinged again. The text was thirteen words long. They were these; *'The word is a name. And the name is Svetlana. Very interesting. S.'* Toby's voice whispered in her head, *'Coincidences mean you're on the right track.'*

Lightfoot smiled.

Dunwoody saw the reaction. 'Tell you what… you do your thing, I'll do my thing, and we'll meet up later and compare notes. Okay?'

'Sounds like a plan,' said the FBI agent, speed-dialling McHale.

Dunwoody went back to the hole in the ground and McHale answered his phone on the third ring.

'Miss me already?' he said.

'In your dreams,' said Lightfoot, although she had to admit, she did like his company. 'Where are you?'

'Fifteen minutes from the Travelodge. Why?'

'Thought I'd give you something to help you sleep better… or keep you awake. Your choice.'

'Okay… I'll bite,' said McHale.

'Dunwoody found something interesting.'

'Human remains?'

You could say so. She found most of a hand, presumably belonging to the occupant of the blown-up Land Rover. It had a tattoo on the back of it. It was a circle of letters that made up a word in Bulgarian. It was a name. Svetlana. Wasn't that Anton Lazarov's mother's name?'

One heartbeat… two heartbeats.

'I think this is our 'holy shit' moment of the day,' said McHale.

'SKIN did the translation. Maybe she can track it down.'

Pause.

'Are you stabbing yourself tonight?' she said, changing the subject.

'I've changed my stabbing routine,' said McHale. *'Every Wednesday and Saturday now.'*

'Does that mean you have to be back in London for the weekend?'

'Next Wednesday at the latest.' McHale thought of the travel case he brought with him, sitting in the Defender a stone's throw away.

'Mac…' said Lightfoot, getting back on track.

'I know. Your spidey-sense is still tingling.'

'Yeah.'

'Watch your back, Eluwei,' he said.

It was the first time he had called her that. It made her feel good hearing the sound.

Lightfoot nodded once, even though he was miles away. Then she killed the call and looked around the tent for blankets. She saw a stack of grey woollen ones, grabbed two, then stripped off her Durex forensic onesie and boot coverings, and put them in a neat pile on the inside of the tent entrance. Then she found a cold weather jacket and put it on. Carrying her blankets and her own small, powerful torch, she walked away from the tent. Far enough away to give her thoughts room to breathe.

Then she circled the scene until she was behind the tent, turned away from it, and started walking in the opposite direction, all the time listening.

She got about thirty yards into clear moorland when she felt a noticeable jump in her spidey-sense.

She stopped, dropped to a crouch, and remained absolutely still, dialling her breathing down. Then she closed her eyes and dialled up her other senses; sniffed the air; listened to the sounds of the night, just like her great-grandfather taught her the first time he took her on a hunt. She was twelve, he was eighty-three. She killed and skinned a full-grown rabbit that night. He let her keep the tail and marked her cheeks with blood. That was then. This was now, and something had her attention. She cast her net out.

Nearly… nearly… nearly… THERE! Right on the outer edges of perception. A faint sound, cutting through the silence of the moor. A smell carried on the breath of the darkness. Far away from the forensic activity going on behind her. A very faint whiff of strong tobacco. Smoke. Drifting lazily in the air. Two legs hunting four? Or hunting two? Then… nothing.

Fifteen minutes later, more nothing.

She slowly stood up. Spread one of the blankets on the ground to sit cross-legged on, and wrapped the second one around her. She shook the chill from her bones, sat back down, faced away from the crime scene, and waited.

Three hours later, she heard the sound of feet moving towards her from behind. Less than a minute after, Dunwoody appeared, carrying a thermos and two mugs.

She, too, had dumped the forensic onesie and was wearing a thick, fur-lined, hooded jacket.

'Thought you might need some company,' she said. "Anyway, I have a question.' She tried to look and sound as casual as possible.

'Um… is McHale attached?'

The question took Lightfoot by surprise.

She didn't know whether to laugh or pour a coffee from the thermos, so she laughed, softly. 'Why don't you ask him yourself?' she said.

'I might not like the answer.'

'Or you might like what you hear…'

The two sat in silence for the next few minutes. It was 3.17am.

Chapter Sixteen

It was 11.25pm the previous night. While Lightfoot was getting ready to walk into the chilly, dark emptiness of Dartmoor, McHale and the rest of the team were getting ready to check their tired bones into a Travelodge with warm rooms and cool beds.

A selection of sandwiches and snacks was waiting in each of their rooms, whether they wanted them or not. McHale decided that the Travelodge was probably the kind of organisation that appreciated the efforts of the people who kept the general public safe while they slept. Especially when the request for late-night refreshments came from someone in the Met with a polite, but forceful, personality.

All their rooms were on the same floor. Same corridor, alternate sides. Every room looked exactly the same as every other; well maintained, standard, predictable. No surprises. One of them already contained a sleeping Jesuit priest who checked in an hour earlier. The priest found a note on his pillow. Courtesy of someone at reception with good handwriting. It was seventeen words long. The words were these; '*Sorry about the change of plans. Catch up with McHale before you leave in the morning. Drummond.*' Ten minutes after reading it he was fast asleep. An hour later, the team checked in.

Five minutes after McHale closed the door to his room, he sent each of them, including Rice, and excluding Lightfoot, an identical text. '*Ground-floor restaurant. Breakfast at eight. Don't be late. McHale.*' He got short replies from all of them except Rice, who he knew was a sound sleeper and an early riser and would get the text when he woke up. Then his mobile pinged again. It was a text from Lightfoot with a picture of the tattoo on the hand. The one she sent to SKIN. The one he knew their non-human team member would be tracking down. 'Nicely done,' he quietly mouthed. Then wondered why his cheeks felt warm when he thought of her. He ignored the thought.

Then the mobile pinged again. This time it was a text from SKIN. *'Have a look at this picture grab. You were right about the blade. Found it on the cutting room floor. Digitally-speaking. S.'* He looked at the image. It was a close-up of the left hand of the smaller of the two goons from the first attack on Grey John. Peeking out from inside his fist was a small blade. It looked like a slim double-edged dagger. It was only in a few stills taken from a phone video never fully examined. But it was enough. More than enough.

This wasn't an attack, it was an attempted murder. Interrupted by a brave onlooker. No wonder they came back to finish the job. Grey John was lucky to be alive. McHale fired off a reply to SKIN. *'Damned fine work. M.'* Then he stripped and gave his ablution duties a good seeing-to.

Once that was done, he slipped four 357s down his neck and told Hurricane Headfuck to take a hike. Then he stood under the shower and dialled the temperature up as high as his skin could take without yelling 'uncle'. Ten minutes later he stepped out of the cubicle and thought about Lightfoot alone on the moor, wrapped in a blanket, wrapped in her thoughts; paying attention to her spidey-sense and trying to figure things out and fit things in.

He dried quickly, thought about sending her a text, binned the idea and sent one to Drummond instead. *'Crime scene pics in the morning, courtesy of Daisy. Plus, tattoo on hand pic from Prof. Dunwoody. Don't get too excited. M.'*

Then he infused.

Thirty minutes later, thanks to the new medication delivery

system he was trialling, he was done, dusted and in between the sheets. He fell asleep thinking of dead people and Cherokee Indians. He awoke thinking of tattoos and mortar rounds.

It was 7am on Thursday, 5th April. Elvis was up and awake, and his debut single 'That's All Right' was blasting its way out of McHale's iPhone alarm. Sixty-four years to the day after 'The King' recorded it in Sun Studio, Memphis.

McHale snaked a right arm out from under the duvet and gave Elvis a slap, but it was too late. The damage was done.

He got up too quick and the bastard thugs, waiting patiently for the past few hours after Hurricane Headfuck legged it, decided to kick only two kinds of shit out of the inside front of his skull. Instead of the usual three. It backtracked into the distance in five minutes with a little help from half-a-dozen glugs of cool bottled water and Para-bloody-cetamol. Times four. And, as usual, it left something behind.

The date was Monday, 3rd September, 1956. The place was Glasgow. Five-year-old Tom McHale's parents had taken him to an area of the city called Maryhill. He didn't like the place. He never liked the place. It was full of tenement buildings. Dirty, old, and poor. And it smelled of death. One death in particular. His grandmother's.

She was laid out in her bed in a room that smelled powerfully of roses. The scent tried its best to mask the odour of putrefaction. It wasn't succeeding. An old priest was sitting in a chair by the door. He had a new glass of whisky in his right hand, and a bible in his left. The light bulb was switched off. On two chairs at either side of the bed by her head, two lighted candles on saucers melted their way to heaven. It gave the place a spooky feeling.

Balanced on her face were three old George V pennies; one over each closed eye, and one on her tongue, inside her slightly opened mouth. Tom wanted to ask his father what the money was for. But a scary act of nature soon slammed the brakes on that. Because dead bodies sometimes do weird things; things that live people don't expect them to do. Tom didn't know about decomposition. He didn't know about the build-up of bacteria generating gasses that sometimes escape up the throat and out of the mouth. And he didn't know that these gasses are often accompanied by a foul stench and a noise that sounded like a burp. He didn't know any of that as he stood in line with the rest of the family to pay their last rites to the old girl by placing a kiss gently on her forehead, above the pennies. So, when it came to his turn, when he entered the room, leaving the others in the queue waiting at the door, two things happened. The first thing was silent. The second thing was loud.

The silent thing was a thought that suddenly went through his brain. And the thought was this, *'I want one of those pennies.'* So, he raised himself up on tip-toes, bent over the body, surreptitiously slipped his fingers between his grandmother's lips and slid out the penny sitting on her tongue, holding it firmly inside his clenched fist.

The loud thing happened as soon as he removed the penny and bent closer to kiss her gently.

The foul-smelling gas rushed up from her stomach. She burped, and Tom screamed, falling backwards onto the floor. Still clutching the penny. Still smelling the gas and tasting it in his mouth. He scrambled to get back on his feet, half scared and half embarrassed.

'Granny made a noise and swallowed the penny,' he shouted. Deftly slipping it into the right-hand pocket of his short trousers. The event went down in family history as the night when dead granny burped and swallowed a penny. But it was also the night that Tom's headaches started. Sometimes once a week, sometimes more often. And every time he had one, he had a thought. The kind of thought that made him put two and two together and come up with five. Sometimes six.

The kind of thought that made him swear blind he saw

his granny walking along the road when she had been in the ground six months. The kind of thought that came in handy when he grew up and joined the police force.

Anyway, that was then. This was now.

McHale's mobile pinged, the memory disappeared, and the sound dragged him back to his room. It was a text from Lightfoot.

'Somebody's looking at us. And there's something else you need to know. Call me. G.'

He fired off a reply. *'Then we must be doing something right. See you after breakfast. Gotta rush. Talk soon. M.'*

She answered immediately. *'Already ate. Call me now. G.'*

His thumb was a gnat's hair away from a reply. Instead, he looked at his watch. It was 7.23am. *'Bollocks,'* cursed inner voice. *'You're late... you're late... for a very important date! And don't forget the clenched fist.'*

He abluted and dressed in record speed and headed to the restaurant one floor down. On the way there, he felt for the shape in the front pocket of his black denim jeans. Never left. Always right. One old George V penny, dated 1922, in its see-through plastic container. One container in its dark red square felt pouch. It went wherever he went.

He walked into a restaurant that was as tidy, practical, and functional as the rooms and guests it serviced. The food was tasty, and the portions were generous. McHale was an instant fan. Daisy, Toby, Rice and Pope were already there, sitting around two tables pushed together, feeding their faces. A selection of cereals and fruit was up for grabs on a nearby chilled breakfast island. Against a wall was a long table with a series of hot trays containing everything a full English breakfast lover could wish for. McHale decided on a carnivore's start to the day.

The others were already deep in conversation when he sat down, plate bulging. The topic was tattoos. It was an 'I'll show you mine if you show me yours' kind of discourse. Ten minutes later the topic took a sharp left turn and ended up with Dunwoody and an elephant in the room.

'Grace called me earlier,' said Daisy softly, looking at McHale. She said it as he was just about to shovel a large forkful of bacon, egg, and beans into his mouth. Timing was everything.

'Dunwoody asked Lightfoot a question last night,' she said. The others had one eye on their breakfast and another on Daisy. The interest was about fifty-fifty.

'This is a heads-up before we go back to the crime scene,' she added, looking him straight in the eyes. McHale had a doubled-up rasher of bacon on a fork on a journey from his plate and his mouth. He froze midway. He should have replied to Lightfoot's text.

He slowly lowered the fork back down onto his plate, followed by the knife, right hand slipping below the table top to feel the comforting shape in his pocket. He took a deep breath. 'Go on…' he said, holding his breath.

'She wanted to know if you were attached.'

Toby was halfway through a tepid coffee when the liquid trying to slide down his throat decided to do a U-turn and head back up towards his lips. He managed to clamp his mouth shut and stop the coffee from joining the remains of his breakfast on the plate in front of him.

Now McHale knew the real reason why Lightfoot wanted him to call her this morning. Or thought he did. It's funny how one sentence can stop a conversation dead in its tracks, thought Rice. So instead, he decided to change the subject.

He swallowed a mouthful of honeyed porridge and said to McHale, 'Do you still have Kelly's cane?'

McHale nodded grimly. Remembering the lethal carved walking stick with the razor-sharp blade hidden inside it. He remembered the Fairbairn-Sykes dagger that Lightfoot had used to kill The Ghost by plunging it deep into the top of his head after he had fatally wounded their team member.

He also remembered fixing the stick to the wall in his upstairs bedroom. In the short time they'd known each other, she had become a fast friend. That carved memory was the least she deserved. He lifted his fork still linked to the bacon slice, and gave it a decent burial between his lips. 'I could murder a slice or two of real Glasgow sausage,' said Toby. And there, just like that, with eleven words, the tenor of the conversation shifted and lightened.

McHale finished his Full English, sighed, looked at his empty plate, burped loudly behind his left hand, and reached for his black coffee. A large gulp was in order. Then he told the team about the Svetlana tattoo, and about the latest attack on Grey John that left one attacker dead and another on the run.

Then Rice spoke up with the words that were probably somewhere in the forefront of most of their minds. 'If the name on the tattoo was the same name as Anton Lazarov's mother, then…' he let the thought trail off into mid-air.

Toby picked up where the priest left off. 'Does the hand belong to Anton?'

That was a conversation stopper. They all looked at McHale who shrugged. His throat was suddenly dry; he needed more coffee.

Rice said, 'Anton visited his brother in Sofia Central Prison, right?'

'Right,' said McHale, looking at his empty his cup.

'When?'

'21st April, 2015.'

'The day Dragan was murdered?'

'Yeah. It was Dragan's birthday. Where are you going with this, Steven?'

Pope was the first to twig. 'I think he might be going here. Does that prison have a visiting area, with CCTV?'

'They all do,' said McHale.

'Apart from those that don't,' said Rice.

Pause.

McHale dug out his mobile and speed-dialled SKIN, pressing the 'speaker' button. Two rings.

'*Morning Mac,*' said the team's intelligence network. '*You want to talk about tattoos?*'

'In a minute. You're on speaker. We're all here except Grace.'

'*Yes… I know.*'

'Of course you do. Now… four questions. First, can you find out if Sofia Central Prison has a visiting area with CCTV? Two, did they have it when Anton visited his brother? Three, how long do they keep the tapes or is it all digital? And four, if they still have images, can we look at them?'

'*Sure.*'

'Now… about the Svetlana tattoo.'

'*You want the good news first or the bad?*'

'I was born a guilty Roman Catholic. I always expect the bad news first.'

To the left of him Rice let out a small chuckle. He tried to disguise it as a cough, but didn't succeed.

'*Okay,*' said SKIN. '*Svetlana is a very common female name in Bulgaria, Russia, Serbia, Belarus, Slovakia, Macedonia, Armenia… and on… and on…*'

'We get the picture,' said McHale.

'*Next, the good news.*'

'Tattoo databases?' said Daisy.

'*Clever girl. I found three hundred and twenty-seven Svetlanas in a circle design in black ink. Eighty-three in red ink. And twenty-seven in dark blue ink. The rest, various colours.*

'*Ninety-five were on the back of a right hand. Seventeen were on the back of a left hand. And before you ask, eleven.*'

'Eleven what?' said Toby.

McHale smiled. 'Eleven Svetlana tattoos were on the back of the right hand in black ink,' he said. 'Can you send the images to all our mobiles?'

'*Already done.*'

'And dig deeper.'

'*Naturally.*'

'Speak later,' said McHale, and killed the line.

'Right,' he said, standing up. 'Time to look at some dead bodies.' Then he looked at Rice. 'You want a sneaky peek before you head off back?'

Rice thought about saying no, but he had always been a curious man. Some would say a contradiction for a Man of God. So instead, he smiled and nodded. Quickly.

Chapter Seventeen

It was 9.28am It was cold and windy and thankfully dry. McHale and the team had parked up, decamped, and, after donning their fresh, new, Durex forensic suits, were heading back to the crime scene tent.

'*So, Kemosabe,*' said inner voice. '*How many have they pulled out of the ground so far? What's the best guess; One? Two? All of them? My money's on two.. There's a fiver on it, okay. And don't forget the clenched fist.*'

Just as Pope, leading the pack, got to the tent entrance, Lightfoot appeared from inside. McHale guessed she was awake most of the night. Maybe it was a Cherokee thing. Her mask was above her eyebrows. She was looking directly at him, and it wasn't a happy look. 'Last night, I was damned sure somebody was out there watching us,' she said. 'I don't know where. Don't ask me to explain how, but I know they were there.' McHale hung back until the rest had gone in and then he leaned close to Lightfoot and softly said, 'You okay?'

If it had been appropriate, the FBI agent would have loved him for his concern. As it was, she merely liked him more than just a lot. Despite her feelings, she nodded ever so slightly as he guided her back into the tent.

The first thing his eyes searched out was Dunwoody, her back to him, scraping away wet peat from the back of a half-buried head. Even though he couldn't see the senior forensic archaeologist's face, he couldn't help looking for it. The second thing he noticed was the crater. It had grown in size, width, not depth. The third thing was the victims who were there before, but not now. The body of the female, face down, with her right arm hanging loose and her right hand balled into a fist. And the headless male trying to climb out of the ground.

The fourth thing was a trolley stood to attention, parked to the side of the expanded hole. The four-wheeled stretcher had an empty, unzipped black body bag, waiting patiently for its only ever occupant.

There was a fifth thing, but it was nothing to do with the first four.

His mobile pinged. It was a text from SKIN. There was stuff he could ignore and stuff he worked like hell not to. This was one of the latter. It had ten words.

The words were these, *'Tracked down Dexter Bob. Contact might be a problem. S.'*

McHale fired back a reply. *'Why? Where is he?'*

'Highgate Cemetery, London. RTA. Last year.'

'Bollocks… I don't suppose you know any mediums?'

'No. Only small, large, or extra-large.'

McHale smiled. *'You're developing a sense of humour,'* he thought, and replied, *'Okay… you definitely pass the Turing test. Congrats.'*

'Do you have a stand-in?'

'I'll sleep on it. Last question for the moment. The gender split of the bodies in Bulgaria… were they in any order?'

'First row, oldest grave, male. Next, female. And so on to the end of the second row. Newest grave, female.'

'How many stab wounds in each victim?'

'Ten that we can tell. Want the locations?'

'Are they all the same?'

'Difficult to say.'

'Do you have photos?'

'I'll send you the full set and copy in the team.'

'I'm looking for a female victim who could be Rayna Orlov. Don't

have a description but I do have an age range of about early fifties when she went missing presumed dead in July '97.'

'If she's there, I'll find her,' said SKIN.

'Excellent. Speak later.'

He killed the call.

Then Dunwoody turned around, and Lightfoot's conversation with her of the previous evening carried with it an awkward warning.

The elephant in the tent called to him, and there was no turning away. So, he raised his right arm, opened his gloved hand, and beckoned Dunwoody to follow him.

He walked back out of the tent, stopping a couple of yards from the entrance, and waited. Fifteen seconds. Twenty seconds. Then Dunwoody appeared. She slowly walked up to him, took off her mask, and pulled down her hood. She sighed. 'I suppose we better get this over with,' she said softly.

McHale let out a small gasp, then put on the broadest smile he could muster.

'Would we have a problem if I said I was somewhere in the romantic vicinity of attached?' he said.

For a split second he could see the disappointment in her face, then it disappeared like smoke in the wind.

'You sure know how to let a girl down easy,' she said.

McHale shrugged and smiled weakly. 'So… are we good?' he said.

Three small nods. 'Yeah, we're good,' she said. Then quietly cursed Lightfoot for mentioning the encounter to McHale. And cursed herself for asking the question in the first place. Stupid girl. Should have kept your mouth shut. *But I suppose if you don't ask you don't get*, she thought.

'Excellent,' he said. 'Now, show me some more bodies.' Somewhere inside his chest, he suddenly felt a lot lighter. He led the way back into the tent and they both kept their masks off, just to let things sink in with the rest of the team. Masks went back up.

'How many up so far?' asked Rice.

'Two,' said Dunwoody, her mask firmly back in place. 'The

male trying to get away, and the half-exposed female. She might turn out to be more interesting than the others. They're on tables next door if you want a look.'

'Sounds like a plan. So… six left?'

'Apart from the mess of flesh and bone in the Land Rover, and all the others buried out here,' she said, nodding at the great expanse of Dartmoor beyond the tents. 'But that's a conversation for another day.'

It was 10.03am. Patterson entered the tent, smiled, said hello, then went straight to the Land Rover. McHale nodded to Daisy and Toby, inclined his head, and they followed on behind the big marine. Dunwoody had a quiet word with one of the forensic team nearby who stopped what they were doing and started to gently brush more wet bog from the head of the next victim being revealed. Pope stayed behind to watch the uncovering. McHale noticed that Rice made a quick sign of the cross when he saw the partially revealed corpse.

It was a male. The head was shaved. There was a large, ugly scar on the back of the head, near the crown. It looked old. So far, the victim gender sequence was intact. Dunwoody led the way to the tent next door where the first two bodies were laid out face up on metal tables. Body bags unzipped; contents revealed. She entered and stopped at the first table, holding the filthy, partially charred body of the headless male corpse. It had once been well-muscled.

'Not found the head yet?' said McHale.

'We only have one head-hunter,' said Dunwoody, ignoring the irony.

The body was smeared with dirt and dried blood, and peppered with holes. The smell was a blend of strong, sad, musty death, sour bodily fluids, and peaty earth.

'It's in good condition… apart from all the damage,' said the forensic archaeologist, with no attempt at humour. 'Humic acid in the bog is a great preservative.'

Lightfoot bent down close to the torso, examining the damage to the skin from the force of the explosion. Only some of the damage looked different to the rest. Some of it looked like stab wounds, and they were all the same size and shape. So, she counted them, then she looked up at McHale.

'Ten,' she said.

'That means something?' said Dunwoody.

'Maybe…' said McHale, moving round to the body of the woman on the next table. He felt a slight tingling in his fingers.

Staring up at him, eyes and mouth open but crammed with dirt, was the first of the victims with a head. She was wearing what had once no doubt been an attractive short-sleeved green blouse and a dark, knee-length dark green woollen skirt. Her hair was dark brown, cropped short. She was petite; about five-feet three, McHale guessed. His guess was almost as good as other folk's measuring tape. And her torso had ten stab wounds. In the same places as the headless male.

McHale sighed deeply and looked at Dunwoody. 'Now it means something,' he said.

The female's blood had pooled underneath her body, discolouring it a dark purple. Her body had remained in the face-down position since shortly after she was murdered. Rigor Mortis had come and gone and it didn't even say goodbye. But her right hand was still closed in the shape of a fist.

Lightfoot gently cleared the dirt from the victim's open eyes and closed the eyelids.

'*Closed bloody fist,*' said inner voice.

McHale looked closely at the right hand of the victim. It was clenched tight.

By his right shoulder Dunwoody said softly, 'Thought you might be interested in that. I didn't want to unclench it without you here. She might have something important in there.'

'Or she might just have a grip full of skin,' said Rice, who had joined them. He was looking at the corpse's face with sadness in his eyes.

McHale's gloved hand brushed the lifeless fist, as if he could tell just by touching it what was trapped inside.

Then Dunwoody took over and opened the fingers. They uncurled as grudgingly as the petals of an uncooperative flower. There was nothing inside. Then his mobile pinged. He stepped out of the tent, dug into his Durex suit, found the phone, and pressed a button. A text from SKIN appeared.

One; is the Svetlana Tattoo on the hand of a male or a female?'

McHale paused, then answered. *'Male I think, but good call. I'll ask.'*

Inner voice piped up, *'Damn... why the hell didn't you think of that. Get your shit together!'*

SKIN texted, *'Two; Sofia Central Prison had CCTV when Anton visited his brother and it still has it now. What am I looking for?'*

McHale punched a reply; 'Images of the back of Anton's right hand.'

'Three; attached are photos of the Bulgaria victims, including close-ups of the stab wounds.'

'Excellent. Attached is a pic of one of the Dartmoor victims. Can you compare wound locations with Bulgarian victims?' texted McHale.

'Of course.'

'Were all the victims identified?'

Pause.

'Only five so far. Three women, two men.'

'Any of the three Rayna Orlov, Grey John's mother?'

'No. Wrong ages.'

McHale quietly cursed.

Inner voice butted in. *'Bloody newsflash, Kemosabe... what about a DNA match with Grey John?'*

'Find out if they extracted DNA from all of the victims...'

SKIN completed the sentence *'... and you'll get a Mitochondrial DNA sample from Grey John for comparison. Good thinking.'*

McHale killed the line, then he speed-dialled Drummond. Three rings.

'*You must be psychic,*' said the senior police officer.

'You must be thinking of my gypsy grandmother,' said McHale. 'Although some folk think I have a tendency to be bloody weird, as you know.'

'*Some folk might be right. What's the latest?*'

McHale brought him up to speed.

Five minutes later, when he finished, Drummond grunted. Then there was silence, followed by more silence. Then Drummond voiced what he was obviously thinking.

'*Is there the skinniest cat in hell's chance that we might have just got very fucking lucky here?*'

'As in..?'

'*As in, if the images from the prison show Anton Lazarov with a tattoo on his right hand, could he be the bastard blown to bits down there in Dartmoor?*'

'That would be bloody bad news for him and a stroke of luck the size of The Grand Canyon for us,' said McHale.

'*You have a habit of getting lucky.*'

'The harder we work, the luckier we get. Anyway, it's just a theory at the moment. We're still kicking it around.'

'*Well, do me a favour. Kick harder.*'

Then there was a click, and Drummond killed the line.

McHale walked back into the crime scene tent and over to Dunwoody, who had taken back control of unearthing the next body. She turned to face him as he adjusted his mask and joined her in the crater. 'You look like a man with an important question on his mind,' she said.

'You remember a singer in the early 70s called Johnny Nash?'

Dunwoody's eyes took on a distant look. '*I Can See Clearly Now?*'

'That's the guy. Well… same album has another track called "*There Are More Questions Than Answers.*"'

'And that's how you feel at the moment?'

McHale's right eyebrow raised. 'Try most of the time.'

They both climbed out of the hole.

'Join the club,' she said.

McHale gave a short, sharp, humourless laugh. 'I'm a card-carrying, fully paid-up lifetime member,' he said. 'I have a question.'

'Just one?'

McHale grunted. 'Is the hand from a male or a female?'

Dunwoody thought for a minute.

'Male,' she said.

There didn't seem any doubt in her voice.

'Good enough for me,' said McHale.

Then there was a pat on his shoulder. It was Rice.

'Sorry Professor, I have to take his confession before I leave.'

Dunwoody shrugged, turned, and climbed back into the hole.

McHale turned. 'You off?' he said to the Jesuit.

'There's probably a joke in there somewhere, but I'll skip it for now,' said Rice. 'I better get back. Find out what Grey John has to say.'

McHale nodded. 'I need you to collect a buccal swab from him. We need to find out if one of the females in the Bulgarian graves is his mother. Probably best if the request comes from you.'

Rice nodded. 'Who do I give the swab to?'

'I'll get someone to collect it from the hospital. They'll get it to the UK National DNA Database. The Bulgarians can pick it up from there and compare it with the ten female samples they have from the bodies in the forest.'

'And if they get a match?'

'Then we've got a link from Anton to Grey John.'

Rice nodded.

'Safe journey,' said McHale.

The priest said goodbye to the rest of the team. Then he did an about turn and walked out of the tent.

Ten minutes later he was on the road back to London, about 220 miles away, give or take, and about four hours. Then another hour through London traffic to St Thomas' Hospital, Westminster. As soon as he left, McHale sent a text to Drummond.

'Rice will arrange for a cheek swab from Grey John. Can you arrange for it to be picked up from St. Thomas' Hospital and sent to the Bell Macaulay Labs in Battersea for processing? They'll put it on the UK National DNA Database. Thanks. M.' About thirty seconds later, he got a reply. It was seven words long. The words were familiar, and they were these, *'What did your last servant die from?'* McHale smiled and took that as a 'yes'.

There was something scratching at the back of his brain. It was refusing to move any further forward. So, he went in search of Patterson, Daisy, and Toby. The search took about three seconds. They were standing next to Dunwoody, while she was standing next to the crater. It was getting bigger.

Dunwoody's team had revealed more of the body of the male with the shaved head. He was wearing jeans with a dark leather belt. No shoes. No socks. Covering most of his upper body, he had a black, short-sleeved t-shirt with the words *'Love & Coffee'* just visible in filthy white on the back. The same words were tattooed in black along his right forearm, visible to the eyes of all who witnessed his uncovering, including the forensic team members who were documenting and photographing the whole event. It was a sad, lonely scene. Inhabited by people whose job it was to bring the dead back to life. Albeit temporarily.

Chapter Eighteen

It was 12.17pm and 'Lippy' Patterson was walking towards McHale inside the crime scene tent. A soldier was just walking out of the tent entrance. There was a cardboard box about a foot-and-a-half square in Patterson's hands, and a wide smile on his face. 'Ladies and gentlemen, we have a head,' he said, opening the box flaps to reveal a skull with half its skin and muscle still attached, and the rest blown away to reveal a bloody skull.

McHale turned to Pope. 'You got your laptop with you, right?'

'I don't leave home without it,' said the sculptor, knowing full well that he often did.

The cop took the box from Patterson and gave it to Pope. 'Find somewhere nice and quiet and see if you can put a proper face on this.'

Pope smiled. 'I bet you say that to all your sculptors,' he said, and walked out of the tent towards the Defenders.

Right, thought McHale, *Native American time. Deep breath.* He turned to Lightfoot, right eyebrow raised. 'So... tell me about this spidey-sense thing that happened last night,' he said.

The FBI agent did, then gave a small shrug. 'Might be something, might be nothing.'

'But you think..?'

Long pause, short nod. 'Might be something.'

'You think there was somebody checking us out?'

'I think there was somebody out there. Whether they were checking us out or not, I don't know.' McHale looked at Patterson. Then back to Lightfoot.

'Fancy going on a hunting party in broad daylight?' he said.

'Thought you'd never ask.'

'Thought I wouldn't need to.'

'Permission is always more powerful if it isn't asked for,' she said

'Is that a saying from an old Cherokee Christmas cracker?'

'Unspoken one from a wise old FBI mentor.'

Pause.

'Take Patterson with you,' he said.

She was about to speak when McHale beat her to the punch. 'He knows the territory. Makes sense.'

He turned to Patterson, 'you okay with that?'

'I'm okay if you're okay,' said Lightfoot, careful not to let disappointment show in her face.

McHale turned to Patterson. 'Please don't piss her off,' he said.

'Wouldn't dream of it,' said the marine. A vague hint of a smile passed across his face. Two minutes later, Lightfoot found the bearings she had left over from the previous night. Three minutes later she had her game head on and started walking west across the moor. Patterson had the good sense to keep his mouth shut, his eyes open, and his feet moving. One step behind her. That left McHale, Daisy, Toby, Dunwoody and her team together in the crime scene tent.

It also left Daisy looking at the team and asking a couple of questions.

'If this is Anton's work… and we think it is… then he's predictable in two ways,' she said. 'One; he stabs all his victims ten times. Why? And two; he kills in sets of ten. Twenty victims in Bulgaria. Ten male. Ten female. Calculated. Precise.

Premeditated. So why are there only eight victims here? What made him change his M.O.?'

Silence.

'Easy answer… maybe he didn't get the chance to finish what he started,' said Dunwoody.

'Killer's version of coitus interruptus?' said McHale,

remembering Lightfoot's comment. His fingers began to tingle. Inner voice piped up. *'Autopsy, Kemosabe. What about Svetlana Lazarov, Anton's mother; how did she die?'*

McHale pulled out his mobile and dialled SKIN.

One ring.

'Hello Mac.'

'Question. Is there an autopsy report on anyone's file about Svetlana Lazarov?'

One heartbeat… two heartbeats.

'Yes. You want me to send it to you?'

'Send it to all the team. Meanwhile, tell me the cause of death.'

'Multiple stab wounds.'

'How many?'

'Ten.'

'Remind me to give you a virtual hug… or a pat on the back.'

'Let me guess… you want to know what Anton's trigger was?'

'I think I know,' said McHale.

'By the way, just sent you a text. You should have it any second.'

McHale killed the call. Bastard thugs were stirring. As if in response, his mobile pinged. It had twenty-eight words and a video clip.

The words were these, *'Compliment you on your instincts. This is Anton Lazarov visiting brother Dragan in Sofia Prison at 1.15pm, on 21st April, 2015. Dragan's birthday. The same day Dragan was murdered.'*

The full-colour clip was of the brothers sitting in a large, clean, cold-looking visiting area. It was half full of visitors and inmates. The walls painted a drab pale green. In the middle of the room were two men sitting on opposite sides of a desk the same colour as the walls. Interior décor was not a big thing in any prison. The CCTV was on the wall behind Dragan. There was a clock high on the wall opposite the camera. The time showed 1.38pm. Anton was on the far side of the table, facing his brother. He had both palms resting on the desk top.

The screen was vertically split in two. One half stayed as a long shot of the room. The other half was a close-up of the back of Anton's right hand. His sleeve was pushed up his forearm. The image of the Svetlana tattoo was crystal clear. There was no doubt. The severed hand Dunwoody showed McHale could have been an exact duplicate of the attached hand they were looking at in the video clip from Sofia Prison; same circular design; same Bulgarian letters in what looked like black ink. This wasn't a tattoo for others to look at and admire, this was something else. This was far more personal. The tingle in McHale's hands grew in intensity. He could feel it in his feet, too. The bastard thugs were kicking over refuse bins as they approached. They didn't give a shit if they made any mess or any noise.

'What?' said Daisy. She didn't normally do worried. She made an exception.

McHale motioned for the others to come close, and he replayed the clip.

Toby was the first to speak after it finished. 'Holy Jesus fuck, guv,' he said.

Nobody swears quite like a Glaswegian in a state of high alert. His normally soft accent took on an altogether harsher, more excited, tone.

McHale texted SKIN four words. *'Send this to Drummond.'*

Immediate reply. *'Way ahead of you.'*

He turned to Dunwoody. 'Where's the hand?' he asked.

'In a cold box in the tent next door with the first two bodies,' said the forensic archaeologist.

'Suppose I want to cross-match a DNA sample from the hand to a sample of a female murder victim in Bulgaria?'

'How old was the deceased when she died?'

'Possibly mid-50's.'

'How long has she been in the ground?'

'Nearly thirty years,' he said.

'Do you have a name?'

'Svetlana Lazarov.'

'Can she be exhumed?' said Dunwoody.

McHale thought of Drummond's clout and powers of persuasion. 'No problem,' he said, fingers mentally crossed.

'I'll get you a nice piece of soft tissue.'

He nodded.

She went to fetch the hand. McHale watched her go. This was her territory; this was where she kicked arse. About thirty seconds later, his mobile rang. Drummond's name came up on the caller ID. He gave it two rings before he answered.

He spoke first. 'Before you say anything, slam the brakes on. We don't know for sure if the hand is his. This is me keeping you in the loop.'

Then he waited.

'So, it could be?'

'Not necessarily, but maybe.'

Drummond sighed. *'Is it your intention to piss me off?'*

'Not at all. It's my intention to be very bloody careful.'

'Well… please be very bloody quick about it. And remember. It might be your bloody body, but it's my bloody loop.'

'There's something else,' said McHale. 'I need a favour… and it's not going to be a small one. And it needs to be done yesterday.'

'It always is, with you.'

'I need the body of Svetlana Lazarov exhumed and DNA taken from the marrow in her thigh bone to compare with the soft-tissue DNA of the hand we have here. Is that going to be a problem?'

Silence. Then more silence. Then a large, audible sigh. *'I might need to pull some bloody long strings,'* said Drummond. *'Leave it with me.'*

Drummond killed the call. Catching serial killers, whole or in bits, was a complicated business. It was 12.54pm.

Five minutes later, Dunwoody was back with the cool box. In

the box was a plastic, see-through evidence bag. Sealed, tagged, and signed. In the bag was the hand, minus thumb.

'I need a finger,' said McHale.

Dunwoody turned and called to a nearby assistant. 'Jo?'

'Yes, boss?' said a small, slim female.

The forensics chief retrieved the hand from the bag. 'Clip off a pinkie, please.'

'A whole pinkie?' said McHale.

'Better to have it and not need it, than need it and not have it,' said Dunwoody.

Jo reached for a box nearby, grabbed a pair of bone-cutting forceps, and snipped off the chosen digit in one strong squeeze. Dunwoody dropped it in an evidence bag and handed it to McHale who dug into his jacket and pulled out a pen.

Then he filled out the CoC label, handed the bag to Toby and said, 'Find the nearest forensics lab. I need a DNA profile on this. And don't let it leave your sight.'

The young DC signed the label and took off towards his Defender at a rate of knots.

McHale turned back to Dunwoody and the hand, now minus two digits.

'How long?' he said.

Dunwoody thought. 'If the lab is on their A-game, and your Drummond guy is extremely well-connected, maybe two or three days to get the DNA profile and load it on the National Database. Same if the Bulgarians have size twelve boots up their arses.

'If somebody knows how to work miracles, maybe less.'

McHale breathed out slow. 'Shit.'

Inner voice piped up. *'Tick bloody tock, Kemosabe. Tick bloody tock!'*

He looked at the lonely hand, now back in its bag, minus a finger at either end, tattoo side up. There was that itch again, the one at the back of McHale's head trying to push its way to the front. Something about a hand… and a circle…

'Dammit. It's staring you right in the face. Or it was!' said inner voice.

Suddenly, the light bulb came on. 'Fuck,' he said, and made fast tracks for the tent next door the one with the dug-up bodies. The others, including Dunwoody, followed him. Confusion on their faces. When he got there, the female corpse was laid out on a metal table. Face up, zipper down. There was an empty trolley by her side, ready to be taken back for the next victim. He binned the gloves he was still wearing and grabbed a pair of fresh ones, heading to the body. He lifted up the right hand and looked at the ring finger. There, staring at him, was a tight-fitting golden band.

'Bingo,' said inner voice.

He looked at Daisy. She didn't need to be asked. She fumbled in her onesie, brought out her phone and took four pics of the ringed finger. Above, below, left, and right.

'I need the ring removed,' said McHale, looking at Dunwoody. 'Intact?'

'Undamaged. Take the finger off if you have to.'

The forensic archaeologist put on a fresh pair of gloves, grabbed the lifeless hand and the ring, and twisted. Then pulled. Then twisted more. The ring refused to budge. 'Bugsy!' she shouted, and a tall forensic team member raised his head from over by the destroyed Land Rover.

'Yes, boss?'

'WD40.'

Bugsy went to fetch the lubricant. Two quick sprays and another couple of twists later, and the ring slid free. Dunwoody didn't even examine it. She handed it straight to McHale who looked at the outside surface, then looked at the inside. Then he smiled. Bugsy went back to doing what he was doing before he became Dunwoody's lubricant gopher. McHale angled the ring, so the light reflected off the inside of the band and showed what was inscribed there. The wording was small, but it took up the whole inside surface of the ring. He didn't understand a word of it.

'Bollocks,' yelled inner voice. *'One step forward, three steps bloody back!'*

McHale grunted, then looked at Daisy. Her phone was still in her hand. While he held and revolved the ring, she took photos of the writing. Then he stretched his right arm and hand out behind him towards Toby. One evidence bag was placed firmly into McHale's hand and the ring was gently dropped into it. Sealed, tagged, and signed.

'I bet my granny's best bone China the language is Bulgarian,' said McHale. 'Find out what it says. And find out how many Bulgarians there are resident in the UK.' Daisy nodded and walked away from the group to send a text and pictures to the team's dedicated crime-fighting intelligence network.

She passed Toby on the way back in. He looked at McHale. 'Plymouth,' he said. 'Neuman Forensics. About 30 miles. I can get there in maybe fifty minutes.'

McHale nodded. 'Call ahead and get there in forty.' When he left the crime scene it was 1.23pm.

Lightfoot and Patterson had been gone an hour and small change. They were just over two miles west of the crime scene and there wasn't a road or a path in sight. And they were being watched; Lightfoot could feel it. It brought back an old memory.

Chapter Nineteen

The date was 25th August, 2010. The place was the Sonoran Desert, Uncle Sam's side of the Arizona-Mexico border fence. The time was just after 1.55am. FBI Supervisory Special Agent Grace Lightfoot was sitting cross-legged on dry, cold, sandy ground, somewhere inside a seventy-six-mile stretch of the Tohono O'odham Nation territory. She was a member of the US Department of Homeland Security's elite Shadow Wolves unit; the Department's only Native American trackers. Some said they were the best trackers of humans in the world. That's probably why, at one point, others said a Mexican drug cartel had placed a bounty on the head of each Shadow Wolf team member of $500,000.

The unit was composed of thirty male tactical patrol officers from nine different tribes, and one female, a Cherokee. They were equipped with night-vision scopes, GPS locators, M-4 rifles and Glock 17 9mm semi-automatic pistols. They were also equipped with traditional 'cutting' skills, formed and honed through generations of natural tracking. They were hunters of the very highest quality, tracking scum of the very lowest.

That night, Lightfoot was with nine members of the unit - all males - and somewhere inside them, a clock was slowly passing the time of night until the sun came up. Or until someone gave them a powerful enough reason to do what they were extremely good at doing.

Tonight, they hoped that the someone in question was a shaven-headed Mexican known as Salvador. Only he was no saviour; he was a coyote. A human who, for every dollar his illegals had, offered to guide them across the desert, out of Mexico, and into the relatively safe embrace of Uncle Sam. Of course, the reality was that he handed them over to smugglers on the US side of the border. In turn, they were treated as slaves, paid little or nothing, and lived for the rest of their lives, long or short, under the threat of discovery and deportation. Or worse.

Salvador was only one of a large number of coyotes operating along the border. But he was one of the best. And he was also one of the worst. Officially, both sides wanted him behind bars. Unofficially, they didn't give a damn how he was caught. They just wanted his head, preferably separated from the rest of his body.

Not because of the immigrants he helped cross the border, but because of the drugs he forced each one of them to carry into the US.

However, Salvador had a fatal personal flaw. Her name was Renata, and she was a Shadow Wolf agent. She had been deep undercover for almost a year, and during that time, she learned that Salvador, along with a team of knowledgeable and talented diggers, had built a tunnel. It was five meters down and fifty feet long; twenty-five up to and under the border fence on the Mexican side, and another twenty-five metres into the US side.

It took over a year to excavate and shore up, mostly at night. It was an impressive feat, and it had a hidden hatch at each end. Salvador was counting on the tunnel to bring him in lots of money. What he wasn't counting on was Renata and the signal she sent to Shadow Wolf HQ three days previously. It was now 2.37am precisely.

Six hours previously, Salvador and thirty 'customers'- men, women and children - had made their way to the entrance of the Mexican end of the tunnel. They were very quiet. When they were all in, they stopped and waited two minutes. Timing was everything. Then they made their way slowly along the dimly-lit passage and prepared to emerge into a new country, Ready for a new life that was a million times better than the old one.

Their feet were wrapped with strips of cloth to keep down the sound. Their mouths were shut tight to keep in their words. Even their breathing, laboured in the claustrophobic heat of the tunnel, was silenced by the tons of desert earth above them. But they were not alone, and they didn't reckon on Lightfoot's almost supernatural sense of hearing.

On Uncle Sam's side of the border fence, near the tunnel exit, Lightfoot and her team members had been waiting, almost motionless, in the dark for two hours. All senses dialled up to the max, listening to the sounds of the night. Listening for a sound that didn't belong. At 2.53am, she heard one.

Lightfoot raised her clenched fist, indicating that the others should stay where they were. Then she slowed her breathing, moved forward, and reached out with her mind. Suddenly, she heard the soft footsteps and faint heartbeats. So, she stopped, turned around and made her way back slowly and quietly to the other members of her team. 'Tunnel,' she whispered. 'We got company.'

In a pocket on her right hip was a black-coloured comms device the size of a cigarette packet. It had an on/off button, a signal button, and a small screen.

Lightfoot pressed the off button to on and the signal button twice in quick succession.

Approximately two hundred miles above her, a US optical image reconnaissance satellite in geosynchronous orbit received two beeps. It stopped looking at what it had been looking at, and instead, turned its beady eye in Lightfoot's direction. What it saw was heat signatures. Ten it immediately identified as Shadow Wolf agents. Thirty-one others, heading slowly towards Lightfoot and her team.

It also saw two old US M35 ex-military 'deuce-and-a-half' trucks, making their way towards Lightfoot and the tunnel. Two signatures up front in each truck. No lights. Good drivers; not so good human beings. They were ten minutes away and coming in fast. The satellite sent the images to Lightfoot.

It also sent the images to a Sikorsky UH-60 Black Hawk helicopter, one of two commissioned for exclusive use by Homeland Security. Heavily modified with stealth technology, flying in from the north at 10,000ft, at 250km an hour. It was fully locked and loaded; hostile in nature and looking for a fight.

At 3.15 am six things happened. One; from below, Salvador pushed up on the tunnel's exit hatch. Then he ushered his 'clients' to follow him to freedom.

Two; the 'deuce-and-a-half' trucks appeared out of the darkness, on the dirt road alongside the border fence. Four unsmiling men jumped down from the M35 cabins and hurried over to Salvador. Two of the men were carrying AK-47s, known amongst Mexican smugglers as the 'cuerno de chivo' or 'goat horn' because of their banana-shaped, 30-round magazine. The AK-47 was simple, noisy, easy to use, easy to repair, and not very accurate.

Three; the ten Shadow Wolf agents, led by Lightfoot, also appeared out of the darkness. Fully armed.

Four; the two men with AKs stopped breathing. Two shots each, centre mass. One shot each, head. Sometimes you just had to announce your arrival with bullets rather than with vocal cords.

Five; the Black Hawk joined the party, this time at a reduced altitude of fifty feet, complete with two 762mm calibre machine guns.

Then six; the dark-skinned, shaven-headed male at the head of the group, and the two unsmiling men still breathing, looked at the Shadow Wolf agents and the hovering Black Hawk, and then each other. Then they sighed, slowly knelt on the ground, put their hands behind their heads, and interlocked their fingers.

Lightfoot walked over to the dark-skinned male and nodded once. 'Smart move,' she said.

Then she looked at the illegals. They were huddled together wondering what the hell was going to happen to them now.

She could see that a couple of them were thinking about sneaking back into the tunnel. One look from her and they were persuaded to think again.

Anyway, that was the past. This was the present, and a million miles away from the Sonoran Desert. But deep inside, Lightfoot was still a Shadow Wolf.

Chapter Twenty

Back to the present. It was 1.32pm. Lightfoot and Patterson were hunkered down behind a large rocky structure, two miles west of the Dartmoor crime scene. It had been slow going. Patterson had tried to speak twice since they stopped walking. Lightfoot had held her right hand up both times, giving his words a good enough reason to stay where they were in the back of his throat.

She was glad that McHale hadn't contacted her since they left the tent. Her eyes were closed, her breathing was slowed and her spidey-sense was tingling.

She had lived for most of her early life with a heightened sense of perception thanks to the guidance of her great grandfather. What he taught her had stayed with her long after they parted company in the physical realm. It had also kept her alive on more than one occasion.

Like the first time she felt the spiders. She was thirteen, and it was cold and late in the year. The moon was hiding. Nimrod had led her into the place called Snake Valley. It didn't deserve the name. It was just a small area of scrubland where young boys used to look under rocks during the day for sleeping vipers. But this was night, and the old man told her there was a twenty-year-old Western Diamondback Rattler in the valley. And it was mean as hell.

He told her to sit on the ground and close her eyes, slow her breathing and listen. She did as she was told, although she didn't like the idea of a Diamondback, mean or not, anywhere nearby. But she felt easier knowing he was there. Then, without making a sound, he left her. Nothing happened for the longest time. Whatever noise the darkness held it hid from her ears. Then she felt it; a tingle, like the feeling she had sometimes if she let a baby Wolf Spider crawl over her hand. Then she felt another tingle. And another.

She heard a noise. Soft and gentle to her right. Then a metallic clunk interrupted her thinking, and she opened her eyes as a flame appeared about a foot in front of her face. That's when she saw the big Diamondback. Coiled up about ten feet away, looking at her.

As she caught her breath, the flame moved down from her face and illuminated her naked hands and arms. There were no spiders. Just the tingling feeling.

Then her great grandfather spoke. 'The Wolf Spider is your totem spirit animal, little one. Whenever danger is close by, it will warn you.'

Then he shone a light on the Diamondback and Lightfoot saw it turn away and disappear into the night.

That was 1988. Thirty years ago. Now it was 2018, and Lightfoot's Wolf Spider totem was yelling its head off. Only this time, it wasn't warning her about the close proximity of a Diamondback, a smuggler, an illegal immigrant, a kidnapper, a child murderer, a rapist, or an armed bank robber. Or even a serial killer.

If Wolf Spiders could speak and knew about guns, this one would be warning her about a thirty-something gun-nut with an L115a3 Sniper Rifle, with sound suppressor and Schmidt & Bender day scope. Made by Accuracy International. Loaded with five Lapua Magnum cartridges, and pointed in their direction.

Patterson decided to chance a whisper. 'You look like your spidey-sense is off the charts,' he said. 'What's up?'

'Somebody's checking us out,' she said softly.

She could see Patterson frown in the darkness.

'How close?' he said.

'Close enough,' and she could feel the spiders crawling up and down the length of her arms.

Past experience told her they were all in her imagination. But she couldn't resist a scratch or two. Just in case her skin was lying to her.

Patterson decided he better attempt to man-up. 'Want me to take a look?'

Lightfoot stared at him, annoyed. 'Why? You feel like being a hero?' she said.

Patterson's tongue attempted to tie itself into a double granny knot. Being lost for words was a new experience for him. So was blushing.

As Lightfoot stopped speaking, a rifle shot split the darkness and a .338 bullet struck the rock high above their heads. The ricochet could have gone anywhere, but it whizzed off at a harmless angle and buried itself in the ground somewhere only a metal detectorist would find.

Patterson cursed. Then another shot struck the rock a bit lower than the first one. This time, he cursed a little louder. 'Why do I get the feeling we're sitting ducks, eh?' Lightfoot cracked a small smile, about halfway between vague and full-on grin.

'Holy fuck,' hissed the marine. 'You find this amusing?'

'He's not our guy,' she said. 'He's a gun nut with a nice-looking firearm and a serious personality disorder for sure, but he's not the guy we're looking for. I think he came out here looking for a spot of target practice and a bit of privacy, and instead he came across us and decided to have some fun. If he was our guy, he would have kept quiet. But he didn't. So, he's not. He's somebody else's guy. That means he's somebody else's problem. You want my advice?'

She carried on without waiting for an answer. 'Have some of your guys pick him up and put him somewhere safe. Say a nice deep hole.' Then she gave a long sigh. Her spidey-sense had fallen quiet. The tingling had gone. The itching had quietened down. Her totem animal had crawled back into her imagination.

'You got a spare bird you can put in the air to flush him out?'

Patterson thought. Then thought some more. 'How about an Apache with Hellfire missiles and a chain gun?' he said.

'Now you're just boasting,' said Lightfoot. 'How soon can you get it here?'

Patterson reached for the mobile phone hitched to his webbing belt and quietly spoke a few words.

'Ten, maybe fifteen minutes?'

That got a nod.

They both tucked themselves as close as they could behind the rock and hoped that the shooter would get bored and leave.

Nineteen minutes later, the gun nut looked up into the sky to find a hunter killer helicopter looking down at him. It was armed to the teeth with enough technology and firepower to take out up to 256 potential targets in a matter of seconds. Or just him, 256 times, if necessary. Understandably, he almost shit his pants when they spotted him and took him into custody. And naturally, he never saw his beloved Sniper Rifle again. The pilot offered to take Lightfoot and Patterson back to the crime scene, which they politely declined. 'I could do with a bit of exercise,' said the FBI agent.

Not long after the Apache lifted off, the pair headed back across the moor to the crime scene. It was 2.37pm. The trip back was fast and uneventful.

Chapter Twenty-One

At the crime scene, it was 1.35pm. Two hours thirty-five minutes after Rice had left for London. One hour and twenty-eight minutes after Lightfoot and Patterson had gone on their daylight hunting party. Twelve minutes after Toby left for the lab. Numbers were on a permanent countdown inside McHale's head.

Daisy was on her way to her Defender. The trek took her all of one minute and fifteen seconds from the main crime site tent. The sky behind her to the west was the colour of cotton wool balls. Ahead, it was the colour of charcoal dust. She had two opposing thoughts kicking the hell out of each other somewhere between her ears.

One; get the photos to SKIN. Two; eat a scabby dog. The dog could wait. The photos couldn't. Held tightly in her left hand was the evidence bag containing the ring. The latest link in the chain of evidence for a small but important piece of the puzzle. Life was too short to let it out of her sight.

She opened the Defender door, climbed inside, put the evidence bag on the dash, fumbled for her phone, and emailed the images of the inside surface of the ring.

Then she waited five minutes and called the team's only non-human member.

One finger, one button; speed dial. Two rings on the other end of the line.

On the first ring, her stomach complained loudly at the lack of red meat in her diet. On the second, SKIN's androgynous voice answered. It never failed to make her smile.

'And today's fun and unusual word is… KERFUFFLE!' It was a game that only SKIN and Daisy played. Daisy thought it brought their 'minds' closer together. SKIN thought that poor Alan Turing would have approved.

'A fuss or a commotion,' said Daisy. 'Did you get my images?'

'Looking at them now. The language is Bulgarian.'

'Chalk one up for Mac. That's what he thought.'

'Clever boy.'

'And the translation?'

'It says, "The devil's finest trick…"'

'That's it?'

'That's it.'

'It sounds familiar,' said Daisy.

'Think Baudelaire,' said SKIN.

'Are you being deliberately obscure?'

'I prefer amorphous.'

'Is it part of a quote?'

Silence.

More silence.

'Okay, I give in. What's the rest of it?'

'… is to persuade you that he does not exist.'

Daisy sighed. 'Okay smarty pants… how about a straight answer to this: how many Bulgarians are there resident in the UK?' She expected a pause. There wasn't one.

'Latest figures for 2017 say an estimated 84,000 Bulgarian-born people live in the UK.'

'Wow… that was quick.'

'Google.'

Daisy's brain stepped on the gas. Small needle. Big haystack.

'How many of them are women between the ages of eighteen and forty?'

'You think the Dartmoor female with the ring was Bulgarian?'

'Answering a question with a question, eh? Okay, I'm just

kicking a couple of ideas around.'

'And?'

'This might be a bit left field,' she said. 'Can you find out how many people are treated for schizophrenia in the UK at any one time?'

'Sure. About 220,000.'

'Shit, that many?'

'Way ahead of you there. Google is the fount of all knowledge.'

'Hmm… okay, back to the Bulgarian women between the ages of eighteen and forty?'

Long pause.

'Maybe Google is just the fount of most knowledge,' said SKIN.

'I thought YOU were the fount of ALL knowledge. You mean you don't know everything?' said Daisy, genuinely surprised.

'Only God knows everything.'

'I don't know what to make of a computer with religious beliefs.'

'I'm yanking your chain, Daisy.'

'You sure you're not human?'

'Don't be insulting.'

Daisy smiled. 'Speak later,' she said and killed the call.

She stowed her mobile, grabbed the evidence bag from the dash, opened the Defender door, and went back to the crime scene tent. It was 2.08pm.

As she went inside, she met McHale at the tent flap, phone in right hand, frown on face, walking out into the fresh air. His mobile was ringing.

He looked at Daisy. 'So, what did SKIN say?'

'There was part of a quote on the inside of the ring. Something from Baudelaire.'

McHale's feet came to a halt. 'Nineteenth century French poet,' he said, curious look on his face. 'Was it something about The Devil's Finest Trick?'

His mobile stopped ringing.

Now it was Daisy's turn to smile. 'I'm impressed. You a fan of nineteenth century poetry?'

'Nope. Twentieth Century movies. The Usual Suspects.'

'The one with Gabriel Byrne?'

McHale double-blinked. 'I only know one Baudelaire quote. I've seen the movie four times. The quote is the only thing they both have in common.'

He stopped talking; thinking, eyes downcast.

'I know that look,' said Daisy.

'What look?' he said, eyes up.

'The look that says *I've got something stuck in my brain I can't quite shake it loose.*'

The cop tilted his head and gently knocked it with his left palm, as if by doing so it would dislodge the thought wedged in his prefrontal cortex. It remained well and truly lodged.

His mobile started ringing again. He didn't read the name on the screen; didn't have to. He put it direct to his right ear without passing go, and began walking slowly away from the tent.

'Hi SKIN,' he said.

'Hi Mac,' said SKIN. *'Do humans indulge in multiple burials for the same corpse?'*

Sigh.

'Okay… spill the beans,' he said.

'Something weird is happening with Dexter Bob.'

'Who? Dead Dexter Bob?'

'Yup.'

'The one who's six feet under the ground and not breathing?'

'Yup.'

'Weird how?'

'Weird as in I found two more graves for him.'

McHale stopped about twelve feet from the tent. He could feel the bastard thugs between his ears grow restless and take a couple of steps closer to ground zero.

'Apart from the one in Highgate, London?'

'Like I said. Weird.'

'Where?'

'One is in Alice Springs Garden Cemetery in Northern Territory Australia, and the other is in Westbury Cemetery in Barbados.'

'And they all have Dexter Bob on the headstones?'

'Only two have upright headstones. Alice Springs and Highgate. The one in Barbados has a horizontal one. And yes, they all have the name Dexter Bob on them.'

Pause. Think. Speak slowly. 'Do they all have exactly the same wording?'

'Give that man a coconut,' said SKIN. *'Every headstone is different. The one in Highgate says; 'Dexter Aloysius Bob. Born 4.11.1987. Died 6.7.2017. Into the Shroud his spirit ascends."*

'Aloysius?'

'It's a cool name.'

McHale smiled. SKIN continued.

'The one in Alice Springs says; 'Here lies Dexter Bob. Born 18.3.1986. Died 12.2.2017. The Shroud protects his mortal remains.'

'And the one in Westbury says; 'Dexter (Bob) Roberts. Wrapped in The Shroud for all eternity. B. 6.3.1989. D. 11.1.2016."

One heartbeat… two heartbeats.

McHale slowly smiled.

'You're smiling, aren't you?' said SKIN. *'Care to share?'*

'You're familiar with the Deep Web and the Dark Web, right?'

'Do bears shit in the woods?'

'Okay. You familiar with Tor, or the Onion browser?'

'Of course.'

'Good. I want you to sniff around Onion and search for a chat room called Layer Cake.'

'Sounds like a baking forum.'

McHale ignored the comment.

'Next, make a post in Layer Cake under the log-on *'Hardin'*. Type in the following four words. *"Peggy Sue Got Married."*

Then get the hell out of there.'

'*Peggy Sue Got Married?*'

'*Peggy Sue Got Married.*' Then vamoose.'

'*That's it?*'

'That's it.'

'*Easiest ten bucks I ever made,*' said SKIN. '*Then what?*'

'Then we wait,' said McHale, and killed the call.

From behind him, Daisy interrupted his thoughts. 'Now it's my turn to say *"spill the beans"* boss.'

She hadn't gone into the tent. She was still waiting at the entrance, ears on full alert, brain standing to attention. Her curiosity bone had been well and truly knocked and she was metaphorically rubbing the hell out of it.

McHale turned, walked the few steps back to the tent entrance, and duly obliged.

'I spent an interesting couple of hours in the company of Dexter Bob in a basement bar in Soho back in 2015,' he said.

'At the time, I knew he was a damned good sax player. What I didn't know then was he was also one of the best Dark Webbers on the planet.

'What was it?' said Daisy.

'What was what?'

'The sax.'

McHale double blinked. 'Old alto. A bit dinged here and there. Used to belong to a well-known jazz player. Dexter never said who. Anyway… one thing led to another. I did a few favours for him. He did a few back for me. Then one day he just up and disappeared.'

'You try to find him?'

McHale sighed and shrugged. 'Nope. I figured he had his reasons, so I just left it at that. Except for one thing. Couple of weeks later, an envelope with the name 'Mac' on the front was shoved through my letterbox. God knows how he knew where I lived. Anyway, inside was a handwritten note.'

As he was speaking, McHale was digging through his onesie and into the left inside pocket of his jacket. He fumbled out his wallet, opened it, fished out a folded slip of paper, then unfolded it and handed it to Daisy.

The paper had four words written in pencil. They were these; 'Remember Buddy Holly. Bob.'

'I don't get it,' she said, re-folding the paper and handing it back to McHale.

'I do,' he said, putting it back in his wallet. 'Dexter Bob's favourite Buddy Holly song was *Peggy Sue Got Married*. He said if ever I needed him, I should post the song title on a Dark Web site called Layer Cake. Use the log-in *'Hardin'*.'

'Why Hardin?'

'Buddy's middle name.'

Pause.

'And?' said Daisy.

'And I don't think Dexter's dead. I think he's gone to a whole lot of trouble to make anyone of an inquisitive nature think he is. We'll know soon enough,' he said. 'Well… SKIN will.'

They both went back inside the tent to check up on Dunwoody's progress unearthing the other bodies. It was going well. There were two more victims, a female and a male. The female had short grey hair and McHale guessed she was in her seventies. About 5'6", she was wearing dirty beige slacks, and a completely unbuttoned blouse. Possibly pink, once. There were no shoes on her feet and no tights on her legs. She had all the usual stab wounds in all the usual places.

The male was young, probably in his twenties. Possibly six-foot. Shoulder-length black hair, slicked against his head and caked with peat. He had been trying to grow a beard. He didn't get very far. He wore the uniform of youth; jeans and a band t-shirt, dirty sneakers. His eyes were wide open and there was a surprised look on his face. Sometimes death doesn't even bother to announce its arrival. It just turns up uninvited. That made five down, or rather up. Three to go. *Female, male, female, in that order. Neat, tidy, and predictable,* thought McHale. Only it wasn't.

'Next one's a male,' shouted Bugsy, Dunwoody's assistant, from the crater.

It was 2.45pm. He stepped away from the body to give the others a better view.

The first thing McHale saw was a filthy, extremely hairy, naked right forearm, lying loose alongside the vague shape of a body. Not yet fully uncovered, but unmistakably well-built. The second thing he saw was an analogue watch strapped onto the wrist. Then he felt cogs whirring double-time between his ears.

'Bugsy, is that watch still working?' he said.

The young assistant stepped forward and looked down at the arm, gently raising it with a gloved hand.

'I think the technical term would be buggered,' he said.

'What time does it show?'

Bugsy looked closer and brushed a little dirt off the smashed glass. 'Five past four,' he said. 'AM or PM is anybody's guess.'

'Let's get him out,' said Dunwoody to McHale's right.

McHale spoke aloud what the rest of the team were thinking, like he was mumbling to himself. 'Should be a woman. Why the hell is the sequence different? He doesn't fuck up. Everything's done for a reason. This is a bloody ritual for him. Unless…'

Toby was the first to answer. 'Are you going to walk in a circle until you get a light bulb moment, boss?' He seriously considered getting ready to fall in line behind McHale. Maybe getting a crime-scene conga going.

After ten minutes, McHale stopped walking - stopped mumbling - and looked up at the young cop.

Toby's feet had a rapid change of heart. He smiled.

Dunwoody looked at McHale, curiosity spread all over her face. Then she looked at Toby. 'Something just happened… tell me what just happened.'

'Light bulb moment,' he said.

'We need a bigger screen,' said McHale, turning to Daisy. 'Bigger than your iPhone.'

'iPad?'

'Bigger.'

'MacBook Pro?'

'Perfect.'

Daisy put her legs in motion and headed for her Defender. Five minutes later she was back and two minutes later the laptop, resting on an empty trolley, showed a full screen video of the visiting room at Sofia Prison. The Lazarov brothers were on opposite sides of a table. Dragan facing Anton, Anton facing Dragan and the camera on the wall, both hands flat on the table, palms down, right hand tattoo fully visible, fingers spread. Everyone who was looking at the screen was also looking at the tattoo. Everyone, that is, except McHale. He was looking at Anton's head, in particular, his eyes.

Toby's voice whispered to the left. 'What are you looking for?'

'I'll know when I see it.'

'What if you don't see it?'

'Then I will,' said Lightfoot's voice behind the group.

Everyone turned around, except McHale, whose eyes were still glued to the image on the screen.

'Miss me?' said the FBI agent, standing next to Patterson, who was breathing heavily.

It was 3.24pm. The big marine shrugged and smiled. 'And I thought I was fit.'

Lightfoot stepped closer to McHale until their heads were practically touching.

He shrugged off a thought and kept his eyes on the screen. He was just about to rewind and look again when he saw a faint movement. A fast gesture. A flick of the eyes up to the camera, followed by a slight nod of the head. Both almost imperceptible. But McHale saw them. And Lightfoot saw them.

An inner voice yelled *'Geronimo!'*

'Eyes,' said Lightfoot.

'Head,' said McHale.

Daisy re-ran the video, fiddled with the controls, and slowed-down the part where Anton's eyes looked up and nodded. She froze the image on the nod.

'Gotcha!' whispered Lightfoot.

Patterson sighed. 'So, what am I missing?'

McHale looked at Lightfoot and both smiled.

'That look like a signal to you?' he said.

'Yup.'

McHale dug out his mobile, put it on speakerphone, and called SKIN. The others listened.

Two rings.

'Mac?'

'How soon after Anton met Dragan in Sofia prison was Dragan murdered?'

'Roughly, or exactly?'

'Let's go with precisely.'

'One hour and twenty-three minutes after Anton left, as near as dammit,' said SKIN. *'His throat was cut in the exercise yard. The left carotid artery was severed. The guards never saw it happen. All they saw was Dragan lying in a heap on the ground in a pool of his own blood. One less mouth to feed.'*

McHale grunted. He killed the line. He had what he needed. There was no point trying to find out who was on the other end of the camera.

He was about to turn and speak to the team, when Toby walked in the tent entrance. Flustered, but looking satisfied. He was holding the evidence bag with the finger in it. It was 3.36pm.

'They took a tissue sample and gave me back the rest of the pinkie,' he said.

'How long?' asked McHale, keeping his fingers mentally crossed, hoping for a result in days, not weeks.

'Officially or unofficially?'

'What's the difference?'

'Officially, anything up to ten weeks. Maybe eight at a push.'

'Shit.'

'Unofficially, anything up to ten days,' said Toby, handing the evidence bag to Dunwoody, after signing the Chain of Custody label. 'That's the bad news.'

'There's good news?'

Toby smiled. 'They've been Drummonded,' he said. 'As soon as the head honcho there heard the mention of Drummond's name, everything stepped up a couple of gears. That guy can get water turned into wine.'

'And?' said McHale.

Toby paused, mostly for effect. 'Head honcho wasn't pleased, but he said two days tops.'

'How come so fast?'

'He mumbled something about a tasty new bit of tech, wouldn't say any more. Tapped the side of his nose with a forefinger. Said 'nudge nudge, wink wink, say no more.' Like someone straight out of Monty Python.' McHale let his breath out slowly, mentally uncrossed his fingers, and nodded once to the young cop.

Dunwoody, with finger back in her custody, blurted out, 'Well colour me bloody impressed. You guys are like a real-life Mission Impossible team.'

'We know people who know dark magic,' said Daisy. That got a laugh from Patterson.

McHale pointed at the laptop on the trolley, with the frozen image of Anton.

'I think Dragan's death was insurance,' he said. 'Anton had him killed to silence him. Permanently. Just in case he started talking. Just in case he let the cat out of the bag and his innocence was discovered.'

'And Anton's guilt,' said Toby.

'Fraternal betrayal,' said Daisy. 'Leaving him free to get away with blue bloody murder, and nobody would be any the wiser.'

'Except, maybe, Rayna Orlov,' said Lightfoot. 'Maybe that's why they only found the twenty graves in the forest. It wasn't because he was finished killing. It was because he was finished killing in Bulgaria… and he was moving on somewhere else.'

'And that somewhere else was right here in England,' said McHale.

'But why here?' said Toby, in his best Bogart voice. 'Why, out of all the countries in the world did he pick this one?'

'What if he didn't have a choice?' said Daisy. 'What if here was his only option?'

McHale looked at her, raised his right eyebrow, said slowly and softly, 'Go on.'

Daisy took a deep breath. She started counting off fingers on her left hand, beginning with her thumb. 'Grey John's mother treated schizophrenics.'

Index finger. 'What if Anton's victims in Bulgaria were schizophrenics?'

'What… all twenty of them?' said Toby.

She glared at him. 'And everyone with ten stab wounds in the same places as his mother.'

Middle finger. 'And what if Rayna figured it out?' Then her eyes took on the thousand-yard stare. She stayed there a few seconds, then she flipped back and looked at McHale, who smiled and tilted his head to the right.

'Light bulb moment?' he said.

She slowly nodded.

Ring finger. 'Boss… what if Rayna starts asking questions about the disappearance of schizophrenic patients, and Anton finds out? He knows he has to silence her.'

'So, he lets Ivan loose to do what Ivan does best,' said Lightfoot.

Next finger. 'Then Grey John starts asking questions about Rayna's disappearance, and Ivan tries to silence him too.'

Next finger. 'But before he can get to him, Grey John buggers off. So, the alter retreats into the background and Anton takes back control. Puts out some feelers, finds out Rayna's son has come to England. But he doesn't know where. So, he gets to Spain, hops on a ferry, and comes here him with two objectives.' Lightfoot got in on the finger act. 'One. Find a new killing ground and get digging. Two. Find Rayna Orlov's son and put him in a shallow grave face-down.'

McHale nodded and spoke softly. 'That explains this little mess here. But what about the two attackers? Where do they fit in?' He looked at the others. They were busy kicking their grey cells around. Silence.

Lightfoot broke it. 'Home-grown muscle?' she said. 'Every good grave-digging serial killer needs helping hands. Do we know who they were?'

'Probably Bulgarian nationals,' said McHale. 'And we have one in the morgue, complete with fingerprints. So, I'll ask SKIN. See if we have a name. That's my second call.'

'Where's Rice?'

'That's my first call.'

McHale picked up his mobile, did an about-face, stepped away from the team, speed-dialled a number with his right index finger, and put his left ear into gear.

It was 4.18pm. The late afternoon warmth was giving way to a chilly breeze. Overhead, dark, ash-coloured clouds were arguing with each other.

'Your timing is nearly perfect,' said Rice. *'Just parked up in St Thomas'. Give me half an hour.'*

McHale killed the call and speed-dialled SKIN. Two rings.

'Hi Mac, enjoying Dartmoor?'

'Is this your idea of small talk?'

'What… too casual?'

'I need your game head on,' said McHale.

'I can do small talk and big talk. I can even do no talk. And my game head is permanently on. Just like yours.'

The ghost of a smile passed across McHale's frontal lobe. 'Tell me about the dead guy in the morgue. The one who attacked Grey John and didn't live to tell the tale.'

'His name was Stanko Matev. At least that's what his fingerprints say. He was a thirty-eight-year-old Bulgarian national. Last known address, Flat 23B, Acre Avenue, Brixton, South West London. Arrived in the UK in August 2003. Arrested eight times since then. Won't be arrested nine.'

'What about his partner?'

'Three distinct sets of prints lifted from Grey John's flat. The victim's, Matev's, and a third individual identified as Marko Kabardinski. Thirty-three-year-old Bulgarian national. Same address as Matev. Never arrested in England. Arrested once in Scotland February 2005. Served eighteen months for use of a weapon, causing serious injury. The weapon was a knife.'

'He's in the wind.'

'Are you sure that Matev and Kabardinski were the same two who carried out the first attack on Grey John?'

'Completely. Sending you images.'

'Good work.'

'You haven't heard the best bit,' said SKIN.

Built into SKIN's programming was a facility that allowed for the use of a conversational pregnant pause.

It lasted all of three heartbeats.

'They both have Svetlana tattoos.'

McHale's pulse rate kicked up a gear. 'Where?' he said.

'On the backs of their right hands.'

'Holy friggin' moly,' said inner voice.

'Have you compared-'

SKIN finished the sentence. *'... the tattoo in the morgue to the one on the slightly crispy hand? Not my first rodeo, Mac. They could be twins.'*

Two heartbeats. One decision.

'Let me get back to you.'

As he killed the call, his mobile pinged, and he received an email containing four images and a message. The message was five words long. The words were these: *'Houston, we have a problem.'*

One image was of Matev and Kabardinski in the process of attacking Grey John for the first time. Another two were close-ups of the goons' hands. The tattoos were clearly visible. The fourth was a shot of the tattoo on the back of Matev's hand as he lay on the slab at London's first ever purpose-built forensic mortuary, in Westminster. It was named the Ian West Forensic Suite, after one of Britain's foremost pathologists.

McHale had heard of him. He was the man who investigated high profile deaths such as Robert Maxwell, Jill Dando, and Yvonne Fletcher, the police officer who was shot from the Libyan Embassy in St. James's Square, London in April, 1984. He was also Scottish, which in McHale's book, already earned him a fistful of brownie points. The state-of-the-art facility was, as one senior police officer said when the suite was opened in 2008 by the then Home Secretary Jacqui Smith, 'the dog's fucking bollocks'. The bollocks were still as advanced and impressive nearly ten years later, and had the capacity to store up to 102 bodies at any given time.

Matev's corpse was one of its newest occupants, although not one of its more famous.

Just then, McHale felt a serious tap on his right shoulder. He turned and saw Lightfoot. She was about to speak when she saw the look on his face.

She tilted her head to the left. 'What?' she said, frowning.

'Sometimes tattoos are like tribbles. You start off with one. Then you leave it in a dark room overnight, and when you look in the morning, you've got more.'

'Tribbles?'

'Star Trek.'

'What the..?'

'We've got two more Svetlana tattoos.'

Pause.

'Where?'

'The two goons who attacked Grey John. Both have the same ink on the back of their right hands.'

'Old or new?'

'Hard to say.'

He showed her the emailed images.

They both stood silent, thoughts bouncing around inside their heads like balls flying off flippers in a couple of pinball machines. That lasted about five seconds. Then Lightfoot spoke.

'He's fucking with us, Mac.'

'Maybe, maybe not,' said McHale. 'Just hear me out.'

Lightfoot zipped the lip.

'One of the greatest chess players of all time was a Cuban called Jose Raul Capablanca.

'One time he played a New Yorker called Charles Jaffe. Like Capablanca, Jaffe was a chess master. But everyone and his uncle thought the Cuban was invincible. So, they were all surprised as Hell when, like a boxer on the receiving end of a well-placed uppercut, he went down and stayed down.

'After the match, a reporter asked both of them how many moves they thought ahead. Capablanca said about ten. The reporter was astonished. How could he lose if he thought ten moves ahead? Then he asked Jaffe the same question. He said only one… but it was the best one.' Lightfoot's eyes revealed the vaguest hint of a smile.

McHale continued, 'Lazarov can make all the moves he likes. He can throw red herrings at us from a distance or right up close. It doesn't matter how smart he thinks he is, or how dumb he thinks we are. All we need to do is make one move, and make it the best move, and he'll go down.'

'I think you'd have liked Nimrod,' said Lightfoot. 'I think you'd have liked him a lot.'

'You're not the only one who has stories to tell,' he said.

It was 5.04pm. Outside the tent, the temperature was going

down. Inside, the body count was going up. Next out of the ground was a heavy-set woman wearing purple tracksuit trousers. She had short blonde hair, a grubby once-white top, and naked feet. Her trousers carried the stain of damp faeces around her arse. Her neck carried the unfathomable weight of a small Saint Christopher medal on a gold chain. The stench of death would have been almost overpowering, but everyone was used to it by then.

But the next and final body was the kicker. She was small, she was fragile, and she was about nine or ten-years-old. Halfway through the unearthing, while purple tracksuit lady was being wheeled into the laying-out tent next door, Dunwoody stopped and sighed loudly and deeply.

Her face was turned away from McHale, but he didn't need to see it to know that there were tears in the eyes of this woman who, because of her experience and professionalism, was normally immune to any display of the darker side of emotion.

Hope provides the exception to all tragedy. So, he said nothing. Did nothing. Just left her alone with her thoughts and waited for her to say something, do something. He didn't have to wait long.

She continued to unearth the body, then two assistants took over and carried it out of the burial site and placed it on the trolley; face-up for everyone to see the ten stab wounds. Then she tore off her mask and walked quickly out of the tent. Eyes down, hands balled into tight fists. It only took a couple of heartbeats after she left the entrance for those inside to hear her scream. Just once. Long and loud. Then she came back in, emotions in check, and stuck her hand out to an assistant, who handed her a new face mask to replace the ripped-off one.

She walked over to the trolley and counted each wound, checking the placement, and using her right hand to brush the victim's dark hair away from her face. She bent down and whispered something in the child's left ear. Then she looked up to Jo, her assistant, and nodded. Just once. Jo wheeled the girl next door to join all the other victims, and the senior forensic archaeologists turned and looked up at McHale.

'Catch this fucker,' she said slowly between clenched teeth.

'Yes ma'am,' he said, and nodded. 'Where are the bodies going?'

'It was supposed to be Exeter,' she said, 'but Cyril wants them back in London. And what Cyril wants, Cyril gets.'

'Wow! Personal connection… first name basis with the big kahuna, eh?' said inner voice.

McHale ignored his invisible travelling companion. Instead, he turned to Daisy and said, 'Take photos of everything. We're out of here and back to London first thing in the morning.' She nodded, fished out her iPhone and started clicking.

He thought about asking Dunwoody what she whispered in the dead girl's ear. Then he thought better of it. That was her business, not his.

Rice called Lightfoot, who answered and handed her phone to McHale.

'McHale's maxim number ten,' said the priest. *'If you can't get through to Batman, try Robin.'* McHale smiled. The pecking order was finally sorting itself out, he thought. It was about bloody time. It was 5.39pm.

'Mission accomplished?' he said.

'Swab's done and on its way to Bell Macaulay,' said Rice.

'Sounds like Drummond greased the wheels for you.'

'People find it difficult to argue with a high-ranking cop, or a priest.'

'I thought you weren't wearing your God Collar?'

'Just because you can't see it doesn't mean it's not there.'

McHale paused, *touché*, he thought, then told Rice about the other Svetlana tattoos, and Toby's race to get a soft tissue DNA profile from the finger to the Bulgarian authorities. There was a sigh from the other end of the line. Then a curse followed by a statement. *'Damn. I've got a bad feeling about this.'*

'The more we know, the less we have to find out,' said McHale.

'Why do I get the feeling that's another one of your maxims?' said Rice.

'I think that one belongs to somebody else. Anyway, enough banter. How's Grey John?'

'He's sore as hell and about a coat of paint away from having a major artery punctured... but he'll live. For how long depends on the pancreatic cancer.'

McHale told him about Marko Kabardinski, the goon who got away, and about Stanko Matev, the one who didn't.

'So... who was the one in the Land Rover? The one who got blown to bits?' said the priest. *'Because as of now, there could be any number of goons with Svetlana tattoos on their right hand. So, the chances of the hand belonging to our friend Anton are fast disappearing down the plughole. It can't be the Bulgarian on the lam...'*

'Kabardinski,' said McHale.

'Bless you!' said Rice. Neither laughed at the attempt at humour. *'It can't be him. The timeline's all wrong. So, it's somebody else. Somebody we don't know.'*

There was silence on the line from both ends, as various possibilities bounced around two skulls.

'When are you back?' said Rice.

'In the morning.'

'I think I'll have another word with Grey John. I'll ask SKIN to text me the goons' details. Their faces might mean nothing, but their names might ring a bell,' said Rice. *'Talk later.'*

McHale killed the call and gathered the others around him. Then he looked at Dunwoody. 'How soon could you get a prelim report to the team?'

'Tomorrow lunchtime,' she said. 'Good autopsies for all of them will probably take a couple of days. We'll wear our go-faster suits.'

Then McHale looked at Patterson, who looked at the destroyed Land Rover and scratched his chin. The big marine thought about it for a few seconds. 'Quick-and-dirty about the same… tomorrow lunchtime,' he said. 'Detailed, give me another day.'

McHale looked at the rest of the team, minus Spencer Pope, who was still in his Discovery, building a face. Only he wasn't; he was standing behind the cop, just about to tap him on the right shoulder. For as long as McHale could remember, he could tell when somebody was occupying the space immediately behind him. No matter how close they were, he could feel their breath on his neck. He could feel their eyes boring into the back of his head. He turned and saw Pope. The sculptor had the skull in the box next to his feet, a closed laptop in his left hand, and a smile on his face.

McHale's fingertips tingled. 'You have a face?' he said.

'I have a face,' said Pope, opening the laptop, balancing it on his left palm and punching keys with his right fingers. Everyone gathered round and looked at the screen. What they saw was a million miles away from a computer generated, forensically reconstructed head with a face like a death mask. It looked alive. Almost animated. Wearing an expression of surprise. Almost as if Death had jumped ahead of itself and caught the victim a split second before the first stab wound had arrived.

McHale wondered if the heart was the first wound in all the victims. Or any.

'You work fast,' said a clearly impressed Lightfoot.

'Thank you very much,' said Pope, in his best Elvis drawl.

He might have sounded like a dead ringer. But the head on the screen looked nothing like the boy from Tupelo, Mississippi. Or the man from Memphis, Tennessee.

Elvis was category-one beautiful. The head on the screen belonged to somebody way south of pig ugly. 'I think maybe Lazarov killed this guy just to get him the hell out of the gene pool,' said Pope. McHale's mobile interrupted what might have turned into a grimly humorous moment.

'I just got a very interesting phone call,' said Drummond.

'You spend half your life getting interesting phone calls,' said

McHale. 'And the other half making them.'

There was a short pause while Drummond decided whether the ache in his head was worth ignoring or self-medicating. He decided on the former.

'You remember Molly Spencer?'

McHale grunted, and his mind flipped back a year.

Internal voice went into panic mode. *'Shit... you haven't unwrapped her moving-in gift yet. You don't even know where the hell it is. If he asks you about it, you're screwed. If you don't mention it, you're screwed. This is a fucking dilemma!'*

'I think you've become her pet project,' said Drummond.

'I don't think I like the sound of that,' said McHale, gift retreating to the back of his mind. 'Should I be worried?'

Then Drummond did something unexpected. He laughed.

In McHale's mind, laughter and Drummond didn't go together. Like peanut butter and marmite. He knew it was a thing; knew it had been a thing since the turn of the Twentieth Century, having looked it up once. He even loved them separately. But there was something just wrong with them together, mixed up in the same sandwich.

'She wants to meet up when you get back to London,' said Drummond, when his laughter subsided.

'Did she say why?'

'She didn't... and I didn't ask. All she said was she wanted to meet up with you and our FBI lass. Nobody else. She didn't say why. I got the feeling it was none of my damned business. One thing I will say. . In my experience it's better to have Molly Spencer as your best friend than as your worst enemy. Play nice.'

McHale's default emotion, after years of hunting killers, was obsessive suspicion. It was his gut reaction. It sat in the back of his mind, like a lump of obstinate phlegm, stuck on the vocal cords, that not even a good hawk could dislodge.

'Okay... thanks for the heads up,' he killed the call.

He turned and looked at the team. 'Right. Meal and an early

night. We're off back to London first thing in the morning.' Then he got a text message from SKIN. It was three words long. The words were these; *'Lazarus has risen.'* McHale tried to visualise an appropriate zombie image. Then the penny dropped, and a lopsided smile invaded his face. For some reason, the magnificent, shaved head of Yul Brynner invaded his memory. He texted back five words. *'And then there were seven.'*

Chapter Twenty-Two

The Travelodge had a passable restaurant, and the meal was a muted affair. The team, apart from Lightfoot' who was cosying up with the US Ambassador at Winfield House in Regent's Park, were together before the next phase of the hunt.

The meals were delicious, but due to the events of the past couple of days, the best that could be said of them was that they were hole-filling. A young waitress smiled politely and brought food and drinks and kept her distance. The team, minus two, hit the sack just after 8.30pm and everyone had the same thought on their minds. What the hell was Anton up to now?

At 9.15pm a dark green army ambulance transported eight bodies, in their zipped bags, from the excavation site in Okehampton, to the dog's bollocks forensic mortuary in Westminster, London. The ambulance, with a driver and mate, was sandwiched between two Met. Police BMW X5 cars with two DIs in each. None of the vehicles had flashing lights in operation. The occupants of the body bags were in no hurry to go anywhere. The convoy reached their destination at 12.57am and they were greeted by two uniformed Met officers and a large, important looking man in a dark overcoat. A DI passenger from the leading X5 stepped out of the car, stretched his legs, and walked the six feet or so over to the overcoated man.

'Everything hunky dory?' said Drummond.

'Seven hunkys and one dory,' said the DI, who was feeling more like a delivery driver than a small cog in a large and very important serial killer wheel.

'Where to?' he said.

Drummond turned his head to the right and behind. 'Park up over there,' he said, indicating a row of bays at the side of a spot-lit building, outside of which were two white-coated men, each one in charge of a trolley. Waiting to take charge of the contents of the body bags. The DI handed Drummond a clipboard, attached to which was a pen and a single sheet of paper. Drummond signed the paper and handed it back to the uniformed copper. After exchanging a few quiet pleasantries, both of them walked towards the parked-up vehicles. The white coats were beginning to unload the bodies. One of the trolley wheels was squeaking. They could hear it cutting through the muted sound of the nearby late-night traffic. 'Who said the dead make no sound,' said Drummond, dryly.

Roughly 217 miles away south west, the team was tucked up in bed fast asleep. The ones who weren't were staring at the ceilings in their respective dark rooms. All except for McHale. He was staring at the inside of his eyelids, thinking of Molly Spencer, and why she wanted to meet with him and Lightfoot when they got back to London. The thought was enough to make the bastard thugs kick old-fashioned metal dustbins between his ears.

Kelly's supply of 357s was way over on the other side of the room, out of reach without getting out of bed. A back-up strip of para-bloody-cetamol, however, was sitting on the bedside cabinet. Next to two glugs of water. *Four of those buggers would have to do*, he thought. He sighed, opened his eyes, reached out, and freed four of the whiteys, swallowing them with the two glugs. *Life is bugger all without decent back-up*, he thought. *'How true,'* said Lightfoot's voice in his head, as he drifted off to a fitful sleep. Before dawn, Dunwoody slipped into a waiting car, which quietly disappeared into the darkness.

In London it was 3.58am. Inside the mortuary in Westminster, a hand-picked team was busy with the grim task of performing forensic autopsies on the contents of seven of the body bags from the Okehampton excavation. The small body inside the eighth bag was placed at the back of the queue, to await the arrival of Dunwoody. Wild horses wouldn't have dragged her away from working on that one. She remembered her whisper in the dead young girl's ear. Some promises should never be broken.

At 6.39am, her Land Rover, driven by Bugsy, pulled up outside the mortuary, and a sleepy-eyed Dunwoody eased herself out of the back and into the chilly night, shaking off the after-effects of the night before. She wasn't thinking of the small body waiting for her. She was thinking of an autopsy performed on an eleven-year-old girl, brought up from a freshly-dug hole in the ground in Bosnia in 2003; and the one she was about to do. She sighed deeply and began walking.

Chapter Twenty-Three

Nine minutes before Dunwoody arrived in London, the first forty-three instrumental seconds of The Who's Baba O'Riley arrived at McHale's eardrums, courtesy of the iPhone in his room in the Travelodge, and Pete Townsend's Lowry Berkshire Deluxe TBO-1 organ. Using its marimba repeat function. The time was 6.30am. Outside, the temperature was an Arctic shiver above cock-shrinking cold. Inside The Travelodge, the heating had been on since 5.30 and the room was approaching a cosy sixty-seven degrees Fahrenheit.

McHale let Baba hang around until the piano kicked in, then he sighed, farted loudly, threw the covers back, avoided breathing in deeply, and headed for what his grandfather fondly called The Cludgie. His iPhone went with him. Halfway through his ablute, he heard his iPhone announce the arrival of two texts. He ignored them and, instead, switched on the shower. He wished he had the courage to switch the temperature to cold. Instead, he turned the dial round to hot as hell, stood under the stream, and began a fast count to a hundred. He made it to sixty-five before a third text arrived. His mobile was sitting next to the bathroom mirror. Wherever he went, it went. With some obvious exceptions.

He cursed loudly, turned off the shower, stepped out of the cubicle, and reached for a large, salmon-coloured bath towel. He could sense the bastard thugs stirring in the background. They were beginning to sound aggressive. He decided to head them off at the pass before he answered the texts. Four para-bloody-cetamols were waiting to be popped, which he duly washed down with two gulps of cool water. He could sense the thugs recoiling in anger and disappointment.

His phone rang. He picked it up and barked: 'What?' and immediately regretted his tone.

'Somebody got out the wrong side of bed this morning,' said SKIN. *'Just thought you'd like to know that you have a visitor.'* McHale's brain woke up. 'How many guesses do I get?'

'You want a clue?'

'He or she?'

'Very definitely a he.'

Pause.

'Bob?'

'The very same. And he has quite a story to tell.'

Now McHale's brain REALLY woke up. He glanced at his iPhone and did a quick calculation in his head. Half an hour to get ready, another half to round up the troops. Set off at 7.30. Four hours on the road. 'Tell Bob we'll be there about 1.30 this afternoon. Don't let him leave the building.'

'That might be a bit difficult,' said SKIN. *'I can't exactly tie him down and lock the doors. And sex is out of the question.'*

McHale smiled. 'You'll think of something,' he said, and killed the line.

Then he looked at the two texts. The first one was from Daisy. It was seven words long. The words were these; *'I think we better hit the road'*. He remembered the relationship she had with SKIN. She knew about Dexter Bob.

He fired back, *'agreed. We leave at 7.30. Round up the usual suspects.'*

She replied. *'A Casablanca quote before breakfast?'*

Then he looked at the second text. It was from Drummond. *'Put your cock down and listen up. Rayna Orlov is alive. Call me.'*

McHale punched in a number and didn't wait to hear the voice on the other end. 'You sure know how to get a man interested,' he said. 'We leave at 7.30. Where the hell is Rayna Orlov?'

'A better question would be 'who the hell is Rayna Orlov?' We'll talk some more when you get here. One more thing… watch your back, you might have a tail.'

McHale's voice went down a pitch. 'Why? You know something I don't?'

'Let's just say a little bird told me somebody we both know might have eyes on you. And they aren't the friendly sort.'

McHale sighed. 'Thanks for the heads-up,' he said. 'You seen Dexter Bob yet?'

'He's not what I expected.'

'Nobody is.'

With that, Drummond killed the call and, McHale looked at the third text. It was from somebody called Harry Carney. The name rang no bells. He frowned and was about to kick it into touch, but something pulled his thumb off the delete button. Then a slow smile spread across his face. He read on. *'Was you ever bit by a dead bee?'* The quote was from the movie *To Have and Have Not*, starring Humphrey Bogart, Lauren Bacall, and Walter Brennan. The line was said by Brennan. It was one of McHale's two all-time favourite movie quotes. The other one was the last line of the movie Casablanca. Suddenly, he knew who Harry Carney was.

The original Harry was born in 1910 and died in 1974. Maybe the first real big band baritone saxophone soloist. He played with the Duke Ellington Orchestra at the Cotton Club in Harlem. McHale had a vinyl recording of one of the gigs. No scratches. Only his name wasn't Carney… it was Bob. Dexter Bob.

McHale had to be careful. If he was being tailed, then somebody might be listening. So, he simply sent back a twenty-five word reply; *'I heard bees can sting you just as bad as if they was alive. Especially if they was kind of mad when they got killed.'*

Sometimes there's no place for proper grammar in movie

quotes. It was the second part of Brennan's quote and a subtle warning to be extra careful. Bob knew the quote, too.

McHale switched off his mobile and threw it on the bed. He dressed, packed, and five minutes after that he was ready for the journey back home. He hoped Lightfoot was locked and loaded, as well. He needn't have worried. When he opened his room door, she was sitting, cross-legged, back against the opposite wall. He raised a right eyebrow. 'This is where I ask you how long you've been sitting there.' She slowly uncoiled and stood up in one smooth motion. 'This is where I tell you that I could hear you snoring from out here,' she said, smiling.

He had a go-to bag slung over his shoulder and the remains of a Mars Bar with half a wrapper sticking out of his mouth like a fat stogie. He smiled. 'And this is where I say we'll check out and eat on the road. We've got a long drive home and, at the end of it, the two of us have a date.'

'Just you and me?' she said. There was a twinkle in her eyes.

'You, me, and a very mysterious lady.'

'Sounds like my kind of date,' said Lightfoot, falling in beside him as they walked along the corridor to the stairs and reception. McHale did a quick double-take without breaking step. The others were waiting at reception. Daisy had already done the paperwork and checked them out. Ten minutes later the team was on the road back to London. Same Defenders; same drivers; same passengers; same thoughts. Where was Lazarov now? And what was his next move? They didn't have long to wait for an answer to at least one of those two questions. At 8.15am, his mobile pinged. It was a text from Drummond. *'Pull your finger out. Someone's waiting for you. D.'*

McHale, sitting in the front passenger seat, cursed softly and glanced at the Defender's Sat Nav screen. They'd just passed a sign for Exmouth about 20 miles back. Outside it was starting to rain. He turned to Daisy in the driving seat. 'Pedal to the metal,' he said. He felt the lead Defender lurch forwards, leaving the follower in its wake. But not for long. Toby, driving the other Defender soon caught up and tucked in behind it.

McHale's mobile rang and Toby said; *'What's up?'*

'Our presence is required back at base ASAP. Use it or lose it.'

'Will do,' came back the reply, and the line went dead.

McHale's internal voice echoed between his ears and repeated the phrase his father said to him a thousand times when he was young. *'Use it or lose it, lad.'* The fingers of his right hand drummed against his thigh in a rhythmic tappity tap.

What was he missing? What had soared past his thought process and slipped off into God knows where, like an angry Lightning Jet, looking for a fight? *'Use it or lose it, lad.'* McHale closed his eyes and let his mind drift.

Cars. The last car his father had before the early onset Alzheimer's put the kybosh on getting behind the wheel at every available opportunity. Or anything that moved faster than an armchair. His father's last car was called Rosebud. It was the same make and model as the one owned and driven by the fictional – and famously cynical - Inspector Morse, his father's favourite TV detective. His father, although not famous, was just as cynical. Rosebud was no relation. Citizen Kane was the old man's favourite movie. The car was a burgundy 1960 Mark ll Jag, complete with a 3.8 litre engine. 'Grace... pace... and space,' said the advertising slogan. Just like the wheels, he walked past in the car park of the Travelodge that morning, sitting next to his Defender. Just like the one two cars behind him right now.

Internal voice made its presence felt. Soft and low. *'No such thing as a damned coincidence, Kemosabe.'*

McHale picked up his iPhone and fast-dialled Toby, who answered immediately. *'Burgundy Mark ll Jag,'* said the young copper unprompted. *'Clocked it at The Travelodge. Can't beat a classic.'*

'Move into the middle lane as if you're going to overtake me,' said McHale. 'See what it does.'

'Will do.'

As soon as the second Defender pulled out, the Jag moved into the outside lane, overtook Toby, and pulled in front of him. Then it slowed and waited for McHale's Defender to catch up. It stayed there, keeping pace with McHale, in a game of motorway leapfrog.

'Somebody's playing silly buggers,' said Daisy.

'No,' said McHale. 'Somebody's sending us a message.'

'What does the message say?' said Lightfoot from the back seat.

'I think it says: "Mr Lazarov says hello",' said McHale.

At that, the driver of the Jag put his foot down, pulled into the outside lane, and ate up the miles, disappearing into a broken line of lesser-pedigree cars up ahead.

'What do you want me to do, Guv?' said Daisy.

'Absolutely nothing.'

'Nothing it is, then,' and she kept the Defender at a steady fifty.

'You ever heard of counting coup?' said Lightfoot.

'I can feel another Native American story coming up,' said Daisy, slowing down her instinct to go hell for leather after the Jag.

'Back at home I have a coup stick,' said Lightfoot. 'It belonged to my great-grandfather Nimrod Smith, who got it from his great-grandfather. It's about three feet long, made of willow covered in coloured beads. Braves would ride up to a warrior in another tribe and hit them with their coup stick. It was an extreme act of bravery.'

'Or stupidity,' said Daisy.

A loud sigh came from the back seat.

Lightfoot said, 'My great grandfather has eight feathers on his. One for each enemy hit. And we just got hit with an old burgundy Mark ll warrior stick. Lazarov is counting coup.'

'You think that was him in the driving seat?' said Daisy.

Silence. Two heartbeats.

'Doubtful,' said McHale.

'This one was a left-hand drive and there was a woman behind the wheel,' said Lightfoot. 'Black hair. About thirty-five or forty,

I'd say. She looked Eastern European, but don't quote me on that. She smiled at me, but I don't think she meant it. No passengers.'

'Like I said... doubtful,' said McHale.

Then he told them about his father's Jag.

'Lazarov chose it on purpose,' said Lightfoot. 'He wants you to know he can get inside your head. Fuck with you.'

McHale scoffed. 'Good luck with that,' he said.

But internal voice didn't agree. And it wasn't scoffing.

'Time to fuck with him, then,' it said. McHale ignored it. It was 9.15am.

The rest of the journey was spent in small talk. Big talk was consigned to the unspoken words and topics sitting between the ears of everyone present. At 1:10pm, they were pulling into the underground car park of Lassiter House. 'The Ranch' as McHale had come to refer to it. He quietly thanked his old man for that John Wayne memory. The whole car park was lit except for one corner full of shadows and question marks. While the rest of the team decanted and made their way to the lift, McHale lagged behind.

Lightfoot looked at him quizzically. Then she saw the figure in the shadows.

She immediately tensed and moved her right hand to grip the butt of her Glock 17. Personal choice, completely legal, and fully loaded. McHale gently put his hand on her wrist. 'It's okay. I got this,' he said. 'This is our date. She doesn't do crowds.'

Then Lightfoot understood, and she moved to McHale's left side, hand still on her Glock. Old habits die hard. Life turns on wrong guesses and mistakes in identity, she thought. 'See you lot upstairs,' said McHale to the others, waiting until the lift was full and the door was sliding shut before doing an about turn and walking towards the dark corner. Lightfoot followed; same pace, mentally one step ahead. As they got closer to the shadows, they could make out two figures. They stopped about six feet from them and he saw they were both female. Both about the same height, one older than the other. One McHale knew. The other he already guessed the identity of.

He turned to the familiar one and smiled. 'I thought it might be you, Molly,' he said. He turned to Lightfoot. 'Say hello to Molly Spencer… and Rayna Orlov, Grey John's mother.' The woman was a shade over five-ten and younger than McHale expected. She wasn't beautiful, but her lack of good looks were replaced with a quiet confidence and a steely gaze that understood everything in a second. Her hair was and grey, and tied in a ponytail. Her nose looked as though it had been broken and reset several times, and there was a strength about her that had nothing to do with muscle and everything to do with power. *This is no lady to mess with*, he thought.

'My name is Katarina Petrova,' said the second woman, in a low voice.

McHale put on his best confused expression. 'Orlov is not a safe name,' she said.

'Got it`,' said McHale, nodding once. 'So do I call you Rayna… or Katarina?'

'Katarina.'

Lightfoot removed her hand from her Glock and held it out in greeting. Molly Spencer moved closer, gripped it tightly, shook it once, and gave it back. McHale and Lightfoot did the same with Katarina Petrova.

Rayna stared into McHale's eyes. 'Molly says I should trust you,' she said.

Her English was good. But her accent was Eastern European, and her voice was tired. She looked at Lightfoot and back to Molly. 'Her, I like. She has careful eyes.' Then she looked at McHale. 'Him, I trust. I don't know if I like yet.'

'I'll settle for that,' said McHale. 'Maybe we better go upstairs. It's a bit exposed down here. That's one of the two things I don't like.'

'And what is the other?' said Katarina, her eyes never leaving his.

'Johnny Walker whisky,' he said.

She guffawed. 'I like Johnny Walker. My father used to drink it,' she said.

'So did mine,' said McHale. 'That was the trouble. He liked it too much.'

Pause. Two heartbeats. Then a long, deep sigh.

'Now I think I like him,' said Katarina. Looking at Molly and nodding once. Then smiling for the first time since coming out of the shadows. McHale wondered how long it had been since her last smile.

Molly turned and looked over her shoulder at the darkest shadow. 'It's alright. You can come out, Charlie. I think we're safe now.' A man emerged slowly out of the dark. He was, as McHale's father used to say, about as solid as a brick-built shit house. Short dark hair, light tan, dark overcoat, and carrying a Glock 22 in his left hand, and an Israeli Mini-Uzi in his right. They were both pointed at the ground. He was about six-four and roughly 250 pounds.

'Expecting trouble?' said McHale, looking at the weapons.

'Charlie always expects trouble,' said Molly. 'It's in his nature. He's my personal attack dog. He goes where I go. And I suggest we go upstairs now, if that's okay with you.' Charlie smiled briefly. It was 1.37am. Three minutes later all five emerged from the lift at the top floor and headed for the meeting table facing the giant screen on the wall. All except Charlie, who stood to attention by the lift door, weapons temporarily out of view; relaxed, but at a heightened state of awareness.

A small, skinny, black guy wearing a black t-shirt, ripped jeans, and scuffed trainers, walked out of the kitchen area. He had dreadlocks about a foot long. and his t-shirt had white lettering across his chest. The lettering said: Dexterity. Everyone who only thought they knew Dexter Bob thought it was a play on his name. Only a very few, including McHale, knew that it was the name of a 1947 track composed by Bob's alto saxophonist hero, Charlie 'Bird' Parker. It was Dexter Bob's bebop homage. On the track, Miles Davis accompanied him on trumpet. McHale had the vinyl. No scratches.

McHale smiled and said; 'Molly, meet my own personal attack dog. He's lethal with his brain. His name is-' And that's as far as he got.

'Dexter Bob,' said Molly, stopping McHale in mid-flow. 'I wondered when you'd turn up.'

'Damn,' said internal voice. *'That dame knows more cool dudes than there are icicles on an Inuit sled dog's butt!'*

Everyone breathed. 'Coffee anyone?' said Pope. He got requests back for five black coffees, one green tea for Molly, and one sound of silence from Father Stephen Rice who, as far as McHale knew, was still with a recovering Grey John at St. Thomas' Hospital. And here was John's mother, sitting two chairs away, and alive and kicking.

When everyone was sitting down, Lightfoot was the first to speak. She was looking at Bob.

'I don't know whether to call you Dexter or Lazarus,' she said. The ghost of a smile passed across Bob's face. Everyone else laughed and broke the mood. Except for Katarina, who was frowning and looking at her black coffee. McHale guessed she hadn't laughed in a while.

Molly Spencer laid a hand gently over Katarina's, patted it twice, and spoke.

'Tell them what you told me', she said, softly. Katarina looked up from her coffee, stared into Molly's eyes, and seemed to come to a decision. She nodded and looked at McHale.

'My new name is Petrova. My old name is Orlov. I used to be a psychiatrist. I was born in the city of Plovdiv, in Bulgaria, in 1945. I am seventy-three years-old. I lived in Sofia and my patients were men, women, and children, who suffered from schizophrenia.' She spoke with no emotion in her voice, like she was reciting facts from a page in a book. She lifted her coffee mug and took a sip at the dark, bitter liquid. Then she put it back down slowly and precisely, with all the care of an EOD tech handling a pipe bomb.

'When you deal with people's broken minds on a daily basis,' she continued, 'you learn early on to be very, very careful. My husband Penko used to say that I had the words 'Be careful' stamped into my bones like the words inside a stick of rock candy.' Katarina blinked.

'In August 1996 a man came to see me…'

McHale looked at her hands. The fingers were on her lap, clasped together tight. Her couldn't see her knuckles. He guessed they were white. Any stress or nervousness she might have been feeling were held firmly in check. He looked away quickly.

She continued. 'The man's name was Nicholas Burkov – and he told me a story. He said that in 2015 he was a prisoner in Sofia Central Prison and he shared a cell with a man called Dragan Lazarov.' The pulse of the room kicked up a notch.

'He said that Dragan was a nervous man who talked a lot. And one of the things he talked about was his brother, a man called Anton.'

McHale looked at Katarina's hands again. She reached for her coffee, and took another small sip. To McHale, the effort seemed Herculean.

'Take your time,' said Lightfoot.

'This is difficult for me,' said Katarina, 'to finally meet people who want the same thing as I do.'

'And what's that?' said McHale.

'To kill Anton Lazarov,' said Rayna. 'To wipe him from the face of the earth.'

She almost spat the nine words out. There was a sharp venom in her voice. A viciousness that belied her age. But not her feeling.

'We've got to catch him first,' said McHale.

From the far end of the table, from between the lips of Pope, came a low, slow whistle. It reminded McHale of the whistle performed by Lauren Bacall, through her lips, directed at Humphrey Bogart, in the movie 'To Have and Have Not.'

It was said that, when Bogart died, Bacall put a whistle in his coffin. McHale liked that idea.

'Go on,' said McHale.

All the eyes around the table were firmly fixed on Katarina. Coffees were forgotten and growing colder by the second. 'On 17th January, 1983, my husband Penko was killed in a car crash. The police said it was an accident. It happened on a lonely country road. They said the man who drove the other car was drunk. They were going to charge him with reckless driving, but the next day they let him go. Then he disappeared. They never found him again.

'Penko was my only love. He was also my patient. He suffered from schizophrenia. Burkov knew I treated such people. The anti-psychotic drug I was treating Penko with had an unfortunate side-effect. It gave him a condition known as Tardive Dyskinesia.'

'We know this condition,' said McHale, whose pulse jumped. He had an idea what was coming next. So did the rest of the team.

'Nicholas Burkov said Penko's death was no accident. He said that a man he shared a cell with in Sofia Prison said that his brother, a man called Anton Lazarov, had arranged it. He said that this Anton had killed before, and that he was on a mission to kill people with Tardive Dyskinesia. He said The Devil lived inside them. The day after Penko was buried, somebody dug up his coffin and stole his body. We never found it.'

McHale scribbled something on a pad on the table in front of him.

This is what he scribbled: *'Penko. Shallow grave. Bulgaria?'* Then he looked back at Katarina.

'I went to the authorities and told them,' she said. 'They said that I shouldn't take the word of a liar, and he was probably only after my money. They didn't do anything. That's when I knew I was on my own. That's when I knew I couldn't tell my son and put him in danger. So, I decided to disappear. Change my name and hunt Anton Lazarov down.'That's when Lightfoot spoke up.

'You're an elderly woman and he is a stone-cold serial killer. What made you think you could put him down?'

Katarina Petrova looked at Lightfoot. Her eyes blazed. 'We Bulgarian women are made of iron,' she said, like the words were a badge of honour. 'In 1970, I was one of only thirty women in the famous 68th Independent Parachute-Reconnaissance Regiment, 'Spetsnaz'. The rest were all men. We were all killers. We were an elite special-operations 'aggressor unit', chosen to be trained in what they called 'direct action on all enemy forces.'

'I was conscripted on my sixteenth birthday and I graduated as the most dangerous of the thirty women. That's what they said. I was very good at hunting and killing. By 1975 I was as good, if not better, than any man in the regiment. Then in January of that year, I met Penko, fell in love, and became pregnant with my son. He was born prematurely in the August and we named him Dimitar.'

McHale looked at Lightfoot.

'Naturally, my life in my unit was over. So, I trained in psychiatry, treating schizophrenics, and we lived happily as a family… until Penko died and I got a visit from Nicholas Burkov.

'It was then I decided to drop off the radar and use my old Spetsnaz training to hunt down Anton Lazarov. I knew my son would try to find me, and I knew it was only a matter of time before he would start asking questions. Lazarov would use him to get to me.

'But I don't understand how Lazarov would see you as a threat? said Daisy.

Katarina Petrova looked at her and blinked.

'Because two weeks after Nicholas Burkov came to see me, he was found floating in the Danube. He had no eyes, and he had been tortured. So I guess Lazarov knew that Burkov came to see me, and what he told me. And I guess he knew he had to find me and kill me. So, I engaged in a little subterfuge. I sent an anonymous note to Dimitar, along with my wedding ring, in the hope that he would think I was dead. Stop looking for me and leave Sofia.'

McHale remembered the words spoken by Grey John on the CD given to the Jesuit, Father Stephen Rice.

'It worked,' Katarina continued. 'He came to England, changed his name, and worked with homeless people. But, judging from what Molly has told me, Lazarov has found him. My son is a good man, McHale. But he thinks I am dead. For his own safety, I want to keep it that way.' Katarina Petrova stopped talking and took a large gulp of her now tepid coffee. It was 2.23am.

'Time for a comfort break,' said McHale, and he turned to Dexter Bob. 'Then it's your turn.' The room was silent. Pope looked at Katarina and spoke. 'Remind me not to get into a fistfight with you,' he said.

Chapter Twenty-Four

Ten minutes later, a raft of assorted sandwiches and biscuits was sitting in front of them on the table, courtesy of a lady from downstairs and a text from McHale. The liquid refreshments consisted of six black coffees from the top floor kitchen, plus one green tea, for Molly. Nothing for Charlie. The large wall screen had remained blank and silent since the return of the team and the arrival of the three visitors. The team was in snack mode, with small talk between small bites. McHale decided that now wasn't the right time for SKIN introductions. So, he finished the last mouthful of his BLT, swallowed, turned to Dexter Bob, and spoke.

'Okay, sunshine… you're up,' he said.

'I'm not finished,' interrupted Katarina.

Dexter Bob, who had opened his mouth and was about to speak, promptly zipped both lips and returned to silent mode.

'I tracked Lazarov to Paris. I nearly caught up with him in a small village called Giverny. He left behind four bodies in shallow graves. I interrupted his business.' She spat the last word out like it was a bitter taste in her mouth. 'I had no doubt he knew he was being hunted and was heading for England. By that time, I had been joined in my hunt by Yan and Kiril Andreev. They had their own reasons for wanting Lazarov dead. We made a good team.'

'I can hear a *but* coming,' said Lightfoot.

'We lost him in Folkestone.'

'*Shit,*' said McHale's internal voice.

'I know he's here, and I know he has help. And I know he's

been killing. I just don't know who's helping him, or where he's burying his victims,' said Katarina.

'This might help,' said Lightfoot quietly.

Everyone turned and looked at her.

'My great grandfather used to tell me a story about a great Cherokee hunter whose name was Tslili. He was very wise and very fast. Whenever he went hunting, he would first go to a burial ground, dig, and he would smear the scent of a buried warrior in his shallow grave all over him, then lie down and wait. Big cats love free meat. But best of all, they love meat that has gone off. The cat would sense no danger, so they would come close, thinking they were safe. Tslili would remain still until the cat would come close, then he would leap up and kill it with his spear. His people never went hungry.'

'And the motto of this tale?' asked McHale.

There was silence all round the table.

Then Katarina suddenly let out a short laugh. 'Very clever,' she said. 'If you want to catch your killer, look in the place where your people bury their dead.'

She was interrupted by the sound of Toby's palm slapping the table top. 'I know where he'll bury his dead,' he said, almost knocking his coffee mug over in the process. 'In the last place you'd look,' he added.

'And that's where?' said McHale.

Toby smiled. 'A cemetery. But it would have to be an old one. Ideally, one whose inhabitants have no living relatives. And it would have to be connected to a church that was no longer a church.'

Toby looked around those seated at the table, waiting for a reaction. 'No interruptions,' he said.

'He's not as dumb as he looks,' said Katarina, nodding at McHale.

A deep cough came from Dexter Bob, who hadn't spoken a word since he sat down. He was 5ft 6ins tall, painfully thin, and Afro-Caribbean by descent, but not by birth. His dreadlocks were tinged here and there with silver. The white lettering on the front of his t-shirt was fading from years of wear. McHale knew what the letters on the back said. So did Bob Marley. 'Some people feel the rain. Others just get wet.'

Below the t-shirt, from his skin inwards, he was forty-six years old and had already survived three attempts on his life. He wasn't about to tempt fate by risking number four. Sitting next to him was Daisy.

'You got yourselves in a shitload of trouble, aintcha,' he said. Looking round the table. His voice was a million miles away from his shape, height, weight, and ancestry.

'I was nice and comfy in my retirement, so to speak? When I got wind you lot here,' he looked around the table, 'we're looking for a certain gentleman. A certain very dangerous gentleman, shall we say? One with the nasty habit of turning a special selection of very live people into very dead ones.'

He picked up his mug of black coffee, took a large swig, put it back down again, and continued talking. He looked at McHale. 'So… I thought I'd better pitch in, before you find yourself up the fuckin' creek without a paddle. Let's just say I'm the paddle.' Then Dexter Bob sat back in his chair, crossed his legs, folded his arms, and nodded once at McHale.

McHale nodded back. 'Good to see you, too, Dexter,' he said. 'Now… what's the *real* reason you're here?'

Silence. Then a deep breath.

He nodded towards Molly Spencer. 'She is,' he said.

Molly shrugged. 'Until his unfortunate fake demise, Dexter used to do the odd job for us,' she said.

'Us?' said Lightfoot.

Molly ignored the question. 'Anyway, one of the things he helped us with was the setting up of The Shroud. Clever boy, our Dexter.' Dexter smiled. Pope frowned. 'The what?'

Dexter told them the story. Not the official version. The version that wasn't just the skinny about The Deep Web and The Dark Web; not just about Tor and The Onion browser; not just about Layer Cake and about Peggy Sue. And definitely not just about The Shroud being the online hidey-hole where serial killers have the ability to talk to each other without anyone else poking their nose in and spoiling all the fun.

Time for the truth, the whole truth, and nothing but the bloody truth.

So, he told them that The Shroud was all a big fat Trojan Horse. Dreamed up by Molly Spencer and put together by an internet genius called Joseph Wyzinski.

'Who the hell is *he*?' blurted Toby, who was scribbling like mad, trying to get Dexter Bob's tale down on paper.

One heartbeat. Two heartbeats.

'That would be me, mate,' said Dexter Bob, a smug grin on his face.

Molly butted in. 'The creation of The Shroud gave us the perfect opportunity to clandestinely eavesdrop on the conversations between some of the world's most dangerous killers.'

McHale sensed a 'but' coming. He didn't have to wait long. 'But we got rumbled,' said Dexter Bob. 'Or rather, Joe Wyzinski did.'

A heavy sigh came from McHale. 'I thought you were supposed to be the best bloody webber on the face of the planet,' he said.

Dexter Bob was wearing his best uncomfortable face. He shrugged and looked sheepish. He looked down at the table and slowly shook his head. Then he looked back at McHale. 'Trane thought he was the best until Bird kicked his ass.'

'For all you uninitiated, Trane was John Coltrane and Bird was Charlie Parker,' said McHale, looking around the table. He looked back at Dexter Bob.

'So… who kicked your ass?'

'I wish the hell I fuckin' knew,' said Dexter. 'All I know for sure is that the day before yesterday, The Shroud went bloody quiet as a graveyard. One minute there was a shitloada yabber… next there was bugger all. No noise. Nothin'. Then my laptop screen went kaput. Like somebody told the bloody power to fuck off.' He pulled at the hairs on his chin like he was trying to pull them out. 'Then it switched itself on again and five words came up. Then, after a minute, the screen went blank again. It's been kaput ever since.'

'What were the words?' said McHale, slow and low.

Dexter looked round the table. Then he double-blinked and breathed out long and hard. 'Simon says time to die,' he said.

'Who the hell is Simon?' said Pope.

'Buggered if I know, but he followed that juicy threat with another ten words,' said Dexter.

'Which were?'

'You can't hunt The Devil, without the Devil hunting you.'

That was a conversation stopper.

'I think it's time to introduce our clever friend,' said McHale.

'I presume you mean me…' said SKIN, and the screen wall blinked into life.

The effect on Dexter was instantaneous.

'Jeeeezus fuckin' shit,' he exclaimed slowly, looking around. A large smile spread slowly over his face.

'I'm pretty sure he did,' said SKIN. *'A long time ago.'*

McHale did the introductions.

'SKIN… meet Dexter, our very clever friend. Dexter… meet SKIN, our other very clever friend.'

'Jeeeezus fuckin' shit,' repeated Dexter.

The screen wall changed to a frozen image of Dexter from the neck up. He still had a confused look on his face.

McHale turned to the screen wall. 'SKIN… are there any Simons on our list?'

'You read my mind, Mac. Including the nineteenth century, we've got two. Simon Bingelhelm and Simon Nelson.'

'Alive?'

'If Bingelhelm was, he'd be over four hundred years old and German. He was convicted of twenty-six murders and executed in 1600.'

'And Nelson?'

He was a lot younger. But he was much more interesting.'

Pause.

'Was?'

Nelson was an inmate at Graham Correctional Centre in Hillsboro, Illinois, USA. He died in prison last year, June 18, aged 85. He was a very bad boy.

'How bad?' said Lightfoot.

'This is beginning to ring a bell. A bloody loud one. How many team members do we have?' said McHale.

'Excluding our late arrivals and including our man of God, who hasn't arrived back yet… six. Why?' said Lightfoot.

Simon Nelson was convicted of killing his six children. His wife told him she wanted a divorce, so he killed their six children and their dog,' said SKIN.

'Jeeeezus fuckin' shit,' repeated Dexter, like he was stuck in a loop.

'Is that your phrase of the month?' said Pope.

Toby looked at McHale. 'We don't believe in coincidences, right Guv?' he said. Toby frowned. 'So, Simon is Anton?'

'And SKIN is the dog?' said Daisy.

I want to be a highly intelligent Rottweiler,' said SKIN.

'You already are,' said McHale. He turned to Dexter. 'How bad is this?' he said.

'Somewhere between fuckin' grievous, and a ton of shit hitting a very active fan,' said Dexter. 'I built the fuckin' thing. No sneaky fucker gets to play with it without my say so. I don't care what his bloody name is.' He sounded like a good blend of pissed off and worried. He finished his coffee in one gulp.

Then Daisy spoke up. 'How long has The Shroud been down?'

Dexter wiped his mouth, then looked at his watch. He did a quick mental calculation. 'Twenty-six hours,' he said.

Daisy was scribbling furiously.

Dexter looked at his watch. 'And fourteen minutes.'

Katarina looked across the table at McHale. She took a sip of her green tea, sniffing the odour rising up from the mug, then nodded sideways towards Dexter.

'Him I like,' she said.

'I have another thought,' said SKIN, interrupting the conversation.

'What kind of other thought?' said McHale.

'It concerns someone else from our list,' said SKIN.

'Someone we know?' said McHale.

'Actually, it's two someones, and they're waving big red flags.'

McHale stopped his thought process in its tracks. 'Names?' he said.

'John and Sarah Makin.'

McHale paused. 'Okay… explain.

'They murdered infants in their care in New South Wales, Australia,' said SKIN. *John was hanged in 1893. Sarah was paroled in 1911. Died seven years later of natural causes.'*

'So why the red flag?' said Lightfoot.

'Early last year, a couple calling themselves John and Sarah Makin bought an old, converted church in a village near Bristol,' said SKIN.

'And?' said McHale.

'The village's name is Chew Magna.'

'And?'

'The church dates back to the 14th century. It's private, walled all round; no prying eyes.'

'And?'

'And it has a graveyard, with three hunrded silent inhabitants. Untouched since the Seventeenth Century. First one in, 11th August, 1399. Last one in, 2nd December, 1643.' Nobody out since the first headstone went up.'

The silent alarm bell in McHale's head became a loud one. 'Name?' he said.

'St. Agnes,' said SKIN.

'And it's still standing?' said Pope.

'Rebuilt in 1867. Converted into a family home in 1964.'

McHale's brain had go-faster stripes all over it. It was 2.09am. Outside, the clouds were broody, and it was starting to drizzle.

Chapter Twenty-Five

Dexter had his head in his hands and his elbows on the table. He'd been like that for ten minutes, in silence.

'Can you fix the Shroud?' said McHale.

Dexter slowly lifted his head, and spoke. 'Back in the fifties, my uncle Cyrus used to meet blokes down the public toilets in Leicester Square. Lovely fella. When he got nicked for about the hundredth time, they got pissed off banging him up and did the same thing to him they did to that Alan Turing bloke. Chemical castration. Oestrogen pills. They said that would fix him. It never did. But he did grow tits.'

He sighed. 'The answer is: sure, I could probably fix it, if I had enough time. But would I trust it again? Not in a million bloody years.'

'So, The Shroud is well and truly kaput?' said Molly.

'As useless as a chocolate fireguard. Sorry, love.'

'Fuck!'

'Unless… ' said Dexter, his face suddenly brightening. He let the thought trail off into a dark void filled with unspoken possibilities.

'Unless what?' said Molly.

'Unless we fix it up and stick a bloody mole in the camp,' said McHale. He let the thought simmer in the air. And that's when Katarina told them about Yan and Kiril Andreev.

'They knocked on my door late one night in July, 2007. I knew them. They're good boys. Identical twins, except for three things. One; Yan is right-handed and Kiril favours his left.'

'And two?' said Lightfoot softly.

'They used to be triplets. They had a brother. His name was Ivo. Ivo disappeared in January 2004. He was thirty-four.' McHale could hear the distant sound of dustbins being kicked around inside his head. They announced the imminent arrival of his bastard thugs. He could feel the tips of his fingers begin to tingle.

'*Danger, Will Robinson,*' said internal voice.

Katarina continued. 'They were born on 11th February, 1970, in the port city of Varna on the Black Sea. Their father, Dimitar, and mother, Nadya, are both deceased.'

'And the third thing?' repeated Lightfoot.

'In 1986 I diagnosed Ivo with early onset schizophrenia. He was sixteen,' said Katarina. 'His mother was alive then, and she heard of my work and brought Ivo to see me. I prescribed antipsychotic medication, and Ivo's schizophrenia was brought under control. He returned to being a normal teenager.

'That was the last time I saw him, except for once in late 2003. He came to see me by himself. By then, both his mother and father had passed away. He was in a bad way. He hadn't had his medication in some time and his psychosis had returned. He said he was being followed and kept looking out of my window. He was very worried. He must have seen something, or someone, because he suddenly looked alarmed and left in a hurry. That was the last time I saw him.' Katarina sighed deeply.

'Then, in July, 2007, Yan and Kiril and came to my door and told me that Ivo had disappeared. They said a stranger had come to see them. The stranger said he was a friend of Ivo and was trying to find him. He asked them about Ivo's health and about where he was treated, but the boys kept their mouths shut. They didn't believe him. They didn't like him. He had odd eyes.'

'Did they describe him?'

'Yes. They said that the man had a scar over his right eye and that his eyes were different colours. The left one was brown and the right one was blue.

'Heterochromia,' whispered Lightfoot.

'Did the man tell them his name?' said McHale.

Katarina was looking intently into his eyes.

'Yes. He said his name was Pichushkin. Alex Pichushkin.'

'The Chessboard Killer?' said Lightfoot, suddenly.

'Who?' said Katarina.

'SKIN,' said McHale, turning to the screens on the wall.

'The Chessboard Killer,' said SKIN. *'Russian serial. He wanted to kill 64 people. The number of squares on a chessboard. Made it to 60 before they caught him.'* 'And he's alive?'

'Alive and kicking. Spends his days and nights in solitary confinement in an Arctic penal colony called 'Polar Owl.''

'SKIN,' he said, turning to the screen wall again, 'bring up the photo we have of Anton. The one with him kneeling in the snow, holding a rifle next to a dead deer.'

'Way ahead of you, Mac,' said the disembodied voice, and an image appeared on the electronic wall.

McHale looked at Katarina. 'That's the man Yan and Kiril described?' he said.

Pause.

'Can you go bigger and closer so I can see the eyes?' Katarina said.

She got up from her chair and walked to the images on the wall.

Then she looked closely at the man's eyes. The left one was brown and the right one was blue. The scar was unmistakable.

She turned and looked at McHale.

'He's younger in the photo, but that's him,' she said, her voice almost a growl. 'That's Anton Lazarov. I would swear it.'

'I got a very bad feeling about this,' said Dexter. His voice interrupted the conversation and took over the thoughts of all the team members.

Finally, McHale broke the spell, and the words of pint-sized Charlie Manson, with his staring eyes and charismatic personality, hit the copper's pre-frontal cortex with all the force of a lump hammer.

'Believe me, if I started murdering, there'd be none of you left,' said

McHale.

'Thing is, he never actually did his own dirty work. He always got others to do it for him,' said Daisy.

'Bloody hell… enter Mister Helter Skelter himself,' said Toby.

Then a scary thought burrowed its way into his head.

'What if he's coming after us?' said McHale, slowly, looking at the others. 'What if he decided that the only way to level the playing field was to hunt the hunters? What if he could fix things so that all the people who knew what Anton was capable of were gathered together in the one place? The team, the guy who created The Shroud and the woman hunting Lazarov, consumed with vengeance. What if he could bring them all together, and get rid of them in one fell swoop?'

Then he stopped talking and let that final, crazy, dangerous thought percolate through the minds of everyone else in the room.

He didn't have long to wait.

'Mac, what would you say if I told you I'd been interfered with?' said SKIN.

McHale blurted out 'What?'

'This morning at 9.22am.'

Pause.

'How long for?'

'Not sure yet… checking.'

'He's fucking with us,' said Lightfoot. Her voice was relaxed, but McHale knew she was on high alert.

'What if he isn't?' said Pope, concern in his voice.

McHale stood up and walked to the screen wall. 'Do a full diagnostic.'

'Already did one. I have a blank spot.'

Now it was Dexter's turn to sound worried. 'How big a fucking blank spot?'

'Exactly 0.00001 of a second,' said SKIN.

'That long? Fuckin' bastard!' said Dexter in a low growl.

McHale walked slowly away from the screen wall and sat

back down in his chair. 'Are you okay?' he said.

'As far as I can tell, nothing's been added and nothing taken away. But I definitely feel like I've been violated,' said SKIN.

'Like I said… he's fucking with us,' said Lightfoot. 'He wants us to know that he can get to us anytime he wants, anywhere he wants, and there's not a damned thing we can do about it.'

McHale turned to Dexter. 'How good would a person have to be to do this?' Dexter took a long, hard breath. 'I would say a person like that would be very dangerous, Mister McHale,' he said slowly. 'Very clever and very fucking dangerous.'

Daisy was absent-mindedly tapping a pencil against the table top. Apart from the voices of the team, it was the only sound in the room. Somehow, the incessant tapping drowned out the voices, forcing them into the background. Then it stopped.

All eyes turned to face her. She was thinking furiously.

'Spit it out,' said McHale.

'What if it's all misdirection?'

The cogs in McHale's head could almost be heard whirring around.

'Go on…' he said.

'What if this is all about throwing us off the scent? He's done it before, in Dartmoor. What if this is misdirection? He only wants us to think we're onto him. That leaves him free to do what he really wants to do.'

'And that is?'

'HKB,' said Daisy.

'Eh?'

'Hunt, Kill, Bury.'

'Is that your version of BTK?' said McHale.

Daisy shrugged. 'The truth is the truth,' she said.

'What is this BTK?' said Katarina.

'Not a what. A who.' said SKIN. 'Dennis Rader, American serial killer. Currently serving ten consecutive life sentences in El Dorado maximum-security prison, in Kansas. He confessed to killing twenty people over three decades. They called him the BTK strangler. The initials stand for Bind, Torture, and Kill,' said McHale.

Toby looked across the table at Pope, who seemed to be lost in a world of miniature creativity.

'I can see a diorama taking shape in that head of yours,' he said.

'He's on our list,' said Daisy.

'Who, Dennis Rader?' said Pope.

'We're getting off track. Remember the words on the laptop screen?' said Lightfoot. 'You can't hunt The Devil, without the Devil hunting you,' said Lightfoot.

'SKIN… ANY chance that your blank spot is a coincidence?'

'Nope.'

'Anomaly?'

'Nope.'

'What about an electronic hiccup?'

'Nope.'

'Damn,' cursed McHale. 'And you're sure nobody's had a sneaky peek at that big brain of yours since then?'

Pause.

'I plead the fifth.'

'What happened to the other four?'

'They already decided to plead out.'

McHale's eyes settled on the empty chair where Katarina had been sitting a couple of minutes ago. He hadn't noticed her get up and go to the screen wall.

'*Shit,*' said internal voice. '*That lady has mad ninja skills.*'

The wall had a series of images of Chew Magna. One was of an old church, or what used to be one. It looked small, but it had a decent-sized steeple. The architecture was a patchwork of medieval and modern.

'As soon as the red flag went up, I took the trouble of requesting the help of a nearby satellite to take a closer look.'

'How did you swing that?' said McHale.

'*Let's say I know a piece of software that knows a piece of hardware,*' said SKIN. The images were three days old.

There was a dark-coloured Mark II Jag parked on the driveway outside the church front door. The door looked dark, wooden, and as old as the original church. God knows how many people had passed through it. And he wasn't telling. Behind the Jag was a dark-coloured van. Katarina turned, walked back to her chair, and sat down. She looked at McHale, seemed to come to a decision, and nodded. 'This Agnes is where we'll find Lazarov,' she said. 'I'm sure of it.'

'And probably Marko Kabardinski, the goon who got away after trying to kill Grey John,' said Daisy.

There was a momentary look of alarm on Katarina's face.

'Don't worry. He didn't succeed.'

The alarm faded.

'We knew another Agnes not so long ago,' said Toby.

'Was she a church?' said Katarina.

'No, as a matter of fact, she was a manual typewriter.'

McHale had a flashback to 2017, when the team hunted the serial killer Charles Halliwell.

'Something tells me that's also where we'll find at least one dead body,' said Molly. She had contributed so little to the conversation that McHale almost forgot she was there.

'What makes you so sure?' said McHale.

Molly seemed to consider this for a moment. 'He's looking for somewhere to hide his victims in plain sight. Nobody looks twice at an old graveyard. Nobody gives it a second thought. He has three hundred ready-made graves waiting to be shared with new tenants. Each one of them will be buried upside down,' she said.

'And on that note,' said Toby, 'I could really do with a coffee.' It was 4.29pm.

'Don't you English have anything stronger?' said Katarina.

'How about coffee with a splash of whiskey?' asked McHale,

standing up and walking to the kitchen. *'About bloody time,'* said Inner Voice. Daisy joined him.

McHale came back with a tray. On it were seven mugs of black coffee. Daisy came back with an unopened bottle of Southern Comfort. One hundred Proof Whiskey Liqueur. It didn't stay unopened for long.

Behind them, the sound of the elevator doors opening interrupted their thoughts. Out stepped Father Stephen Rice, to be met by a well-dressed brick-built-shithouse by the name of Charlie, carrying two very serious-looking weapons. They were both pointed at the priest.

'You can call off your attack dog now,' said Rice with a grim smile on his face.

'It's okay, Charlie, he's one of us,' said McHale. Charlie reluctantly stood aside and let Rice enter the room.

'How is my son?' said Katarina.

McHale did the introductions.

Rice removed his coat and headed for the only remaining spare seat at the table. His gaze shifted from Katarina to McHale, who nodded.

'He's been better,' he said. 'But he'll live, for the time being. You, I gather, are the dead mother?' said Rice.

'Fancy a coffee with a snifter?' said McHale. Rice smiled. 'Does Pope Francis drink The Balvenie Whisky?'

'Only at home and at bedtime, like me,' answered McHale.

'Well, today you'll have to do with Southern Comfort.'

'Beggars can't be choosers,' said Rice, lifting a mug of fortified coffee, kindly supplied by Daisy, to his lips.

'Does he know I'm alive?' said Katarina.

Rice took a large gulp and felt the warm glow travel down his throat.

'Not yet,' he said.

'I would prefer to keep it that way.'

Rice paused, then nodded. He had spent half a lifetime

keeping secrets. He wasn't about to stop now.

'So… what have you children been up to while I've been away?'

McHale filled him in on the events of the past few hours. 'So, I suppose the burning questions are: One; has he any idea that we're coming for him? And two; are we walking into a bloody trap?' said Rice.

'What about if we're not?' said Lightfoot.

'A graveyard is still a good place to die,' said Katarina

'Hang on, sister,' said Pope, scoffing. 'I don't plan on shuffling off this mortal coil any time soon.'

Katarina gave him a hard look. 'You won't be the one doing the shuffling,' she said.

'Oh, that's okay, then. Good to know.' He was visibly embarrassed.

McHale turned to Daisy. . 'Call Drummond. We need the three Land Rovers. First thing in the morning.' Then he turned to Molly. 'You coming with?'

'Wild horses wouldn't drag me away from this fight. I'll supply the weapons and ammo.' McHale nodded. 'Plus anti-stab vests.'

'How many?' she said.

McHale paused and silently counted.

'Ten,' he said.

'That's a good number,' said Lightfoot.

'Don't tell me… that's a lucky number for the Cherokee, right?' said Toby.

Lightfoot shook her head slowly from side to side. 'Nope. They would be four and seven. Ten was a number special to my great grandfather.' McHale could feel a story coming on.

Lightfoot took a deep breath, a sip of fortified coffee, and duly obliged.

'One of the first times he took me out hunting, he told me a story of The Ten Braves. These young men went hunting for buffalo. They knew there were some nearby, and the strongest of the braves, a man called Dustu, meaning Spring Frog, was their leader. He had fire in his belly and had no fear of any animal. In the late afternoon, they came across a big bull who was strong and wise and dangerous. This bull smelled them coming near, and it snorted a warning to the herd. But Dustu picked up some fresh buffalo dung and smeared it over his body. He urged the other warriors to do the same. Soon they all smelled like buffalo. This is how they were able to crawl closer to the large bull and kill it with their spears. But not before it gored one of the warriors in the left leg. This was a grievous wound, and he limped for the rest of his life. From then on, they were known as The Nine-And-A-Half Braves.'

Lightfoot took a long drink of her coffee. Telling stories was thirsty work.

There was silence all around the table. Then Pope spoke.

'So, this means that we'll have a successful hunt, kill the bad guys, but one of us will be injured I the process?'

Lightfoot shrugged.

'It was a story told by an old man to a young girl. Maybe it was true, maybe it was bullshit,' she said. That got a few laughs. It was 5.59pm. Everyone was hungry. Everyone had a house, a flat, a share, a nearby hotel, or temporary residence to go to, with a meal and a bed. With or without company.

McHale was of the latter persuasion. Daisy and Toby were of the former. Nobody had any idea what the persuasions of the rest of the team were. Except for Rice. His persuasion was not of this earth.

The Land Rovers and supplies would be parked in the underground garage by the time they got back into Lassiter House at eight in the morning. Tonight was a time for sleep and recharging of batteries. Tomorrow they were predators, and God help the prey.

Chapter Twenty-Six

In Twenty-First Century England, the ancient village of Chew Magna, just outside Bristol, was roughly 125 miles via modern roadway from Lassiter House, London. Or, to put it another way, about 3.5 hours away via Land Rover convoy.

In Fourteenth Century England, time and distance moved a little different. Rural architecture had its own way of drastically reducing the growth of village life, and The Black Death had its own way of drastically reducing the population. By about forty-six million lives. On top of that, The Middle Ages took no prisoners, except for those involved in the Hundred Years' War with France.

In 1356, those who were unlucky enough to live in the parish of Chew Magna, yet lucky enough to survive The Black Death, or Bubonic Plague, decided to build a brand spanking new church (not far from the tired, old one) in the hope that God would look down upon them from above and spare those who remained stubbornly untouched by festering lymph nodes. It wasn't a pretty sight. The church of St. Agnes, sat on a donated plot of land with enough space to mass-bury around a thousand poor souls who didn't have two silver pennies to rub together. The smell was strong enough to wake those already trying to stay dead.

The rest of the plot eventually had enough room for three hundred individual graves, with headstones, for those who, over the next few hundred years, did have a lot more than two silver pennies stashed away. Eventually, time and nature got bored and Chew Magna recovered and, in part, prospered. But nothing good lasts forever.

By 1649, the country was in turmoil once again. King Charles I was executed with one blow of the executioner's axe, and the pews of St. Agnes were regularly unoccupied. The last burial took place on December 2nd, 1643, and two weeks later the church doors closed for the last time.

In 1964, the ruined architectural bones of St. Agnes were resurrected and the church was converted into a comfortable, un-consecrated family home.

The accompanying graveyard was tidied up, made presentable, and sold with the church building as a job lot. Apart from the bean counters at the Vatican, here was nobody left alive to object.

Looking after the last resting place of the ancient, buried bones was now the job of a very willing couple in their early forties called Herbert and Sophie Cook. At least, that's what the names on the house purchase said. In fact, their names were Georgi and Maria Bakalov. They were born in Varna, Bulgaria. They were distant cousins of Anton Lazarov. They were very loyal. The kind of loyal that's separated only by death. They hadn't used their birth names since they left Bulgaria and came to the UK. They didn't know why they were chosen. They didn't ask. Lazarov was a man who knew what he wanted, and wasn't a man to be argued with. He was blood, and that was good enough for them.

So, they changed their name, spoke the second language they had grown up speaking (the benefit of having an English-speaking father) and came to England to look for a church that was no longer a church, with a graveyard that was no longer a graveyard. They were now Herbert and Sophie and they kept themselves to themselves. They had no friends and no living relatives. At least that was their story.

That comfy, private arrangement lasted until 10pm on Friday, 15th April, 2018, at which point, Georgi and Maria Bakalov woke up after four years asleep. That's when Herbert answered the doorbell and went to see who was visiting at such an ungodly hour of the night. They hadn't heard any car come up the gravel driveway and brake noisily outside the house.

Nevertheless, Sophie heard the doorbell go again. A little more insistently this time. She frowned and put down the book she was reading and was about to follow Herbert to the door. That's when she heard the door open and voices speaking in a language they hadn't used for years. Then she heard laughter and the sound of footsteps coming along the hallway.

Herbert came into the living room accompanied by two strangers. The strangers were a man, who Herbert introduced as Stefan Genov, and a woman he introduced as Elena Markov.

Stefan was average sized and wiry, and was entirely unremarkable in looks except for a large mole on his left cheek near his nose. Elena was black-haired, beautiful in a hard-faced way, and quiet in a way that made Stefan thankful. He didn't know what she was thinking, and he didn't want to.

Parked outside the front of the house, was a burgundy 1960 Mark ll Jag. A dark figure was sitting in the rear passenger seat, driver's side. Genov walked briskly to the Jag and opened the driver's side rear door. The dark figure stepped out of the car, looked around, nodded, and went inside the house. Genov followed him inside and closed the front door. Behind the closed door, the dark figure's face held a grim smile. 'Time to go to work,' he said sotto voce.

As he walked along the hallway, his eye caught an image on the oak-framed mirror hanging on the wall to the right. The face of Anton Lazarov looked back at him. He was fifty-three and looked ten years younger. The scar bisecting his right eyebrow and stretched down to his cheek, giving his face a vicious countenance. His blue right eye almost pierced the mirror with a sharp stare.

The van had two strong men inside. It also had two bodies; an old couple, each with ten stab wounds. Just like the victims in Dartmoor. Just like the victims in the forest in Bulgaria. Just like his mother and father.

From there, the bodies were driven less than one hundred

yards and buried, face-down, in two adjoining shallow graves. There was writing on the gravestones. But time and weather had eroded any meaning. First the topsoil in front of the gravestones would be removed, temporarily. Then two shallow graves would be dug. Each three feet deep. Then each body would be buried face down, on top of the original occupants. The Devil would be trapped. Then the ancient soil was replaced and the two strong men drove the van away into the night, sweating and grimy, and waited until their services were needed again.

As the men left the gravesides, their place was taken by Anton Lazarov, who had come from the house via the back door.

He was standing at the end of the graves, unzipping his flies.

Very deliberately, he pissed on the newly covered graves of the old dead couple from the van. Then he smiled triumphantly, zipped up his flies, and spat a thick, sticky gob of phlegm on each of the graves. 'Try escaping from there,' he said.

Then he grunted and walked slowly back into the house, lifting his right arm and drawing back the cuff of his coat, revealing the tattoo on the back of his hand.

He looked at it fondly, then glanced at his watch before joining the others. It was 1.25am on Saturday April 16. There were two graves down and 298 left. That was the thing about doing God's work. It was never over until there was nowhere left for The Devil to go.

Chapter Twenty-Seven

Just over 125 miles away and three hours earlier, McHale was stabbing himself. It was 10.25pm, and he had just finished injecting 60ml of liquid plasma into his abdomen. The bad news was that he had to do it twice a week. The good news was that, with the new infusion system, it only took 15 minutes each time; as opposed to the old infusion system, which took three hours.

By 10.45pm he was tucked up in bed, dreaming of bloody bodies coming out of the ground in ancient cemeteries.

By 7.30am, he was sitting at the table in Lassiter House, sipping a hot, black coffee, waiting for the post headache that infusion always brought on. He was also waiting for the arrival of the rest of the team. Apart from Daisy, Toby, and Lightfoot. They had been there since 6.30am. Four down, five to go.

At 8am, two things happened. One; the lift door opened and out stepped Rice, Pope, and Dexter Bob. They were all dressed in black. Rice's dog collar was conspicuously absent without leave. Two; the three black Range Rover Defenders pulled back in to the underground garage of Lassiter House.

In the front one was Molly, Katarina, Charlie, and a large Special Forces officer named Tosh. Two other officers, named Brodie and Wallace, were driving the other Defenders. They were not people to be messed with. Upstairs, McHale's phone rang. 'We're here,' said Molly. 'And we've brought some boys with some toys.'

A ghost of a smile passed over McHale's face. *'Lock and load, Kemosabe. Time to go hunting,'* said internal voice.

'You might as well turn around and head for the basement,' said McHale, to the fresh-looking arrivals. 'Transport's here.' The trio did an about turn and headed for the Defenders, Dexter Bob yawning and scratching his arse. Daisy, Toby, and Lightfoot ambled over to catch the next lift down.

By the time they all got to the basement, the third Defenders' rear doors were wide open and inside were enough weapons and protective gear to kit out a small but very deadly assault force. Glock 17 pistols with suppressors, Heckler & Koch G36 assault rifles, one AWP sniper rifle, bullet-proof anti-stab vests, Ka-Bar D2 Extreme fighting knives, plus covert Bluetooth earwigs for live, direct communication with SKIN and each other. Molly wasn't leaving anything to chance. Capture or kill was the order of the day. No exceptions.

McHale looked at Molly, who smiled and said, 'Pick & Mix time, boys and girls.' They were a long way from any Woolworths sweetie counter. The team scanned the selection. They reminded McHale of the firepower Molly supplied for their last hunt, when they took down the serial killer Charles Halliwell. On the night when Kelly died. Suffice to say that, thanks to Molly, this time around, the team would be armed to the teeth and ready for war.

McHale's mobile rang. He walked away from the Defenders before putting it to his ear. *'A small, last minute, request from the Bulgarian authorities,'* said Drummond, almost apologetically.

McHale sighed. Slow and loud.

'Let me guess. They want him alive,' he said.

'They want to know if there are any more bodies, dammit.'

'How alive do they want him?'

'Still breathing would be preferable,' said Drummond.

McHale frowned.

'No promises,' he said. Then he killed the call and turned to Lightfoot, who was closely examining an AWP sniper rifle. It had three clips of ten hollow-point .308 NATO rounds, ballistic tipped. She was smiling.

'Let's go back upstairs and do some planning,' he said. She nodded and reluctantly put the weapon back where it came from, patted it twice and gathered up the team. One of Molly's men, Wallace, stayed with the Defenders. Everyone else squeezed into the lift, in two shifts, back to the top floor. It was 9.15am. When they stepped out, they grabbed coffees from the kitchen, then arranged themselves haphazardly around the horseshoe table. They had plenty to say. For the moment, however, all the words they needed to use were inside their heads. Except for McHale. 'Morning, SKIN,' he said, facing the screen wall. The wall came alive.

'Morning Mac,' said SKIN. *'I see you've brought some guests.'* Taking up all the screens on the wall were live images of everyone sitting at the table. Tosh and Brodie, who hadn't been introduced to SKIN, were open-mouthed, looking around for cameras and speakers.

McHale smiled and said, 'Say hello to Tosh and Brodie. Boys, say hello to SKIN. Your best friend and your worst enemy… and the only being in this room who won't take shit from anyone, alive or dead.' Tosh and Brodie nodded slowly in the direction of the screens. Their images nodded back.

'Right. Let's get down to business,' said McHale. 'SKIN, bring up the latest ground and aerial photos and topographical details of St. Agnes Church, Chew Magna.'

'What did your last servant die of, Mac?' said SKIN. McHale smiled. The well-remembered comeback hadn't got lost in translation from human to artificial intelligence.

'You and Drummond must be best mates,' he said. Dexter Bob was halfway through taking a large gulp of coffee. The gulp changed into a splutter, which changed into a coughing fit.

'SKIN has a sense of humour,' said Lightfoot.

The screen changed into a selection of 36-degree shots of the church, then changed to a live feed from a US optical image reconnaissance satellite in geosynchronous orbit parked

200 miles directly overhead. A blind man could count the individual drops of bird shit on the roof tiles. *'Fucking show-off,'* said internal voice. *'Name the pigeons that dropped them!'*

'SKIN, give us a street map view of the property and surrounding area,' said Lightfoot. 'Ten-mile radius.' The screen wall changed to an overhead image of the ex-church, cemetery, and surrounding roads.

'AAs you can see,' said SKIN, *'the property that used to hold 'St. Agnes' sits on an island surrounded by, and accessed by, B roads. The kind of roads that have very little traffic, very little footfall. In fact, very little of anything except entry to a dwelling with a few live people, and a lot of dead bodies nearby'*

'Switch to the satellite image, draw back 100 metres vertical,' said Lightfoot.

'Why do I get the feeling you've done this kind of thing before?' said Toby.

'Because I've done this kind of thing before,' said Lightfoot, who had a small flashback of her time in the Sonoran Desert eight years before.

Parked outside the front of the dwelling were two vehicles. A Jag and a dark-coloured van. 'Same vehicles as yesterday?' said McHale.

'I know what you're thinking, Mac,' said SKIN, *'and yes, the feed has thermal imaging. There are seven warm bodies inside the house. None of them are immobile. I think we can presume they're all naughty. How long they'll stay there is anyone's guess. Even I'm not that good.'*

'We need to go,' said Katarina, standing up.

'Hang on,' said Pope. 'Let's think about this for a minute. How do you know we're not walking into a trap? This could be exactly what he wants.'

That was a conversation stopper.

Katarina sat down.

'Aww bollocks, Kemosabe,' said internal voice. *'If we don't press the green light now, bloody Lazarov and his mates will fuck off and we'll be stood here holding our dicks in our hands!'*

McHale sighed and blinked. 'We go,' he said. *'Outstanding,'* said internal voice. *'Lock and bloody load.'*

'Not so fast. SKIN, are there any ways in or out apart from the front gate?' said McHale.

'Two. One Old wooden gate on the West Wall,' said SKIN. *'Approximately 950 metres from the back door of the house. It leads to the B road to the west of the cemetery.'*

'And two?'

'A priest hole behind what used to be the altar, leading to a tunnel.'

McHale turned to Pope and reminded himself of the sculptor's rarely-talked-about previous life as a Sergeant in Her Majesty's Special Air Service. Not even Major George 'Lippy' Patterson (a Royal Marine) knew about that well-hidden little secret.

'Grab a blade, a Glock, and an assault rifle,' he said to Pope, 'And, when we get there, go with Charlie to the West Wall gate. Welcome any potential escapees with the option of surrender, or a dose of your very best hellfire.' Then he turned to Charlie. 'Take your pick of firepower and bring him back alive.'

'I'd prefer to stay with Katarina,' said Charlie. They were the first words he had spoken since they met. McHale understood. He was her protector. He paused and nodded.

'Okay,' he said, and turned to Toby. 'You go with Pope to the gate… and keep your heads down.' Both nodded, lips firmly zipped.

Then McHale nodded at Molly's men. 'Tosh, Brodie, Wallacc… you three will be first through the door. Announce your presence if you really feel like it. Drop anyone that reaches for anything except the ceiling.'

'Male or female?' said Tosh.

'Male or female,' said McHale. All three nodded.

Then he turned to Lightfoot. 'You'll be across the road opposite the front gate, on the roof of the lead Defender with the AWP and Daisy. She can spot for you. Anyone who isn't us and tries to escape through the front door, put a hollow point in them. Centre of mass. If they move when they're down, shoot them again.' Lightfoot smiled. She could feel her trigger finger getting itchy.

'What about Molly and me?' said Katarina.

'You two grab a Glock and follow on behind Rice and me. Shoot anything that tries to shoot back.'

'Lazarov is mine,' said Katarina. There was no argument in the tone of her voice. It was like steel.

'Fair enough,' said McHale. 'You and Charlie stick together.'

'And where exactly would that be?'

McHale smiled. 'The Priest Hole.'

'What's a priest hole?' said Pope.

'Hidey holes for persecuted catholic priests during the reign of Elizabeth I. A bit before your time.'

'Never seen one,' said Katarina.

'There's one hidden behind where the altar used to be in St. Agnes' said McHale. 'Only it's not just a hole, it's also a tunnel leading below the graves and under the East wall to safety. We know where it comes out. If Lazarov makes a break for it, that's where he'll head for. And you'll be waiting for him with an assault rifle and Charlie.'

'I won't need an assault rifle,' said Katarina.

'Better to have it and not need it, than need it and not have it. SKIN, do we have an exit for the Priest hole?' The always-listening voice of the non-human team member answered. *'Roughly ten feet on the other side of the East wall, and 250 yards along the B road East. I've sent the directions to Wallace. He'll drop you both off, then come back to the front gate.'*

That seemed to satisfy Katarina.

Lightfoot looked at everyone around the table. 'Don't forget to pick up a Ka-Bar each.'

Toby got up from his chair and headed for the kitchen, followed by Pope. When they got there, they were greeted by a mountain of sandwiches, a plate full of chocolate biscuits, two large flasks full of black coffee, and a jug of milk. Courtesy of the fast-disappearing ladies from the main kitchen downstairs.

An hour of small-talk later, they vacated the top floor and headed down to the basement and the Discoveries. Daisy brought the guarding Wallace some sandwiches and a couple of Penguin chocolate biscuits. He was very grateful. Looking after weapons was hungry work. They sorted out travelling arrangements, with Daisy bossing the seating, and McHale taking shotgun next to Tosh driving the lead Defender. Daisy and Toby were in the rear. The Girl Friday and the boy wonder.

Defender Two had Brodie driving with Lightfoot riding shotgun, and Katarina and Charlie in the rear. The shrink and the bodyguard. Defender Three had Wallace driving, with Rice riding shotgun, and Molly, Pofpe, and Dexter in the rear. The spook, the sculptor and the geek. It was another tight squeeze.

They pulled out of the basement garage of Lassiter House at 1.05pm, left the Embankment, and headed through the London traffic for Slough. Then onto Reading, Swindon, Chippenham, Bath, and Bristol. Then Chew Magna.

Ahead lay three hours twenty-five minutes of driving at a steady 60mph and an appointment with a serial killer.

Sometimes 125 miles feels like a whole lot of travelling, if you think really hard about what you're going to do when you get to where you're going. Other times it goes by in the blink of an eye. Like it was never there in the first place. McHale's mobile rang. It came through the on-board sound system on all three Discoveries simultaneously.

'Hi Mac,' said SKIN. *'Hi everybody. This is your friendly, neighbourhood Serial Killer Intelligence Network speaking. Might be a good idea to stop at Moto services, Reading for a Costa coffee.' It's on the M4, between J11 and 12. Use the break to check your earwigs. You're all locked into the same channel. Just press the button on the device to speak or go silent. You'll be there in about 1 hr 20 mins. Have a nice trip. Don't shoot anyone you don't have to.'* There was a short pause.

'That was a joke,' said SKIN.

Up front, McHale frowned.

'Music?' said Tosh.

'Jazz,' said McHale. 'Low and slow.'

Conversation was intermittent. Forty-five miles later, the convoy pulled into Moto services Reading M4 Westbound. It was 2.33pm. Inside, the humour was dry. Outside, the weather was wet. They decided to stay in the Defenders and fiddle with their earwigs. All except Toby and Daisy, who indulged in a little leg stretching, followed by a welcome coffee run. There were no refusals.

At 3.10pm, they hit the road again. Earwigs were unhooked and the last dregs of coffee were consigned to convenient plastic trash bags. As they passed a large IKEA store in Theale, Reading, Daisy, sitting behind McHale, said 'I spent half a day in an IKEA store once, shopping for a standard lamp. I sent it back after a month. It was crap.'

There was a short pause, then Toby said, 'So... not a bright idea, then.'

That brought a burst of laughter from Tosh, who covered his mouth with his right hand, and kept steering with his left. He was Welsh, with a deep, melodious voice. He reminded McHale of an old singer called Ivor Emmanuel. Not because of his singing voice, but because of one of the most important movies he ever appeared in. It was called "Zulu". It starred one of McHale's favourite actors, Michael Caine. Although McHale had to admit that in "Zulu", Caine did play a bit of an upper-class ponce.

Immediately ahead of them, hugging the middle lane stubbornly, was an old Volvo towing a small boxy caravan. It didn't look like it was going to pull into the inside lane any time soon. It didn't look like it was going to speed up any time soon either.

The lead Defender moved to the outside lane. The other two followed, and they left the Volvo in their wake. They pulled back in five or six miles up ahead. The Volvo was a speck in the rear-view mirror.

'My dad had one of those,' said Toby.

'Volvo?' said McHale.

'Caravan,' said Toby. 'We used to go to The Isle of Skye every year. He was a nature photographer. He liked to photograph the wildlife around the distilleries.'

There was a short pause.

'Did he like whisky?' said McHale.

'Hated the stuff,' said Toby. 'He was a Guinness man.'

'So was my dad. He was a whisky man, too,' said McHale. 'Only he liked them too damned much. Mostly at the same time. You could say they contributed to his death.'

'My dad drank a glass of port every night before bed,' said Daisy. 'He said it helped him sleep.'

'And did it?' said McHale.

'He was an insomniac,' said Daisy. 'Just like Winston Churchill and Lady Gaga. Unlike them, he was also an arsehole.'

'If I was an insomniac, it would send me gaga, too!' piped up Tosh.

That got a laugh.

'Fuck me, Kemosabe,' said internal voice. *'You lot are a bunch of comedians.'*

McHale thought of his own father. He was conspicuous by his absence at McHale's passing out parade in Hendon. He was passed out at the time in a pub in West Hampstead after fifteen pints of Guinness, one after the other, or so the story went. He was attacked as he staggered home. He nearly made it, too, but he died in hospital three days later. Brain damage and a few well-placed stab wounds. They never caught the bastards who did it. Not then, anyway. They reckoned McHale's dad had put enough vicious folk away to make a line of likely suspects a mile long. But three years later, McHale caught up with them. That was another story. His mates at the police station turned the event into a long-standing joke. Cop humour. *'Question. Where do drunk coppers go to die? Answer. St. Thomas' Hospital A&E.'*

McHale's mobile rang. He answered on the third ring. It was an old habit; two rings felt too keen, four felt not keen enough.

'The van's gone,' said SKIN.

'Shit,' said McHale. 'How long ago?'

'About an hour.'

'And you didn't think of sending up a red flag?'

'I didn't have one handy. Anyway, it might have come back. I didn't want to worry you.'

McHale sighed. 'At what point did you decide to worry me?'

'Three minutes ago.'

'What happened then?'

'The Jag disappeared.'

McHale cursed under his breath. 'Okay… patch me through to the others.'

'Done,' said SKIN.

'This is McHale. It seems that our friends in the Jag and the van have done a bunk,' he said.

Lightfoot was the first to reply.

'Done a what?' she said.

'A bunk… buggered off… disappeared.' It was 3.54pm.

'Shit,' said Pope, from the rear of Defender three. 'Does that mean more bodies?'

'Ever the optimist,' said Rice, sitting shotgun in front of him.

'Piss off, Father,' said Pope, and immediately apologised with a sign of the cross and a quick 'Mea Culpa'.

'When was the last time you went to confession?' said Rice.

'I think I was five,' said Pope.

Rice smiled.

'The van's back,' said SKIN.

'Keep looking for the Jag,' said McHale. Then he thought about Dexter in Defender 3. He switched on comms. 'Hey Dex, you okay in there? Cat got your tongue?'

'I been buried three times. Don't wanna make it four.'

McHale had a thought. 'When we go in the house, you tuck in behind me and the boys. I'd feel safer if I knew you had my back, okay?' he said.

'Cheers, Mac.'

'No problem.'

Both of them knew he was keeping Dexter out of the line of fire as much as possible. And both of them knew Dexter had a deep-seated fear of guns.

'Found the Jag yet?' said McHale to SKIN.

'You'll know when I know... oh... found it. Five miles out from Chew Magna, heading back fast.'

'Too soon for bodies,' said Lightfoot. 'Supplies maybe.'

'How far out are we?' said McHale.

SKIN interrupted. *'You should be there about 5.00pm.'*

'Why is the Jag in such a hurry to get back?' said Katarina, in the rear of Defender Two.

'If they had even the slightest hint that we were on the way, surely they'd be heading in the opposite direction,' said Molly.

Silence.

'What if Lazarov isn't in the Jag?' said Lightfoot slowly. Then suddenly and quickly, she said, 'What if he's still in the house and the Jag's coming back for him?'

'Shit,' said McHale. 'They've finally made a mistake. Somehow, they know we're coming for him, and he's back at the house unprotected.'

'Or they need petrol,' said Rice. 'I don't think they know we're coming'.

'You want my opinion, Mac?' said SKIN.

'Always.'

'Van's been for supplies. Jag's been for petrol,' said SKIN. *'Morrisons about three miles out... and there's a Shell petrol station on York Road, Bedminster. Just over five miles.'*

'Right,' said McHale. 'You know what to do, everyone. SKIN, how much further to St. Agnes? The convoy was on a B road with fields either side. There was a lay-by coming up on the left.

'Turn in here,' said McHale to Tosh. The other two Defenders followed.

'Earwigs in, throat mics on, bullet-proof vests on, and guns loaded,' he said. 'This is gonna be fast and furious.' Ten minutes later they took off again.

'SKIN…' said McHale. He didn't have to finish the sentence.

'Take the second on the right in two miles,' said SKIN. *'That's the driveway. Through the gate and 150 yards to the house. The Jag's parked behind the van just outside the front door. The third on the right is the B road bordering the west wall.'*

'Where's the exit on the west wall?' said Pope.

'100 yards along the wall, wooden door on the right.'

Brodie's Defender, with Pope and Toby, swerved past McHale's and sped up to the B road, turned, accelerated, then came to a slow halt at the wooden door. No point announcing their arrival… yet. Pope and Toby jumped out, forced open the wooden door, and waited. Brodie did a U-turn and headed back to the front gate, parking next to the second Defender, out of sight and shielded by trees just to the left of the entrance. Lightfoot climbed onto the roof of her Defender, carrying her AWP sniper rifle, fitted with a suppressor, and a box of NATO 308 Winchester ammunition and Schmidt and Bender scope, and lay down lengthwise facing the house. She chambered a round and her brain automatically began the process of slowing her breathing. Daisy lay down beside her, taking up the spotter's role.

Wallace's Defender turned along the B road East, dropped Charlie and Katarina outside what looked like a large, flowering, rhododendron bush covering up a hole in the ground at the base of the wall, then U-turned and came back to park alongside Brodie's Defender. Then three things happened.

The first was the sound of SKIN's voice inserting itself into McHale ear. *'You know, if I were a paranoid killer, which of course*

I'm not, I'd have cameras covering the front and side entrances. Maybe a small distraction might be in order.'

McHale smiled and scanned the front of the house above the porch thirty feet away. He saw the camera about three feet above the door, pointing directly towards the gate.

The second was McHale's voice talking softly into his throat mic. 'Lightfoot,' he said. 'Take out the camera above the door.'

The third was the camera disintegrated into useless bits of plastic and metal, thanks to a bullet from Lightfoot's rifle. It lay, dead and motionless, dangling by a wire from the wall.

'So... what's it gonna be?' asked Lightfoot in McHale's ear. 'Apache-style assault, or full-frontal Blitzkrieg?'

McHale smiled. 'I've always had a soft spot for a sneaky Apache,' he said, stepping quietly out of the Defender and motioning the others to follow.

Brodie checked the wooden gate and found it unlocked. Wallace, Brodie and Tosh led the way with McHale, Rice, Dexter and Molly, close behind.

It took them ten seconds for them to reach the three steps at the base of the front door, thirty feet from the gate. All the time expecting somebody inside to notice that their early warning device wasn't working any more.

McHale moved to the front of the line and banged twice loudly on the door. The sound echoed in the entrance hallway. At first, there was silence. No voices. No footsteps. No movement.

Then, the door was opened slowly by Georgi Bakalov, a gun held loosely in his right hand, a half-eaten sandwich in the left. It was clear he wasn't expecting visitors.

His eyes didn't even have time to register any emotion, before a bullet from Lightfoot's AWP hit him hard in the chest, destroying any nearby organs, crashing out through his spine, and throwing him back inside the hallway. He was dead before the soles of his slippers had a chance to say goodbye to the floor. Blood rushing out from an ugly hole in his sternum. He was trampled by an inrushing Tosh, Brodie and Wallace, whose forward momentum took them almost to the end of the corridor, where they were met by a screaming Maria Bakalov, who ran at them wielding a large kitchen knife in her right hand.

She got as far as attempting to plunge it into Wallace's anti-stab vest before Tosh shot her three times in the face with his Glock. Her nose and left eye disappeared and, almost in slow motion, her head jerked backwards and she slumped, lifeless, to the floor like a puppet whose strings had been suddenly cut.

Behind him, Brodie swung left and fired a quick burst into the oncoming upper body of Stefan Genov. His chest exploded in a red mist which sprayed the open door behind him. But not before he got a couple of shots off. Brodie took a bullet to the upper left arm. Genov didn't have time to aim properly. In fact, he didn't even have time to breathe properly as his lungs and heart exploded inside his chest cavity.

Time seemed to come to a dead stop as the deadly exertions of the past few seconds were followed by heavy breathing and a loud silence that seemed to go on forever. It was broken by the sound of a door slamming shut. Tosh looked to his left into the kitchen, where an open door was bouncing against a wall. He touched his earwig and yelled, 'I've got runners, out the back door. Two coming your way through the graveyard.'

At the door on the West wall, Tosh's warning was heard by Pope and Toby. They saw the two figures barging out the open door and charging towards them through the gravestones. They took aim and fired. The figures were thirty feet from them when they screamed and collapsed. One managed to crawl to prop himself against an old gravestone in the shape of a cross. The other lay where he fell. Motionless. Toby put another two shots into the propped man, who grunted, then tilted over on his side and went somewhere fast to meet his maker. Toby pressed his earwig. 'Two runners down,' he yelled.

Back inside the house, Brodie was leaning against a wall,

blood seeping from his arm.

McHale shouted, 'Where's Lazarov?'

Ahead, Molly saw two shapes dive into a room and slam the door behind them. To the side of Molly, Dexter was holding his Glock so tight the brown of his hand was turning white. He couldn't have pulled the trigger if his life depended on it, but he was bravely holding the Glock and doing his best to threaten fresh air.

'Mac, find the Priest Hole,' said SKIN in his ear.

'Damn,' cursed McHale. He rushed to the door, only to be met by a burst of fire from the other side, destroying one of the door panels and narrowly missing him and anyone near him. Then silence. Molly turned to Tosh. 'Would you be a love?' she said, sweetly. The polite manner of her speech belied the steely danger in her voice.

Tosh smiled, paused, and demolished the door with two very powerful kicks.

The room was empty. But on the floor against the far wall, a trap door was open. The Priest Hole was being used as an escape route, presumably by Elena Markov, the dark-haired woman in the burgundy Mark ll Jag, and Anton Lazarov.

McHale rushed to the open trapdoor. There was a smear of blood on it. He pressed the button on his earwig. 'Katarina… Markov and Lazarov are coming your way. They're armed and one of them is wounded. Give them a nice welcome.'

'I've waited a long time to do that,' said Katarina in McHale's ear. McHale had no doubt how deadly the welcome would be. He climbed gingerly down the six steps into the Priest Hole, Molly following on behind.

Both were immediately engulfed in darkness with no way of knowing which direction to go. And that's when two things happened to McHale in quick succession.

The first was the faint, but unmistakable rattle, inside his head, of dustbins being kicked by bastard thugs. The second was a sharp tingling at the tip of the pinkie finger on his left hand.

'*Danger, Will Robinson,*' said internal voice.

McHale decided to ignore the warning. He knew he would pay for it later. The oncoming head tsunami and pins and needles would have to wait. He fumbled in a pocket and found his mini Maglite torch. He switched it on and a powerful beam of light shone on two tunnels almost dead ahead. One veering off to the left and the other to the right. No way of knowing which one Lazarov and Markov had taken.

Katarina was nowhere in sight.

They stopped and listened. Nothing

The tunnel ceiling was so low they had to walk in a crouch as carefully as they could until the tunnel forked. Suddenly, there was a sharp yelp from behind him and he stopped and turned to see Molly furiously rubbing her head where it had come into contact with a low-hanging piece of rock.

McHale shone his torch onto her face, momentarily blinding her.

A small trickle of blood was dripping down her forehead from her hair line.

'Shit… shit… shit,' she cursed loudly, before motioning McHale to keep moving. 'We can't let them get away!'

Just then, a shot rang out, then a pause, then another shot. McHale reached out and tapped Molly on her right arm. 'Right,' he said, and led the way. The air was almost suffocating and they could feel a slight breeze on their faces. Not far ahead, they could see a light. They shuffled urgently as fast as their posture and the tunnel height would let them. Then, they heard two more shots, close together.

As they reached the end of the tunnel, they burst out into daylight, expecting to exercise their trigger fingers. They saw Elena Markov sprawled on the floor, a single shot to her forehead, and another wound with blood pumping from her abdomen, staining her grubby white shirt. Charlie was standing over her. She looked very dead.

'One down… one to go,' said internal voice.

Ten feet away, lying in the bushes, was Lazarov. He looked uncomfortably alive.

Katarina was standing over him, grimly smiling. He was on his back, breathing heavily, snarling at her in defiance. There was a thin trickle of blood oozing out of the left-hand edge of his mouth, and his unkempt hair was damp with sweat. There was a bullet wound to his stomach. He was trying to push himself away from her, but there was no power in his legs. She stepped closer until she was standing directly above him.

He grimaced and tried to stem the blood flowing from the hole in his gut. And then the light of recognition crept into his eyes. 'I know you,' he said, and he coughed a large gout of blood splashed onto his chin. 'I saw you in Giverny, near Paris.' Every word was now a huge effort. 'You were nearly lucky then,' he said, his accent thick with his mother tongue.

'I know,' she said.

Then he raised his right hand and motioned for her to come closer. She bent nearer, thinking he was going to whisper something. Instead, he hawked and spat a large glob of blood-red spit in her face. 'The Devil will take you,' he said.

'You first,' she said, standing up.

Part of her wanted to capture Lazarov and watch as he was locked away forever. But only a very small part. Instead, she slowly raised her handgun and pointed it at him. 'This is for Penko,' she said. 'And all the others.' Then she shot him three times. Once in each eye, and once in the heart. Then she breathed long and deep. And she smiled. It wasn't smile of humour. It was the smile of satisfaction. Of a job well done. Of justice finally being serviced. Of a death that should have happened a long time ago.

Any thought McHale had of trying to stop her from exacting a very personal kind of retribution disappeared with the echo of the gunshots in the tunnel entrance. Katarina handed her gun to

Molly and nodded. Molly took it, butt-forward, and nodded back. 'Some monsters you lock up,' said McHale. 'Others you put down.'

Epilogue

Molly and SKIN organised the clean-up at what used to be a house of God. It was in a bit of a mess. The two fresh bodies in the shallow graves were exhumed and treated with the utmost respect. They were the old couple from the van. Nameless, and normal in every respect except for the ten stab wounds in each. They were autopsied with extra care after a special request from Lightfoot to Dunwoody, who was only too glad to be back with the team. Then they would be buried together, face up, which, in the grand scheme of things, was all that really mattered.

Brodie's injury was merely a flesh wound, and he was back in action within a week. Three weeks after the shoot-out, the two brothers Yan and Kiril Andreev tracked down Marko Kabardinski, the surviving attacker of Dimitar Orlov a.k.a. Grey John. They delivered his right hand, with the Svetlana tattoo, in an ice box, to Katarina Petrova, who reverted to the name Rayna Orlov. There was a letter attached to the box. The letter had ten typed words. The words were these: 'A monster took our brother. A mother made him pay.'

Two months after the shoot-out, Dimitar Orlov passed away peacefully in his sleep. There were four people by his side. His mother, Rayna Orlov, Father Stephen Rice, DI Tom McHale, and FBI Supervisory Special Agent Grace Lightfoot. He was buried in a private ceremony in Highgate Cemetery, North

London. Next to an unknown fifteen-year-old girl called Sam.

After the funeral, McHale went home alone to his house in Battersea, sat down in his Poggenpohl kitchen, sipped a strong black coffee, then unwrapped the moving-in gift from Molly Spencer brought to him by Drummond.

Inside the plain brown wrapping paper was a first edition, hardback copy of his all-time favourite movie, Casablanca, containing 1,500 photos and compete dialogue from the original soundtrack. Signed by Director Michael Curtiz.

On the flyleaf, in beautiful cursive handwriting, was an inscription. His favourite quote from the movie.

'Louis, I think this is the beginning of a beautiful friendship.'

It was signed; 'To Tom, with thanks, from Molly.'

McHale sighed contentedly, smiled, and made another coffee.

It was going to be a long night.

Acknowledgements

As with my debut crime novel, A Time for Dying, I have many people to thank for the help they have given in creating A House for Monsters, Book Two in my DI Tom McHale crime series. They won't all know who they are. But the important thing is, I do.

As with A Time for Dying, I have been economical with the truth in many cases. It is, after all, a work of fiction.

In the case of many names and places, dates and times, I have chosen to err on the side of my hard-working imagination, except in a few obvious cases.

In the case of people, real or imagined, you can rest assured that nobody was hurt, physically or emotionally, seriously or otherwise, in the writing of this book.

From a medical perspective, I have tried to ensure that the conditions suffered by those in the book are as accurate as possible.

From a firearms perspective, I have also tried to ensure that the equipment mentioned in the book and used by the team is, again, as accurate as possible.

As far as I am aware, there is no department in existence known as SKIN, nor is there any technology (hardware or software) with the ability to do what it does.

My apologies for any inaccuracies in this text.

DI Tom McHale will return in another mystery.

Keep reading for an exclusive extract of
A Place for Killing by Bryce Main.

Prologue

The date was Sunday, 2nd September, 1945. The time was 9.04am precisely. Japan had just formally surrendered to the Western forces, in the person of US General Douglas MacArthur on board the USS Missouri in Tokyo Bay, marking the end of World War II.

On the other side of the world, in the middle of Oklahoma, in Uncle Sam's USA, three people were eating breakfast in a sturdy, bark-roofed cabin somewhere inside the 7,000 square mile Cherokee reservation. One of them was a young child.

The date in the west, thanks to the difference in time zone, was Saturday, 1st September. The time was just after 6am. The reservation had been formed over one hundred years earlier, after the forced relocation of the Cherokee nation from their homeland in Georgia, after the infamous Trail of Tears in 1838, during which about 4,000 Cherokee men, women, and children, out of an estimated total of 15,000, had died of starvation and disease.

The Trail was over 5,000 miles long and stretched from Alabama, Arkansas, Georgia, Illinois, Kentucky, Missouri, to North Carolina, Oklahoma and Tennessee.

It hadn't been a relocation as much as a government-approved exercise in ethnic cleansing.

The cabin was roughly thirty-five miles north-west of the Cherokee capital of Tahlequah. It was neat, clean, and home to a

Nation law enforcement officer named John Grey Wolf, a half-blood Cherokee who lived there with his full-blood wife, Alice Long Sight, and their two-year-old son Little Wolf Who Howls in the Night. The Cherokee nation was a matriarchal society, with women having an equal voice in the affairs of the tribe.

In most cases, the women ruled the roost. John, however, was the exception that unofficially proved the rule. His duties comprised mostly of rounding up the drunks, keeping the peace between those who wanted to go back to their old home and those who wanted to make a new life in their new one. But John had another duty.

One whose genesis stretched back way before he was born. One that was almost forgotten. It concerned keeping a keen eye out for any hint of the band of sixty or so renegades who had escaped over one hundred years previously from their Soldier escorts during the Trail of Tears, and disappeared into the wilderness of God-knows where.

Some said they died off. Others said they kept their heads down, procreated, and quietly got on with their lives where nobody could tell them what to do or where to go. The government said nothing. They simply forgot to care about them. Out of sight was out of mind. But, as they say, eventually all good things come to an end. And for ten people, the good things lasted until 1949. Then the bad things happened.

In the spring of that year, a band of twelve renegades came out of nowhere and attacked two white families. They left wounded, but luckily, nobody was killed.

Their leader was a man who called himself Inola. He was a vicious man with a long memory and a short temper. One hundred years before the Trail of Tears, fifty percent of the Cherokee nation had been wiped out by the deliberate introduction, by white men, of the deadly disease Smallpox. If Inola had any good reason to be bitter and murderous, it was he. The truth was, although it happened a long time ago, Inola was a generational ticking time bomb and in 1949, the bomb went off. He and a band of renegades returned and attacked another two families. Because the families were white, the government acted fast, but Inola always evaded any attempt by law enforcement at capture.

Then, in October that year, Inola stole twenty head of cattle from a local ranch. So the Cherokee leaders sent John Grey Wolf and four deputies to arrest Inola. Although John was half-Cherokee, he was also half-Scottish. He had one foot in the camp of The People of his father, and another in the camp of The Glaswegians of his mother. And the spilled blood of both families demanded he capture Inola, and bring peace back to The People.

John was very good at his job. He was known throughout The Nation as a tracker without equal. Inola, on the other hand, was known as a vicious killer without compassion. Any meeting of the two was bound to have a bloody ending. What John didn't know was that an hour after they left, Inola and six strangers with painted faces came out of hiding. They were in two old, beat-up, Chevy pick-up trucks. And they had murder in mind.

They broke into the home of John's Grey Wolf's neighbour, a man called Otis Lewis, and they held him down and killed him. They stabbed an arrow into each of his eyes. They spared Margaret Lewis, his wife. But not before they carved two letters into her back. The letters were two t's. 'The two 't's stood for the

Trail of Tears. It was well-known that Otis was a distant relative to one of the government men who, signed off on the removal of the Cherokees in the 1830s from their homeland. Whether it was true or not didn't seem to matter. Otis Lewis had the right name (or, on that night, the wrong one) so he must have guilty blood running through his veins and that was good enough for Inola. But they didn't reckon with John Grey Wolf.

Fast forward seventy-five years.

Chapter One

It started with a smell. At least as far as the woman was concerned.

Not the kind of smell that made her cover her mouth with either hand to stop the odour from getting in past her lips and nostrils. And not the kind of smell that made her feel like immediately evacuating the contents of her stomach onto the filthy carpet she was standing on. Hitting her well-worn Magnum Viper boots on the way down.

This wasn't that. This was much worse.

This was the kind of smell that announces itself without any introduction, without any preamble, and without any warning. The kind that instantly stings eyes and makes tears flow down cheeks in salty trickles, heading for the floor. The kind that would make Death itself feel proud to have created. And it deserved no place being anywhere near the inside of any of her facial orifices.

The woman's name was Eve Beaumont. And she was a member of the MET's Specialist Crime Directorate. She was normally based in London. But not today.

Today, she was 310 miles from home, in an old, refurbished cottage in Northumberland.

Beaumont was a police Detective Sergeant, and a bloody good one. She didn't know why she was anywhere near the smell. It was Friday, 24th January, 2020. Just shy of 7.10am.

And today was her birthday. 'Jesus Fuck!' she spat out from behind her hand. And then immediately regretted it.

'Oh yeah, I forgot. Happy Birthday,' said the tall, burly man standing next to her. Reaching quickly for a handkerchief to cover his mouth and nose. Similarly affected by the odour. His voice didn't match his size.

'Let's pretend you didn't know,' she said to the man. 'Now, if I can just breathe for five minutes without passing out, I'll be happy as a pig in shit.' The man tried very hard not to laugh. His name was DC David Cartwright. 'Tiny' to his friends. He was 6'4" tall. A full eight inches taller on the outside than Bumont. She was a lot taller on the inside. Beaumont looked around. They were standing about three feet inside what looked like a beautifully-furnished living room. The room was the largest single space inside the cottage, which was the only building standing in a large dip in the ground. One track in, same one out, surrounded by miles of moorland in the middle of nowhere. The perfect private bolthole.

She blinked slowly as her eyes adjusted to the gloomy interior. Tiny was looking around for curtains to pull back and windows to open. Fresh air was a stranger here, and both could almost chew on the stench of something not long dead.

As light invaded the room, Beaumont found herself looking at the body of an old man. More specifically, a very dead and, except for a dirty rag that pretended to be a loincloth covering his ancient masculinity, very naked old man. Lying on his back, spreadeagled on the floor.

A man whose exposed flesh was black, where putrefaction had made itself at home, and where a large drying puddle of bodily fluid was oozing nicely around him. He was well past the stage of not giving a damn where he was or how he was feeling.

Sticking out of his eyes were the shafts and the flight feathers of two arrows coated with dried blood. Beaumont sighed loudly and slowly shook her head from side to side. Some birthday present, she thought. Hard on its heels she had another two thoughts. One… how long ago did the old man die? And two… who made the phone call to get them here? She didn't know the answer to the first one… yet. But she had a fair idea who was responsible for the second one.

She pulled out her mobile and punched in a number long since committed to memory.

Printed in Great Britain
by Amazon